THE SIREN OF SAMSARA

THE SIREN OF SAMSARA

NEMAIN'S REVENGE
BOOK TWO

MCKENZIE A HATTON

The Siren of Samsara is the pirate fantasy sequel to
The Captain of Nemain's Revenge.
This book is intended for mature audiences.
It contains some sensitive elements such as violence, torture
scenes, depictions of sexual assault, profanity, abuse, slavery,
sexual explicit scenes, death, and race related discrimination.

PRONUNCIATION GUIDE FOR MAP

Samsara: sam-SAHraw
Kheli: KHEE-lih
Carriwitchet: karr-e-wIHtch-eht
Brettania: brit-AY-ni-ah
Koi No Yokan: koy-noh-YOE-khahn
Draiocht: drah-ou-SHET
Keraunos: kAIRa-ounohs
Toska: TUH-skah
Sumerian: suh-mAIR-ian

TANOIA

SUMERIAN SEA
NERII CASCADES
ATLAS
DEAD MAN'S WASTES
QUARAFA
RUINS OF OLD KALON
CARRIWITCHET ISLES
SAMSAR

TOSKA
BREVIS
BRETTANIA
PYRIA
LUCIS
KOI NO YOKAN
DRAIOCHT
KHELI
KERAUNOS SEA

MCKENZIE A HATTON

Editing by Rachel Ohm (www.rachelo300.wixsite.com/website/work)

Cover Design by Maria Spada (www.mariaspada.com)

Scene Art by Hanna @sovana.art

 Created with Vellum

For those who are looking for the right song

CHAPTER I
OLD DOOR, NEW MAN

It might have been the longest boat ride of Phantom's pirate career. The Fortress stood high above him on the cliff face. Part of the cliff *was* the Fortress, fog circling the stones in a lazy haze.

It reminded Phantom of when he was first brought here. Memories crashed into him like waves. He was a boy, no older than thirteen when they dragged him from the streets of Samsara and into the Fortress's throne room. Every forgotten boy of Samsara kneeled before the Prime Minister that day. There was no shortage of orphaned children. The Necromite War made sure of that.

They were taken under the Minister's care, leaning to read, write, and history, all per his instruction. At the age of fourteen, every orphan graduated to basic officer training.

The Minister liked to groom young boys into becoming officers; boys who had nothing, given a place and purpose. It made them strikingly loyal. Especially since they had no families to return to. They tested those boys in the every manner of the word.

Mentally. Physically. Politically.

Phantom was called James Hawkins then, and he was favored by the Minister's. During years of grooming, James had come out better than the rest of the boys in all categories. Stronger, faster, smarter, and the Minster had noticed. He gave James all kinds of rewards for doing well.

Until one day, they brought in a Mokshan boy. His brown skin was dirty, and his eyes were dark and scared. A look he would see on his crew member Tick. Even for the orphaned boys of Samsara, the Mokshan boy wore rags for clothes. The Minister stood before James, handing him a leather whip.

It was another test. A test graver than any that came before it.

A test of obedience.

"This boy," the Minister had spat, his wrinkles much less pronounced and his eyes brighter. "Is guilty of trespassing on Samsara, bringing disease to our shores. Whip him until I tell you to stop." With the dark look in the man's eyes, James knew he would only say *stop* once the boy was dead.

James had refused, tossing the whip to the ground. He could nearly taste the disappointment rippling off the Minister that day. "Are you sure you want to be doing that, Hawkins?"

James narrowed his eyes at the Minister. A man he had felt indebted to. Who brought him food and sweets and told him he'd be great one day.

The Minister's eyes shifted from the Mokshan boy to him. "He will be whipped regardless of whether or not you do it. Your choice is if you will join him."

When James said nothing, a frown appeared on the Minister's face. He bent down to retrieve the whip and tossed it to the Commodore. A tall war weathered man with grey hair and a permanent frown.

James stepped in front of the boy, not letting the Commodore gain one inch over him. But the Commodore did not care who stood in the way of his whip.

Phantom could still recall the sting of the whip, the crushing defeat it inflicted on its victims. Shuddering to himself, scars decorated his chest and back from that brutal whipping. The Mokshan boy lost his life that day, folding quickly under the Commodore's cruelty. The Prime Minister carried on with the needless tests, but he removed his favor and instead placed it upon James's best friend, Bash.

The boys only knew Sebastian Ashby on the streets of Samsara as Bash. A fleeting word. A passing glance. Nothing worthy of note. Not until the day the Minister dragged in another boy, this one was from Draiocht. His skin darker than James had yet seen. His eyes like pools of ink, terrified.

Once again, the Minister shoved the whip into the hands of a groomed orphan, giving Bash the same decision. James had searched for his eyes, begging his friend to look at him, to choose something else. But he also knew, the Minister would not allow a defiant officer in training to be pardoned for disobedience again.

Bash wouldn't make it out of there alive if he chose to stand up for the Draiocht boy, but James fumed from the balcony they trapped him on, far enough away that he could not intervene. He would save Bash, to save them both. He'd risk everything just for the chance. He'd let the beast out and they could—

But Bash didn't allow him the chance.

With every ounce of strength in his teenage arms, Bash whipped the boy bloody. The putrid sound of leather hitting flesh remained with James until he sailed the seas as a pirate captain.

That day changed both their lives. Bash stepped onto the road that would lead him to become Commodore Sebastian Ashby.

And James to become Captain Phantom of the Eleven Devils.

The large stone doors to the Minister's Fortress opened, a

prison surrounded by the sea. It was as if he were a boy all over again, but there wasn't a cavalry of orphans behind him. He entered not as a boy, searching for his place in life, but as Phantom, a man clad in black, silver buckles lining his sword belt and leather coat, rings decorating his dirty fingers. There was so much evidence of what he had become, what he had fought for, and what he had earned. Especially the tattoos circling his flesh. He had so much more than the boy who first entered those doors.

But that boy had Bash.

Now, Bash stood decorated as well, but in the uniform of the Commodore for his Prime Minister's Navy. His coat was white with embellishments of blue and gold. The blue to symbolize that he belonged to the Navy, but the gold warned civilians that he earned his position.

Ashby nodded dutifully at his old friend upon entering, but through his mask of decorum, he huffed. The only sign he didn't agree with the Minister. He likely wanted to see the pirate captain hang. To ease the people's mind that the threat was gone. Not to orchestrate their fear.

Ashby extended his hand out to stop his old friend. With a sideways glance, Phantom let a smirk paint his face, right before it shifted into fake innocence.

"What seems to be the problem, Commodore?" He purred, letting the title leave his lips like an insult, not showing a hint of respect. Any admiration he might have held for his old friend faded the moment he let Robin bleed under his knife. It was the moment he knew Bash no longer existed.

Ashby tossed his head to a nearby table.

"Disarm," he commanded, letting his gaze fall on Phantom's sword belt and pistol.

Phantom let a single eyebrow raise. "Make me."

Ashby's eyes narrowed, tempted by the notion.

"Play nice, boys," a sensual, irritating voice slammed into

Phantom. The voice made every muscle in his body tense. A voice that belonged to the Priestess Ravana.

Phantom struggled to keep his affable demeanor as she approached. She dripped in jewels that dazzled in the fresh morning light. Her silver skintight dress hugged her generous curves as she walked. And she always walked with a prowess. There were only three colors she would wear. Silver. Lilac. Crimson. The color choice would occasionally relate to the state of the moons, or what the Goddesses supposedly told her. But mostly, they reflected her moods. Silver told Phantom that she felt powerful, untouchable, and controlling.

Her vibrant red hair was a silken sheet that fell down her back. For a woman she was tall, standing nearly eye to eye with Phantom.

The priestess had a proclivity for the orphaned boys the Minister brought to the castle. He was not the only one grooming the boys.

"Yes, my lady," Ashby cooed out of habit. When Phantom was still living at the Fortress, Ravana had taken to Bash. No doubt she instilled more than respect into him.

Phantom kept his face disinterested.

She kissed her teeth at him. "Always were the defiant one, James," she purred.

He stiffened further as she encroached upon his space, circling him with a hand on his shoulder. She let her hand drag with her around his shoulder, across his back, then to the other shoulder. She was mentally undressing him. If it was any other woman, he would have flirted back, he would have teased her. But it was *her*. He'd rather shove her off a cliff than give her one ounce of satisfaction.

She breathed out, "Oh, I've missed you, James." The words sent a shiver along his spine. She squeezed his bicep. "My my, you've grown into a man." She finally rounded, facing him again. If it weren't for the Commodore's presence, he'd gut her right there. Her breath was far too close as she leaned in, "I will enjoy reacquainting myself with your," she trailed off, "talents."

Finally, Phantom let a smile break his stoic stare, but it held no warmth. It was only a mockery of a smile. "You're fooling yourself Ravana, if you think I'd ever invite you into my bed."

The Priestess's eyes did not fade with disappointment, instead her eyebrows rose in challenge. "We shall see, Captain," she hissed, but she somehow made it sound sensual and bitter all at once. Then her hands were on his sword belt, unbuckling it. Her eyes snapped to his as she handed the entire sword belt to Ashby. He would rather have the Commodore rip them from his body than this.

Her hand curled around the pistol at his side. The beast growled in his core, and he let a bit of it come out his throat. Her answering smile was sickening. After handing the pistol to Ashby, she took a step back, examining Phantom with a hand on her hip.

As quick as a minx she swiped the small blade from inside his boot and grinned devilishly. "You may look different, James, but you're still up to the same tricks." With the dagger's hilt between her pointer finger and thumb, she delicately handed that to Ashby too.

"Anything else, pet?" She cooed.

Phantom sliced her a look, wishing he could unleash the beast on her. He'd enjoy every second that it would take to rip her throat out.

"No?" She turned to the Commodore. "Sebastian," she said his name slowly, like it was a poem. "I'll let you take it from here." She turned to walk away. He thanked Nemain that she had not sported crimson that day. It was a disgrace to the Goddess of Death when she did, because it meant she was out for blood.

CHAPTER 2
FORTRESS OF DREAD

Towering doors opened with a groaning creak that spoke to the building's age, although the intricate designs on its frame illustrated its reverence to Brettanian architecture.

The Prime Minister lined the throne room with officers, each displaying a pistol and a longsword. Phantom chuckled at the sight. The Minister thought Phantom enough of a threat to lend two dozen officers to his defense. He supposed it was fair given what the Minister had done the morning before, what he had ripped away from Phantom.

He was becoming a desperate man, volatile and unpredictable.

But flattery surged through him at the Minister's precautions against one man. A dark voice in the back of Phantom's mind told him it wouldn't be enough. If Phantom truly wanted the Minister dead, all he had to do was let the beast out to take care of it. He would slaughter the entire room in minutes. He'd done it before. The only reason his devils lasted as long as they did was because they meant something to him. The beast knew at least that.

Unleashing the creature on his enemies would breed a more nefarious result.

Phantom shook the thought from his mind. Even if he killed the Minister, he could not guarantee the safety of his devils. The safety of the Khelitians. One wrong move and the Commodore would ship out to decimate the island.

He kept his hands to himself as he sauntered through the room, landing before the Minister with a stomp. After all, making a spectacle of the situation was the only thing he could do to keep the illusion of control.

"I knew you'd be back," the Minister said with a small, controlled smile. He leaned his forearms against the armrests of his polished stone and velvet throne, his hands folded together before him. His body dripped in an array of jewels, and he reeked of expensive perfumes. Phantom thanked Nemain that he was not in beast form now. The heightened scent of that stench might throw him into a frenzy alone.

Phantom squinted his eyes at the man. "Truly? You knew the man who committed treason would work for you again?" He spread his arms out. "You wanted that?" Doubt etched from his tone. He couldn't quite figure it out. After all he had done, the Minister should want to see him hang, instead he blackmailed the pirate into becoming his own personal lapdog.

The Minister put a finger to his lips, studying the pirate captain before him. Or rather, he studied the lieutenant who had gone rogue.

"Waste not, want not. I only kill what I cannot use." The Minister took a sharp breath. "I'm not in the business of forgiving deserters, mind you."

Phantom nearly choked. He was many things, but a deserter was the least of them. A thief, a traitor, a liar, a rebel, but he didn't leave because he wanted to. After leaving the Navy to save the Kalonites, he couldn't return.

When Phantom didn't answer, the Minister continued.

"But." His pitch hitched. "You were exceptional, Hawkins." Phantom blinked at the compliment. "Your skill with a sword is as if you'd been born with it."

Black's skill would astound him. "I've been bested."

The Minister continued, ignoring Phantom's comment. "Your capacity for knowledge and problem solving — unbeatable."

Ramirez would have doubled over at the idea. "Oh, I can be quite idiotic."

"But it was your talent of manipulating speech that truly caught my eye."

Phantom could not refute that claim. He often got what he wanted with words and the right timing. It was a talent that came more naturally to him than anything.

"I saw it when you were a boy. You were popular among the orphans when I dragged you out of Samsara's armpit. Not for anything you did, but how you made them feel." He leaned back on his throne. "You proved it with this," he waved a limp hand, "this crew of yours."

Phantom ground his teeth. He could defend his devils. His instincts raged to but defending them would point out his weakness. The devils were his family. The first family he ever truly had. If the Minister caught a whiff of that, he'd use it against him. Just as he was using Kheli. It was best the Minister believed Phantom cared no more for them than the orphans he left behind. Those orphans were now the officers standing around him.

That was why Phantom only shrugged.

The Minister paused, but only briefly before continuing. "I am quite fond of you, Hawkins." His voice trailed lazily, as if speaking to one of his entertainers.

Phantom let a breathy laugh escape him. "You must be joking."

His tone sharpened. "I am not. You'd be wise to seek my

affections, Lieutenant. One day, they will not be so easily given." Those pale eyes of his narrowed on Phantom, as if he wanted to retract the sentence. He put a quizzical finger to his lip. "I enjoyed that boy from the streets of Samsara, who thought of answers to tests no one else could. I loved to watch your mind work because it always solved riddles in the most interesting ways."

Phantom swallowed. At the time, he was seeking the Minister's attention. He wanted to be noticed. Just a boy, searching for a lost father figure he never got.

The Minister pointed that finger at him. "I prepared you to take the position of commodore when you were in the Navy." The thought made Phantom shiver, even if a younger version of himself wanted that. "But alas, you choose to liberate the shipment I assigned you."

The shiver grew down his back, stirring the beast within. "People aren't cargo," he whispered.

"Oh, don't fret, Lieutenant, I've forgiven you for that treason. Your journey into piracy has been quite worth it."

Phantom swallowed, even his piratedom had been exploited by the Minister.

Sharply, the Minister stood from his throne, a mockery of a king with that finger in the air. "You know, the War was too long ago." He stepped up to the decanter and drinking glasses beside him, resting on a serving cart. It surprised Phantom he poured the drink himself rather than allow his servant to. The servant was one of his ladies, dressed up in a rich costume of gold to please her master.

He reached for the decanter, but with a sharp flip of his hand, she stepped back with her eyes fixed firmly on the floor. They were orphans, too. Although the girls were in a separate wing from the boys, nearly imperceptible to each other, it was the same story. All of them poor orphans taken in by the Minister. He must have thought himself a saint.

He poured the amber liquid into the glasses. "Many of my people are too young to remember the War and the horrors that plague the mainlands. Since it is not something they encounter, they do not fear it." He set the decanter down and descended from the dais. "You," he chimed, handing a glass to Phantom. "You have given the people something new to fear. Something they must depend on me to help with." Hesitantly, Phantom accepted the glass, but he did not drink.

In all their raids, in every pillage of Samsara, Phantom went easy on the people. He had rules for the devils to follow. They couldn't hurt anyone unless they took up arms against the devils. A few officers had died, but they often spared the civilians, especially the ones from low town.

Often, they didn't even plunder the innocent. Their targets were the worst of Samsara.

Still, rumors took flight of Captain Phantom's ruthlessness. There were stories of his pirate crew slicing open helpless victims in bloodlust. Of them looting homes, destroying more than taking. Some rumors even said they kidnapped women.

In three years of pirating, Phantom only stole one woman, and she made it home intact. Phantom resisted the urge to search for her. If the Minister found out he cared at all for the songbird, her life would be in danger. He saw it in the set of her jaw as she walked away from him.

I should have begged her to stay.

"You started the rumors." The Minister sipped at his glass and blinked up at Phantom. "That's where the rumors came from. You orchestrated them." Not a question. Only a realization. One the Minister did not deny. He laughed into his glass.

"I couldn't allow the opportunity to slip. Now look. My people are compliant. I provide. We are all happy."

Except the Khelitians.

Except his crew.

Except the Samsarans.

Except Phantom.

The only one winning was the Minister. And most likely, the Priestess.

"Then what—" Phantom started, his voice dangerously low. "What do you want from me?"

The Minister hummed in amusement, satisfied he received an emotional reaction from Phantom. The Minister watched him straighten himself, with that finger over his mouth again.

"Your crew will continue as normal. Pillaging and providing supplies and protection for the Khelitians. But you will remain here. You are to be my lieutenant again."

Phantom burst with laughter. He wasn't sure if that meant he was hysterical. "Am I?" The Minister's gaze was piercing as he reclaimed the dais. "And what purpose would you have for a treasonous, newly reinstated lieutenant?"

"As I said," the Minister recounted. "I admire your talents. And I have use for them. It remains to be seen how." He laughed coldly. "Make no mistake, you are not rejoining the Navy. But you will do as I bid."

"And how's that?" It was bait. He wanted the Minister to admit he took Serena, using the little dragon as another way to control him. The fact that he wasn't was more concerning. What purpose did he have for the beastie?

He stared at Phantom for a long moment. "There is a significant difference between the orphan I knew and the man who stands before me now."

Phantom lifted his brows.

"You have more to lose now, Captain," he whispered. "Quite a bit more." Phantom blinked at the man. He wasn't wrong. In three years, he made everything for himself, a family, a home, a purpose, a desire. All of which the Minister could wipe away. "I imagine that passion I witnessed from you before has not abated; you will do as I say."

Phantom stared at him with steely eyes. He didn't outright

claim to have Serena, or maybe he wasn't willing to mention her in front of witnesses. Either way, he had to get her out fast.

"Now, Lieutenant, am I going to have any trouble with you?"

Oh yes, loads of it. A knowing voice echoed through his head, green sparking in the back of his mind.

"No," Phantom said dryly.

"No, what?" The Minister snapped. Suddenly Phantom was back at training, facing the old Commodore. The one who took pleasure in the blood on his hands and didn't even have time to scream when Phantom snapped his neck.

"No, Your Grace." Phantom bit out.

The Minister leaned back, relaxing where he stood. "Good," he breathed, studying Phantom. He held out a hand to his servant. "Natasha will show you to your room. Write a letter to your crew, detailing their instructions and your stay here." He lifted that finger again. "But no hidden messages. I will examine the note before it ships off." He nearly rolled his eyes. As if the Minister hadn't threatened him enough. "Once you're settled, dress properly, and meet the Commodore at the front door. He possesses your first assignment."

Delightful. Bloody Commodore Ashby himself.

The servant girl, head still bowed, walked from the dais to a nearby staircase. Phantom stepped to follow, glaring at the flashy marble around him.

The Minister sat back in his throne, a king all but in name. As Phantom was about to climb the steps, he added, "Don't worry over the Kalonites, Lieutenant. Someone collected them soon after you liberated them."

Phantom stilled completely. The air left his lungs as he stood at the base of the stairs. He didn't dare look back at the Minister. His eyes had surely dilated. The monster roared beneath his skin, begging to rip into the Minister. The only thing that doused his anger was the overwhelming sadness.

Tick. Ramirez. He had narrowly saved them. But they believed their families had survived. That they had escaped Samsara.

Phantom sent a prayer to Nemain. No, a promise. That he would burn the entire Fortress to the ground.

CHAPTER 3
RELUCTANT OFFICER

It was a room by the sea.

The gesture was both kind and cruel, to be so near to that with which he longed for, but no way to reach it. He tried to ignore the burning thoughts of a certain songbird in likeness to that statement. The sea breeze drifted through the black curtains with fresh sunlight. The morning fog had cleared, rewarding the day with a clear blue sky. It made the ocean dance and glimmer with light.

The room itself was mostly stone. Grey, cold stone that felt like a prison compared to wood planks. The bed was simple, with a dated black chest beside it. On the bed laid a newly minted naval officer uniform.

Before the servant, Natasha, had left, Phantom broke the silence. "I suppose it is required of me to wear the uniform?" He said, not bothering to hide the irritation in his voice. The last naval uniform he wore, he burned.

She only nodded, her dark curly hair nodding with her. Her skin was a dark sepia, like Angelica.

Natasha kept her head down as she pointed to a writing desk at the other end of the room. It contained parchment, along with ink and a quill. The Minister had prepared for his arrival. The man was overly confident, but he laid the terms bare on Bashtir. There was no doubt where Phantom's priorities lied or the lengths by which he would go.

Hopefully, those loyalties disguised the rest of Phantom's secrets. The monster brewing under his skin, for one. It wasn't in control, not even close. He suspected it would stay close to his skin while he lived in the Fortress. The place stirred up unwanted memories.

Natasha swept from the room without a word.

Once the door shut, Phantom's gaze traveled back and forth from the uniform to the writing desk. He'd delay his time in uniform as long as possible, so the letter it would be.

He sat at the small desk and took up the quill. It had been some time since he'd scratched words on parchment, other than the maps he frequented. He found strings of words on parchment more difficult to conjure than speaking.

> Devils,
>
> My presence is required to remain here. However, Kheli will need a new shipment before I can return. Jon is acting captain until Earhart can rejoin.
>
> Your Captain

He glanced at the note from afar. Hardly a letter, but there wasn't much to be said. Especially since he knew every word would grace the Minister's eyes. Part of him wanted to drone on for pages to spite him, but he didn't have the patience for such antics.

The other part of him wanted to tell his devils to run. To take the Khelitians and go far away. But the devils wouldn't leave, not with Phantom behind enemy lines. The Commodore would finally get his wish to see Phantom hang.

Besides, they had nowhere to go. Kheli was a coveted land, and they knew that better than anyone.

It was precisely the reason the Minister required his presence. Sure, he'd keep the Captain busy, but the devils were loyal to Phantom. He was the hostage. At least until the Minister no longer needed him.

Phantom wouldn't let it get that far. He'd get his devils out of this, and he'd finally leave Samsara in his wake. The thought used to give him much-needed relief, but now, a hint of sadness tightened his throat. He'd have to leave Rose behind, but he couldn't care for the songbird. This was her home, but it could never be his.

He pushed away from the desk and returned to the dreaded white and naval uniform. With a heavy sigh, he disrobed and unbranded himself, replacing it will the officer he once was. A man he thought he left behind years ago.

With the last button, he finished, and he wanted to burn it all over again.

The new cloth itched at his skin, the shoulders too narrow and the cuffs too short. He'd hardly pass an inspection, but he doubted the Commodore cared much for the accuracy of his uniform. Only that he wore it. It felt like a goddess-damned leash.

A glance in the mirror surprised him. He expected to see the boy who joined the Navy. A boy with wide eyes and even wider hopes, but the man standing in that mirror was much more broken than that. Bits of the pirate underneath still showed.

His collar wasn't high enough to cover the tentacle wrapping around his neck. Kohl from his time in Draiocht lined his eyes, and rings still decorated his hands, but more than that, it was the raging seas in his eyes.

Phantom stepped out to the hall, ready to meet the Commodore and find out precisely what kind of torture the Minister had in store for him.

Along the halls of the Fortress, paintings lined the grey walls, bringing some warmth into an otherwise dreary scene. In fact, the paintings stood out more than anything, as if their beauty should have never belonged in a place such as this.

Phantom stared at one painting in particular. It was of the sea with *Davina's Will* pressed upon the waters with its proud silver sails. He mourned the loss of such a beautiful ship, even if it was his actions that caused its downfall, but as he stared at the painting, there was a strong sense of adoration, of pride—

The beast reared its head, bashing those feelings before they crawled further under his skin. He blinked and red washed his vision until he stepped away. The beast went back to its slumber and Phantom could breathe evenly.

He narrowed his eyes at the painting, this time with an air of suspicion. Something had changed in this Fortress since he lived here and if he was going to have any chance of finding Serena and escaping, he'd have to figure out exactly what that was.

Footsteps came from around the corner. On pure instinct, he ducked into an alcove, shadowed enough to hide. Two sets drew nearer. As they passed, Phantom noted a blonde head of hair. His heart nearly stopped in his chest.

She was here. Rose was living in the same place he was, if only for a moment. Of course, he knew he'd run into her, but he didn't suspect it to be so quickly. He knew what she was to him, even if he didn't fully understand the bond between them. Some part deep in his soul recognized hers from the beginning. There must have been a part of her that recognized him as well. It was too soon, and she was too impossible for him to get his hopes up.

He steeled himself, allowing her to pass, letting her go, allowing her to descend into his memory as a pleasant ghost. All he had to do was stand there as they passed.

Green flashed across his vision as a force pulled him from the alcove.

"Hello love."

Dammit. A voice in his mind bellowed with laughter just as the green dissolved.

Her head whipped to his so quickly her hair fanned out around her. She stood in a pale floor length dress that floated about her. She styled the long golden tendrils of her hair half up and away from her face, brightening her eyes.

Those eyes. The pure magnetic energy of them. How did he not see it before?

Phantom realized he'd never seen her here before, in her natural environment, even if it didn't seem natural to him at all. She was so much more than this prison could give her. Although he could admit that the sight didn't make her any less beautiful. In fact, her pristine dress made Phantom want to mess it up, get her dirty, free her locks from the pins—

Focus.

Phantom blinked. *Right, thank you.*

Beside her, a woman with dark brown hair stood with her mouth gapping. She was shorter than Rose, but possessed a gentle, questioning gaze.

Rose's eyes slid down his uniform, and he wondered if her mind tumbled into a similar process. If his new appearance affected her at all, she didn't show it.

"Officer?" She prompted, as if she didn't know who he was. An act for the benefit of her companion, no doubt.

"Hawkins." Phantom hated the name. It wasn't even a family name. It was a common last name given to orphans.

Without uttering a response, she turned to her companion, and her hands started moving. He wasn't sure what she was doing at first until he recognized the signs for *new, officer,* and *hello.* She was signing to the woman.

The woman responded, her dark hair tumbling over her

shoulder as she moved a hand before her mouth then drew it away. Phantom recognized the sign for *hot*, but he concluded from the context that she wasn't referring to the temperature.

He cleared his throat until Rose looked at him, catching her companion's gaze. His hands moved with familiar movements. He hadn't used the hand language in some time, so he feared he wouldn't be understood.

"Pleasure to meet you. I am officer H-A-W-K-I-N-S." He spelled out each letter to her with his fingers. *"And you are?"* He intensified his gaze, and the woman blushed.

She spelled out her name as he did. *"L-A-R-A."*

Phantom smiled, bowing low at his waist and she blushed further. He would have put a kiss to her hand, but he was too aware of the songbird next to him, and he suddenly wanted nothing to do with Lara.

"Are you settling back into your life again, love?" He signed as he went along. Mama Owen would have smacked him for leaving a deaf person out of the conversation so rudely like that. But he let a satisfied grin reach his lips as he brought his fist to his heart. Lara would have plenty to ask her friend once he was gone, and the thought of them talking about him once he left filled him with satisfaction.

Rose refused to blush, waving off his endearment easily. She signed as she spoke. "I am not your love." She signed clearly and decisively, but Lara's gaze filled with a playful skepticism.

Rose ignored her. "As well as can be expected." She paused for a moment, seeming to consider something. "How is it you are here?"

He wanted to say more, but he wasn't sure what he could. If the Lara knew who he was, she didn't reveal it and Rose seemed to keep it from her. Far be it for him to foil a woman's intentions.

"I've been assigned to a new venture with the Commodore."

He made a foolish face as he signed for *commodore*, dragging a laugh from Lara.

Rose blinked.

Mention of the Commodore had his mind trailing back to that beach, where his fate sealed. And the pinch he swore he saw the Minister inflict on his daughter. A daughter he got back, yet he didn't offer her any warmth or familiarity, just pain.

He braced himself for the beast to rise, but with the songbird before him, he only had room for concern. What was it like to have a father like that? He wanted to rake her body for bruises, wondering if the Minister had inflicted any pain since her return.

Something red flashed in her eyes, but it vanished in the next blink.

"Well, I hope you have fun on your date," she signed with a smile. He smirked at her attempt to bait him, but it was not an effortless task, and he would enjoy every second she tried.

Phantom let a dark chuckle escape him. "Oh, I will." He planned on punishing his old friend for his performance on Bashtir and for stealing Serena away. Of course, he couldn't kill the Commodore, but he knew exactly how to get under Ashby's skin.

He stepped closer to her, but she didn't step back. There was a gleam of challenge in her eyes, so he stopped signing, knowing the words would only be for her. "However, I much rather be taking you with me. Finding out what spots in Samsara are your favorite, what foods make your taste buds sing, what views make your heart soar." Her lips parted with his admission, a blush rising to her cheeks. It wasn't a lot, but she needed to understand at least this. That he *saw* her, and he would not look away.

He smiled and leaned away as Lara shifted anxiously beside her friend. She at least read some words from his lips. Lara would undoubtedly pressure her friend for what he'd said. He wished he could watch the interaction himself.

Phantom stepped away from the songbird. "Farewell, love." He signed that part again, making it clear the endearment was going nowhere as he stepped further down the hall with a grin pulling at his mouth.

A quick glance behind him showed the girls walking. Lara signing vehemently.

Yes, there was one highlight to this whole situation, and her name was Rose Davenport.

CHAPTER 4
FIRST MISSION

Commodore Ashby stood at the gates of the Fortress with a permanent scowl threatening to inflict early wrinkles into his chin and eyes. Phantom nearly bellowed at the sight. Even their time together in the Navy hadn't brought that scowl to his face. It was everything that happened since that made his old friend look ten years older than he was.

He stood with his giant arms crossed in front of himself, glaring at Phantom.

"What? Do I have something on my shirt?" Phantom made a show of glancing down at his uniform with a frown and swiping at the tightly woven fabric like there was indeed something upsetting his look.

Ashby grunted before moving to straighten his jacket and tuck the collar of his white undershirt. "You were in the Navy long enough to know how to appear in uniform." He straightened and buttoned Phantom's cuffs right before he began plucking every ring off his fingers. Phantom expected the interference, of course. Just like he knew his collar was tucked and cuffs undone. He would take every small rebellious opportunity he could. Although the benefit might have been purely for the distaste in his old friend's eyes.

The Commodore pocketed the rings, then made a lap around Phantom for inspection. "It'll have to do." He began walking away with a curt nod, gesturing for Phantom to follow. With a slow breath, he marched behind Ashby. It had been some time since Phantom followed orders from anyone, let alone a naval officer. It took every ounce of his self-control not to rebel against the command.

Phantom skipped up beside Ashby instead, clutching his hands in front of himself.

"Where are we off to? Collecting tax debts? Removing unsavory characters?" Phantom's eyes lit with an idea while Ashby remained silent. "Perhaps, we're visiting a doctor to dislodge the stick firmly stuck up your ass?"

Ashby let out a breath that bordered on a growl, fixing Phantom with an impossibly deeper scowl.

Phantom blinked, bowing his head slightly. "I apologize." He cleared his throat. "To dislodge the stick firmly stuck up your ass, *sir*."

Ashby grunted his disapproval before walking on, not waiting to see if Phantom followed. "This is not a joke. If you're going to pass as an officer, you'll need to walk and talk like one. I hope you remember how."

"How could I forget? They beat it into us." It occurred to Phantom that the man walking beside him was now the conduit for such offenses. Although, part of him always wondered if Ashby still treated the orphan boys like his predecessors did, or did he make things better after all? He stared at the man in question, whose only reaction was to clench his jaw. Whatever the answer, he wasn't proud of it.

"When we reach our destination, you'll need to keep your

mouth shut and your eyes sharp." Phantom opened his mouth to remark on the entertainment of doing those things in reverse, but Ashby had a hand up to stop him short of it. "You will act with the principled manners of an officer, nothing more and nothing else. Remember what is at stake."

The reminder only set Phantom's blood ablaze. Playing the part reminded him of how powerless he truly was. Yet, he had no other choice. For now.

"No need for a reminder, Commodore." He raised his hand in a mock salute that he didn't wait to be reciprocated before trudging down the path to high town. The Commodore gave a small, irritated grunt at the blatant disrespect. It was all too easy to rile the man. It was practically irresistible to watch the annoyance redden his cheeks and cause his teeth to grind. Phantom had been his personal irritant since they were children in Mama Owen's orphanage.

The path winded down the hill from the Fortress. It was all kept very close together, even if there was a lot of unused land. Samsara was extremely barren compared to the lush forests of Kheli. The town below was bustling with late morning shoppers and storekeepers. Most of the housing was closely stacked, as if huddling together would make them easier to protect. The houses were heavily slanted on account of the downpour storms would bring. Even the streets were lined with trenches to guide the runoff away from the homes.

After a storm, Samsara would look like a city made of waterfalls with streams of water falling down the sides of cliffs. A beauty few seemed to recognize since many never had the chance to see it from the sea.

A few townspeople called to Ashby, either recognizing his face or the many pins and decorations on his special uniform. Dutifully, Ashby inclined his head to them, but made no move to stop and sample the various delicacies offered to him. One woman brought out a fine set of Yokan porcelain teacups. It was common knowledge among Samsarans that women only brought out their finest wares for the most important of guests, even if Ashby politely declined.

"The people here are very grateful to you," Phantom whispered soft enough where only the Commodore would hear.

"They'd be less inclined if they knew the company I keep was the very monster they thank me for defending them against." The words bit and usually Phantom would let something like that roll off him. He knew what he stole from these people, but it was only what the Minister took from Kheli. It was just harder to witness the people who had to endure the middle of it.

Phantom was aware he chose which people to lay his kindness with. He chose the Khelitians all those years ago, because the Samsarans had Sebastian Ashby. But in equal measures, they all needed to be saved from the veritable monster who occupied the Fortress.

"Perhaps they would be less inclined to fear if the Minister hadn't exaggerated the stories. Though I'm flattered; he's spread my name enough to make me legend. It's made my conquests all the easier."

"James," Ashby started, taking a subtle glance to see if anyone was listening, but the people gave him — and subsequently Phantom — a wide berth. "I haven't the patience for your false bravado." Phantom's brow shot up even as he considered his old friend's words. "We are going to see Lord Desmond."

Phantom opened his mouth, but before his beautifully strung insults towards the rich noble could spill out, Ashby had a finger up to stop him short.

"I will hear none of it, Officer." Phantom bit his cheek. "When we reach his estate, you will act like a dutiful officer accompanying his Commodore on a routine security check. Desmond needs his treasure safe from infamous pirates and you are going to tell him exactly how to do that."

A mocking chuckle left him. "And how do you figure that?"

Ashby's dark eyes gazed slightly down at Phantom. The man only surpassed him by an inch or so to Phantom's utter annoyance. "Because if you don't, I will report back to the Minister on your failure, and he'll find the best way to punish you."

The fight didn't leave Phantom completely, but the idea of standing his ground for something as insignificant as this was laughable. If he was going to enrage the Minister, he'd spend it on something far more useful than his pride. Besides, playing good little officer might just gain him enough information to burn the entire system down.

"Fine," Phantom spat, letting a little of his dignity fall at the Commodore's feet. The submission was enough to earn a dimpled smile from his old friend. It brought back memories of a smaller, but just as dimpled smile as they ran across the muddy streets of Samsara post storm.

The Commodore resumed marching towards Lord Desmond's estate, but the feeling of submission fell flat and bitter in Phantom's chest, so he did the only thing he could think of to temper it.

He swiped a bandolim from a nearby merchant kart. The man standing behind the kart didn't even notice the thievery. Phantom wasn't exactly being subtle. Perhaps the merchants were used to forgoing their goods to officers.

"Put it back," Ashby grumbled, clearly losing patience and every bit of victory he felt at Phantom's submission.

Phantom painted on a blinding grin. "No." He fiddled with the metal coiled strings, testing their notes and how tuned the instrument was. It had been a while since he'd laid his hands on a bandolim, but the feel of metal against his callused fingertips was all too familiar. He'd played endless songs for the officers back when he was a willing participant of the Navy. The instrument had gained him many friends there even if he lost them not long after that, some of them to the clutches of the monster.

"My apologies." Ashby placed a pair of silver coins on the kart in place of the bandolim, the merchant's eyes beaming with gratitude.

"There's no need, sir," the man blubbered, his wide eyes stuck somewhere between awe and fear. So, the officers did swipe at karts. Although Phantom was hardly one to judge. "W—we are honored to provide music to the heroes of the island."

Nemain, spare him.

Ashby flashed his most noble smile. "I insist."

The man's eyes brightened, his slight frame quivering with excitement. "Thank you, sir." Ashby nodded before returning to Phantom's side.

"It's been a while since I paid for something," Phantom lied. He'd passed out coins plenty of times in Kheli and even in Samsara, but he wasn't about to sully his legend.

"You didn't pay for it." Ashby's tone took on a lower register that signaled the end of his patience. There wasn't much more Phantom could get away with without consequence.

"Oh good, still got it then."

Ashby growled a sigh which was a warning all its own, but Phantom ignored him, strumming at his new instrument instead.

"Do you remember the songs Mama Owen taught us, brother?" The chords blended together as Phantom searched for a pleasant melody.

"I'm not your brother."

"She always was off key, considering she couldn't hear a goddess-damned thing, but I still remember the words. It would always cheer you up." Phantom let a chord vibrate as his fingers danced across metal coils. Soon his voice carried out along with them.

> WHEN THE SUN CAME UP AND THE MOON FELL DOWN
> DOWN TO THE RIVER RUSH DOWN TO THE SEA
> THE WORM BREATHED IN AND THE SPARROW CAUGHT HIM
> DOWN TO THE RIVER RUSH DOWN TO THE SEA
> THE SPARROW FELL DOWN AND THE FOX DID POUNCE
> DOWN TO THE RIVER RUSH DOWN TO THE SEA

Ashby sighed as Phantom sang, but he didn't miss the way the Commodore's eyes lit or how his shoulders relaxed. The memories filled him too. The way they'd stay up and laugh at the ridiculous songs Mama Owen used to sing terribly. Tone deaf didn't come close to describing that woman, but she didn't seem to care that she couldn't hear herself or that she was bursting the eardrums of the children at her orphanage. She wanted to sing anyway.

There was something freeing about singing, especially if one didn't care about doing it well.

> THE FOX WALKED ON BUT THE WOLF CAME UPON
> DOWN TO THE RIVER RUSH DOWN TO THE SEA
> THE WOLF FELL ASLEEP AND THE BEAR DID REAP
> DOWN TO THE RIVER RUSH DOWN TO THE SEA
> THE BEAR CAME TO TOWN AND THE PEOPLE BROUGHT
> HIM DOWN
> DOWN TO THE RIVER RUSH DOWN TO THE SEA

The song continued telling of the cycle of life and how one creature's death meant another would live another day until they fell into the cycle again. Phantom always thought it was a ridiculous concept because there was one creature that defied this process entirely. Necromites were already dead, so they couldn't be another's prey and yet they were the predators to everything.

Phantom caught Ashby singing along with him. A small mumble, but even with the song's eerie theme, it was a reminder of a simpler time. A time when 'commodores and pirates' was only a game they played.

CHAPTER 5

REVERIAN BOURBON

The minutes ticked by as Phantom played songs from their childhood and the Commodore either resisted singing or mumbled along. At least, until they turned a corner to a large estate. Bushes lined the fences to keep nosy eyes off the house itself, but with two naval officers approaching, a pair of personal guards opened the gate.

Ashby snatched the bandolim from Phantom's hands and tossed it to the nearest tree. It banged against the trunk, but somehow remained intact while Phantom cringed.

"You could just ask nicely."

Ashby didn't respond, instead he puffed out his chest and straightened his shoulders. Phantom resisted rolling his eyes as he mimicked the same movement, lifting his chin to really sell it. He'd mostly have to not laugh at this nobleman for letting in the very monster he wanted protection from.

As the path stretched on, it came to a mansion big enough to house a tenth of the population of Samsara. It was a gleaming white estate with large pillars decorating the front and surrounded by lush green grass. The house was built before the War, which wasn't unheard of. Anything ornate came before necromites. This nobleman had enough luck and money to keep it that way.

The Commodore painted on a winning smile as they approached, but he leaned in so only Phantom could hear. "Keep your wit to yourself. Convince Lord Desmond you are a proper officer, and I can let the Minister know you succeeded."

Phantom couldn't stop his nose from wrinkling at the suggestion of wanting Daddy Davenport's approval. His disapproval was much more appetizing. If there wasn't so much at stake, he'd do his very best to ruin this interaction.

A man stepped out of the ten-foot front doors with his arms outstretched. "Commodore Sebastian Ashby. At last, you've come." He was a spindly man with a wiry white mustache and a grey councilor's suit. Even if Samsara didn't have politicians who could rival the Minister, the noblemen of the island liked to think they could.

Lord Desmond let out a bellowed laugh as he clapped his hands on either side of Ashby's shoulders. "You've grown bigger, my boy. What is Thomas feeding you at the Fortress these days?"

Ashby let a dark chuckle escape him and Phantom couldn't quite tell if his smiles were forced or if he felt a friendship with the nobleman. The latter seemed both impossible and laughable for a boy of Mama Owen's orphanage.

"The same rubbish as always, my lord," Ashby admitted.

Desmond nodded, but his attention drifted to Phantom. Even with the rings gone and the uniform up to code, he stood out. Perhaps it was the lick of a tentacle peeking out around his neck, the kohl still rimming his dark blue eyes, or the eyes themselves showing the soul of a free man.

"And who is your companion, Commodore?"

Phantom extended a hand and let his mouth spread into a warm smile. "Officer Hawkins at your service, my lord." It was too easy. To the untrained ear, he sounded like a dutiful officer, but he laced the words with sarcasm. With a glance at Ashby's less than impressed face, he caught onto it.

Desmond accepted his hand and shook it fiercely. "Hawkins you say?" The man's eyes narrowed. "Any relation to the late lieutenant turned rogue pirate?"

Phantom let his smile become genuine as he reassessed the man. He was smarter than he looked and clearly heard enough gossip from way back in his glittering mansion.

"I'm afraid they often give that name to orphans, my lord." It wasn't untrue. Many of the children who left Mama Owen's care had the last name Hawkins, as if they all came from the same family. Since Ashby's parents died while he was old enough to remember them and their last name, there was no need for him to be assigned one.

Desmond's eyes slid to the Commodore's for a moment, who nodded his confirmation. Clearly, he trusted Ashby enough to accept he wasn't letting an infamous pirate into his home. They followed him into the ridiculous house that really should have been called a palace.

The doors closed with a thunderous clap as Desmond lifted his arms to showcase his wealth. There were situations in which Phantom could control his basic instincts, but this was not one of them. After years of pick pocketing as a boy, then adulthood spent as a thieving pirate, every beat of his heart told him this was the perfect man to rob, and he was about to get the inside look on how to pull it off.

"Welcome to my home, gentlemen. Come." Desmond gestured for them to follow him up the eye-catching grand staircase, the focal point of the foyer.

First, Phantom noticed the abundance of staff on hand. The questions remained: where did they stay, and what protocols did they follow in the event of a burglary?

"Officer Hawkins is our expert in security measures, my lord. He'll ask you a few questions to be sure your assets remain yours." Ashby followed the man who rounded into a smoke-filled room that instantly reminded Phantom of Ramirez. With the abundance of old books lining the walls, a stash of bourbon on a cart to the side, and the island's finest selection of cigars, it would indeed be the old man's favorite room in the house.

"Ask away, my boy."

Desmond strolled up to the cart and poured a finger measure of bourbon into a crystal glass before handing it to Ashby, who held up a dismissive hand.

"Not on duty, I'm afraid, my lord."

The man seemed disappointed but tipped his head regardless. "Shame. What about you, Hawkins? Any reservations about drinking on the job?"

"Normally, yes, but I could not say no to a thirty-year aged Reverian Bourbon if I was hung by my toes in the market, my lord." Phantom swiped the drink and sipped at its contents. The drink was easily worth more than that bandolim merchant would earn in his lifetime, so naturally Phantom couldn't pass it up.

Desmond chuckled. "The man has taste, Commodore. I dare say, he's much more entertaining that most of the officers you collect. I swear you teach those boys to be boring."

Ashby seethed a bit at the unprofessionalism Phantom displayed by accepting the drink. "Boring can be efficient, my lord."

Desmond waved him off and turned back to Phantom. "Ask your questions."

Phantom swirled the dark amber liquid in his cup for a moment before lifting his eyes to the nobleman as if he didn't already have the questions. "How many staff members you do you have on hand at night?"

The man sighed loudly. "I don't like to be surrounded by hired help when I am trying to sleep, so only my butler stays; in case I have need of him. Dear old Farley has been working for me since before the dreadful war."

Phantom raised his brows. The beginning of the war was about as old as the bourbon in his cup. His butler would have to be in his fifties or sixties, hardly a sound defender.

"But you do not have guards at night, my lord?"

Desmond tsked. "Of course, I do, boy. They man the gates at all hours of the day and night." He sat down on an expertly threaded couch that screamed of wealth.

"But you do not have any of them within your home at night, my lord?" Could the man be so arrogant to believe that gate security was enough? Phantom chastised himself for not robbing the foolish man sooner. Even if the gate guards could get to him in time, two would not nearly be enough.

The man scowled at Phantom's tone. "I am reluctant to entrust strangers with access to my home at night."

Phantom nodded, but with a pointed look from Ashby, he knew what he should say. "My lord, if a staff member robs you, you can track them, find the culprit, and punish them for the audacity they must have in trying to steal from you. But if a stranger you've never met robs you, the task becomes much harder."

"I will not be swayed in this, Officer. So don't waste your breath."

I was hoping you would say that.

"Well then," Phantom started, downing the rest of his over-priced bourbon. "Shall we look at what you want to protect most of all?"

Desmond's smile returned as he downed the rest of his bourbon and lifted from his seat. He clapped a hand on Phantom's shoulder. "With pleasure, my boy."

They followed the nobleman as he turned into the hall.

Second, Phantom noticed the abundance of discreet servant passageways buried in the walls, hidden by tapestries, but visible towards the edge at the bottom where a dark shadow suggested an opening. Desmond clearly liked his servants to remain unseen, but another question drilled into him.

"Do you have any children, my lord? Perhaps a wife?" Phantom spoke the question like it was causal small talk rather than an interrogation. Children enjoyed hiding spots and if there was one who lived in the mansion, that child would know exactly where each passage let out.

"I'm afraid not. Davina did not gift me with such a prize."

"Then where will your wealth go in the unfortunate event of your demise, my lord?" Phantom tried to word it correctly. It was more of a curiosity than obtaining knowledge for a heist or outwardly the protection of a heist. But if he were investigating a robbery or a murder, it would be the first question he would ask. Especially without a clear successor.

Desmond's head snapped around. "The Minister, of course." Phantom let one eyebrow shoot up. No wonder the Minister wanted the best thief in Samsara to tell this man how to protect his treasure. It would all be his soon.

They rounded into a large glass domed room with the light of two moons shining down onto the museum of treasure below. The glass looked out over a cliff that dropped off into the ocean. Phantom had to keep himself from smiling. It wasn't hard to scale a cliff face and as far as he could see, there were no fences lining it. The man was asking to be robbed.

Third, the treasure surrounding the room was all locked away in heavy glass cages. All pre-war glass, which despite its age, was still the most indestructible the man could have gotten his hands on, but not impenetrable. Desmond had to have some way of accessing the treasure.

"How do these displays open, my lord?" The man shouldn't give up this information no matter how much he trusted the receiver, but Phantom betted on the man's gullible nature and his arrogance in showing off his toys.

Desmond raised a single finger to encourage patience, then he strolled over to the nearest display. On it sat a crown encrusted with rubies and sapphires so large they took over the surface entirely. The weight alone meant anyone who wore it could not do so for long.

He pressed his hand to the glass and whispered, *"Anoixe."*

The glass instantly shifted, the top opening for him to reach in. He had to use two hands to lift the weighty thing and could only pop it on his head for a second with the largest grin he could muster before returning it to its perch.

"Interesting. You hired a witch, my lord?"

"Of course. The spell only reacts to my voice and that of the Minister in the case of my unfortunate death. Here, come Commodore, try it yourself." The man was giddy with excitement. Phantom often thought the wealthy used magic too easily. Witches rarely had use for assisting noblemen and could put all kinds of loopholes in their magical barriers. Desmond was likely trusting the witch too wholeheartedly.

Ashby walked to the nearest glass case; enclosed was a golden chest with intricate designs that was propped open to reveal a wealth of gold coins and jewels inside. It was practically a pirate's bloody wet dream.

He pressed his hand to the glass and whispered the word, *"Anoixe."* But the glass didn't budge. Desmond clapped as the witch's spell worked to perfection.

At the very center of the glass room stood a pedestal with a gleaming necklace on display. It was clearly of great importance. Even its surrounding aura made the air thicker. It was in the shape of a circle emanating silver light. A brief look to the sky confirmed that it was mimicking Davina's moon perfectly. The moon was half-waned, and the necklace only illuminated half of its pendant.

"Remarkable, isn't it?" Desmond cooed as he noted where Phantom's attention had landed.

"How did you get ahold of a Goddess pendant?" The necklaces were infamous and lost to time centuries ago. The magic in them was enough to rival any witch. It was a wonder the witch didn't steal it for herself when casting the barriers.

Desmond ignored his question. "It is said the pendants can amplify a witch's magic. In the old days, there were Goddess witches who would wield the pendants and were arguably the most powerful people in the world." The words sounded directly out of a children's tale, which made Phantom question its accuracy, but all legends came from somewhere.

"Arguably, my lord?" The Commodore asked, clearly taking the nobleman's bait.

"Well, they're dead now, aren't they? How powerful could they truly have been?" Desmond began walking away as if the treasure did not differ from anything else in his collection. To him, it must not have been. Desmond was no witch, so the necklace would do no more for him than any of the other treasure. Its religious attachment alone meant its worth was far greater than anything else in that room. Arguably, only the Stone and the other two lost necklaces were worth as much.

Something hummed inside Phantom's chest as he stared at it, as if he was destined to take it.

Desmond escorted them back to the front of the house with a small goodbye. With the sun setting, he clearly was eager for the removal of their presence. Ashby nearly cantered out of the gate, picking the bandolim up and handing it back to Phantom.

"I knew you missed the songs." But something in Ashby's eyes gave him pause. There was an intensity and a challenge in them which made Phantom grin deviously. "You want me to steal that necklace?"

Ashby grimaced at Phantom's accusation but nodded. "The Minister wants you to steal that necklace."

CHAPTER 6

WITCHES & PAINTINGS

There were many things Phantom had to do before robbing Lord Desmond. First on his agenda was tracking down the witch who cast those barrier spells on the glass cases. After living as an orphan and pick pocket in Samsara, he knew his way around its slums.

The lowest elevated land of the city, which was nearly sea level and had beautiful white sand beaches, was where the vilest of creatures inhabited the island. Of course, this was where the witches were, not because they chose the slums, but because the Minister drove them to live here. Much like Phantom's situation, their usefulness was the only reason they weren't strung up, but it only took one crystal out of line to change his mind.

An onyx building housed symbol after symbol of runes and other deity worshiping markings. Witches did not solely follow the Triple Goddesses, but the Draiocht Gods as well. The symbol of Hect, a crescent moon with a single dot in the middle, stood at the entrance to the building. Witches were well known and used often in Samsara. Small tricks for the commoners and expensive spells for the wealthy. Specifically this building, which advertised its expertise on the protection of precious possessions.

Phantom forwent his uniform for his usual pirate garb, including the silver rings he pried away from Ashby and his long black leather coat. These were the parts of Samsara he visited the most. Ashby was reluctant to let him go, but Phantom had to reassure the Commodore that the stakes alone would keep him on the island and in order to complete the task appointed by the Minister, he needed to visit the witches. A visit that the Commodore's presence would make immensely more difficult.

He strolled into the onyx building and immediately had to adjust to the dim lighting. Candles were lit around the expansive welcoming room, along with burning incense strong enough to choke. Phantom was grateful that his beast slept, or he might not have been able to endure it.

A woman rested across a sloping red chaise. Her fingers were blackened to the knuckle, small burn marks decorating her forehead just above her brow. The dress she wore was as black as night, with lace that extended past where her legs were and fanned across the arm of the couch. She propped herself up on one arm, examining Phantom with a critical eye.

"Hello, I'm—"

"A man with many names and yet no name at all." Her accent rang stronger than Phantom had ever heard before, telling of places further than he had been to. Further than was even on a map. "A man with a purpose and yet no purpose at all." She reached for a candle next to her, but no flame danced upon the waxy stub. "A man." With a wave of her hand, the candle lit with a fury, blazing against the wax. "And yet, not a man at all." She blew out the candle as suddenly as she had lit it, a rising column of smoke the only evidence of the flame's existence.

"Right," Phantom started, unsure what to do with the witch's riddles. "And you are?"

The witch stood, her dress descending from the couch to trail behind her. "A woman with many names and yet no name at all." Phantom narrowed his eyes at her, but she only offered a dark chuckle. "We are alike Phantom of the Devils." Her hand drifted to his face, grazing across the stubble there. She was indeed a beautiful woman, but not in the way Rose Davenport was. This witch was beautiful, like a snake. A wonder to see, but dangerous to touch. She tossed his head away suddenly as if he spoke his thoughts. "You are not ready." She turned from him and pointed to a curtain on the side of the room. "Who you seek is there."

Phantom tipped his head at the strange woman. "Thank you, dearie." He stepped toward the curtain to pull it to the side.

"We will meet again Phantom of the Devils."

Phantom turned to respond, but the witch was gone. The only thing left was that smoke trail still burning out of the candle she blew out.

The scent of sandalwood hit Phantom from beyond the curtain. Incense was lit in a bowl in the middle of the room at the center of a sand circle. The white sand was littered with small lit candles, carefully arranged crystals, and small animal bones. A woman dressed in a dusty deep blue dress sat cross-legged in the sand before all her items. Her eyes were delicately closed, and her hands rested on her knees. A string was wrapped around each of her hands in the pattern of a star. Rings covered her hands, and her chest was full of adornments.

He considered the woman in her peaceful state. Her dark ebony hair cascaded over her shoulder in soft curls, her skin was sun worn and freckled. There was youth to the woman's face, yet when her eyes opened, something old swirled within them.

"Captain," she started, taking in Phantom's appearance and perhaps something hidden beneath it all. "But that isn't right. For what is a captain without his crew?"

Phantom resisted the urge to roll his eyes. "Do all the women here speak in riddles?" Acid burned in his gut at the thought of being without his crew. He might not be with them, but they were still his.

Her eyes closed again. "You know about the spells I placed on the rich man's treasure."

"Right." His annoyance slipped at the idea of getting what he came for. "Tell me how to get past the barriers and I'll be on my way."

She huffed, but it also sounded like a laugh. "You cannot get what you seek for nothing. Even you Maahes." There weren't many people who knew of the Draiocht legends, but if anyone did, it would be the witches.

Phantom spread his arms. "What can I do for you, my lady?"

She narrowed her eyes, clearly not enjoying his teasing. "You may call me Indigo, and that remains to be seen. I've yet to decide what I want from you."

He placed his arms before himself, regarding the witch further. "You expect me to trust you enough to owe you a favor?"

Indigo smiled; her teeth traced in black as if she had been chewing on charcoal. "I know what's at stake for you, Captain. You stand to lose everything you love should you fail the Minister. Is that not worth a pinch of trust?" She pinched a few granules of sand to display her point. The sand traveled over candle, bone, and crystal alike.

"Fine," he bit out. "Just tell me."

"Ah ah," she chastised. "Surely, Captain, you remember how to make a deal with a witch?"

He let out an exasperated grunt and reached for the knife in his boot. It was the only weapon Ashby allowed him to take after tedious convincing. The knife's edge bit into his palm as he sliced it open. He balled his hand into a fist and let the red liquid drip from his hand to the incense bowl below. After a few drips, the sting in his palm ceased.

Indigo swirled the blood inside the bowl with the incense stick, then offered her own blood to the mix. The moment her blood hit his, the candles flared around them.

"It is done. The spell I placed on the rich man's treasure was designed to keep humans out, but you are not human, are you, Captain?"

"What do you know of the beast?"

She smirked. "Do you wish to grow your debt to me, Captain?" His instinct was to demand the information, but he did not know what he would sacrifice for it. Indigo, knowing the full extent of his abilities, made those favors even more risky.

"No, I do not."

She sighed as if she both expected the answer and was disappointed by it. "When you visit Lord Desmond's estate, keep your beast close and the barriers will not stop you."

He nodded before pivoting for the door, leaving the witches in his wake and wondering what exactly he'd agreed to.

***

The heist would have to wait for nightfall, so Phantom took the time he had to explore the Fortress for any signs of Serena. He doubted the Minister would keep the beastie in the same building as Phantom, but it was worth checking. That is, if he could go anywhere.

Even back in his officer uniform, they guarded most rooms with strict orders to keep Phantom out. Normally, he could find a way around the guards, but with a Fortress lacking windows or other exits, sneaking in was less than achievable. Only those beautiful bloody paintings lined the walls, with the occasional window in the hallways. It was giving him a headache to look at them. He should have asked Indigo about it. No doubt the Minister had them enchanted to ensure loyalty.

As a result, he was glad it didn't work on him.

Phantom's exploration brought him to the sunroom, named appropriately for its towering windows and abundance of sunlight. It was as if the Minister congregated every window that should have been in the Fortress to this one room. It was no surprise that it was the most popular room for courtiers and off-duty officers alike. Raucous laughter from surrounding courtiers filled the glass room that overlooked a sun shining sea.

Phantom's gaze instantly fixed on the back of a blonde head right next to the window with the sea expanded beyond her. In her grasp was a paintbrush as she swiped strokes on the canvas before her. Phantom's mouth parted. She was the artist of the paintings on the walls? With the apparent skill of her brush strokes and style of the painting, he had to assume he was correct.

It would explain their recent appearance in the Fortress halls, since her presence was a fresh addition as well. During his old days in the Fortress, their paths never crossed.

He willed his footsteps to remain quiet as he stalked behind her, peering at her work. It was a beautiful blue ocean on the cusp of dusk with dark jagged cliffs and a ship bravely sailing between them. He nearly gasped at the sight of red sails.

"Reminiscing are we, love?" The words were soft, only for her. He realized a moment too late that he leaned in, saying those words directly into her ear. She tensed and relaxed all within a second, hardly perceptible, but he would notice anything about her.

Rose continued her brush strokes, adding sea foam to the

waves to make them appear wilder. "Please, Captain." Her words dripped disdain like they did when she first boarded his ship, not when she left. He wondered when they had taken steps backwards. "One can admire the beauty of a ship and its environment without daydreaming of its tranquility."

Phantom scoffed. "Tranquility?" He couldn't help the grin it brought to his face of her recounting the time she spent on *Nemain's Revenge*. "Hardly the word I'd use to describe a rogue pirate ship, especially the one on which I held you captive on." With her back to him, he found himself tempted to draw closer. He wanted to run a hand across her arm, down her back, wrap an arm around her waist and pull her flush to him.

"As you like to remind me, I was a well-treated stowaway. The only moment I felt captive was when you locked me in your quarters."

He stopped himself before his hand landed on her waist, her words pulling him from her spell. "Yes, how *did* you escape from there? I've been *ever* so curious, little songbird."

She glanced over her shoulder, and time stopped. There was no one else around, just a pirate and his songbird. She leaned in closely, and he couldn't help it this time. His hand landed on her waist. She did not object.

"A lady never reveals her secrets." A small smirk lifted the side of her mouth as she shrugged his hand off and returned to her work. This woman was going to be the death of him.

"Well then, since you are so adept with a canvas and paints and you destroyed my very expensive portrait, I shall require a new one. Do you take commissions, Miss Davenport?" He didn't miss the way she bristled at her last name, but she covered it with a sly smile.

"What can you offer in exchange, Captain?" Her brush continued to stroke as if she only half paid attention to his presence.

Phantom leaned in closer, brushing a gold lock of hair

behind her ear to whisper. He had to contain his smile when she sucked in a breath in reaction to his touch. "What do you require? To sail across the sea and never return? Perhaps you'd like to see the oasis plains in Draiocht? Or the snow-tipped mountains in Meraki? Your wish is my command, love. You need only ask, and I'd take you anywhere my ship can carry us."

She cleared her throat. "You aren't in a particular arrangement to be promising such things."

"I'd do it still. I'd defy Nemain herself if you asked it of me." The words were out before he could stop them, but he couldn't deny their truth. Rose gasped at the notion. She knew what the Goddess of Death meant to Phantom.

"Why?" The words spilled from her in a way that made Phantom's heart break.

He whipped her around to face him, keeping only a hand on her waist. "What makes you think you aren't worth it?"

Her lips parted, staring up at Phantom like he was a miracle and a ghost all at once. But the expression was gone as soon as it came, replaced with narrowed eyes and her lips set into a hard line. She set her brush down and rushed away without another word. Something felt amiss between them. Although Phantom knew she was holding back many things from the man who tricked her, this was something more.

The delicate fabric of her dress carried in her wake. A few eyes were on them as she walked away. A few officers and curious courtiers, but they soon resumed their conversations.

Phantom somehow felt colder with her no longer in the room.

A prickling sensation, like the feeling of a spider crawling on his back, made him turn. Ravana stood next to him witnessing Rose's abrupt departure. The Priestess wore a lilac silk gown, her crimson hair spilling like a river of blood over her shoulder. It told Phantom she was in a playful mood, which usually involved drama of some sort, but no matter what dress she wore, it always meant trouble.

"James dear, don't pine. It doesn't suit you." Her voice took on a lower register.

"I really prefer Captain Phantom now." The last thing he wanted to hear from her was his name. Even if he didn't claim it fully, it was the name he had as a child. A name for a simpler version of himself and this venomous woman was anything but simple.

There was a glass of red wine in her hand that she swirled absentmindedly. "Not here, you don't." Her words were quiet enough to only be heard by him. "Although, I do say, I prefer your brooding pirate compared to this doe eyed officer."

A low growl escaped his throat. "What do you want, Ravana?"

She chuckled darkly. "See, we are on a first name basis."

Phantom glared down at her, but the reaction only seemed to amuse her. She reached out to place her palm on his arm and he fought his instinct to shrug her off or bash open the glass behind him just to throw her off the cliff. But getting on her bad side would be a sore mistake.

Yellow flickered at the edges of his mind.

Not unless the fall killed her.

"Relax, James. I want nothing from you." He didn't dare release a breath. "Yet," she added. There it was. This woman wouldn't leave him alone if it gave her the world. Tormenting him was much too fun for that.

"Excuse me, my Lady." Phantom offered her a small bow, enough to satisfy any onlookers, but the glare still present on his face should have been warning enough.

She stepped forward before he could pull away gracefully. "If you do not listen to anything else I say, James, listen to this." He grunted, but she ignored him. "Stay away from the Minister's daughter. Your losses will outweigh whatever conclusion you've envisioned. For you and for her."

If Rose did in fact decide to leave this Davina-forsaken rock, he'd gladly be her vessel, but he couldn't let Ravana see that. Ravana would make it her mission to stand between them and *that* he couldn't allow.

Instead, he nodded and bowed again, slipping away from her pawing hands. He still had a beastie to find and a heist to complete. Hopefully, that was all the Minister needed from him.

CHAPTER 7

ONE VOICE, ONE BROTHER

EIGHTEEN YEARS AGO

It didn't get this cold on Samsara, not normally. But a nippy wind, as Mama Owen liked to put it, came through rather strong last night and the orphanage had little in the way of holding off the bitter air.

A few blankets, and a wood fireplace was the most of it.

James rubbed his hands together to stave off the numbness settling into his fingers. He was still a gangly boy with little meat on his bones thanks to the meager rations provided by the Minister. Mama Owen did what she could with minimal ingredients, though.

The fire roared in the opening of brick and mortar. It was late in the night, so everyone, aside from a stray orange cat that took up residency next to the heat of the flames, slept in their beds, huddled together for warmth. But no one would go near James, so the fire it was.

He didn't blame them. They had good reason to fear him.

James was stronger and angrier than he should have been, tearing apart clothes, trinkets, and flesh alike at the smallest inconvenience.

Now, you know that isn't true, said the green voice in his head that went by the name Sam.

Many voices occupied his mind, chattering and taking up space so he'd distinguish his own thoughts from others with colors. He didn't know all their names, but he knew their colors. The colors were the only way to tell which one was speaking. It was brief and faint, but there was a slight coloration when a voice that wasn't his, spoke. Or when they were too close. So close that they could use his hands, his teeth—

James snapped his eyes closed against the memory. That was the red one. The red one didn't speak. It knew only violence.

One voice he heard more than the rest was the green one.

Sam was what James imagined having an older brother was like, kind, protective, annoying. James hadn't quite decided if the voice was some sort of comforting illusion he'd fabricated, but it was certainly nice to have someone to talk to.

But that meant the red one was him, and the destruction he caused, his to own.

It's not your fault. It never was. The beast is only trying to protect you.

It was nights like these, James was inclined to believe Sam and his pretty lies.

"Meow."

James's attention flicked to the orange ball of fluff curled a bit too close to the fire. The creature purred as James stroked its matted fur. The thing desperately needed a bath. When it butted its soft head against James's hand, he felt Sam flinch away from the little beastie.

It brought a smile to his face. "What's the matter? Afraid of cats?" James spoke aloud even though he didn't have to. It helped him separate his voice from those in his head.

Sam hesitated before answering. *If you saw the felines I am used to, you'd be wary of them as well.*

The notion of Sam being afraid of anything was ridiculous enough to bring a smile to his face. It made him feel a little more powerful, not fearing something when someone else did. Not much made him feel that way anymore.

"Maybe you can tell me about them sometime." The cat leapt away, James's only warning, before a voice came from behind him.

"Talking to yourself, demonio?"

James's head whipped to the boys behind him. All of them were skinny like him, but they were taller, a little older. He looked like them: dirty faces, unevenly chopped hair, and ratty clothing. But their faces contorted with hard lines and sneers.

"No, I was talking to the cat."

The boys laughed loudly. There wasn't a purpose to remaining quiet. Mama Owen couldn't even hear a scream, let alone a few boys looking to make trouble.

"What do you want, Felix?"

The middle boy's laughter died, his eyes darkening. "What makes you think you can say my name?" The boys advanced, crowding James and cutting off anyway around them. Soon, he was cornered, the heat of flames beating against his backside.

James tried not to show fear, but it was an impossible task.

A cruel smile curled up Felix's face, a single dimple combining with a mole on the right side. The boys reached for him, fear shooting through James's veins. Red washed his vision.

He pushed one boy away, tossing him further than he should have been able to.

But Felix only scoffed at him, his blonde hair falling into his face. "I know what you are. It's what the officers come looking for. A witch's son."

The words hit like a death sentence. A witch's son would be enough to cause panic across Samsara. They were known for their brutality and ruthless nature, not to mention their affinity for dark magic. Captain Pike was the most well-known son of witch, appearing out of nowhere, seemingly invincible, escaping all odds. He was unnatural and feared above all others.

Witch's sons were hunted by officers and killed.

James knew that's what he was. There was no other explanation. Still, he didn't want to die.

"I'm not. I swear it." He'd had to be a good liar. His life depended on it often lately.

"Then how do you explain the red eyes?" The boy advanced further, causing James to take an instinctual step back.

He had no explanation, he never did, and in the face of a boy who could turn him over to the officers, he felt helpless.

"Don't worry. Mama Owen would throw me out if I turned you in." James let a breath of relief leave him. "But I'm going to be an officer, someday. When that happens, I'll be bringing you in as my first prize."

Not if I have something to say about it.

James didn't dare respond to Sam. He couldn't give Felix or the other boys anymore reason to suspect him. But Felix's gaze shifted from the roaring fire back to James again, red blurring the edges of his vision again.

He knew the boys saw it.

"Or I could just take care of you now."

Felix moved faster than James could register, hands landing on his shoulders. But James resisted before Felix could push, fear flooding his system, the beast roaring beneath his flesh.

He struggled against Felix's hold while simultaneously shoving the beast deep into himself. If he ripped apart the boys before him, there wasn't anything Mama Owen could do. He'd be taken away before morning.

"Noooo!" He screamed against the beast. But more hands came down on him as the other two boys came around him. Six hands now pushed him towards the fire, the heat becoming unbearable and the beast becoming too powerful.

He fought and struggled against two fronts and screamed at the beast, the boys, the world and whatever cruel fate Davina inflicted upon him.

Maybe he deserved it after all.

No, yellow shouted.

The thought ricocheted in his mind enough that it woke something up. It distracted him enough to lose one battle. His body gave in, searing heat and biting metal greeted him.

James woke at the foot of the fireplace. The fire had long since died and the cold bit at his naked flesh.

Naked?

James's hand roamed his skin, finding only smooth skin, but no burn marks, just a few soot stains and a few scraps of clothing. The flames didn't burn him at all.

You're welcome.

James leapt to his feet.

The voice was unfamiliar, completely different from the other three. This one felt like sunlight.

"Who are you? Where did you come from?"

The name's Kayden. I've been here for a while, actually.

"No, you haven't. It's my head, I would know."

You really wouldn't. You should get some clothes on.

Right, that would be a good idea. James headed for the chest where Mama Owen kept the extra clothing, nothing greater than what the other orphans were wearing, but it was better than no clothes at all, especially on this chilly night. He put on the warmest clothes he could get his hands on.

"I need to get out of here."

A wise choice.

James ran out the front door before anyone could find him. He needed air.

"What happened?"

I saved you from the fire and taught those vermin a lesson.

James's heart raced in his chest, but it wasn't from running. He stopped in an alleyway. "What did you do to them?" he whisper shouted into empty air.

I only bruised them. No one will believe you managed it on your own and nothing resembling a witch.

He let out a breath of air. The relief he felt so consuming he nearly fell to his knees, but he held onto the ladder beside him instead. James looked up the ladder.

Probably not a good idea. A storm is coming.

Indeed, he could feel the first drops of rain gracing his cheeks, but storms made him feel more alive. He climbed the ladder, ignoring the annoyed sigh coming from Kayden.

James looked over the dark Samsaran streets, the rain growing harder by the second. The streets of Samsara would soon run with fresh water, filling reserves and having plenty left over to spill into the sea in waterfalls off the cliffs. Rain poured above James's head. The way it felt on his skin was both calming and exhilarating, and calm was something he needed in droves.

He let it wash over him, soaking in the peace it brought him. It washed away his problems, if only for a moment.

A crash broke in the alley beside James, but it was nothing like the thunder beginning to rumble.

"You must know something, kid." The dark voice of a man followed several heavy footfalls and a pair of light ones. "Mommy and Daddy must have had a place. One they told you to never to tell anyone about."

"Please." The small voice of a boy who had been crying carried through the rain. James shouldn't have been able to hear it from that distance, which told him the monster was awake. "I don't know. They didn't tell me anything."

Another male voice laughed cruelly. "He expects us to believe that. The little shit is holding out on us." Water splashed as if a large boot had stomped in a puddle.

"No," the boy cried. "Please, I did nothing."

"Well, it's not about what you did, innit?" More footsteps in the same puddle said they were advancing, backing their prey into a corner. James crawled over the roof to get a look. There were three men slowly walking towards the boy, each were heavily armed, but only one held a knife out. The boy started sobbing, the tangy scent of his fear hitting James harder than the storm raging. "This is about who your parents were, and you'll be growin' right into their shoes, won't cha?"

"Please, I—I don't know what you mean." The sobs grew fiercer, too strong for him to form words anymore.

This isn't right. You need to help him, green interjected.

James breathed heavily. "If I go down there, what will happen?"

Death, but it looks to me, that'll happen anyway, yellow said.

"Bah, this one is useless, boss. Let the street have 'em." Lightning flared overhead as if Davina herself was in outrage, but the men didn't so much as flinch. No one grew up in Samsara without learning to weather its storms.

"Nah, the streets are too good for him. Slaver blood runs thick and strong. We'll take the little shit out here before he can become one of 'em."

The boy started screaming, but it was useless against the rage of the storm. The three men advanced, the other two drawing their own blades. James's recent experience with three boys and a fire had him on edge, but this was worse—so much worse. Red flared at the edges of his vision, quickly overtaking him.

Are you a coward, boy? Jump!

James leapt off the roof, landing square before the three men, who paused at the intrusion. His hand was to the stone below and his head was down. If he looked up, he knew precisely what they would see. Red already tinted his vision. The monster was hardly leashed, too close to banish completely. There was no calming it once everything turned red.

"What's this?" One man asked.

"Run," James said in a voice that was both young and old, contained both one and many souls. Yellow, green, orange, red—James. All five of them spoke at once. The boy behind him needed no more encouragement than that. He took off down the street, one of the men jumping after him.

"Oi, he's gettin' away," he protested, but a calmer voice seemed to halt him.

"We'll find him again. It's a small island. I'm more interested in the *hero* who dropped out of the sky." In the tone the man said *hero*, he believed in no such thing. Perhaps he was right, because James was no hero. He was the monster, but maybe the monster could do something good for once.

When the footsteps came into his downcast view, he finally lifted his head, looking through a curtain of black hair that was dripping with rainwater. He found all three men staring at him with what could only be described as a morbid fascination.

"What are you? A witch's son?" The calmer man asked. His eyes narrowed into slits, unmistakably seeing the red eyes that made him a target amongst the bullies of Mama Owen's orphanage.

The other two men grew pale, staring at the wrongness of him.

"What do we do with it?"

James stared at them, hoping the eyes would be enough.

The man in charge scrunched his nose as if the very sight of

James ignited a visceral reaction in him. "Kill it. Nothin' good can come from a witch."

James prayed to Davina that they believed in some god that would take them.

The men reached for him, but James let the leash fall and we smiled at them a second before we tore out their throats from their necks with our fangs.

James stood in the middle of an abandoned street in Samsara, letting the water wash away everything he had done. Rain trickled along his skin, washing blood from him to the cobblestones of the street, all the way to the waterfalls that rushed to the sea.

His hands shook under the weight of what he did. When he was a child and the beast first came out, he didn't know that would happen. This time, he chose those men's deaths. It was murder, even if they were horrid men.

Red images flashed in his mind, and he knew sleep would be harder to get in the coming weeks.

A soft sob broke into the air and James knew the monster hadn't left him completely, but it was sated for now, curled up like that stray cat before the fire.

James followed the cry to a wheeled kart on the side of the street. That tangy scent of fear filled the space, but not as potent as it was before. He rounded the kart to see the boy huddled next to the wheel. He really didn't have anywhere to go. Maybe Mama Owen had some room.

"Hey," James said softly, but loud enough to be heard over the rain. The boy snapped his head up, locking eyes with James. "Do you need a place to stay? I have—"

The boy pounced on him, flinging his arms around James's waist and pulling him in tight. He was only slightly bigger than the boy, but he continued to sob into James's chest like he was heaven sent.

"Thank you." The boy sniffed. "Thank you for saving me."

James's heart clenched. Saving him? He slaughtered three men. The boy only held him tighter as if trying to convince himself that James was real, that those men were really gone.

"Look, I know someone who can take you in." He nodded against James's chest. "Hey, what's your name?"

The boy looked up at him with constellations of freckles across his cheeks. "Sebastian, but most people call me Bash."

"Well Bash, let's get you out of this rain." He nodded, squeezing impossibly tighter to James's arms.

James had to wonder if this was what it felt like to be a hero.

CHAPTER 8

BEGGING FOR A ROBBERY

"I look ridiculous." Seeing Ashby dressed in black robes fitting a Draiocht *cerbalus* was beyond laughable, but if the Commodore was to pass as Phantom's first mate, it would have to do. Ashby shifted and plucked at the fabric as if it offended him by existing on his frame.

"Oh, stop your fussing," Phantom drawled and fixed the shawl around Ashby's head to hide his too light face and lack of facial hair. "The Minister insists that the robbery be credited to pirates, and you'll have to do."

Ashby groaned deeply in a way that resembled a growl. It brought a smile to Phantom's face to see his old prudish friend outside his realm of comfort.

"You know, Commodore, this new direction of yours is worrisome. I never thought I'd see you take the advice of witches, and plunder with a pirate. I'm beginning to think I'm a bad influence." It was difficult to keep a straight face, but Phantom managed.

Ashby glowered. "Let's just get this over with."

They stood on the cliff's edge with the night in full bloom around them, silver and lilac moonlight mixing at different angles. Lord Desmond's estate awaited beyond the bush lined fence beside them. They could climb the fence, but the expanse of grass and rock beyond it wouldn't offer much in the way of cover. The Minister was clear about making sure Phantom was seen in the act, so Desmond wouldn't suspect the Minister of the crime. He didn't want to be caught until the necklace was firmly in his clutches.

Phantom nearly pointed out that stealing an artifact after their visit regarding security was hardly covert, but in truth, he cared very little about the Minister's precious reputation.

The cliff side would provide them with the proper cover. The seas raged below; white foam abundant among the many rocks. It would be a fatal fall. The cliff itself would be mostly smooth and slimy due to its proximity to the ocean. It would be an arduous climb.

They each stabbed a stake into the most solid land they could find and tied a length of rope to it, which they promptly tied to their waistbands. An extra belt anchored the rope even more efficiently so that they could let out more rope when needed.

"Are you sure this will hold?" Ashby kicked at the stake, reassuring himself that it was solidly stuck in the earth.

"Only one way to find out." Before Ashby could react, Phantom kicked his chest sending the man sprawling backwards over the cliff. He gasped, but disappointingly didn't scream as he cascaded down. Phantom chuckled to himself but went still when he noticed his own rope falling down the cliff after the Commodore. "Bloody he—"

The rope tugged him off the cliff, straight after Ashby. The wind rushed by Phantom's face, pulling his hood off to rustle his dark hair before Phantom got ahold of the rope to steady himself. His gut twisted as the sea grew closer.

He jerked as the stake held, stopping his descent. Ashby

swung beside him, already trying to get a foothold on the slip-pery cliff side.

"You pulled my rope," Phantom accused, but Ashby gave him a blank stare.

"Then don't kick me off a cliff. Either of our ropes or stakes could have failed. Did you even consider that before planting your boot in my chest?" Small rocks and debris rolled from the cliff at their less than subtle movements.

"And now I know they won't fail." Ashby's eyes narrowed like he was picturing cutting Phantom's line. "You're welcome."

Ashby grunted before continuing his climb. Phantom's stunt cost them some distance but scaling rock faces was a familiar task that Phantom easily found a rhythm for. This was when he felt most alive, with the sea breeze spraying salty air at his back, dirt and rock crumbling around him, dirtying his nails.

As they climbed closer to Desmond's estate, Phantom found he didn't like the silence.

"Remember that day we broke into the Temple?" Ashby was a couple of feet away. He'd fallen back a fraction, clearly not as used to the task as Phantom was.

"Not particularly."

Phantom paused for a moment, letting the Commodore catch up, so the wind didn't muffle his voice. "You remember. We dressed as guards and painted the Goddess statues."

Phantom smiled at the memory. He had covered his palms in red paint then placed his hands under the statues' breasts and other choice body parts.

Ashby huffed as he caught up. "The Priestess thought it was such an atrocity that she sacrificed three goats to the Goddesses the next day." Phantom cringed at the memory. The Priestess's idea of a sacrifice included draining the blood from those goats and bathing naked in it under the light of the moons. It was a morbid and *public* affair.

Ashby quirked a brow. "Are you forgetting that the Minister

had us strung up by our ankles while the other recruits threw rotten food at us?"

"It was worth it."

"You always did enjoy getting me into trouble." Ashby groaned, a flicker of amusement in his stony gaze. "Somehow that hasn't changed."

Phantom smiled to himself, recalling the many times that was true. "You always did enjoy me getting you into trouble. Or was it the trouble, I wonder?"

The cliff's edge was close in sight as they covered the last few feet. Ashby didn't answer as they crested the edge and found themselves right outside Desmond's mansion.

"I only wanted to impress you," Ashby admitted.

Phantom paused, taking in the Commodore dressed as a devil, but there was a glint in his eye that reminded him of Bash, the boy Ashby used to be. At that moment, Phantom had to wonder if leaving his best friend behind all those years ago was really the right decision.

But the Commodore's mask shifted into place as he lifted his shawl back over his head. They both untied the rope at their waists and let the ropes fall. If someone saw the ropes, it could blow their cover before they were ready, so that escape plan was forfeit.

They crouched low, keeping to the shadows along the wall. Phantom reached out a hand, rubbing against the smooth stone.

"What are you doing?" Ashby whispered low enough that Phantom almost didn't hear, but he expected the question.

Phantom let his fingers trail the crevices of the wall, searching for a particular—there. Air sucked into the wall, signaling an entrance. He looked back at Ashby. "This." He pulled at the stone; it shifted, opening to a long, dark hallway.

Ashby's eyes widened. "How did you know this was here?"

"Desmond likes his staff to remain as unseen as possible. It was clear by the amount of servant halls in his home, hidden by furniture and tapestries." Phantom slithered inside, towing Ashby behind him and closing the hidden door. In the next breath, he lit a match, lighting a torch mounted to the wall, then sliding it from its perch. "The servants need to leave the house unseen. Since this side of the building faces away from the most visible areas, it would stand to reason this was where they would come and go."

Phantom shifted the torch in his hand, letting his eyes adjust to the light before leading the way.

"You got all that from a few hidden servant's halls?" Ashby stalked after him, taking in the oddly clean corridor that remained hidden without windows.

"That, and Desmond's disinterest in having so many servants. Sometimes a man's paranoia is exactly what makes him vulnerable." Phantom grinned in a way that had Ashby scowling at him again, but he didn't dwell on the Commodore's discomfort. He pulled out a compass, knowing the treasure sunroom lay in the furthest room in the west wing. They followed turns and corridors in the west direction until they ended up in the hall closest to the sunroom.

The door was locked, but Phantom made quick work of it as he pulled a lockpick from his pocket. It was a dull grey metal with two separate picks for the more complicated locks. A faint clicking noise ran through the halls as Phantom worked.

"Could you do that any quieter?" Ashby insisted, looking back to the halls as if he excepted Desmond himself to pounce on them.

A prickle of irritation ran down Phantom's spine. "Perhaps if you didn't speak, my hands would work faster."

Ashby's answering glare told Phantom exactly what he thought of Phantom's tone. A final click resounded, signaling Phantom's success but the grin on his face only made Ashby's scowl deepen.

He needed to bed someone. Preferably someone who wasn't his betrothed.

The door opened with a creak that seemed much louder now that he wanted it to be quiet. It was truly a shame, the lack of security around the treasure room. Only one locked door in a room lined with glass. Desmond was practically begging someone to rob him. Phantom had even suggested how to prevent thievery, though he would have found a way, regardless.

The nobleman relied too heavily on his fences and magic. There were far too many people who believed magic to be infallible when, in fact, it was the most unpredictable.

The silver moon of Davina shone proudly and brightly through the glass of the sunroom, almost as if highlighting the necklace itself. Surrounding the necklace, Desmond's treasure seemed to glitter even more astoundingly, reflecting the twinkling stars above as the clouds parted.

"Any chance I could take something more than the necklace?"

"No," Ashby retorted without hesitation in his most commanding voice.

"Come now, it would be much less suspicious if more than the necklace turns up missing." At Ashby's cocked eyebrow, Phantom pulled his prey in further. "It will make the Minister look suspicious if Desmond knows he wants it, and we stole nothing else from his precious collection." A beat of silence passed as Ashby's eye narrowed. "It's not hard to sort out that the Minister must have negotiated for the necklace already. Reaching for my help, well, it just reeks of desperation. I'll bet he tried every other avenue before reducing himself to piracy."

"You are committing the crime, not the Minister," Ashby snapped, but it was enough for Phantom to know he was right, though he hardly needed the confirmation.

"And yet," Phantom started, "I would not be here without

him. And speaking solely on my behalf, I would not rob a place like this and only take one trinket. You wanted a believable cover story, then make it real, and he'd have no reason to suspect the Minister."

"Fine, take whatever, but—" Ashby raised an accusatory finger. "Your spoils will belong to the Minister."

Phantom let his smile grow catlike. "I'm disappointed, Commodore. I knew you were the Minister's loyal lapdog, but I thought you would be cleverer than that." Ashby's anger grew visceral, flushing his cheeks red. "If the treasure were to be found in the Minister's possession, he would be accused, or if his reserves had a significant deposit, it would raise suspicion, especially after such a magnanimous robbery."

Ashby's anger melted away, replaced by a cruel smile. "Fine, *Captain*. Take what you want. The Minister owns you anyway. So long as there are people you care about, everything you are, everything you take will belong to him."

Rage was a fire that burned deep within his core, waking the beast beneath his skin. Phantom knew his eyes were dilating, filling his blue irises until crimson flooded the corners of his vision. He let the change happen. Let the monster stretch its legs. Although he had no intention of allowing the beast full access to his body, the closeness of the monster was exactly what he needed.

Ashby blinked at Phantom's reddening eyes. "You never told me why your eyes change like that." He had never witnessed Phantom's beast for himself, although it had appeared around him. Ashby never saw the truth, and Phantom would keep it that way if he could.

"I don't know," Phantom lied.

"Yes, you do," Ashby countered. "But if you wouldn't tell me while we were friends, I don't expect for you to tell me now." He passed Phantom, striding into the moonlit room.

The words hit Phantom harder than he expected, but he brushed it off.

"What did you find out from the witches?"

Phantom let a smile come back, although it felt more forced now. "Watch and see, old friend." He let his gaze snag on the crown encased in glass and witch's magic. He let his beast rise to the surface of his skin, enough to be close without breaking the surface.

The surrounding smells became all too potent. Some of the sandalwood still stuck to Phantom's clothes from his visit with Indigo, but beyond that he could smell the sun still baked into the floorboards. Even at night, the smell of the sun's influence still filled the room. Beyond that, the metallic smell of gold was so potent the taste lingered on his tongue, like a pool of blood in his mouth.

Then there was the scent of the salty sea air which wafted around Phantom and Ashby, but as his old friend drew closer to him, memories poured in with his scent. He smelled of suede and moss. It was an odd combination, but it was subtle enough that a human nose could not scent it on him. It was a dual scent that reminded Phantom of something that was meant to be wild but was tamed.

Phantom opened his eyes, and they were wholly red. Ashby inspected him from beyond the crown's case as Phantom continued to lift the glass and the top popped open for him.

Ashby's eyes widened as Phantom reached in for the weighty crown and placed it on his head. He knew he was a sight to behold in the glittering gold crown with red rubies matching his eyes. Not to mention his black leather contrasting terribly with such over the top finery.

"What do you think, Commodore?" He grinned, realizing too late that his fangs were out, his beast was too close to the surface to hide them. Ashby's eyes widened impossibly larger as Phantom let his tongue roam over the sharp peaks, drawing more attention to them.

"You are a demon," Ashby breathed in a trancelike state.

The crown weighed heavily on his head, but he enjoyed the way the Commodore was looking at him, a mix of awe and fear. With great effort, he pulled the crown from his head and placed it in a black bag he had brought with him, but he kept the beast close.

"Perhaps you'd be wise to recognize the fox you let into your house of hens." Phantom strode to where Ashby stood. He straightened at Phantom's approach, recovering from his shock.

"Is that a threat, *Captain*?"

Phantom frowned dramatically. "A friendly warning, *Commodore*. I don't respond well to cages." He turned his back on Ashby, heading to the object they came for. So long as he was doing what was asked of him, the Commodore would not heed his words, and he would pay dearly for it.

He performed the same act on the glass encasing the Goddess necklace. His monster growling in the presence of the Goddess of Fate. Davina had not done them any favors.

The glass popped open, and Phantom reached for the necklace. Ashby watched him closely as if he would steal it away, but the necklace had to be received by the Minister. That much was clear enough. He had plenty of other treasures to keep him happy.

As his fingers pressed into the cool pendant, the ground shook. Treasure tumbled from its perches, resounding in loud crashes as panels of glass above their heads cracked.

"What's happening?" Ashby shouted.

"I don't know," Phantom growled, struggling to keep his beast under the surface as the world grew more unpredictable around them and Davina's presence pulsed in his hand as if fighting against Phantom's hold.

The world grew red as if they stood in a lake of blood.

Ashby's eyes went to the sky and Phantom followed his gaze. Nemain's moon revealed itself overhead, but it wasn't due for another five months. Phantom's breathing grew rapid as more treasure clattered around him.

He gazed down at the necklace in his hand and noticed the blasted thing was omitting its own red hue and growing hotter in his hand.

A blow like fire entered his gut and pushed him to the ground, flashes of images impeded into his eyes. A life he did not remember. A name he no longer possessed, yet felt like the exact name he'd been looking for his entire life.

The Goddess of Fate stood before him, a body that was no longer his. She had blood dripping on her hand that he somehow knew was not hers, the knowledge of that making him so full of wrath that it burned. Davina chanted words that locked down his very soul, words he couldn't quite hear. Her bloodied hand slammed into his chest, her long nails digging in and causing him to bleed along with it.

But it was more than a blood oath she was forcing on him. Since she was a Goddess, this oath would attach to his very soul and follow him throughout all his lives. There was a woman on her knees only a few feet before him with tears streaming down her face. Her eyes were fierce, wild, and as amber as a burning fire. Her hair a gold so true it glittered, behind her feathered wings unfurled as if raging with her. He couldn't quite place the woman until he smelled wildflowers and campfire smoke.

The image faded from his mind the moment the necklace fell from his grasp, the world returning to normal. The ground no longer shook, and the sky was no longer red. The last thing to register were sounds, specifically the sound of Ashby shouting at him.

"Get up, you clumsy thief!"

Phantom blinked away the fog and noticed his beast was gone too, completely settled and locked up tight within him.

Ashby tucked away the necklace, which had returned to its silvery state, as he reached out a hand for Phantom.

"We must hurry. Desmond will check here first," Ashby snapped.

Phantom nodded and Ashby pulled him up, but as he reached for the door, Phantom stopped him. "Not that way, brother. It's too late for subtly."

Ashby looked back, pulling off a panicked scowl, the only sign he feared discovery. The Commodore couldn't be caught here.

Phantom tossed his head to the large windows that overlooked the sea. A small stretch of grass filled the space between the two, much of the glass already shattered in the earthquake.

"Come on," Phantom yelled back as he bolted for the most cracked of the windows, using his elbow to finish the job. Once the glass shattered, they slipped out, scattering bits of glass along the floor and grass. The door unlocked as Desmond came barreling into his precious treasure room.

"Thieves! Pirates!" Desmond shouted, but it was night, and his only guards were at the gate. The man paled as he realized it. Ashby took off, careful not to look back and expose himself. Phantom bowed to the foolish man, his hood kept up to shadow his features, but his look was recognizable enough. The theft would be credited to Captain Phantom and his Eleven Devils.

CHAPTER 9
DAVINA'S INFLUENCE

"What was that?" Ashby had kept his mouth shut the entire trek back to the Fortress even if he was brimming with questions. Not that Phantom had answers to any of them. He suspected that the small moon pendant in Ashby's pocket was the only thing with the ability to clear that fog, but since his touch elicited Nemain's moon to appear, it wasn't worth the risk. Or rather, the attention. "Was that the price you paid to get into Desmond's cases?"

"Unfortunately, no," Phantom mused, wishing his debt to Indigo was that simple.

Ashby put a hand on his shoulder as they climbed the steps to the Fortress, the dead of night still thick around them. "Then what happened?"

Phantom wet his dry lips. "Would you believe me if I told you I haven't the faintest idea?"

Davina had seemed as real as Ashby standing before him. She especially felt real when her bloody claws sank into his skin. If he didn't already detest the Goddess, this would have been enough to convince him. She always seemed cruel to him, yet that version of him didn't feel her cruelty. Her anger felt warranted. His past self seemed to accept her vengeance as punishment.

"I wouldn't have believed you even if you said birds sing," Ashby spat, his eyes angry and full of something else that burned brighter, but Phantom couldn't piece it together.

"Then why ask, *Commodore*?" He spat. There was no teasing Ashby this time, he didn't have the energy left for it. He wanted to go to Ramirez, talk to his mate about the vision. Maybe the stars held some insight.

Ashby sighed and dropped his gaze. "I don't know," he admitted, defeated by even trying to have a conversation with Phantom. At least one that meant anything. He tried not to let the blow sting. "I have to deliver this to the Minister and report what happened."

The thought of Ashby telling the Minister that they caused the impromptu Nemain moon was a less than appealing subject. Phantom scrunched his nose in disgust as the Commodore put a finger in his face.

"Head straight back to your room. The Minister may call you again before the sun rises to get your explanation, so I suggest you try to understand what happened."

Phantom nodded curtly but headed into the Fortress without uttering another word. No matter what happened, he was more certain that Rose Davenport was the woman haunting his dreams. The soul his was irrevocably attached to, but he couldn't find it within himself to be bothered by that fact. She was perhaps the sweetest curse Davina felt inclined to smite him with.

That's not how this plays out, friend, Sam reminded him.

Phantom froze as a crawling sense of dread washed over him. Even if he wasn't allowed the details, he knew how this story ended before. It wasn't the first time, and it wouldn't be the last. He turned down the hallway, making sure no bystanders were in earshot.

"Do you know what that was?" He whispered to the voices in his head, trying not to appear as crazed as he was.

That was an original memory from our first life and ultimately where we first met her. Sam's voice rumbled. Phantom could see Sam sometimes, in his mind's eye. When he was alive, he was taller and broader than even the Commodore. A beast of a man, like Jon.

"Who were we?"

Sam spoke very little of their original life, but he was the only one inclined to give him any answers.

Unfortunately, I don't know. I never gained the knowledge. I believe it has been lost to us since we were cursed.

Phantom stopped abruptly in the hall. "Cursed? Why do you say cursed? Is it the beast?"

The monster growled at the mention of him.

The lion is not your curse, James.

She is. Kayden chimed in, his yellowish aura hinted his anger and ambition.

Sadness. Overwhelming sadness hit him like a wave of bricks. It wasn't Phantom's, but it belonged to every other soul sharing his body.

"How can Rose be my curse?"

Sam sighed, as if not wanting to let the information slide.

That's what Davina did to us that night; cursed us to reincarnate with her repeatedly, meeting each other, falling in love, then losing each other again.

Phantom stopped, snapping his eyes shut.

She is your end, and you are hers.

The Minister did not call on him that night or for the next four days. Phantom was going stir crazy, forced to join the new recruits and pretend he didn't know exactly what he was doing.

But he was kept separate from the older officers with the fear he could be recognized as the defected lieutenant turned pirate.

Enlisted officers differed from the orphans raised in the Fortress. It was much harder to gain favor and standing as an enlistee since men couldn't enlist until they were eighteen, so the raised orphans had at least a four-year head start on them.

It was demeaning, learning basic sailor skills that he had mastered since he was fifteen, but the Commodore insisted he didn't stand out amongst them.

But he could only "accidentally" fail basic tasks for so long before he would grow mad.

In his free time, he roamed the Fortress and the Temple de Angeles as often as he could, seeking Serena's cage. She was a wild creature too and soon she wouldn't stand being locked away, either.

Serena wasn't the only thing calling to him; he could feel Davina's pendant nearby. The beat of it pulsing like his own heartbeat, but he couldn't locate where it was. He hadn't quite decided if he wanted to experience the pendant's visions again or the dramatic consequences of them. The Commodore would instantly know it was stolen by Phantom the moment he touched the bloody thing, but there was a lure he couldn't quite ignore, as if the blasted necklace wasn't finished with him.

But what he searched for more than anything was a glimpse of his songbird. He'd hardly known her more than a week and she had completely consumed him. Although it wasn't a surprise given who she was to him. He could feel the bond he had to her now, pulsating beneath the surface of his skin, urging him to go to her. Or maybe it had nothing to do with Goddess magic.

Stay away from her, Kayden's voice echoed in his mind. Every time he thought of her, Kayden would come to chase those thoughts away.

The assembly of officers gathered in the field outside the

Fortress for weekly mass. The Temple was abuzz after Nemain's Moon appeared in the sky over five months early. Ravana had taken it as an omen of death and promptly bathed in goat's blood to abate the Goddess's wrath. The spectacle had required all officers in attendance and Phantom was still working to burn the images of a very naked Ravana covered in goat's blood from his mind... again.

He hardly thought Nemain would appreciate it, but many of the officers did. Probably ones that weren't molested by her as a boy, but he could forgive their clearly addled minds.

But this assembly was wholly different because his songbird stood on a balcony overlooking the crowd. She looked heaven sent in her white lace gown. Her neck, ears, and wrists dripped in gold finery and her head was adorned with a crown of blue roses.

Blue was quickly becoming his favorite color.

There was something in her stare, though. Even from a distance, he could see the creases at the corners of her eyes and the downward tilt of her mouth. She didn't want to be standing there. The knowledge nearly made him want to leap from his skin, run to her, and pull her from the balcony, but that wouldn't achieve anything with so many officers surrounding him.

His gaze snagged on a familiar form. Felix had grown from the child he once was in the orphanage. The same two nameless goons stood on either side of him. Felix's blonde locks fell over his brow in a way some might think was handsome, but Phantom recognized his hollow gaze. A moment passed as Felix's eyes narrowed, then widened in recognition.

Phantom broke the contact.

Rose's eyes found Phantom's and something sad shadowed them that made his skin prickle.

"Gentlemen," the Minister started, drawing the attention of the crowd. "Let us pray together. Pray to Davina for our good fortune. For the food we eat. For the water we drink. And for the safety Davina has entrusted you with providing for us." The Minister continued, but Phantom didn't hear a word of it because Rose trembled. It was a slight motion, but he could see it in the hand she kept loose at her side.

He itched to take her away, especially since her eyes had not left his, as if pleading with him, but he couldn't quite tell what they were begging him to do. He needed action.

"Let us begin," the Minister finished, turning to Rose. She flinched under his gaze and that made his blood boil. Something in the man's eyes subdued her because she took his place at the railing of the balcony, calming herself with a heavy breath.

Her eyes closed for a moment and the air grew still and quiet as if the entire world was waiting on bated breath.

BRING THE STARS DOWN TO THE SEA
BRING US HOME, LET US FREE

The hymn was new, unlike he had ever heard before, but the way Rose sang, it was like listening to a lullaby that used to put him to sleep as a child. The newness and oldness of the song blended, giving it an eerie air.

OH GODDESS DIVINE,
HAVE HEAVEN WAIT FOR EVERY MAN

He watched closely as Rose's gold irises blended into cerulean blue. The surrounding crowd was unaware of the change. In fact, the officers seemed entranced, even ones he suspected of harboring disloyalty to the Goddesses. Felix's suspecting brow had softened, along with the rest of the officers.

WHEN WE HAVE COME TO TAKE YOUR HAND
HAVE MERCY, DAVINA, HAVE MERCY

As she sang on, his beast grew ravenous beneath his skin. She didn't want to be on that balcony. She seemed inclined to run rather than sing.

Phantom had suspected the songbird possessed more power than to heal, but he never imagined it was being regularly used on officers. No wonder the naval officers had such unwavering loyalty.

As the thought occurred to him, he checked his own thoughts, his own emotions, for signs of intrusion, but nothing was amiss. Although, he was sure he wouldn't know the difference; all the other officers were frozen in place, staring at Rose as if she were the sun, burning their eyes, but still, they could not look away.

But he could still look around and turn his head. Was she shielding him somehow?

Phantom glanced at Rose again and a tear slipped down her cheek as if it took great effort for her to remain singing. He recalled how she had fainted after administering her gifts to Angelica. Was it taxing to her every time she sang? The Minister wouldn't care about the toll it took on his daughter, but he doubted the Minister even noticed what it cost her.

The thought of that made his anger spike, the monster beginning to blur the edges of his vision in red, but he continued to stare at her. A presence was missing from behind her. The Minister had retreated into the Fortress, likely before she began singing. A subtle glance around told Phantom the Commodore was also suspiciously absent.

Whatever Rose's gift was doing to these officers was severe enough for them to have to leave the area entirely to avoid it.

The song grew to a crescendo and Phantom's anger burned red hot like an iron brand, searing his insides. It was odd for the beast to rise so quickly. These officers were in danger, not from the songbird who manipulated them, but from the monster ready to burst from his skin.

When fangs grew from his gums, he took to his feet.

He tried to keep his gait calm; it couldn't look like running. Part of him ached at leaving Rose to face this alone, but the day would end bathed in blood if he remained a moment longer.

He reached the edge of the crowd of neatly lined officers as a manicured hand reached out to halt him. He nearly growled at the sight of the freakishly long red nails that could only belong to one woman.

Ravana stepped into his path with a coy smile playing at her lips. "Wherever are you going, officer?"

He kept his gaze averted from her eyes, so she didn't see the red growing more urgent there. "Forgive my heathen ways, Priestess, but the Goddess Davina would smite me for standing amongst her honored like that."

"Ah," she cooed, raising her hand to the lapels of his uniform and twirling her fingers. "Where do you belong, then?"

"The sea and wherever Nemain instructs, for I am but Her vessel." The words were too holy, too honoring for Nemain, and Ravana knew that. No one spoke with as much respect for Nemain as for Davina or even Macha.

But Ravana knew there was truth in that. She hummed, seeming to chew on his words as if they contained a sweet flavor. Her hand moved to his chin, forcing it to raise, but he kept his eyes downcast.

"Look at me," she ordered with enough volume to prickle the hairs on his back.

He relented, meeting her icy gaze with the fire in his own.

But she smiled. Bloody hell, she smiled. "There you are."

Finally, she moved out of the way, letting Phantom pass. He grasped the opportunity, stepping around her. The moment he had, he shot to the beach, needing the peaceful chaos of the sea and feeling like he made a fatal mistake.

It took Phantom three hours to recover the beast after its untimely appearance at weekly mass. He swam in the waves by the shore, trying and failing to keep his mind clear. But he had little hope of that on a good day.

If he didn't know better, he'd say Ravana knew about his monster, but that couldn't be right. Perhaps she was only looking for the ruthless pirate Captain she expected him to be. If she pushed him hard enough, that's exactly what she would find.

Then there was Rose with her scared eyes and trembling hands. He'd never seen her more scared, yet there was no tangy scent of fear on her. Had she shielded herself? Or was it not fear at all?

But what blasted his mind more than anything was the trancelike state of the other officers. There was something happening to them, something his beast kept him from. Maybe he was a witch's son after all, and it was the magic in his blood deflecting hers. But what was she doing to them?

Something else occurred to him that should have occurred a long time ago. He lifted his head out of the waves, flipping his hair back as it plastered to his nape.

Where are the men of Kheli? Sam echoed his thoughts perfectly.

The men were stolen from Kheli years ago, even before Phantom was sailing the seas with his devils. It was the reason Kheli needed their protection, at least until the angels took over that responsibility. Phantom's memory was foggy with the faces of those men. He'd only briefly met them before they were his enemies in the Navy. If they were receiving the same "mass" treatment, did they even remember where they truly belonged?

Too many bloody questions. Not enough bloody answers.

Asking the witches was too costly. Asking the Commodore was too risky. Going to the source would have to do.

The officers took their meals all in the mess hall, a dank common room in the bowels of the Fortress. It was windowless. Apparently, one didn't need natural light to eat. Torches lined the walls during mealtimes. If one were to miss a meal, there was no retrieving it. Not that meals were worth much, slop really.

The common room was mostly quiet, even with the abundance of officers. A few chatted, some excitedly, some seriously, but the sheer number of officers with blank stares was troublesome. How had he not seen it before?

Not paying attention, that's how, Kayden mused from his dark corner of Phantom's mind.

As helpful as usual, Kayden, Sam sighed.

Phantom ignored them. It wasn't worth the officers noticing that he was insane. His gaze roamed the room, landing on a few tables that were filled with loud and laughing officers. Felix was at the center of one of them, his gaze shooting to Phantom as if he could sense the ghost.

Phantom turned his attention to a quieter table.

A lanky man with short, cropped hair sat by himself, slowly shoveling slop into his mouth. Phantom would not be eating the inhumane dinner. He'd swipe something from the Minister's personal kitchens later, but he picked up a bowl to blend in before taking a seat in front of the shell of an officer.

Phantom let out an exasperated sigh. "Quite the tedious day, if I do say so myself." He hardly looked at the man, using a charming tactic to talk to the man as if they had been friends for some time. "Although I do think the Commodore needs a straight kick to the ass." The man continued to stare at the wall, face impassive as he shoved the slop into his mouth. Phantom furrowed his brow. "What's your name, sailor?"

Finally, the man turned to look at him. His eyes glazed over without truly centering on Phantom. "Sailor? I was a sailor once." It was sadness creeping into the corners of his eyes, drooping his face.

"You are a sailor. Part of the Prime Minister's mighty Navy." He tried and failed to sound genuine.

"Yes, I am." That was all he said before lifting the spoon to his mouth again.

Since that question didn't work, he thought to try another. "Where are you from?"

The man drew his brows together as if he didn't understand the question. Then his eyes turned confused like he couldn't recall the answer.

"What?" He mumbled.

Phantom looked at the man's uniform, seeing the word "Smith" stitched into his jacket. He hated using given names when he didn't know if the individual had chosen it for themselves, but he was running out of options.

"Officer Smith."

Smith straightened as if ready and waiting for orders, even if he remained sitting, his spoon clanking against the bowl as he abandoned it.

Phantom straightened his own spine, coming up with a theory to test out. "Officer Smith," he repeated with more command. "Who are you?"

"Navigator to the Minister's Navy, sir." His eyes pinned to the wall behind Phantom, listening, but not looking.

"And who were you before that, officer?" The command felt weird in his mouth. When he commanded his devils, it wasn't so formal. But he remembered being a lieutenant in this very Navy. It wasn't hard to revert, even if every bone in his body screamed against it.

"A sailor in the Minister's Navy, sir."

Phantom pursed his lips. Why was it so hard to get information out of the man? Would every conversation with these men go this way?

"And before that, officer?" The man shook his head a moment, hesitating. Phantom stood, towering over the man. "Answer me, officer." Phantom's voice bellowed loud enough for other nearby officers to notice, but instead of turning to watch, their backs straightened as they awaited their superior.

All except one table, who all watched like a pack of wolves. Felix's stare bored into the back of Phantom's head, causing gooseflesh to form down his back.

The sadness returned to Smith's face. "There was nothing before serving in the Minister's Navy, sir."

Phantom's stomach dropped as if he was falling. Smith remembered nothing of his life before the Navy. He didn't remember who loved him, only his duty as if it were the sole reason he was alive.

"At ease," Phantom barked before he drew too much attention. The entire room relaxed, including Smith, and they returned to their bowls.

Phantom abandoned his bowl. He couldn't stand another moment around them, fear and pity creeping in. He both felt sorry for them and dreaded his mind being taken away. The Commodore was a part of this?

Even if he could figure out which of the officers were from Kheli, would they even remember their families?

As he turned, he noticed Felix was the only one still staring at him. His gaze darkened as he caught Phantom in his snare. Phantom's brow furrowed at the curious freedom of his old board mate, but he only nodded once before disappearing down the corridor.

CHAPTER 10

WHERE TO FIND A ROSE

All the officers were called to the gardens later that week to "watch" over the tea party guests. But they were just as decorative as the flowers in the garden.

The officers lifted their swords in honor of the Minister, not that they would give Phantom a sword. He was firmly planted in the back of the display. It was perhaps the first sunny day that had graced Samsara in some time. Even the women wore hats to shield their eyes from the blinding sun they weren't accustomed to.

Phantom snickered. He'd like to see how the noblewomen of Samsara fared on the dunes of Draiocht. They were out in masses near the Fortress gardens, fanning themselves and giving their attention to lucky or unlucky officers and nobles alike.

He ignored the batting eyelashes flitting his way. At one point, he would have gladly taken the offer, soaking in their attention more than the rays of the sun currently beating down on his cheeks. But he only had eyes for one, no matter the torment she caused him.

The object of his desire strode behind the Minister, her

ladiesmaid, Lara, on one side, the Commodore on the other. A pang of jealousy he quickly covered with a scoff as he witnessed the prized pig of the Minister's Navy stride beside her, a vision of propriety and all things decent.

It made him sick.

But the feeling washed away as his gaze traveled over Rose's soft pink dress that drifted in the wind like the clouds of a warm sunrise. Her hat brimmed far enough to shadow her face; her blonde locks tied back at her nape. She was a vision, the perfect daughter to the Minister, and he wanted nothing more than to ruin her.

Instruments blared, breaking Phantom's focus on the songbird. Would she sing at this gathering? He doubted it. This interaction was for show. The Minister wanted the nobles to see his dutiful daughter playing her part, unharmed and uninfluenced by the pirates she was captured by.

He watched from his spot in the blazing sun as she sat with her father and the other noble families, Lord Desmond included.

Desmond didn't even bother to acknowledge his existence, which was fine with him. It wasn't his fault the man had inadequate security measures.

His focus drifted back to the songbird, who smiled brightly at Ashby. Phantom's gut churned as he groaned inwardly. Another officer glanced at him with disdain.

Right, perhaps it wasn't as inward as he thought, but the two were insufferable. Her gloved hand landed on his arm, and he overlapped it with his. Lara smiled gently at them as Rose raised her hand to clue her friend in on the conversation. Even Ashby used his hands to talk. At least he didn't lose that from his childhood.

Phantom wanted to gag at the overwhelming display of domestication. Give him a sword fight or storm over this. It wasn't like her smiles and laughter were real, anyway. Her nose scrunched when she laughed, and her smile made her eyes glow like the morning sun. None of which he saw at that table.

Finally, Rose broke away from the hollow laughter and fake smiles, drifting into the rose garden beside the tea tables. Since most of the officers were mingling with the noble ladies of the court, he broke off to see what Miss Davenport was up to.

What are you doing? Kayden demanded, but Phantom ignored him.

The rose garden was more of an overgrown maze; fashioned with bushes that were large and thick enough to block other outlets from view. It was the perfect place to hunt a songbird.

She strode inside, glancing behind her to see if anyone followed. Hiding behind a nearby tree, he trailed after her as she continued her quest.

The bushes separated out into different paths, but there was a lingering scent of smokey sweetness that kept his feet in the right direction.

Turning a corner, he finally spotted the songbird standing before a statue in the garden. The marble statue, fashioned to look like a delicate woman with soft, loving eyes and a gentle demeanor. A soul that was dignified and pure of heart.

He had thought of a million things to say to Rose. A million different ways to make her understand what she meant to him, but none of them mattered as Rose's legs folded and she pressed a single red rose to the base of the statue.

"Who is she?" The words came out gently, but they still made her jolt.

She didn't turn, though. He knew she recognized his voice. "She was my mother."

Phantom froze. Of all the things he expected to find in the rose garden, it wasn't this.

"My father had this garden made for her." Still, Rose did not turn, so Phantom lifted his gaze to the gentle eyes of the statue. Yes, he could see it now. The gentle curve of her mouth, the slight hint of mischief in her eyes. It was all in Rose. Phantom never met the lady, she was dead before he made it to the Fortress.

"This is where she died."

Everyone in Samsara knew very little of the Minister's late wife. She rarely left the Fortress when she was alive. When she died, lanterns were lit in her honor, but no one seemed to know how she died.

"How?" Maybe it was insensitive of him, but he wanted to know every detail. Everything that made Rose who she was.

"Her heart gave out. At least she died seeing her favorite flower."

He couldn't imagine what this place meant to her. It was simultaneously her mother's favorite place, and where she took her last breath.

Rose stood, seeming to recover. "What are you doing here, James?"

He hated anyone else saying his childhood name, but now it felt like hers. Like his name was the secret only she held, even if that wasn't true. There was a truth in her saying his given name rather than his chosen name.

Phantom was the villain. A monster who plagued these waters. The darkness in a fairytale.

James was a man. A man who made mistakes, but still a man.

And Rose was the woman who treated a monster as a man.

"Am I not allowed a stroll in the garden?"

"No, you are not," she snapped, and one of his eyebrows shot up. He got too close, discovered too much. Now the songbird was defending herself.

He could play along.

Phantom clasped his hands behind his back, but instead of inching away, he sauntered towards her. She stiffened at his approach. A glance down at her gloved hand, and he spotted a raspberry sized ruby on her hand. Jealousy burned bitterly in his gut.

"Sure, that isn't an enchanted rock itself, love."

She let out a weary sigh. "I'm not your love. In fact, I am some else's." He inched towards her as she spoke, ignoring the rising jealousy that came. "Sebastian is quite the gentleman."

"Really?" He purred, her eyes shifting across his face as he drew closer. "And that's what you want? A gentleman?"

He never would be. Even if she asked him to, it would no longer be him.

She pushed off him, heading deeper into the garden. "What I don't want is a lying, cheating thief."

He had to contain his grin when he saw the blush on her cheeks. "You forgot to mention a dashing rogue. When you describe me, be sure to mention that I am a ruthless pirate Captain. I shan't have my reputation defiled." His tone was full of jest, even if he didn't want her to think of him that way.

She scoffed, almost sounding like one of those fake laughs she used at the tea table.

He put a finger to his lips. "Though I remember you were quite comfortable in my arms not too long ago. You can't be *that* repulsed by me."

"A momentary lapse of judgement, but I am interested in much more than a pretty smile."

He smirked. "You think my smile is pretty?"

She turned away from him. "It won't work," she called, so he could hear her with her back turned to him. He followed her as she found her way through the maze, clearly knowing where she was going.

"What won't?"

"Charming me. Seducing me. It may work on tavern wenches and maids, but not me."

He caught up to her, slipping a hand around her waist, turning her around and holding her in his arms. He hovered so close to her, they were only a breath's width apart. By the focus of her eyes and the parting of her lips, she could feel the heat of his stare as much as he felt hers. As powerful as the surrounding sunlight.

"I haven't even begun to seduce you." His voice was so quiet, his words only for her, making it feel much more intimate. "I assure you, when I do—" he pulled her closer, brushing a hand along the small of her back, causing her to suck in a breath. "You'll feel it."

His hand made lazy strokes against her spine, trailing up and down. It took all his will to not brush his hand lower, but he contained himself at the sight of her fluttering lashes. She soaked in his touch like a sunbathing feline.

"Is that what you are doing now?" she breathed.

"Doing what?" He feigned ignorance, but she was too consumed by his touch to retort. He wasn't sure how he had her melting with so little, but part of him could feel the familiarity in the touch. As if he instinctually knew how to touch her.

"Seducing me," she mumbled.

He wasn't sure how to answer.

Yes. No. Perhaps.

None of the answers seemed adequate.

Instead, he asked, "Do you want me to seduce you, Rose?"

He watched the sound of her name snap the enchantment on her. She blinked several times, realizing where she was, who she was with, and where his hand was now frozen on her back. He wanted to close the distance between them. Find out exactly what her lips would taste like.

But she stepped away—and it felt like dumping ice water over his head.

Her chin raised, her eyes unyielding.

"No, Captain," she bit out.

"Back to 'Captain', are we?"

"I do not want your attention in any form."

Phantom's smile dropped. He examined her features, the hard lines, her steady breathing. She was too calm, too controlled.

"You forget, love. I know when you're lying to me."

Her lips pressed together hard as her jaw clenched. He loved it, watching her calm demeanor fall away and the real woman emerge.

"You think you're so good, taking from Samsara so you can give to Kheli?" His brows rose. "But have you ever stopped to think what those actions are doing to the people here?"

She sounded like the Commodore. "The Samsarans aren't my concern."

"What would you have done if it worked?"

"If what worked?"

"Trading me back to my father for Kheli?" The words came out too bitter for him to turn the conversation around. Whatever it was, it was too late.

"I would have given the island to the people to live there, and I would have made my own way." He let the words come out neutrally. There was nothing he owed to anyone but his devils.

"You mean you would have left two vulnerable islands to fend for themselves while you gallivant the seas at your leisure?"

He smiled humorlessly. This time, he was the one to turn his back on her. He wasn't exactly sure where to go. He would be stuck in the maze for hours if she didn't show him the way out. But he needed to walk away from her.

He'd forgotten how she could easily irritate him. Curious, since it happened so often.

"There are those better suited to take care of the islands than I."

"And look where that got them." The most irritating thing was that she had a point. If he was a selfless man like her precious Commodore, maybe her words would have worked. "Samsara will starve without the shipments from Kheli."

"Kheli will starve if Samsara continues to take too much." Her face turned white for a moment as the reality settled on her. "The islands are running low on resources. Soon, there won't be enough."

"Then what is the answer?"

"Doesn't matter. We won't be the ones choosing that fate."

There was something akin to hurt in her eyes. "So that's it then? You're just going to sail away on your little ship and forget all about us?"

"Assuming your father doesn't kill me first," he grumbled. He wasn't sure he would make it out. There was too much at risk, but he'd always escaped before. Who's saying he wouldn't again? "What would you have me do, anyway? You think people will listen to a pirate?"

She stared at him, unblinking for a moment. Then a humorless laugh left her. "I'm such an imbecile," she mumbled to herself. Hearing the words leave her lips, he expected it to be directed at him, then paused when he realized she spoke of herself. But he didn't have time to respond before she spoke again. "You're just a selfish prick. You only care about yourself, don't you?"

"I beg your pardon?"

"All you care about is your ship and your precious freedom. I bet your devils are only bodies to man your ship. You'd sail alone in a heartbeat if you could."

When he started out, yes, she would have been right. He needed bodies to manage his ship. He even would have let Earhart return to his family and sailed into the sea alone if he could. But that was years ago. Now, he'd be heartbroken if any one of them left.

He narrowed his eyes at her. She was there. She saw what it

did to him, the weight of his devil's freedom, Kheli's protection. She witnessed it all, yet she accused him of this.

"At last, you show your true colors," he whispered softly, barely contained rage edging at the surface.

Her brows rose. "Excuse me."

"This is what I expected when I captured the Minister's daughter." His ability to be quiet was quickly diminishing.

"Oh, we're admitting to it now, that I wasn't truly a stowaway? Tell me, Captain, what did you expect?" Her hands rested on her hips, a paltry attempt to make herself seem bigger, but all it did was make him painfully aware of the curve at her waist.

He gestured to all of her. "This entitled spoiled princess who hasn't known poverty a day in her life. Who sits at tea parties and offers fake laughter. Whose content to wander about the Fortress, not even considering there could be a world out there waiting for her!"

Phantom watched the words hit home. He knew he was wrong the moment the words left his lips. She was trapped here, same as him. He had seen the look on her face when she saw Kheli for the first time.

"Well," she breathed. "If that's what you truly think of me." She walked away, a slight sway to her hips that he was learning came when she was angry. If that be the case, he'd start making her mad on purpose.

But a flicker of guilt—or a boulder of it—crashed into him.

He reached for her, but before his fingers could curl around her arm, she whirled, clearly not done with him.

"I thought you differed from what they said about you. And you do."

He hummed. "Yes, it is bigger in person."

She scoffed, ignoring his comment. "But not in the way I thought. When I learned what you did for Kheli, I thought you were the hero disguised as the ruthless villain. But I misjudged you *twice*. You're not some hero. You're just clearing your conscience before you leave everyone in the dust."

"Cute of you to think I have a conscience—"

He'd call it a handful of annoying siblings even if they were all himself in different lives. All of which were uncharacteristically quiet right now.

"Second, you're not the depraved pirate either. Oh no no no, you are much too scared to be that."

One eyebrow shot up, his chin raising so he could look down on her. "Scared? Tell me, what exactly am I afraid of?"

"You tell me, *Captain*," she said sweetly, leaning into him so closely that a wave of that smoky sweetness swept over him. "Is it the fear that you will cause the deaths of everyone around you, or that none of them cared about you in the first place?"

Anger boiled out from his core, but somehow his beast stayed silent. The anger was purely his own. He lifted his hands, wanting to wrap them around her throat.

"You insufferable woman."

"Egotistical bastard," she retorted.

She was so close with her bright eyes and intoxicating scent; it made his head fuzzy.

He growled low in his throat. "I just want to—" His fist clenched right next to face. She was just too bloody close.

"You just want to what?" She practically shouted at him, daring him to do whatever was on his mind.

His hands came around either side of her face as he crashed into her.

Their lips met in a fury of passion. She met him instantly, deepening the kiss like their bodies knew exactly what to do with one another. Her hands landed on his arms, but she didn't push him away. It was more like she tried to get his body closer, hating the distance his arms created between them.

He leaned in deeper, and she opened for him. He plundered her mouth, keeping one hand on her nape while the other trailed to her waist, pulling her flush to him and obeying the silent command of her body.

She was absolutely *everything*.

It was like that moment he first saw the garden at Koi No Yokan, or what he imagined seeing the colorful waterfalls of Kalon would be like. It was just a kiss, but he was utterly wrapped up in her.

Until she—squealed.

She broke away with a gasp. "What? No. Did you? Did I?"

"Yes," he purred, inching closer. "Would you like to do it again?"

He expected a more positive reaction, one that had her in his arms again, preferably with his lips against hers.

"No," she squeaked out. "You can't just kiss me and expect me to fall at your feet."

"I'd gladly do the falling, love, if you'd prefer."

She scoffed like he said something offensive. Had he? He didn't even know, and she was marching away. Not swaying her hips like before, no, she marched like she was in the Navy herself.

"Wait," he pleaded, trotting after her. "Am I mistaken in believing we just shared a moment?"

"Yes, you would be mistaken."

They rounded a rose covered hedge to reveal a glittering fountain. One he had not seen during their approach. Or maybe this was an entirely different way? Frankly, he couldn't tell if they were heading deeper into the garden or towards the exit.

But he didn't care.

He grabbed her arm, gently pulling, so she'd face him again.

"That was—"

"Just a kiss. Something that will *never* happen again." Her finger came up to him, right in his face. "One that no one will hear of. Is that clear?"

"I don't kiss and tell." He let his smile fall. "However, I'd wager you'll be back in my arms soon."

Her gaze hardened and a single finger rising from her clenched fist. A cute gesture she must have considered offensive.

"How ladylike," he breathed.

Rose's gaze turned deadly. "Stay away from me."

It was childish; he knew that. But he also knew she would not walk away and forget this ever happened. Not after he was through with her.

Before she could march away, he dipped down, grasping her waist and throwing her over his shoulder.

"What are you doing?" She didn't scream, just struggled as he hauled her through the maze. "Put me down now. I'll scream."

"No, you won't," he dared her. He wasn't entirely sure she wouldn't scream, but from everything he'd seen of her, he doubted it. It wasn't something she would do lightly, and he hoped by now she didn't fear him.

A feminine growl tore from her lips, and she ceased her struggling. It was pointless anyway.

"Good girl," he praised, and she groaned. He gave her a light smack on her perfect ass for it.

It distracted her enough that she didn't notice when they came up to the fountain.

He threw her in. She squealed as she splashed amongst the rose petals and lily pads. A laugh rolled out of him. The first genuine laugh he had since arriving at the bloody Fortress.

And her face—she was actually pouting.

A pang of guilt greeted him as he thought of her walking to the Fortress completely drenched. He held out a hand for her. "Come on, let's get you dried off."

She accepted the hand, but he realized his error the

moment a deviant smile appeared on her face. With alarming strength, she pulled, dragging him into the water with her.

He nearly breathed in a mouthful of scummy water as he splashed into the fountain, too. Breaching the water, he realized the fountain had a dedication to Davina. How pleasant. Of course, it would be the Goddess of Fate looking over them now.

He looked at Rose, hoping to share a laugh over the ridiculous situation, but she stood, stepping over the rim of the fountain.

"Rose, wait," he pleaded, but she was walking away, this time with her head held high, trying to counteract the humiliation she was about to face.

He clamored out of the fountain in time to follow her out. There were only two bends before they were back at the tea party. He spared her the embarrassment of walking out in a similar state, leading to questions neither of them could answer.

She had been honest with him when she pointed out his willingness to leave everything behind. For his disregard of the Samsarans, even as he played hero to the Khelitians, not that he ever wanted to be the hero. With his beast a constant reminder of what he really was, he never considered it a possibility.

Now here she was, asking him to be the hero for everyone.

That wasn't who he was. He was the monster, the legend that people feared, not their savior. She expected too much from him. Saw too much in him.

She knows you better than you think, Sam rumbled from the back of his mind.

"Well, that's just unhelpful," he whispered, replying to the ringing in his ears. "You're already driving me to madness. Let's not help the process along."

An echoing laugh in his head responded. *You're doing that well enough on your own.*

He rolled his eyes, which he knew Sam could see — or feel — but Phantom turned his attention back to Rose.

Ashby had run to her aid, wrapping his coat over her shoulders. A gesture that stoked a fury in him. He'd rip that bloody coat to shreds.

But she also needed it.

Her pink tea dress was completely soaked through and clinging to every part of her. Parts he didn't have the proper time to admire before the coat wrapped around her. But he had caused her enough humiliation for one day. Showing off those perfect curves to the world was not his ideal form of torture.

But as she walked away, a sense of foreboding swept over him.

What just happened? Did he start something with her or ruin it before it ever began?

Does it matter? It's for the best that she is gone.

But could he accept that? Let her walk away, releasing the prey before he ever made the catch?

Two words returned to him. Words that had haunted him from the moment Ramirez said them.

It's her.

CHAPTER II

THE BLACK SHADOW

ONE YEAR AGO

It was a sunny day, albeit rare for Samsara at this time of year, but it was nice to walk on sunbaked streets rather than dodging rain puddles.

Phantom examined the building before him. One built of brick and mortar like any other, but with black windows and a sign to indicate it housed a butcher shop.

Meats were the only trade profitable for Samsarans, with butcher shops on nearly every street. With Samsara being surrounded by the sea, livestock was hard to come by. The market for them was governed by Lord Castellanos, who took advantage of the demand to over price the sale of them.

The witches tipped Phantom off that there was some suspicious activity around this building. Other than the blacked-out windows and blood stains, many had reported people being dragged into the building blindfolded.

The crime circles in Samsara were not to be underestimated. Slave trade ran rampant since the War had decimated human decency.

He had witnessed it firsthand when he stole *Nemain's Revenge.* Yet the trade was still practiced in Samsara.

Phantom entered the building, Earhart steady at his side with one hand on his pistol. "Is your plan really to just walk through the front door?" Earhart seethed under his breath as if he hadn't already crossed the threshold to the meat market that reeked of carrion. Clearly, the establishment was lacking in pride and hygienic workers.

"If it isn't, I'm going the wrong way." Phantom smirked and Earhart's brows lowered, clearly unamused.

He charged through the door, his senses assaulted by the odor of the strung-up carcasses lining the shop.

Phantom clapped his hands together in friendly greeting. "Good sir," he addressed the man standing behind the counter with large hairy arms and a permanent scowl. "How are you on this fine Davina-blessed day?"

The man only stared, deepening a glare at Phantom's apparent cheery attitude. He wore less conspicuous clothing for this raid. It was best not to be recognized, at least at first. He wore dirty brown trousers and a white sailor's shirt, easily blending in with the citizens without his signature black leather. That is, as long as he covered his neck tattoo with a scarf.

"Yeah, you're right. It's quite disgusting." Phantom leaned his arms on the counter before the man. "I prefer the dreary rainy days, don't you?" The man still showed no reaction other than heavy breathing, like his patience was waning.

"What can I get for you?" The man said with the most pained tone Phantom had ever heard.

"If you don't mind terribly," Phantom said as he withdrew his own pistol, pointing it at the man's head before he could blink. "I'll take everything."

The man flinched, reaching for his own pistol, securely strapped to his hip.

Earhart's gun cocked loudly next to the man's ear. "Ah ah, I wouldn't do that if I were you."

The man raised his arms, overall calmer than a typical shop keeper should at a robbery.

"That box behind me has all my coins. I don't want any trouble. Just take it and go."

Phantom nodded to Earhart, who investigated the box, spying a handful of coins, then tucking it under his arm, keeping his pistol aimed at the man's temple the whole time.

"Oh George, can I call you George?" The man's name was in fact Robert Westerwood, but Phantom enjoyed watching the vein pop out of his forehead. "See, the problem is, I came here for trouble, as you so quaintly put it, but I am a simple man." The man's brows furrowed, and it was clear Phantom was losing him. "For example, it was simple to discover that this building is owned by Lockness, the infamous crime lord of Samsara, however this business is run by none other than Robert Westerwood, ever heard of him, George?"

The man gritted his teeth, his jaw clenching, but he still said nothing.

"You see, Mister Westerwood is the right hand of Lockness and often oversees the important warehouses that store their most prized possessions. The ones that are worth the most. Particularly the breathing ones."

"I know who you are," Westerwood blurted, his voice as rough as one would imagine by his equally brutish appearance.

"Do you, now?" Phantom's veins buzzed with giddy energy. "You hear that Earhart? We've grown recognizable. How exciting is that?"

"Invigorating, Captain," Earhart responded dryly, more for Westerwood's benefit than Phantom's.

"Now, George, if you'd like to hold on to your miserable, goddess-damned, cod-rotten excuse of a life I'd suggest—" He cocked the gun. "You show me exactly where you keep them."

With the barrel of two guns facing the burly man, Phantom expected him to deny his involvement, to lie, or to cry like the lily-livered urchin he was, but he didn't expect him to laugh.

Westerwood's laugh was grating and scratchy, eliciting a growl of frustration from Phantom.

"You do not think you can do this." Westerwood's accent came out heavily. "Lockness will find you, shadow. Even if you can get them out, do not make an enemy of him."

He stalked the man, rounding the counter with his gun still keenly pointed at his forehead.

"Do not think yourself immune, shadow."

Phantom pushed the gun into the man's face until it sat between his eyebrows. He knew that his position had him more vulnerable. It would be more tempting for Westerwood to snatch the gun from him or land a fist to his face, but with Earhart now firmly pressing his gun into the back of the man's head, he knew he had no chance. But some part of Phantom wanted him to try. He wanted a reason to blast Westerwood's head open.

"Then I'd better get a head start." Phantom raised his pistol, using the handle as a club to ram into Westerwood's temple, knocking him out cold.

Earhart jumped backwards as the man's burly body dropped to the ground. "Was that really necessary?"

"No," Phantom holstered his gun and stepped over the man. "But it felt good."

"Robert?" A male voice called from the stairway across the room. "Is everything alright down there?" The floorboards creaked as a man descended the steps.

Phantom caught Earhart's gaze and put a silencing finger to his lips, then he used two spread fingers to point to the door. The first mate nodded, clearly understanding the signal. The two of them crept to the doorframe, where the staircase would let out.

"Lockness won't like it if you're asleep on the job again."

Phantom and Earhart put their backs to either wall, hiding from the sight of the approaching man. From the sound of his voice, he couldn't have been older than thirty. It was an oddly young age to involve oneself in such a devious crime circle, but Phantom started his own pirate crew in his middle twenties, so he wasn't one to judge.

He reached the landing and peeked out of the door frame. "Robert?" This time, his tone was more hesitant, finally sensing the danger.

Once he came out of the doorframe, Phantom and Earhart pounced on him from behind. He turned as both their fists collided with his head, knocking him out cold.

Phantom drew his sword next, the metal singing against its sheath. "We have little time. They'll send more." Earhart drew his next, the cutlass a broad and heavy weapon.

"Perhaps we should wait. Pick them off one by one," Earhart whispered.

Phantom eyed the staircase, but he knew what he would do if two of his devils weren't responding. "The next wave they send down will expect us. It's best to get to them before they can suspect that something is wrong."

Earhart nodded, and Phantom led the way, creeping up the stairs with cutlass in hand. It was the more silent weapon over a pistol, although the small contraption worked better as a threat. These men would need to be taken out as quietly as possible.

A stair groaned under Phantom's weight, and he froze, cringing at the sound. He held up a hand for Earhart to stop a second too late. The wood creaked under his boot, too.

"William, is that you, boy?" This man sounded older, more seasoned, and likely understood his instincts more acutely. A couple of heartbeats passed before metal sung with a weapon drawn. So much for an ambush.

A crash of glass echoed from the chamber at the top of the staircase.

"Who the hell are—"

Metal clashed against metal in the telltale sound of a sword fight. More swords drew and Phantom leapt at the chance, Earhart close on his tail as they burst from the top of the stairs and into the fray of swinging swords.

He caught the blade of one man as it swiped at him, ducking low to dodge the attack of another that Earhart promptly parried.

Phantom danced with the man, stepping into him and swiping at his stomach, but he jumped back. He spun, sweeping his sword at the man's side, cutting through the fabric to the flesh below. He cried out, grabbing his side. Phantom wasted no time, kicking him in the chest causing him to stumble into the stairs. Phantom swung back into the fray; a smirk permanently etched into his face at the satisfaction of hearing the man groaning at the bottom of the steps.

Earhart was still locked in battle, metal crashing against metal, but the battle to his side stole his attention.

A hooded figure, opposed to the slavers, battled three men at once with apparent and enviable ease.

Phantom was sure the figure was not one of his own, but for the time the stranger appeared to be on their side. He stepped into the chaos, stealing a blade fighting the hooded figure.

His new opponent was older, but fit and ready for battle, eagerly tossing Phantom's blade before striking. Phantom righted himself in time to jump away, but swiped in retaliation, slicing at the man's wrist, right along the vein.

The man cried out, slapping his opposing hand against his wrist. It was a vital area; if left open too long, it would cause him to bleed out. He glared at Phantom, clearly unwilling to give up. With one hand on his wrist, he advanced, but his balance was all off. With a quick step to the side and a swipe, he tripped on his own feet.

His stumble drew him closer to the blacked-out window. Phantom smiled, then charged the man with a battle cry. The shift caught the man off guard, sending him another step back before Phantom collided with him, sending him straight out the window, breaking shutters and glass.

Phantom watched him fall a single story. It wasn't a high enough fall to kill him unless it knocked him out long enough for his wrist wound to bleed out. The man, unfortunately, could sit up.

Phantom hummed, but before he could reevaluate his surroundings, a door crashed to his side. A giant of a man barreled in. He was about the size of Jon, with a less than handsome face. His arms and shoulders were wide enough that he had to shuffle into the room sideways, but the man didn't have a sword. He had a length of chains in his arms, and he set his sights directly on Phantom and chuckled, low and deadly.

The giant made Phantom feel about two inches tall.

"Hello," Phantom mused. "You are a magnificent beastie, aren't you?"

The man huffed like a bull before a matador, throwing his length of chains. Phantom jumped to the side, dodging the bite of metal, but the giant hadn't aimed for him. Before he knew it, his cutlass was ripped from his hand and slid across the floorboards to the opposite side of the room. *Behind* the beast.

Phantom stared dumbly at his lost weapon. "*Mierda.*"

The man lunged, tossing the chains again, this time aiming for Phantom's neck. He ducked, tucking his legs in and rolling away as the chains crashed against the wood. When he was far enough to jump to his feet, he pulled out his pistol, but that too was pulled from his hand. The man laughed even louder at Phantom's dumbfounded face. He was steadily losing all his weapons.

Before he could blink, the giant tossed his chains again, this time wrapping around Phantom's neck. The cool metal was nothing compared to the pressure on his windpipe as the giant pulled on the chain. It forced Phantom to take steps towards him, no escape in sight.

The monster woke, stirring beneath his skin, locked in his chest just like his breath, begging to be released. Phantom borrowed the monster's strength, pulling at the chains enough for oxygen to sweep in. But before he could get a second breath in, the giant pushed him down to his knees, the chains wrapped around his knuckles, pulling the leash taut.

Red started sparking at the edges of Phantom's vision. The monster raged at the submissive position, being at another man's mercy. A growl, low and vicious, tore from his throat unbidden.

The giant laughed again. "Where is your cunning now, shadow?"

Phantom's brows knocked together. *Why does everyone keep calling me a shadow?*

"Right here, you overgrown sea bass."

The man turned his head in time to see the hooded figure plunge a sword into his belly. Death made the man jerk the chains at Phantom's neck harder, but the figure put a booted foot into the man's chest, knocking him to the floor. Finally, he released the chains and Phantom inhaled sharply, falling to his hands and knees.

After catching his breath, he glanced up at the hooded figure, but shadows covered their face.

A look behind the figure confirmed Earhart was alive and retrieving the slaves from the adjacent room. He unlocked the Kalonites who were terrified; uncertainty and distrust evident in their eyes, with the evidence of their enslavement showing in their gaunt features. They seemed to understand Earhart was there to help. He had a natural calming effect on people that Phantom simply did not possess.

Phantom stared at the hooded figure again. "Shadow, I presume."

Their arms came up, letting the hood fall. "Black Shadow actually, but mostly I go by Black."

For the third time, Phantom was struck dumb.

Beneath the hood was a stunningly beautiful woman. Inky black hair fell in waves behind her with sharp feminine facial features. Her eyebrows were thick and manicured along with a straight and sloped nose.

The hooded figure was a woman, and she had taken three skilled swordsmen on at once. Warmth consumed him like a nearby fire, yet at the same time, a coolness caused shivers along his spine. He knew the feeling well.

A smile grew on his face.

"I trust you will get them to safety." Phantom noticed her voice was deep for a woman, commanding enough that no one would question it.

Phantom climbed to his feet with an exaggerated grunt, then bent at the waist. "Captain Phantom at your service, milady."

She bristled. "Don't call me that."

"Then what is your name, love?"

She stomped across the room to the window. Even her gait was more masculine than feminine. If he hadn't seen her face, he wouldn't have considered her a woman at all.

"Black," she said dryly. "And don't call me 'love' either." She turned, a pistol cocked and pointed between Phantom's legs. He flinched at her choice of aim. "If you must call me something other than Black, call me mate, sir or *senor* and if I hear that either of you have told anyone that the Black Shadow is a woman, I will find you and make good on this threat. Is that understood?"

He resisted calling her ma'am, the manner turned instinct, ingrained in him by Mama Owen, but he knew the result of that mistake.

"Yes, sir." Phantom said with a flicker of a smile. She narrowed her eyes, then turned her gaze to Earhart.

He saluted. "Yes, sir."

She nodded, lowering her weapon and turning for the window.

"You really trust a band of pirates with the slaves you risked yourself to save?"

She let out an exasperated sigh. "Listen, I came here in a hurry. I've yet to secure their safety. And the witches speak highly of you, *Captain*." She turned to face him. "That, and I am late."

"We shan't keep you then, mate." Phantom smiled to himself, already picturing Black amongst his devils. "But I will be seeing you again."

She jumped onto the broken windowsill, a rope dangling from the roof, evidence of her grand entrance. "For your sake, Captain, I hope not."

His smile settled further as she slid down the rope. He stepped to the window, gazing down in time to see the man he had tossed out. He still hadn't stood, which likely meant he couldn't move his legs. She came up to him as he reached for her, begging for help. But her hood was still down.

"Wait, you're—"

She plunged her sword into his throat before he could utter the rest. The gurgle of blood at his throat spilled out as she retrieved her sword. She lifted her hood once more then ran into the shadows of the building.

Earhart stood beside Phantom, leaning out the window to spy the tailcoat of the Black Shadow before she disappeared. He looked back at his Captain's still present smile.

Earhart's shoulder sagged. "She's a devil, isn't she?"

The gears in Phantom's head turned with ideas, contriving plans to get her on his ship.

"She will be. We are exactly what she needs."

Earhart stared out the window again. "We could use a woman aboard."

"That, mate, will not happen. Not unless Angelica has finally accepted my offer?"

Earhart let out an airy laugh. "Not in this lifetime."

"No, the Black Shadow is going to be the greatest swordsman to ever board *Nemain's Revenge.*"

CHAPTER 12

A BARMAID AND A SHADOW

Out of luck and patience, Phantom made his way to low town. Tonight, the rain was soft and forgiving. Not that it mattered. He tried to find the closest tavern he could, but he took one step into a high town pub and stepped right back out. There was no place for him among the wealthy nobles of Samsara. Not unless he was picking their pockets, but he decided that to be ill-advised.

Phantom turned to see a bustling building clearly setting up for their dinner rush.

Posada Gato Mojado, meaning 'Wet Cat Inn', seemed to be the right place to go despite its repelling name, too fitting for a tavern in low town. He shoved the doors open to find mostly empty tables. The night was young and more would file in soon enough, but the emptiness left a foul taste in Phantom's mouth. He hadn't realized he was searching for a chaotic atmosphere until he didn't get one.

A group of old Quencerian men sat at a table with a round of beers and cheery smiles. Quencerian people occupied most of Samsara.

"Oh ey!" The men shouted in unison, lifting their glasses

before tipping them back and drinking as fast as they could. It brought a half smile to Phantom's face. Once he did that with Jon, Black, Earhart, and Russet. Naturally, the competition involved who could finish their glass the quickest. Russet won. The man had unhinged his jaw, his throat taking the alcohol like a waterfall. No need to swallow.

Merakesh men were another breed entirely.

He chuckled at the thought before a wave of sadness crashed into him. He missed his devils. Part of him hoped they ran. If they ferried the Khelitians and found another sanctuary, then the Minister could have the island—and him. But they would be free, just like he promised.

At least someone would be free.

"Oh please, Captain. Black is your color, not blue." The familiar voice had Phantom turning to the bar. A barmaid stood behind the counter, adorned in scarlet and wiping a beer glass with a rag. Her eyes brightened with a knowing look and a smirk.

"Clare?" He whispered, almost not believing he saw a familiar face.

She let a soft chuckle escape at his astonishment. "Truly, you must work on your vigilance." She didn't miss a beat behind the counter, throwing her rag over her shoulder and mixing a drink right before him.

He shook his head as reality settled. "Why? How?"

Clare set the glass down with a sigh, as if catching Phantom up to speed was a chore. "We needed to check on you and they were hiring here." She continued mixing, the concoction having something to do with rum, but Phantom was too stunned to pay attention. "It wasn't hard to determine which piece of shit tavern you'd end up in."

"Don't you have people to take care of on Kheli?"

"This *is* me taking care of them." She set the finished drink on the bar in front of him. Finally, his mind caught up. She was checking on him to make sure her people were not in peril. It was ironic. As much as he loved Roger, Clare did more for that island than Roger ever could.

He lifted an eyebrow at the drink before him. "Miss Clare, I am a man of propriety now."

A small smile hitched the corner of her mouth. "No amount of fine clothing and fancy title could ever achieve that." His smile broke, seizing the drink and tipping it down his throat. The amber liquid burned all the way down, warming his insides. "That's more like it." Her eyes glittered. There was a strange camaraderie he had with the huntress. The way he would imagine having a sister was like, but it was more than that. It was more like Davina had paralleled their paths, yet he couldn't find it within himself to be upset at the Goddess's interference. This time.

Clare leaned down on the counter. "Now, tell me why you seek a shitty tavern in low town."

He smirked and lifted his empty glass, tapping his finger against it. "I'm going to need something stronger, barmaid."

"Ah," she hummed. "Does this have to do with a certain songbird?"

Phantom's gaze snapped to hers. He wasn't sure he ever said the nickname before. Her answering smirk told him she had made the connection on her own.

"It does." He straightened, watching her reach for the rum to make another drink. This time he watched her add orange and lemon juice along with a couple of light-colored spices. The smell reached him in time to recognize nutmeg and ginger. He smiled to himself, hiding it behind his hand. Samsara didn't deserve her.

She slid the finished drink into his hand. This time he sipped at the drink, enjoying the flavors.

"Alright, out with it. What did you say to her?"

He nearly choked on the biting liquid. "What makes you think I said something wrong?"

She answered with a single raised eyebrow.

"I offered to take her anywhere she wants." He sipped at the rum again. "Then I might have called her a spoiled princess."

Clare tipped her head forward with a heavy breath escaping her, black hair sliding down her face. "You offered to kidnap her again." Not a question. "Then you reminded her what she was worth to you."

"No—" Phantom started, realizing that might have been exactly what he did.

"Not only that, but *Nemain's Revenge* is not yours to command right now. You're not even allowed on the ship while under the Minister's control. Taking her anywhere is out of the question." Clare leaned on the bar, getting closer to the undercover pirate. "But maybe try to find out what she wants and try not to insult her this time."

Phantom blinked in quick succession, shocked he hadn't thought of that. The freedom and adventure speech usually worked. Plan B wasn't one he usually had to think of. He failed to mention the whole throwing her into a fountain incident.

People began filing into the bar, chatter and music permeating into the air. A bard in the corner strummed his guitar, singing a jolly tune.

"Listen, Captain," she said with a heavy breath, making him lock eyes with her. "Freedom comes in many forms, and you only offer one. But perhaps some need a unique form of it."

Phantom's brows knocked together as he considered that. He saw Samsara as the cage. He never considered it wasn't that way for everyone.

Clare's head shifted, tipping to the floor behind Phantom. With some reluctance, he turned in time to see a magnificent creature stride through the tavern door. She was tall and slender, her black shirt fell loosely around her chest, revealing a V of décolletage. Tight-fitting trousers hugged her generous thighs with leather boots that crawled up to her knees. A sword adorned her hip and a triangular hat rested on her head. The woman's dark hair curled around her temples and nape, her dark eyes glittering in the candlelight.

But he recognized her face—

He knew her like he knew his own face.

Black.

"Some of us," Clare's voice came in as a whisper behind him, "need freedom from ourselves, or at least, who we think we should be." Phantom turned to look into Clare's eyes, but her gaze firmly was fixed on the woman who strode in. "Freedom to be who we are."

Black's gaze searched the crowd until it landed on Clare, then her eyes widened when they landed on *him*.

Phantom cleared his throat as Black approached. There was a time when a woman as beautiful and fearsome as Black was precisely what he needed to lift his mood for the night. But Rose had changed him in the short time they'd known each other. Phantom no longer felt the desire to distract himself with the flesh of a stranger. As for Black, he knew where she stood, the evidence was obvious in Black's eyes as they softened when looking at the barmaid behind him. A longing look that was returned in full force for once.

"Captain," Black addressed in a soft voice.

Phantom tipped his head. "I must say, this ensemble suits you."

Black beamed, smiling widely, and turning to Clare. "I required an angel for assistance." A smug sort of grin etched the corner of Clare's mouth. She went back to creating another drink.

"Tell me, mate, how should I address you now? You were once insistent on the way I spoke of you. Have you changed that, along with the clothes on your back?"

A haunted gleam dulled Black's dark eyes.

"No." Clare stilled completely, but Black continued, "You may refer to me as a woman here, but once we are aboard again, you will return to addressing me as you did before."

A glass slammed against the counter loudly as Clare set it before Black with a stern crease to her brow. Clare lifted the apron from her head and set the ratted cloth on the counter.

Black seemed to shrink under Clare's gaze, the tension in the air suffocating.

"Sophia—"

"Don't." Clare raised a hand to halt Black's plea, then she turned her gaze to Phantom. "Captain," she said by way of dismissal before striding away.

Black watched her back as she went, her mouth falling open as if still ready to plead to Clare. But something stopped her.

"By the moons, what did you do?"

Black's broken gaze landed on her Captain, releasing a heavy breath. "Clare believes there are two versions of me. The one I am now and the one I pretend to be when I'm with the devils."

The thought made Phantom's gut churn. He'd gone through great effort to see his devils were in a place they could be themselves.

He narrowed his eyes. "Is that true?"

She cleared her throat, taking on the lower register he was accustomed to hearing. "Of course not."

Phantom raised a single damning eyebrow as Black bit her lip, a nervous habit she often fell prey to in Kazeboon. It was how he beat her at the game, and it appeared he'd have to use it to beat her here as well.

"Which do you want to be?" Black's gaze hit the floor, avoiding his stare. "Because I, for one, would be honored to have the world's best swordsman among my crew in any form you choose to take."

"It's not you I doubt, Captain," she let slip.

"The devils? You think them so shallow as to care what clothes you wear or what name you go by? Half of them don't go by their true names, anyway." Doubt flashed across her face, creating shadows in her dark eyes. He put a hand to her shoulder and squeezed firmly, as he would have with any devil. "Anywhere else in the world you may deny yourself, but on *Nemain's Revenge*? She was created for *you*. For anyone needing a place to be themselves. If this is who you are, be her. If the strapping pirate I know is who you are, be him. Either way, the devils will accept you or I will damn them myself."

A small smile curved her beautiful face.

He gave a pat to his mate's shoulder before lifting his hand away. "Don't allow Clare to sway that decision either, mate. There are other lasses out there."

Black chuckled softly into her drink. "Speaking from experience, Captain?"

Ouch, Sam responded.

"Alas, I am predestined to pine after one alone and the last time I saw her, I threw her into a fountain."

Black's eyes flared.

Phantom snickered and was about to explain further when an awareness drew his eye. It was an odd feeling, like the hand of Davina guiding him. A realization that made him want to ignore the pull completely. How dare Davina interfere with his life? Fate could do no more damage than it already had.

A shadowed figure slipped passed through the corners of the tavern before disappearing through a door. If he were to guess, the door would lead to the rooms of the inn, not uncommon for a stranger to enter. There were many people walking low town with their hoods up and their heads down. Nothing was out of the ordinary.

Except, the way the stranger crawled around the corners of the room like a shadow, trying not to draw attention.

Bloody hell.

Phantom tipped back the last of his drink before setting it on the counter. He nodded to Black, who understood the dismissal, before following the little shadow.

Music and dancing surrounded him as he crossed the floor. A woman with a broad smile and orange hair leapt at him as he passed.

"Looking for company tonight, officer?" Her voice was light and sweet. With her proximity, he could see a sky's worth of freckles making constellations across her cheekbones and nose. Before, he would have happily taken the offer, but now, all he could see was gold and blue.

"No," was all he said as he shrugged her off. The woman recovered quickly, returning to dancing before the bard as he played.

Finally, he made it to the door. There was still a pull in his gut he tried to ignore. If he thought too much on the hand of fate, he'd turn right around and forget the shadow, but curiosity was stronger.

Beyond the door, stairs led up. He checked behind himself to make sure no one was looking or following him. It wasn't likely, unless Davina was guiding someone else too. To the tavern goers, he appeared to be headed to his room.

He climbed the steps as quietly as possible, as to not alert the cloaked figure.

The stairs emptied into a hallway. Staggered rooms lined either side of him with numbers decorating their doors, but the figure was gone. He tapped into his monster for its enhanced hearing, listening to the bustling within the rooms. Part of him wished he hadn't.

The struggled breathing of a snoring man.

A couple in the middle of passionate throws.

Another couple bickering over—blankets, of all things.

He reached the end of the hall with no sign of the shadow

and no idea what to look for, so he closed his eyes and focused on the sounds around him.

"I am not sleeping with your mother's quilt."

"*Oh, Fernando, mi amore.*"

"If the Minister raises taxes anymore, we'll be out of a home."

"It's good luck. It's been in my family for generations."

"Sí, *señorita, beane de vida.*"

"Precisely why you should burn it."

Phantom growled in frustration, the beast crawling too close to the surface. With its nearness, so came the scents of the inn. Cleaning supplies, fresh sheets and old dirty ones, musky scents and perfumed ones. Then smoky sweetness, like smelling fresh flowers in a burning room.

His eyes snapped open. That scent could only belong to one person. Following the trail, it led him to the door of a guest room. With the beast's advanced hearing, it didn't take much to hear his songbird inside.

"How is she doing?"

"*No beano, mija.* I fear she won't last the night."

"Bring me to her."

He knew that voice like he knew his own soul.

"What are you up to, little songbird?"

He waited for the steps to recede further into the room before gently trying the doorknob. It was locked, of course, but nothing was ever truly locked. He pulled a double prong pick from his pocket and went to work on the door. It had been sometime since he picked something so simple. Most of his conquests of late included much more complex locks, but a small inn in low town would be the easiest.

The lock gave only after a little encouragement, clicking open.

Opening the door softly, he peeked inside, finding a single candle on a table, lighting the simple room. He shifted inside, closing the door soundlessly behind him. Keeping to the shadows and the edges of the hall, he followed down the only opening.

Voices swept over him.

"How long has she been like this?" He could hear Rose's melodic voice, but there was a mountain of concern lacing it.

"She hasn't woken in three days. The welts appeared this morning."

Phantom peeked through a bedroom door to see a candle lighting the sad scene. A large chested woman stood with a hand over her heart as her brows curved into a furrow of pain and worry. Her amber hair fastened behind her head. She wore a governess uniform.

She looked down upon the bed, which cradled a girl, no older than eight. The girl was Mokshan, with thick dark hair and warm brown skin, although the skin was more ashen than should have been possible. Large angry welts peppered her face in red splotches, sweat coating her brow.

Phantom immediately recognized it, the locals called it Crimson Death. The disease was highly contagious and brought to Samsaran shores by Mokshan people. It was why the race was so harshly handled. If anyone found out this girl was here, she would die, and the inn would burn as a "cleansing".

Yet, here was his songbird, patting the girl's brow as if she had no fear of the disease herself.

"Can you heal her?" The woman asked.

Phantom's brows knocked together. Could the songbird truly heal without the Stone?

"I can try." Rose lifted her delicate hand to rest on one of the girl's. The touch alone enough to condemn her, but she was willing to risk it. She hummed softly at first, singing the song she once did to Angelica. Blue swirled in her eyes, then her ribbons of light emerged from her hands, filling the room and wrapping themselves around Rose and the little girl.

HEAVEN NEED NO MORE
HELL CLOSE YOUR GATE
HEAL ALL THAT WAS TORN
BREAK THE LOOM OF FATE

The song was as beautiful as he remembered it, only this time she seemed to have more control over it. Last time, the Stone seemed to possess her, controlling the flow of magic in her veins. This time the ribbons of blue light obeyed her, dancing in time with the melody of her voice.

The song ended and the blue light faded, but the girl still laid motionless and ashen.

"Did it work?"

Rose put her hand to the girl's sweat laden forehead. "Her fever is broken, but it will come back." She rose, readjusting her cloak as if readying to leave.

"I don't understand."

"That was a song of healing. It repaired the damage done by the disease, but it did not kill the infection. I must find the right song for that." The way she spoke so easily took Phantom by surprise. He was so used to the way she spoke to him that this was—odd.

"What does that mean?" The woman clutched her apron to her dress.

Rose noticed, taking a moment to reach her arm out to the woman, placing it on her shoulder. "I bought her time. She will be alright for a few weeks, but the disease will come back with a vengeance. Nemain doesn't like to be cheated." Rose pulled gloves onto her hands. "I will be back with the right song to destroy the infection within her."

She crept toward the door where Phantom was, but he called on his orange counterpart to hide him in the shadows, slipping out of the room before she was any wiser. His vision tipped with orange and shadows drew into him as Draven's power aided him.

Unfortunately, Phantom didn't have time to re-lock the door. He watched her hesitate with the lack of resistance as she exited the door, looking up and down the halls on either side for her intruder.

Mercifully, she walked away, toward the inn entrance. He stalked after her, curious that she had to find "the right song". He had a feeling it had something to do with the Stone, but he was determined to find out what secrets the songbird kept.

CHAPTER 13

WATCH YOUR FOOTWORK

Black followed Sophia to the back alley behind the inn. It wasn't the most romantic location, with a slow trickle of rain and the stench of piss spoiling the cool, crisp night air.

"What are you doing out here?" Sophia leaned up against the brick of the building, smoking a cigar she likely lifted off a patron. Not that they would have complained. Sophia's outstanding good looks, fierce eyes, and full bosom got her away with murder on a bad day.

Davina knows Black would help her hide a body in a heartbeat.

Black sucked in her bottom lip before leaning against the building beside Sophia.

"What does it look like I'm doing?"

A false smile brightened Sophia's beautiful face. "Taking up my breathing space." Yet she did not move as Black inched closer.

"This doesn't make sense, Sophia." The barmaid's head turned so fast, Black nearly laughed. "Why does it matter what

I wear or how I have people refer to me? Why should it matter at all?"

Sophia puffed smoke into the damp air. "You really don't see it, do you?"

Her brow raised. "See what?"

Somehow, Sophia looked down her nose at Black from a few inches below. "How do you think a woman should be treated, Gwen?"

Gwen.

Sophia and *only* Sophia could get away with calling her that, and only out of public earshot.

"What do you mean?"

Sophia tossed her used cigar into a nearby puddle. "I think it's a simple enough question. How do you treat a woman?"

Black's brow lowered in contemplation, taking in the severity of this one question, but her mind went blank, completely empty when she needed it to be full.

"With respect," Black blurted before she could stop herself. It was the simple answer, but perhaps it was the right one.

"Good. Now, think back on all the moments you were a man. How did you treat me?"

Black's brows scrunched together. When the devils were around and her armor was firmly in place, she played the part they expected of *him*. He had yelled at Sophia, sensually, but hardly respectful. He pinched her ass in public. Crowded her. Mocked her.

Black deflated as all the moments, she soon after regretted, came to mind. "Poorly."

"Now, think about how you treat me when the devils aren't present."

Black didn't have to think about it. She treasured those moments because every one of them involved Sophia. It started as using a disguise for information from the innkeeper, but it had felt right. It felt easier to walk around as a woman with Sophia than to walk as a man with the devils.

Two entirely different lives. Ones she couldn't allow to cross over. If they did, she'd have to let go of her armor.

"I'm sorry, I can't—"

Sophia jerked back. "Can't? Or won't?" A single moment of silence was all Black could offer her. "Do what you want with your life, but leave me out of it." She pushed off the brick to stride down the alley.

Black wanted to go after her, but what could she say? This decision was hers, and she wasn't even certain she needed to make it. What was so wrong about being both the fearsome swordsman pirate of *Nemain's Revenge* and the swashbuckling maiden who frequented the bars of low town? Why couldn't she have both?

"All alone, sweetheart? I haven't seen you around here before." The deep vibrato of a man's voice faintly came from the direction Sophia went.

"I won't be needing your company, sailor," Sophia's sharp tongue dripped with repulsion. A cacophony of boos suggested more than one bothersome low towner facing off with her.

Black kicked off the wall, strutting towards the voices with one hand on the pommel of her sword.

"Feisty, I like my women that way." The man lunged for her, but she slapped him hard across the face before he could touch her. The two men resembling drowned rats, bellowed at his failure.

Black drew her sword, drawing the attention of all three men.

"Are these men bothering you, *señorita*?"

Sophia drew her fur shawl tighter around her shoulders to block out the cold. "I can handle these street urchins."

"Urchins?" The first man said with mock offense, widening his arms. He was older, likely in his forties, and wore clothes he probably thought himself proud of. Black assessed him as a man who found joy in asserting his dominance without the nature of a leader. "You wound us, sweetheart." The man's eyes found Black through Samsara's infamous fog. "You're welcome to join the party, my lady." His eyes grew weary at the sight of her blade. "But put your sword away."

"Funny. I reckon I would tell you the same thing."

At his expense, his friends laughed again. The man's jaw grew tense. "I wouldn't talk to me in such a way, lass."

Sophia's eyes brightened. "Well, if you get along with yourself so well, perhaps your hand would be better assistance than we would."

The men laughed harder this time, doubling over and pointing.

He gritted his teeth a moment before drawing his own sword. He swung at Black's still drawn weapon, but his advance was sloppy, his footwork that of an amateur. Black parried his swing easily enough, forcing the metal from his hand and placing the end of her blade to the man's chin.

"I'd advise you to rethink that decision."

The three men behind him snapped to attention, drawing their own blades at the threat to their friend. It must have looked easy. Sophia wasn't carrying a sword, so it would be three against one.

One man reached out for Sophia, forcing her back to his chest as he pressed a knife to her throat. But Black only smiled. Her Sophia wasn't so easily subdued.

Before he could utter a threat, Sophia bent her knees and pushed off them to smack her skull into his nose. He cried out in pain before her foot came down on his boot. He screamed, backing away and releasing her. She spun in place, striking between his legs with her knee.

The other men cringed as he fell, a pained moan leaving him.

Two men lunged at Black at once, but she could handle two easily enough. She caught both their blades at once, shoving them back. Before she could stop the barmaid, Sophia snatched the first man's fallen blade.

"No, I've got this. Go inside."

"Like I'd run from a fight." Sophia tucked part of her dress into her waistband, exposing one leg. The man facing her whistled. "You like that?" She ran toward him, swiping her sword and nicking the side of his face. "What about that?"

The man gritted his teeth, then swung, which she quickly deflected.

Black caught the sword of the one facing her, but he was wiser with his position and footwork. He had seen his friend make the mistake of underestimating her and adjusted his perspective.

Black spared a glance at Sophia but couldn't keep her eyes off her opponent long enough to assess her. "Keeping your feet apart?"

Sophia grunted. "I didn't learn yesterday."

"Yet still, your feet like to keep together." Black parried her opponent's next attack.

"You think right now is a good time for a lesson?"

"Now's the perfect time for a lesson." Black risked a glance to see Sophia's shoulders square to her opponent. "Keep the target narrow."

Sophia growled at Black's commentary but adjusted anyway.

Black smiled at her reluctant obedience. Her opponent shoved off her advance, backing her up a step.

"Oi," he barked, twisting his head. "I've seen you before, 'aven't I?"

She narrowed her eyes. "No, you haven't."

"Yes, I 'ave, but somethin' be throwin' me off."

Black advanced quickly, bouncing off the wall to cut a

bloody line down his arm. He cried out with the pain. "Say another word, and I'll stop toying with you. You won't make it out of this alley with your tongue."

His eyed widened and she could tell he placed her face. "Understood, lass." He turned tail, running away from her. "Come on," he shouted back at Sophia's opponent. The man trusted his friend enough to abandon his fight and sped off with his friend.

Black let out a huff of air, but she was hardly winded. They didn't put up much of a fight, but she dreaded what would become of someone recognizing her.

Sophia's breath was heavier, but it might have been from anger. She turned her back on Black, heading back to the inn.

"Wait," Black pleaded. "What if I chose? What if I remained like this?"

Sophia's eyes narrowed. "Would you treat me with respect?" At Black's confusion, Sophia continued. "I don't care what form you take. Be a man. Be a woman. Switch between personas. I don't care what you choose to look like or go by as long as you do it for you. Not for the devils, and certainly not for me."

"Then you'll stop fighting me?"

Sophia's beautiful face tipped with a sad smile. "When you figure it out, come find me." Then she turned, heading back into the inn and leaving Black in the cold.

LOCKNESS'S ESTATE

ONE YEAR AGO

It took some time locating the Black Shadow.

Phantom asked around low town, but the reports varied, saying he was a ghost avenging those wronged by Lockness or other noblemen abusing their power. Some said he was a devil sent by Nemain to collect overdue souls, while others, swore he was an angel sent by Davina to crush the wicked.

But there wasn't a single report claiming the Black Shadow was a woman. The Black Shadow left no witnesses and no evidence. There were so many rumors surrounding her, considering how very few people had seen her. It begged the question of why she left Phantom and Earhart alive when they could easily spill her secret.

To Phantom, it sounded like his little shadow friend liked him, which was good considering he had every intention of getting her aboard his ship.

After enough research, he found that the Black Shadow appeared near Lockness suspiciously often. Phantom knew from experience how well the man hid his involvement in the slave trade and other black-market dealings. It was nearly impossible for the Navy to get hold of any evidence to condemn him, let alone discover his hiding spots laid out throughout the city. And yet, the Black Shadow had been successful at finding ten of them in the last few months, which meant one thing.

The Black Shadow was an inside man — or woman, rather. Since everyone had been looking for a man, she blended right in. Probably a maid or kitchen servant. No wonder the secret of her gender was so closely guarded.

Phantom stood before the infamous mansion of nobleman Lockness himself. For once, he had an invitation.

Phantom had dressed himself and Earhart in the finest threads he could steal. Apparently, Niklaus Lockness was taking suitors to meet his daughter. As she was the richest heiress in Samsara, suitors flocked to his doors. Eventually, he would find one he thought could handle his fortune the way he wanted and marry them off to his daughter.

Earhart stood a step behind him, itching at the bright green silks on his arms.

"Stop moving, mate, or I swear to Nemain, I will deliver you to Her personally."

"Did you have to steal the most uncomfortable thing you could find? There are noblemen who prefer to wear simpler things." Earhart lowered his arms, flexing his palms at his sides.

"We will not impress the man with less than the best finery," Phantom leaned over to inspect Earhart's tie. He truly was in the best clothing money could buy. His suit jacket alone could feed an entire family for a year. Formal dress-wear was hard to get in Samsara, so every scrap was vastly overpriced.

Earhart lowered his brows, inspecting his Captain. "Then what the hell are you wearing?"

Phantom smirked. He opted for something less showy than Earhart's bright green. It was a navy-blue suit with a white ruffled undershirt and embroidered edges. It was still vastly more expensive than anything that had ever graced his frame, but it wasn't the nobleman's clown suit Earhart wore.

"Couldn't we have come as officers?"

Since they were both former naval officers, the feat wouldn't have been hard to pull off. Although, he still would've stolen uniforms. They burned theirs years ago.

"Lockness runs the black market. How kindly do you think he would take to naval officers poking around his home?"

"Fair point," he admitted before the gates to Lockness's mansion opened.

Phantom straightened his back and puffed up his chest, Earhart following his lead as they walked right through the main gates. He handed a folded invitation to the guard at the gate.

"Mr. Castellanos," the guard addressed, mistrust showing in a sneer curving his mouth. No doubt a guard charged with protecting its wealth and inhabitants wouldn't take kindly to strangers. "Welcome to Lockness Estate."

Skepticism strained the guard's face, dragging down the edges of his mouth.

"Apologies, my lord, but I need some proof of your legitimacy. We can hardly trust every stranger that appears at our doors, especially with pirates lurking about our shores."

Phantom resisted the smile that threatened to creep up his face, opting for an exaggerated frown. "It is hardly customary for your master to invite a guest and immediately question him upon arrival. Do I appear to be a pirate, good sir?"

The security guard regarded Phantom, taking in his fancy clothes and turned-up nose. Phantom's tattoos were hidden away, of course. A white silk scarf that matched the suit perfectly hid the kraken tentacles that crawled up his neck. Luckily, it was a common fashion among the nobles.

"Forgive me if I do not take your appearance into account,

my lord." The guard's eyes narrowed, not liking Phantom's delay in providing proof.

"I shall not forgive you, sir, but—" he sighed heavily "—if you must have proof." Phantom tilted his head to Earhart, who immediately provided a paper with the deed to the Castellanos Estate on the opposite side of the island.

The man's brows shot up, so Phantom extended his hand with the signet ring to the House of Castellanos stamped upon it.

The guard took in their appearance once more. "That is quite a long way to walk."

Phantom immediately let his smile break, laughing in a way that was hollow. Earhart joined in the laughter. "I did not walk the entire island. No, I am staying at the nearby inn." He turned back to Earhart. "This man thought I walked." They broke into laughter again.

The guard groaned. "Your invitation was to stay at my lord's estate for the duration of your stay."

Phantom let his smile fade, and the laughter silenced. "I make my own way, sir."

"It's good to hear so," a voice chimed from further down the path. Phantom turned to see a man dressed even more lavishly than Earhart, but in nearly all white, with hints of silver at the edges of his many layers. "Some may take my hospitality. Especially the opportunity to reside in my estate, but it says a lot about a man who wants to negotiate on his own terms."

Phantom's blood boiled, making the monster difficult to hold back. It was Lockness. The very man he had spent endless hours attempting to take down. By the time Phantom turned to face the man, he plastered a smile on his face. "Ah, the man of the house, I presume."

Lockness scrunched up his nose, making his grayish white mustache twist. "Man of the island is a closer description."

Phantom raised his brows, playing along. "Quite the estate, however do you manage an entire island?"

"The same way I manage everything else." His gaze turned up to the sky. "With the help of Davina and an iron fist."

Phantom frowned to himself, but Lockness caught it. "And how would you, Castellanos, manage an island?"

"The same way one manages a woman." Lockness narrowed his eyes, curiosity piqued at Phantom's example. "By understanding her deepest and darkest truths and involving myself in those so thoroughly, there isn't a part of her I do not know."

Lockness's lips turned up slightly in amusement. Then his arm came around Phantom, planting on his shoulder and directing him through the estate. "You may have some trouble with my daughter, then."

Phantom smiled too. "I'm counting on it."

Lockness pulled Phantom into a lavish sitting room and offered him a cigar. The estate was larger than Phantom had ever seen before, other than the Fortress, naturally. White cobblestones made up the outside in a careful display.

In every hallway, Phantom wondered if they dragged Kalonite slaves or children through. No, Lockness would never bring his sins into his own house. The risk was too great. His empire ran on his reputation. That delicate balance of the right people thinking him to be benevolent, and some believing him to be malevolent.

"So, Mr. Castellanos," Lockness mused between puffs while his arms spread over the back of his fine couch, stitched with silk to resemble a mural. "What is it you do on your lonesome side of the island?"

"Come now, Lockness, you should know better than to ask a man's business."

Phantom had stolen the invitation from the Castellanos Estate himself. The man was locked in his room, since he graciously gave his staff the entire week off. He was a stout, skittish man and wouldn't dare challenge Jon, who was tasked with babysitting the nobleman.

From the information Phantom could glean from the man's office; he ran a cow and pig farm to provide meat to the masses of Samsara. He likely supplied many of the butcher houses Lockness ran his black market from. Although, from the reports Phantom found, he overcharged his patrons.

"Although," Phantom began at Lockness's frown. "I will say it is a pleasure to put a name to the face. You are one of my best customers."

Lockness smiled to himself, but it held no joy, only suspicion. "Your goods are highly overpriced, Mr. Castellanos. Do you know why I buy from you?"

Phantom only narrowed his eyes at the man. He was rich beyond reason, so Castellanos likely took advantage of such a capable buyer.

"I buy from you, because you are discreet. You stay in your little castle on the other side of the island, and you never ask questions." Lockness leaned forward, resting his elbows on his knees. "I did not expect you to accept my invitation. So why make this journey when you never have before?" The taste of suspicion was thick in the air. The fact that someone had shown up claiming to be Castellanos was enough to spark his intuition.

"How could I refuse?" Phantom said softly. "After all, you are offering the world."

Lockness's lips drew into a tight line. It wasn't likely the suitors had come out and said it before. They were all there at the chance to inherit his unofficial kingdom, not his daughter.

Before Lockness could reply, footsteps interrupted them.

"Ah, Gwenivere, nice of you to join us."

Phantom's gaze snapped to the woman entering, she was in a decorated gown resembling a cupcake. High fashion for the ladies of Samsara, but a bit overdressed for a casual day. It looked even more ridiculous with her frame. She was tall, lean, with broad sharp shoulders. Her posture and scowl gave away her absolute discomfort in the hideous dress.

He locked eyes with the woman and recognized her easily. After all, how could he forget the best swordsman he'd ever met?

Her dark eyes narrowed for a moment as if trying to place his face, but even he had to admit, he was good at disguising himself. His presence in her father's home must have been outlandish enough that she couldn't connect the dots.

"Gwenivere, this is Mr. Castellanos. He's come from the opposite side of the island to meet you."

She dipped in a curtsy, her dress brushing the floor, and her eyes low. "A pleasure to meet you, sir." Her voice was clipped and rehearsed.

Phantom rose to greet her, taking her hand in his and raising it to his lips. "The pleasure is all mine." He kissed her knuckles, and she tried to hide the upward tilt of her nose, but he caught it, letting out a low chuckle. At the laugh, her eyes snapped to his, and he winked.

Finally, her eyes widened as she placed him.

There they stood, knowing the authentic life of the other, the secret that would earn them a mountain of trouble if Lockness ever found out. But they both knew the other wouldn't say a thing for that exact reason.

Her face smoothed over into her mask again as she glanced at her father.

"Shall we have dinner?" Lockness suggested.

"Sounds brilliant." He held out his arm for her to take, and she did so dutifully.

The Black Shadow. Lockness's own daughter.

Lockness unknowingly led his two biggest enemies through the doors of his banquet hall.

CHAPTER 15

STALKING ALONG

Rose's silhouette flitted through the inn and out the door. Phantom glanced at the bar as he remained at the edges. Black and Clare were nowhere to be found. He made a note to himself to revisit the inn to check on them, assuming they remained on the island.

She slipped out of the door as swiftly as an escaping breeze. No one paid her any attention, even if Phantom himself received a few glances. A few older Quarencian men narrowed suspicious eyes in his direction. A good cue to leave.

Rose, however, slipped away with no one taking a second glance at her. He paused. How was it possible that this creature hadn't drawn a single eye and yet stole all his attention when she entered a room?

He knew the answer. The one staring him in the face, but he wanted to hear it from her.

Breaching the door, he spotted her cloak before it disappeared behind an alley bend. An uneasy grunt left him as he followed. He didn't like that she wandered the streets of low town alone.

As if in answer to his thoughts, a man flicked a cigar to the ground before following after her.

Phantom picked up his pace. "Oh, no you don't."

He followed Rose's new stalker, keeping himself hidden as he watched the figure jump from shadow to shadow. He was clearly male, with the silhouette of broad shoulders, a sharp jaw, and a nose only a mother could love. There was no good reason for the man to be following *his* songbird. Only Phantom was allowed to do that.

If he were a standard criminal looking for easy prey, then his miserable heart only had a few more beats inside his body.

But if he was hired by someone with much more complicated reasonings, then Phantom needed to know what those were. Especially after Rose left a scene that could earn her a fierce punishment.

Phantom followed Rose's tail for a few miles as she climbed steps and hills to reach high town. She was heading back to the Fortress and her tail was more intentional that some petty criminal. He wanted to see where she would go, maybe with no intention of pouncing on her — yet.

The bastard would have to live long enough to scream his story to Phantom. He let out a slow breath. It wasn't exactly how he wanted to spend his night.

He didn't want the man to see Rose slip onto the pathway leading to the Fortress beyond high town. Especially if he was after her chamber's location in the Fortress. Phantom caught up, stealing a spot in the shadows the rat would try next.

Sure enough, he stepped before Phantom like a rabbit hopping unawares into a trap. The man's back was to him, and it was too goddess-damned easy. He pounced on the man, one hand on his mouth, the other holding a knife to his throat.

He jolted, but Phantom held him in place, whispering in his ear. "Scream and I'll let Nemain drag you into the depths tonight." He struggled more but didn't make a sound as Phantom let his mouth go.

Until he decided threats would work. "I'll cut you in so many pieces your own mother won't recognize you."

Phantom guffawed. "Oh, big boy with big promises. You must say that to all the ladies."

The man froze in his arms, clearly confused at Phantom's response. Good, they were more pliable this way.

"Now, tell me. What is a big boy like you, Jimmy—can I call you Jimmy—doing following around a woman in the middle of the night? Nothing nefarious I hope."

He paused for a moment, clearly deciding which lie would be most believable. "I'm desperate. I need a few coins to get me through the week."

Phantom laughed darkly in the stalker's ear. If he had any intention of robbing Rose, he would have done it in low town where crimes were more easily dismissed. In high town, they were harder to get away with. Every criminal in Samsara knew that. "Jimmy, you aren't even a good liar."

He hit the backs of the man's knees, forcing him to the ground and letting the knife drop away. It was enough freedom for him to get the idea to run, but the sound of a pistol cocking let him know to stay put.

Phantom rounded on the man, keeping his gun aimed at the man's head. The man's mouth twisted into a hard frown and determination seeped through his features. Since his acting skills were decidedly lacking, loyal bravery clung to him instead. The look told Phantom he was in for a long night, and he still needed to find Rose.

"Tell me what she means to you, and we can skip the unpleasantries. I may even let you live if you're a good boy." Phantom let a cruel smile tilt his lips. The man looked him over, appraising his opponent.

"Captain Phantom, I presume?" The sniveling voice the man

possessed before was gone, replaced by something stronger. Phantom's smile faded, but he gave no response, letting the man absorb how much danger he was truly in. But he laughed cruelly instead. "I heard you're the Minister's little bitch now. How's palace life, officer?"

A prickle ran down Phantom's back. The man knew too much and the look on his face said as much. He knew he wasn't making it out of this alive, but Phantom needed to find out exactly who else knew he worked for the Minister.

"I don't suppose you'll tell me how you know all that, so I don't have to deal with your ugly face for the rest of the night." The man's face turned to stone, his eyes hard and his breathing steady.

Phantom let out a sigh.

The very fact that this man gave Phantom a reason to kill him was enough to tell him he would die to keep his secrets, but that would change. They all sing eventually.

"Then I suppose we are going to become very familiar with one another."

In a flash of movement, Phantom used the palm of his pistol, ramming it into the side of the man's head and knocking him out cold.

***

After depositing Rose's stalker where he could take a nap while Phantom continued, he followed Rose to the Fortress. She was long gone, but he knew where she would be.

Her room looked over the sea, at the cliff face and the crashing waves below. Davina's silver moon glittered in ripples on the water's surface. The lilac moon was on the opposite side of the sky, creating two shadows on his silhouette.

He knew it to be her room by her scent. He'd picked up on it days ago.

Phantom looked up to the white marble balcony to see Rose, still adorned in her cloak, climbing down the wall of the Fortress to the dirt below. He waited and watched for a moment, crossing his arms as he tried to contain his smile.

The Minister's dutiful daughter had snuck in and back out of her own room, but Phantom had to wonder how often of an occurrence that was. She climbed down like it was muscle memory, like she knew every crevasse and ledge to cling to. It shouldn't surprise him. She stowed away on his ship and that was after he discovered her in the Temple after dark. A time of night she should have been spending in her room.

Phantom felt a tingle of amusement. She was becoming more and more fascinating every time he interacted with her. At this rate, he'd be so taken with her, it would be irrevocable. Not that he minded.

Her shoes crashed into the pebbles below when he finally made his presence known. "You know, you could use the front door."

She whirled, and he glimpsed her golden eyes before they narrowed into slits. He must have been smiling smugly. After all, he was very pleased with himself for discovering her.

"What do you want?" She bit out before walking away from him, her shoes crunching on the pebbled ground.

You, he almost said before he thought better of it. She wasn't ready for that yet. "I want to see what trouble you've gotten yourself into this time."

A humorless laugh left her. "I don't need your help, *Captain.*"

He caught up to her, walking beside her and aching to touch her even if the look in her eyes was equal to the warning rattle of a snake.

"What happened, love? I thought we were past this. Don't get me wrong, your attitude gives me many ideas about how to punish you and *not* the kind of punishment you would hate."

She stiffened as she walked then a tiny grimace wrinkled her nose. "Bold of you to assume you have any claim over me to be able to *punish* me."

He jumped ahead to block her path, reaching out to touch her arm. If she could kill with a single stare, he would be greeting Nemain. "Do I not?"

"No." She pulled her arm back from him sharply.

He let a soft smile grow. "Come now, we both know that's not true."

She scoffed. "Why wouldn't it be? You're selfish, unruly, uncivilized, and a liar. You have only ever cared about what you can get from me."

Phantom frowned. Hurt leaked from her eyes, even if she refused to admit it. He studied her further, hoping to find the answer in her expression. "Where is this coming from?"

She turned, walking away from him, but he reached out to catch her around the waist. A second before he did, cool metal pressed against his throat. The knife he had given her poised at his neck, ready to slice his skin open, and the steely look in her eyes told him she would.

"Ah," he started, letting his words deepen. "We've stepped this far back then. Whatever did I do to lose so much of your trust?"

Although her face was still hard, her delicate brows scrunched. "I never trusted you. The reminder of who you really are is what I needed. I should blame myself, really. It's not like you can help it. You're a pirate."

Her words burned, boiling his insides.

In a movement too fast for her to catch, he tossed the knife away from his throat. It fell to the rocks below them as Phantom's palm came around her throat. Her eyes snapped to his and widened. He backed her up until her back crashed against the Fortress wall. One of her hands came up to his, but she didn't pry him away. Perhaps it was the shock.

"You'll need to be a bit more specific." His voice came out in a growl. His grip on her throat was firm, but gentle. "What exactly can I not help because I'm a *pirate*?" He was used to being judged by what he was, but something about her believing the worst of him felt wrong.

Instead of answering, her knee flinched upwards, but he moved his thigh in time to stop her from downing him with a single blow. He learned from that mistake last time.

"Not going to happen. So why don't you answer the question?"

She remained silent, glaring through her lashes at him. But the look only made his skin grow warm and blood rush to the very spot she had wished to crush under her knee. He wanted very much to know if her body was having a similar reaction. If she did, she didn't let on.

He leaned in closer. "I have no objections to staying like this all night, which is precisely what will happen if you don't give me an answer." He felt her body stiffen in the exact moment she felt how much he liked the position.

Still, she didn't answer. A smile tipped the corner of his mouth as he looked down at her. An adorable frown was her only sign of discomfort. But he knew exactly what form of torture would get her to speak the quickest. The question was, who would it torture more?

The hand on her throat tipped her chin up, letting his thumb land on the pulse point of her neck. He wanted to feel her heart rate pick up. He pressed his lips to the underside of her chin. It was a delicate kiss that left gooseflesh on her skin. Her heart rate picked up exponentially, and he chuckled when he felt it.

Trailing kisses down the column of her neck, his other hand came around her waist, drawing her closer to him. He growled against her flesh, letting the vibrations absorb into her body.

"Wait," she said breathlessly. It was curious that she didn't say *stop*, only to wait.

He chuckled again, then pulled back to look into her eyes. "Are you ready to speak then, love? If not," he purred, "maybe I'll get back to it." He moved slowly, keeping his eyes on hers as long as he could until his lips reached her neck again. He swore he glimpsed her eyelids flutter shut.

"Wait," she said more firmly this time, but made no move to shove him off. "Please."

A smile tipped his lips. He wondered what exactly she begged for, because it didn't sound like it was a plea for him to stop. Still, he paused, even if all he wanted to do was continue, but he kept his breath on her. "Are you ready to tell me what's wrong?"

She breathed heavily, stopping and starting a few times before words finally tumbled from her. "You—you don't care about me." The words seemed to give her strength, firming her belief. "All you want is your precious treasure."

The words pierced him sharper than any knife. She pushed him off and he let her, taking a step back, but not enough that she could slip away.

"What gave you that idea?"

Her features hardened with the newfound coolness on her skin. He felt it too. Even though they were still so close, the distance was too much.

"Two. Things," she bit out. He recalled one of the first conversations he had with her. He told her that only two things motivated him. Freedom and coin. Both of which he thought he'd get when he ransomed her.

But by then, everything had changed.

He abandoned his flirty tone, letting his voice become sharp. "I nearly risked everything for you. I would have turned that ship around and never looked back if that's what you wanted."

Her eyes steeled, building a wall to keep him out.

"Was that before or after you learned what I could do?"

He took another step back. There it was. The reason she distrusted him again was because of what she thought he wanted from her.

"You think I want you because of your voice?" She didn't run, only stared at him as if waiting for him to deny or confirm it. "Apparently, I haven't made myself clear." He inched toward her again, letting his approach be slow like a lion stalking its prey.

"I want you, Rose Davenport. But it has nothing to do with what you can do." He seized her chin, making her look at him. "It has everything to do with who you are. The woman who stows away on the most dangerous ship on the Sumerian Sea to retrieve a stolen treasure because it reminds her of her mother. Even though she shouldn't know how, she learned how to wield a knife. The woman who challenged a pirate, not only with the crossing of blades, but to a liar's game." Her lips parted as he went on. Part of him wanted to sever the distance, but he resisted. She needed to hear this.

"I want the woman who risked her life, then her secret for a woman she only just met. I want the woman who got drunk on a beach because she could." He stared at her for a moment. "And I want the woman who sneaks off in the middle of the night to heal sick children."

Her eyes widened then narrowed. "How long have you been following me?"

He smirked. "I think you know. You had a nasty tail on you since the inn."

"Was it you?"

He chuckled. "Yes and no, but he is a bit tied up right now."

She furrowed her brow, coming to terms with the idea of having not only one, but two stalkers. "Did you kill him?"

"No," he said, and she sagged in relief. "Not yet."

"You will let me speak to him first."

He smiled, but it didn't reach his eyes. "We went over this. I don't take orders from you."

Yet, some distant voice echoed in his head, but he couldn't tell which counterpart to blame. He was too distracted to pay attention to bothersome colors.

"A favor then."

This time, a smile brightened his eyes, leaning in until he had both arms draped on the wall behind her head. "What exactly would you give me in return?"

She wet her lips, her eyes flicking down to his for a moment before she straightened herself. "I will let you help me with something tonight if you do."

"That sounds like a double win for you." Although he wouldn't deny his curiosity. He caught her escaping from her room, not going back in. She was after something else tonight. Not to mention, the deal would afford him time with her.

"Do you want to come or not?" She challenged, clearly understanding him enough to know he wouldn't refuse.

"Wouldn't miss it." He stepped away from her to allow her the space to move. As she walked away, he wished to be right back in her space again. He wanted to taste her skin on his lips. The feeling of it too fresh to leave him. He hoped it never would.

He turned to pull her into his arms, but she flinched away.

He stopped, witnessing a flash of fear in her eyes. Then something occurred to him. She had flinched away from him several times before. He dismissed it for the uncomfortable environment and that fact that she was face to face with a pirate, but that reaction should be gone by now.

"Why did you flinch?"

She wouldn't meet his gaze, opting to stare at his shoes.

"Rose." He put a hand on her cheek and pulled her face towards him. He found himself being slower and gentler than he was before. There was a pain in her eyes so keen he felt it like a sharp jab to his stomach. The pain ignited a fire that burned hot, then climbed up his body until he felt the monster rumble beneath his skin. Her eyes lined with silver for a second before she pulled her cheek away.

"It's nothing. I'm just not used to people—touching me."

"Rose." She stopped before he reached out again. "I don't know what you've been through, but I swear to you, the vermin responsible for instilling that fear in you will bleed out at your feet and beg you to forgive them." Her eyes snapped to his, drinking in the violence of his words. "And if you trust nothing else, know this. I will never lay a harming hand on you, Rose Davenport. I swear it to you on my life and my crew."

She sucked in a breath, understanding the gravity of that vow.

He let his words settle on her. Her features relaxed, accepting and believing him.

"Come on then, Captain, or we won't make it before the sun rises."

He smiled in a way that could have been cruel as he thought about the satisfaction of ripping apart all the villains in Rose's life.

She nodded, turning away from him, and he followed.

CHAPTER 16
TEMPLE AT NIGHT

Rose silently led the way, but by ten minutes in, Phantom knew exactly where they were headed.

She stopped out of sight of the temple guard manning the front, stooping down behind a boulder. Phantom crouched down with her as she rummaged around in a small satchel she had slung around her shoulder.

"We're here to steal the Stone, of course," Phantom guessed. It connected to her power somehow, that much was clear. If he recalled the earlier conversation correctly, it was something about the right song.

"You think you're the first to steal it?" There was a ghost of a smirk on her lips. "I've stolen it over a dozen times, and no one knows."

Phantom furrowed his brow. Why would anyone *need* to steal something that often?

"Forgive me, love, but how exactly did you manage that?"

Finally, she pulled out a glowing smooth stone from her satchel with glittering lilacs and silvers. Phantom's eye went wide. By all accounts, it looked exactly like the Stone, but there was something missing. Something he'd only be able to recognize because he spent so much time with the bloody thing. The soft hum of magic was absent.

"Where did you get that?"

Her thumb caressed the glasslike surface of the stone. "I made it." Her eyes glittered as the light from the faux Stone reflected in them.

"How?"

She stammered, a line creasing the skin between her brows as she realized she might have said too much.

"T-that's not important. The problem is that ever since you stole the Stone, the Priestess has increased security. It's going to be harder than I'm used to dealing with. Next time you steal something, learn how to be subtle."

His jaw dropped. This songbird was chastising *him* about a heist.

"I assure you, love. The dramatics were absolutely necessary." A single delicate eyebrow raised while her mouth pressed together. The goal was not the Stone, it was *her*.

"Did you *have* to jump off a cliff?"

He smiled, not bothering to contain it. She sounded like Ramirez. "Why? Were you worried about me?"

"If you would have died from the jump and lost the Stone, I would have dragged you back from Nemain's realm myself so I could kill you again."

He couldn't stop himself from chuckling. He must have given her quite the shock when he made that jump.

"I'll keep that in mind." She shot him a look that said she didn't believe that for a second. "Now, how do you propose we get in?" He leaned to look over the boulder. He didn't have to be right behind her but slipping his hand around her waist was much easier this way. She slapped it away as soon as she could feel it. She didn't complain about his closeness, though, so he let that be a victory.

The temple guard was one officer he'd worked with before,

but only briefly. Phantom recognized his reddish blonde hair and soft features. He smirked at an idea, palming the stone and pulling it from Rose's grasp.

"How about you distract the guard and I'll slip in to exchange the Stone?"

She shifted, clearly uncomfortable working with someone on one of her little heists, but he could be subtle when he wanted to be.

Pfft.

"How exactly would I distract him?"

He let a smirk play on his lips. "I know I would be awfully distracted if you strode up to me and started using your feminine charms."

She snorted, but he must have missed the joke. "If using charm is your tactic, then the job would be better suited for you." At his confusion, she continued. "Charles enjoys the explicit company of men."

Oh.

"I'd even caught him staring at you occasionally."

Oh.

Phantom had flirted with Jon, but it wasn't because he was interested. Making Jon uncomfortable was the joy of it, but he had absolutely no intention of bedding a man, especially when there was a woman right next to him that was more than suited to his tastes. Although, he couldn't say he hadn't dabbled in his younger years.

She slipped the stone from his hands back to hers. A smile danced on her lips as she refrained from laughing. "You distract the guard and I'll exchange the stone."

Rose snickered as she disappeared behind the nearby bushes. He hadn't even agreed to it yet.

Phantom stood up, straightening his jacket and ran a hand across his hair to make sure it was in place.

This should be good, Sam teased, but Phantom ignored him.

He sauntered up to the guard with the confidence of a man on a mission.

"Good evening," Phantom purred as the guard held out a halting hand.

"Sorry, officer, Temple is closed for the night. You'll have to come back in the morning." His voice held no amount of softness, only cool calm and dutifulness.

"Good, then there will be no one to disturb us." He watched the guard's eyes grow wide as Phantom tried to remember the name Rose had given him. *Was it Richard? Charlie? Bloody hell.* Sam even gave a mental shrug that was utterly useless. Turned out, every version of him was bad with names. "I've been watching you."

"You have?" The man said, shifting uncomfortably.

Phantom began circling him, keeping his eyes on the dark amber of the guard's. "And I like what I see."

"You do?" The guard kept eye contact with him, turning as Phantom circled him. The man was attractive in a soft masculine way. His reddish blonde hair laid in soft curls around his face, paired with his big brown eyes and lean figure. He would have been one of Phantom's conquests during his experimental era.

"I know you've been watching me, too."

The guard swallowed. "I thought your attention was with women." Considering that recently the only woman he bothered flirting with at the Fortress was Rose, the officer had paid close attention. Not that he was subtle with his songbird, but he had only seen her a handful of times.

Phantom dared to run his knuckle along the threads of the guard's arm. "I enjoy many forms of attention." Phantom didn't see her but rather felt a subtle breeze and a waft of smokey sweetness.

The guard turned slightly, seeming to sense her.

"I—," Phantom started speaking before the words fully

formed in his head, desperate to divert him. "I especially like the attention of blondes."

A red flush crawled up the guard's neck and over his cheeks. He cleared his throat. "I am on duty, sir."

Phantom raised an eyebrow. "Understood. I shan't keep you then." He smiled devilishly and shot the guard a wink before striding away. Internally he was relieved for the guard's sense of honor. He waited until he knew he was out of view before ducking behind the same boulder.

He didn't exactly plan on waiting around for Rose to sneak back out. Since the guards were looking for threats outside the Temple, they weren't expecting someone to sneak out of it, but he'd hardly leave her fate to chance.

Phantom roamed the edges of the brush around the Temple. Trees and bushes lined the area thick enough to provide enough shadows to hide a scoundrel like himself. The guards strolled around the walls of the Temple in waves, but they were close enough that not an edge of the wall was unseen.

Right above where the guards patrolled, Phantom spied the wisp of a cloak. Red flickered over his vision a second before he spotted her in the shadows. She was concealed so well; it was impressive. She stood on a ledge, a story from the ground. The nearby window she must have crawled from was lit with candlelight and the shadow of a figure stood there. It must have been the Priestess, doing some late-night studies.

How had she gotten herself into so much trouble so quickly?

Seems about right. Sam groaned while Kayden grunted his agreement.

If Ravana found her stealing the Stone, the consequences would be severe, even for the Minister's daughter, but they never caught her before. She wasn't about to start now. He'd see to that.

She would need a distraction and not simply flirting with a guard. No, he needed those guards to be somewhere else.

Normally, he had people to command. His first thought was to have Hyne and Tick create a distraction on the other side of the building, possibly with some explosives, but he had no such luxuries this time. He supposed it was a challenge for his creativity.

"Open up!"

Phantom's attention turned back to the main entrance of the Temple. There was a shipment being carted through the front doors, pulled by guards. By the looks of them, former officers, but they bore the triple Goddess colors like a coat of arms.

Ravana's head popped out of the window, inspecting the shipment from her perch. Phantom sucked in a breath, watching as the Priestess was only a head turn away from discovering Rose.

Ravana's sheet of red hair spilled over her shoulder and out the window. The robes she wore were mercifully lilac, but it didn't stop the unease in his stomach at seeing the woman at all. If he could only hate one soul in the world, it would be her blackened one.

She drifted back into the Temple and blew out the candle, darkening the room and leaving Phantom with a wash of relief. The absence of the light made no difference to him since his beast was leaning into him. Night vision was a useful trick.

Beside him was a small sharp rock. It had been some time since he threw rocks from his perch on the low town roofs with Bash, but he could still do it. He closed one eye to get good aim and threw. The rock knocked into one wheel of the shipment kart. It rocked the structure and the wheel fell from the body of the cart, sending boxes flying to the ground.

He swore he heard the shouts of animals and water sloshing as the cart tipped, but no trilling or ear-piercing screeches of a small dragon.

Guards were made of steel it seemed, moving to rectify the situation without a hint of panic. Ravana charged out of the

Temple, shrieking. "That is delicate, you buffoons!" The guards patrolling the side took notice and ran to help. "Pick this all up and bring it inside. Gently!"

Phantom pressed his lips together to keep from laughing. It wasn't often he could get Ravana in such a fury without feeling her wrath. He felt a pang of regret for the guards who had to deal with her, including Charlie, or whatever his name was.

Rose still clung to the ledge, unable to reenter through the window Ravana closed.

He whistled in a way that sounded like a nightingale, but he knew it would draw the songbird's attention. "Jump, I'll catch you," he whisper-shouted, hoping he was loud enough for her to hear.

"Are you crazy?"

Oh, she heard.

He chuckled under his breath a bit. "What's wrong, love? Scared of a little leap of faith?"

"If you haven't noticed, I cannot see you and I know you cannot see me. How am I supposed to jump, knowing you won't catch me?" There was a hint of panic and a cartful of apprehension.

"Trust, love. Trust me to catch you, and I will."

She didn't exactly have another choice. The guards would be back at any moment. If the sun rose while she was still there, she would get caught and the true Stone returned. Then, people would ask questions about how she got her hands on a replica.

"I promise, I will always catch you." He felt the words ring true right down to his soul, the one that was shared by many names over many lives, but they all had one thing in common. Her. It would always be her.

He held out his arms for her. She closed her eyes and jumped, falling into his outstretched arms. She held her breath, as if that would save her from the approaching ground. He smiled at his girl, having a moment to take her in before she opened one eye to see him staring at her.

Slowly, she opened the other eye and released her very important, life-saving breath. She didn't make a move to crawl out of his arms, so he held her closer, comforted by her warmth and nearness. He was tempted to lean in and close the remaining distance between them, but before he could decide, he leaned forward, pressing his forehead to hers.

She made no move against the action. In fact, her eyelids fluttered closed to soak in the sweet serenity. He breathed in her scent, bathing in fresh flowers while burning, both her smoki-ness and the raging inferno beneath his skin begging to claim this beautiful creature in his arms, as if it were the singular reason he existed.

Phantom dipped his chin to taste her lips, but she pulled away a moment before he could, yet she still didn't move from his arms. He pulled back to inspect her face and found it hesi-tant. She was torn. He had already offered all he could, and she rejected it. There was a reason she had to stay.

"I—" she started before shaking her head like those words were no good at all. She still didn't completely trust him yet. He'd have to prove it to her. That he was worth trusting.

"You don't have to tell me yet, love. But know this, if it takes a few more days, or a hundred years, I will always want you and I'll be waiting for you to realize it too. When you choose me," he squeezed her, "I'll never let you go." The words echoed through his head and the speech he gave the angels came to mind. If she let him, he just found his reason to fight.

Footsteps crunched gravel yards away. They were out of time. He let her feet reach the ground, then immediately put a finger to his mouth to make sure she stayed quiet. He wasn't too worried about it, though. His songbird was stealthy.

Unwilling to release her completely, he grabbed her hand to

guide her to the brush where they could make their way back to the Fortress.

———

The sky warmed to soft pinks as dawn crept up on them. They spoke little as they made it to her balcony, hand in hand.

Phantom had never held onto a woman's hand for so long before, but he couldn't help wanting to keep her close. There was something serene about holding her hand. If she gave him nothing more than that, he would be a content man. But Nemain knows he'd give quite a lot to have every bit of her.

They stopped just below her balcony, letting the night's bitter wind surround them. The clouds parted for a moment, letting silver moonlight drift down. It softened her features. Her mouth opened and closed with unspoken words.

"You needn't fret, love," Phantom spared her from deciding. He wasn't even close to finished with her, so waiting for her to be ready was hardly a deterrent. "I understand you have secrets you aren't willing to divulge." He tipped her chin up, locking eyes. "I do plan to hear every one of them, and to tell you every one of mine." Something knotted deep in his stomach at the thought of her finding out about his beast, but he'd do it. "I also understand you need to trust me completely before that happens. Allow me to prove that to you."

This time, when her mouth opened, it didn't close again.

He smiled and spared her from responding by pulling the glittering Stone from his pocket. "You will need this."

Her shock melted into an amused smile. "You really need to show me how to do that." She snuffed out the glittering light by shoving it back into her satchel.

This time, it was he who was shocked. "The dutiful daughter of the Prime Minister wants to learn how to pick pockets?"

She frowned as if she forgot who she was and he was sorry to have reminded her, but she cleared it with a shake of her head. "Yes, it seems to be a handy skill for you."

He grinned at her words, then he slipped a hand around her waist and pulled her in. "Well, love, it comes with growing up as an orphan on the streets of Samsara. I'm not sure you could handle it."

She raised an eyebrow. "Trust me, Captain, I could handle it." But a realization swept across her face at the other part of his statement. She looked up at him with wide, golden eyes. "You're an orphan?"

He winced on letting that detail slip. Not because he didn't want her to know every broken part of him, but because it was hardly the time to get into such details. The sun would be up soon; their time together cut too short.

"I'll spare you the stor—"

"No, tell me." She drew closer to him, curiosity making her eyes glitter. He couldn't remember another moment her gaze was so enraptured by his. Had he ever had her undivided attention for so long before? It didn't matter. He'd crave it, even if he had felt it a thousand times over. He studied her face for a moment, the slope of her nose, the way her cheekbones rounded, and the curve of her lips.

"There isn't much to tell." He folded his other arm around her and drew her against him. "Mama Owen found me in a basket on the shore. Not even left at the orphanage. One child with her heard my cries and led her to me. If I had been left much longer, Nemain would have carried me away on the tide."

"As a baby?"

"Aye."

Phantom suspected they saw a child with red eyes and decided he was a demon. The sea would have been a merciful end to a creature like him, even if he had yet to do anything monstrous.

"James," she whispered, and it sounded so sweet on her lips. It might not have been his true name but hearing her say the name he grew up with was far more intimate than a kiss. "You didn't deserve to die."

It was as if she read his thoughts, or maybe their souls recognized each other enough that she could sense it.

Footsteps sounded against the pebbles distantly, breaking their spell. Instinctively, he pushed her against the wall, hiding her body with his own.

"Go, love. I'll see you again soon." He winked for good measure, and she blushed in return.

"Remember not to kill the man before I can talk to him."

Bloody hell, I forgot about Jimmy.

He grabbed her hand and placed it against his chest, right over his heart. The place it was when she finally woke from her nightmare. "I swear to you, he will still have his ability to speak by the time you can talk to him."

She furrowed her brow. "But you will still hurt him?"

"He was following you, Rose." He felt her shiver with the sound of her name on his lips. "If I dislike his answer, he will understand the cost of putting you in danger." She sucked in a breath. "As will every vermin on Samsaran soil." The footsteps sounded closer, creeping in on their location. "Go," he said, pressing a kiss to her knuckles and holding his eyes to hers. "I'll see you again soon, love."

She didn't hesitate a moment longer, climbing the ledges and crevasses of the Fortress wall as she drew closer to her balcony. Her cloak billowed in the wind as she jumped onto it without a look behind her.

CHAPTER 17

ANOTHER DRINK, ANOTHER DEVIL

ONE YEAR AGO

During the dinner with Lockness and his lovely undermining daughter, Phantom slipped a note into her palm at his farewell. He needed her aboard *Nemain's Revenge* before the week was out.

She had been so discreet about the note; he wondered if she saw it at all, but he wasn't worried about it ending up in the wrong ends. To any outsider, it would look like an admirer encouraging affection, but to Guinevere, or more accurately, the Black Shadow, it would feel like a threat. He knew the secret she had been guarding with her life and he could spill it easily.

His cover was no longer needed, he'd be sailing away from the miserable island by morning. The real Castellanos would report him soon enough, so she had nothing to keep him quiet with. When two moons rose that night, Phantom knew a shadow would visit him.

Phantom sat at the bar with two rum glasses at *La Trinidad*. The bar was close to a low town church and often shared the same patrons. Although the churches in low town were nothing like the Temple, opting for community and charity rather than control and judgement. It was the place he often took refugees he rescued from missions.

It was otherwise a very empty bar. There was a festival that day, so many party attendees would be on the streets dressed for the rain. Samsarans didn't care about a little water. Not on waterfall island.

The door swung open, and a figure clad in red, brown, and black strode in. A large feather hat sat upon her head, a sword decorating her hip where her hand rested on the hilt.

The Black Shadow's eyes landed on Phantom as soon as she crossed the threshold.

The corner of his mouth kicked up. "Can I buy you a drink?"

There was a glint of amusement in her eye as she approached. "You can buy me your silence." The barmaid at the counter took a passing glance at the pants she chose to wear but said nothing as she poured the rum Phantom enjoyed.

"I can keep a secret, Shadow. I'm not here to blackmail you."

She let out a breathy laugh and picked up the glass. "You'll excuse me if I don't take you at your word. I'm not the only one living a double life, Captain." She downed the amber liquid in one swig and set the glass down on the counter. "Let me make this perfectly clear." With a swift jerk, she freed her sword from its sheath. "If you breathe one word, I will gut you open like a freshly butchered cow."

Phantom stared for a moment at the death steaming from her eyes, the promise to fulfill her threat fully.

Oh yeah, I like her, Sam stated.

"Bloody hell, you are magnificent, aren't you?" She blinked at the compliment. Phantom glanced at the barmaid again, then pointed to the Shadow's empty glass. The barmaid seemed hardly bothered by the weapon being drawn in her establishment, but it could be because it was solely pointed at Phantom. He couldn't quite remember what the barmaid's grievance with him was, but her pleasure at his demise was clear. "My friend here will need another drink." The barmaid rolled her eyes before refilling the glass.

Phantom turned back to his target, who hadn't moved from her perfect form and death glare.

"I want you to join me on *Nemain's Revenge*." She scoffed, her sword lowering by a fraction. "I've seen no one handle a sword as you do. You've been taking down Lockness dealings flawlessly for years. I could use you."

Her brows knocked together. "Run off and join a band of pirates?" She grabbed the glass again. "Not in this lifetime, Captain. Do you understand what I'm risking just being seen with you?" She knocked the glass back with little effort.

"What have you got to lose? Fancy dresses? Inherited blood money? Being sold off to the highest bidder?" Her nose scrunched up in disgust. "What I'm offering you is freedom." He let the words sink in, ticking a finger against his glass. "Freedom to do what you want. Go where you want." He looked her up and down, drawing attention to the clothing she wore as the Black Shadow. "Be who you want to be."

For a moment she seemed tempted by the prospect, letting the words melt her steel cold eyes, but the warmth was gone as fast as it came. "That's a pretty dream, but that's all it is."

"Why? Why limit yourself? You could be so much more." Phantom's tone turned dreamy. He could feel her acceptance, but it was out of reach.

"You truly believe your men will accept me as—"

"Yes," he blurted. There was no doubt it would thrill his devils to have her.

He leaned in closer as she put away the sword and took the seat next to him. "That is what She is. *Nemain's Revenge* is more than a ship. She is a vessel that provides absolute freedom. Not just freedom from prison bars and a bit of rope. No. She is freedom from who you must be. You can live and breathe exactly as you choose and nothing less."

She swung the glass back again, then coughed a laugh as she set it down. "That's a lot of pretty words, Captain."

"It's the truth, if you choose to believe it."

She pondered that for a moment. "Even if I believed it, I can't leave. Right now, I'm in the perfect position to take Lockness down. If I leave, he'll know it was me."

He let out a breathy laugh, then sipped at his own drink. "I can make you disappear and inside jobs can't last forever. One day he'll discover it was you and kill you for opposing him. Get ahead of him. With my crew, you can still fight."

"You really think you have me all figured out, don't you, Captain?" Her eyes cast down to the newly full glass. The barmaid was a good one, keeping their glasses full. "You think I'll just abandon my life and start a new one? What about all the people who are counting on me here?"

Phantom put a hand on his shoulder. "Have you ever been to Kheli?" She furrowed her brows, but he ignored her and patted her back before rising. "Come and meet the crew before you make your decision."

With a few moments of hesitation, she stared at her glass.

"*A la mierda,*" she muttered before downing the rest of the alcohol. "Let's go before I change my mind."

"Good," he said before ducking behind a wall. "Because she's about to come after us."

"Who?"

The crash of glass hitting a wall rang out throughout the empty bar. The barmaid started shouting a string of Quarencian curses that would make Mama Owen ill.

"Run!" Phantom shouted at the Shadow. She took little coaxing as the other glass shattered against the wall and the curses continued. They ran together out the door and down the street, the woman's shouts getting lost to the rain and the crowd. The festivities surged around them like crashing waves in a cacophony of colors and wet bodies.

A shot rang, and they both ducked, tucking themselves into a nearby alley. "What did you do to that woman?" The incredulous glare from the Black Shadow made it hard for him to contain his grin.

He pulled a very expensive looking ruby ring from his pocket.

"It's probably not because we forgot to pay the tab."

CHAPTER 18

SECOND MISSION

Phantom got an hour of sleep before a fist pounded against his door.

"James, I know you're in there."

He hadn't even changed out of the clothes he wore the night before. After ensuring Rose had arrived safely to her chambers, Phantom had returned to his room to fall on the hard bed and immediately fall asleep.

He recognized the Commodore's voice as he banged on the door again. "Let me in or I will kick down the door."

Phantom rubbed the sleep out of his eyes and crawled out of bed. Ashby would carry out his threat. It was one of many things he was annoyingly perfect at, carrying out threats. He pulled the door open to reveal a scowling Commodore towering over him.

"What do you want?"

"You were out last night," Ashby spat, venom coating every word.

"Ah, an interrogation then. Tell me, Commodore, did you bring a rope to tie me up? Because I've gotten into bondage since we've last played." Phantom tried to smile, but it faltered with the sleep still clinging to him.

"Rose was missing from her bed last night as well. Did you have anything do to with that?" That broke through the rest of Phantom's morning fog.

"Surprisingly, I did not. I went to a tavern for a drink and spotted your precious princess on the streets. She had quite a nasty tail. As the dutiful officer that I am, I disposed of the bilge rat, so she could make it home safely."

His brow softened by a fraction. "You have this criminal in custody? I didn't hear of you bringing anyone in."

Phantom rubbed at the headache forming at his brow. It was too early for this many questions.

"Forgive me, Commodore," Phantom addressed with contempt. "Since there was someone following her, I didn't think it was the safest to bring him back. I can introduce you. Jimmy would love to meet you."

"Jimmy?" Ashby scrunched his nose as if trying to place the name. Phantom rolled his eyes. Clearly, Ashby had forgotten Phantom's propensity for fabricating names. "Bring me to him."

"Slow down. I will be needing a change of clothes." Phantom looked the man up and down, dressed in a finely pressed and decorated officer's uniform. "So will you."

Ashby looked down at his uniform and frowned. "What's wrong with this?"

"You look like an officer."

"I am an officer. I'm *your* commanding officer."

Phantom let out an exasperated sigh. "Yes, but Jimmy doesn't need to know that." At Ashby's confused look, Phantom continued. "If he knows who you are, he may be less inclined to divulge his secrets."

"What do I wear then?"

"Do you not have any street clothes? Things you wear off duty?"

"An officer is never off duty."

Nemain spare him.

"We're going to find you something on the way there."

Phantom led the way through high town in the mist and fog of early morning. The sky had scarcely changed since he got to his room. Although, the fog surrounding Samsara made telling the difference rather difficult.

Ashby was as dressed down as they could manage. Phantom tried to steal what they needed for his disguise, but Ashby insisted on paying.

"I will be entirely discreet, sir." The shopkeeper beamed as if the Commodore had given him a mission that was important enough to risk his life over. He saluted and Phantom rolled his eyes. "They can beat me, torture me, or send me to Nemain herself. I will not speak of your presence in my shop."

Nemain spare him. *Again.*

Ashby stood stunned for a moment. "Mr. Gomez, I seriously doubt anyone will come asking questions. And if they do, please tell them before they hurt you."

"Now, sir, I may not be an officer, but I can still serve my country and will do so. You can count on me, sir." The man stood as straight as a board, mimicking an officer and failing at it. But there was a spirit to the man Phantom admired.

The Commodore looked like he wanted to say more, but Phantom clapped a hand on his shoulder and whispered, "There really is no use convincing him otherwise. Just don't do anything stupid enough to bring unsavory characters to his doorstep and he'll be fine."

Ashby grimaced before nodding and *finally* saluting back so the man could relax.

The pile of clothing Ashby got from the shopkeeper looked

too new for low town, but anything was better than the decorated officer's uniform. It was a loose brown shirt and black trousers. Other than being obviously new, they were unremarkable.

Now they stood before a pile of ropes and potato sack Phantom had used to restrain the man in the alley.

"I swear to Davina, I left him right here."

"You don't worship Davina," Ashby groaned deeply before pinching his fingers around the bridge of his nose. "And how am I supposed to believe you when your hostage isn't here?"

A crease formed in the middle of Phantom's forehead. "Come now, brother. You know I'm capable of lying much better than that. If I had wanted to feed you a falsehood, you wouldn't even be doubting it right now."

"Except I don't believe a word that comes out of your mouth, *brother*," Ashby spat, but Phantom only grinned at getting the Commodore to say it at all.

"Then why follow me out here?"

"If you are telling the truth, then there was a threat to Miss Davenport that needed to be handled." There was something about the way he spoke about Rose that made Phantom's insides boil. The protective way he spoke of her, like she was his to protect.

She is, Kayden reminded unhelpfully.

"Now you've dragged me out to the worst corner of high town you could find, dressing me as a civilian to show me nothing. Was this a distraction? So, you could kill me out here?"

A strained chuckle escaped Phantom. "If I wanted you dead, I would have done it on the cliff side."

The Commodore's face turned red. "Your whole life is a joke, isn't it?"

"I assure you, I am dead serious."

Ashby scoffed. "Give it up, James. Whatever this game is you're playing."

"There is no game. I didn't have to bring you along, so I suggest you act a little more grateful."

Ashby nearly choked on hollow laughter. "Grateful? To you?" He got up in Phantom's face, the laughter ceasing. "I suppose I should thank you for leaving me on that Davina-forsaken island, too."

"What?"

Ashby's eyes hardened, but Phantom softened, seeing the hurt in them. He was about to acknowledge it when an arrow shot between their faces and into the wall.

Ashby and Phantom's eyes both tracked the arrow, then back to its origin. A figure stood at the end of the alley, too shadowed to be seen properly.

Clare? But no, that wasn't right. She wouldn't have missed.

More figures materialized from the fog, advancing down the alley.

"*Mierda,*" Phantom and Ashby swore at once. Another arrow flew, and they finally ran. They both ducked before the arrow struck. They reached the corner of the wall, using it to take cover as more arrows flew by.

Ashby withdrew the sword at his side. "I think your friend brought back reinforcements."

"So, you believe me now?"

"This seems extravagant for a game, even for you." Ashby leaned against the wall, looking back toward the alley to see where their attackers had gone. "Hold on to your prisoners better next time."

Phantom wrinkled his nose. "I don't *do* prisoners. I'm more experienced in the art that involves—" An arrow zipped by, silencing him.

Ashby's voice came out whispered, which made Phantom's hackles rise. "You had Miss Davenport as your prisoner for three days."

Phantom scoffed. "She was hardly a prisoner."

Ashby shushed Phantom before he could say more, their attackers closing in. Phantom drew his cutlass as silently as he could manage.

"What's the plan?" Phantom whisper shouted.

"Keep one alive for questioning."

"That's not a plan. That's a dream." Phantom leaned out to see they had stopped in the middle of the alley, waiting for their targets to come out and face them.

Ashby moved to do that, but Phantom's free hand flew out to stop him. "Nope, you're not dying on my watch, Commodore."

"We need to take one of them alive. I'm not leaving here empty-handed."

"Did I say we would?" Phantom's gaze took in the surrounding space. The sun was rising and filling the streets with sunlight through the haze of fog. "But if you go out there, sword swinging, they will shoot you down before you can get to them. They really aren't the honor type like you, Commodore."

"What do you suggest, then?"

Phantom winced at the pressure of the decision as he desperately searched for an answer. A few feet beside them, he spied a ladder leading up to the building's rooftop.

He smiled at the metal contraption, then nodded to Ashby. "Up we go."

Ashby's eyes were full of doubt, but he followed Phantom, climbing up the ladder. They kept their steps as silent as possible, reaching the top with little trouble. Rooftops in Samsara were shaped in a pyramid, but there was usually some type of irrigation to control the rain runoff. Those were easier to walk on if they weren't flowing with water.

"This is your big plan?" Ashby complained from behind him.

Phantom glanced behind him. "Have you forgotten so soon?"

Ashby narrowed his eyes for a moment, but Phantom caught the exact moment he remembered. This wasn't their first time on a rooftop together.

Ashby nodded in understanding.

Phantom crept across the roof, leaning down to gage exactly where the attackers were. With the sun's rays beginning to break through the cloud cover, he could see them more clearly. It was three large, tough-looking men. The kind of men who would kill a child in some backwater alleyway.

A small nod from Phantom and they both leapt to the ground below, right behind the three figures.

The attackers whipped around immediately, but they didn't shoot fast enough. Jimmy was the one standing in the middle with the bow, the two on his sides looking like bodyguards with how much they towered over him.

"Come back for more, Jimmy?" Phantom teased.

Jimmy scoffed then nocked an arrow back, but Ashby had made it to one of the side guards. The man moved in time to block Ashby's sword, but Phantom knew the Commodore's swing. He came in like a battering ram. His force of strength was enough to knock any man off balance.

With Jimmy distracted, Phantom swung his sword at his bow, dislodging it from his hand. Jimmy pulled his own blade, crossing it with Phantom's.

The other bodyguard advanced, but Phantom spat, "Need your henchmen to do your dirty work, Jimmy? Or do you not like getting your hands dirty?"

"Stand down," Jimmy yelled at his taller, broader shadow. "I can handle the pirate."

"Oh," Phantom mocked excitedly. "Are you in charge, Jimmy? That seems ill-advised."

Jimmy cried out murderously as he swung, but Phantom jumped out of the way. He advanced again and Phantom laughed as he caught Jimmy's blade with his own and pushed him back.

"Are you really up for this? I mean, you were free, and came back because...?" He paused, making a show of pondering. "Because you missed me!"

"Filthy pirate," Jimmy spat.

"I beg your pardon, but who was following an innocent girl last night?"

A joyless smile etched his sharp face. "Innocent?" He laughed abruptly. "You must not know her very well, Captain."

Phantom kept his face uninterested, but bloody hell was he ever. What could this back street rat know about his songbird? Even if he wasn't privy to the information, he wanted to kill the man for knowing any of her secrets. But Jimmy wouldn't know his death was coming, not yet.

After all, he had a promise to keep.

When Phantom failed to respond, Jimmy continued. "But do you know who knows *you*, Captain?"

He could tell the moron was about to tell him exactly what he wanted to know, so he feigned disinterest. "You, apparently."

Jimmy laughed again. "Lockness knows." A shiver crawled up Phantom's spine like a spider. "Because I told him that the infamous Captain Phantom is in Samsara *without* his ship. I'm sure he'd love to know the new company you keep." His eyes slid to the Commodore, who was still recognizable even without his uniform. He was fighting off both bodyguards at once, but they were slower than him. It only took him a few more swings to down them both.

Phantom put on a bright smile. "Congratulations Jimmy. You've just earned passage aboard Nemain's carriage." Jimmy's eyes widened as he realized his allies were beaten. Phantom used the moment to free the blade from his hand and knock him to the ground. "You best pray she'll be merciful."

Phantom lifted the cutlass when he put up a hand. "Wait." Phantom hesitated as Ashby flanked him. It was a good feeling, Ashby's presence after all this time. "Lockness will come looking for me if I'm dead."

Phantom crouched down, whispering, "I'm counting on it."

Ashby moved before Phantom could react, grabbing the man's hand and placing a knife next to his smallest finger. "Why were you following Miss Davenport?"

The man steeled his face, coming to realize his secrets were the only thing keeping him alive.

At the lack of reaction, Ashby dug his knife into Jimmy's pinky, but before he would cry out from the pain, Phantom stuffed his mouth with a rag. He screamed, but the cloth muffled it. Ashby ran his knife all the way through Jimmy's flesh until the finger fell to the dirt like a bloody carrot.

Phantom whistled. "You're down to nine, my friend." He reached for the cloth, pulling it out so the man could talk. His eyes blazed with hatred as he puffed air in and out.

"I'm not your friend," he spat as Ashby moved his knife to the next finger and Jimmy flinched from the movement.

"Really? Because my friends don't get this kind of treatment. So, I'd reckon you really want to be my friend, don't you Jimmy?" Phantom circled him.

"My name's not Jimmy," he bit out.

Phantom breathed out dramatically. "That's a shame." Phantom nodded to the Commodore, who narrowed his eyes at the command, but obeyed, pushing the blade into Jimmy's second finger.

"Wait." His breaths came out sharply as he stared at his bleeding stub and the knife right beside it. "Lockness sent me to follow her, but I don't know what for."

Phantom sucked in a breath through his teeth, leaning in until he was level with the man's ear. "See, that's not good enough, Jimmy." To further the point, Ashby pushed on his knife, drawing a pained gasp from Jimmy.

"Okay, okay. He thinks he can take the Minister's seat if he has her," Jimmy blurted, halting Ashby's progress.

"And why would he think such a thing?"

Jimmy breathed out a laugh, knowing that he held onto one crucial bit of information, but Ashby dug his blade in, and the laughter ceased.

"Because of what happens when her eyes glow blue."

Ashby snapped up, abandoning the knife and wrapping a hand around the hand's throat instead. "How do you know that? What does Lockness know?"

The man laughed again. "The look on your face, Commodore." His laugh became a roaring tumble. "He will find you, too. He'll go through both of you. Lockness will have her and then he'll have the entire island."

Jimmy struggled to breath as Ashby's fingers dug into his throat. Phantom spied the man's hand as his remaining fingers curled around the hilt of Ashby's abandoned knife.

"No," Phantom yelled, tackling Ashby to get him out of the way as Jimmy plunged the knife into his own heart. A laugh tumbled from him a moment before the light left his eyes and he fell forward into the dirt.

The Commodore and Phantom shared a brief look. If Lockness was coming to claim Samsara, the island was truly damned.

CHAPTER 19
BIRDS OF A FEATHER

Since the morning had only begun, the Commodore did not allow Phantom to return to bed. He stood before the Minister as the Commodore gave his report. He had found his mind lost more than once during the address, thinking of the gold on the pillars or the finely sculpted marble statue of the Minister as a much younger, much more fit man.

He grew up around the gaudy displays without thinking much of them, but after being away from them for so long, Phantom wondered where it all came from.

Samsara made many attempts at trade with other surviving countries, but resources were vastly limited and coveted. Samsara had little to offer in the way of trade, and marble wasn't exactly a local commodity.

"... I believe we should watch her at all times with the danger Lockness imposes on her."

Oh, she won't like that at all.

The Minister stroked his mostly nonexistent beard, deep in thought before his eye landed on Phantom. "What do you think, Lieutenant? Is Lockness a threat to me?"

He never thought he and the Minister would have anything in common, especially an enemy. But the mere idea that he was helping the Minister was enough to let a hollow laugh out.

"You think this is funny, officer?" The Commodore barked with as much authority as he could, but it wouldn't work on Phantom. He wasn't part of Ashby's force.

"I've been laughing since I got here, Commodore." Phantom shifted his eyes to the Minister. "And you're crazy if you believe you can ignore this." The Minister sucked in a subtle breath and lifted his chin, but said nothing, so Phantom crept forward. "Lockness doesn't just have a following of loyal members, they are criminals with a personal vendetta against *you*."

"Criminals are hardly a threat," the Minister spat, turning to sit in his throne. For a man claiming to be chosen by his people, he sure acted like a king. "I'll use them, or I'll exterminate them. I'm sure you understand, Lieutenant." His glare said all he needed to. Phantom was the bear he had tamed and leashed, trained to bite on command. The big dangerous pirate, doing his bidding. Of course, Lockness did not intimidate him.

"I thought you prideful, Minister, but never idiotic," Phantom said too quietly, but both heard it loud and clear.

"How dare you—"

The Minister's raised hand halted the Commodore's verbal defense. The Minister let his stare settle on Phantom for a moment, waiting for the axe to drop on his head.

"If you insist Lockness is a threat, then I charge you with finding out what he is up to." Phantom nearly let his mouth hang open. "But you will be sure to omit my involvement in your investigations. If you slip up, Lieutenant, I will not be there to dig you out. Lockness will not know that I've allocated you with this."

His instinct was to decline, but there was a threat in the air. It was bad enough that he insulted the Minister, refusing him would have consequences. Ones his devils or the Khelitians would pay.

Phantom nodded. The danger of investigating Lockness was both exciting and terrifying.

"Let me make something clear, Lieutenant." The Minister stood from his throne and slowly descended the steps. "If you are captured and tortured to reveal who owns you, or if he finds out in any way that I have sent you, the Commodore will make a trip to Kheli and eradicate every soul on that goddess-forsaken island." He said it so casually, Phantom almost didn't understand it was a threat.

A glance at Ashby's face revealed a flash of horror before it was smothered, replaced by his Commodore mask.

Phantom drew his gaze back to the Minister, but he wasn't certain it didn't look like a glare. "Understood." He couldn't perform the investigations as himself then. Lockness already knew Captain Phantom was the Minister's pet, but luckily the crime lord didn't know his face, at least not associated to his pirate's name.

"Oh Lieutenant, have you forgotten all your manners?"

"Understood, Your Grace." The address burned his insides.

The Minister grinned smugly. "That wasn't so hard, was it?" He turned his back on Phantom like he wasn't a threat at all. With so much to lose, he supposed he was no threat to the Minister.

Not yet, Sam promised.

It was the one thing they all agreed on. The Minister needed to meet his end.

"Let me sleep," Phantom complained as they walked the halls of the Fortress.

"How do you expect to fulfill your duty with your eyes closed?" The way the Commodore said it made Phantom cringe. As if he cared about duty.

With any luck, Lockness would come after the Minister and distract him long enough for Phantom to evacuate Kheli and find a new home for them.

He'd convince Rose to come with him by then, too. Hopefully.

"I suspect I will be able to infiltrate Lockness's plans much better with a clearer head."

For a bright, shining moment, he watched Ashby's face soften. Perhaps he understood Phantom needed some rest in order to work properly.

But as Ashby nodded, a crow landed on the windowsill next to them and squawked loudly. It turned its head in Phantom's direction as if looking for him, then squawked again.

Bloody hell. Bloody Indigo and her bloody calling card.

"James," Ashby whispered, as if a raised voice might encourage the creature to attack. "What is that?"

"A crow," Phantom said with his brightest smile. "Haven't you seen them? They infest the city. It's a problem, really." He continued walking straight past the loud bird. "You really should bring it up with the Minister."

As they continued to walk, the wretched winged beast followed them, flying and squawking through the halls, the sound echoing against the stone walls.

Phantom raised his voice to speak over the creature. "A real nuisance, these things." If he had his pistol, he'd shoot the creature, risking the bad luck with Macha to do it. Alas, that weapon was confiscated at the door by Ravana. But the Commodore...

"James," Ashby scolded.

Phantom reached for the pistol strapped to Ashby's side

while he was distracted. The moment he dislodged it from the Commodore, he shot at the bloody creature. It dodged as the bullet ran directly into the brick behind it, causing pieces of brick and mortar to fall to the floor, dust floating in the air around them.

Ashby swore, ducking at the sound of gunfire before he realized what Phantom was shooting at. Phantom attempted to aim another shot at the creature through the dust, but Ashby swung at him, wrestling the weapon away from him as the crow squawked more intensely with the action.

All he wanted was some decent sleep. Not a bloody summons.

Finally, Phantom pulled the pistol away from Ashby and shot the bird down.

"Ha!" He jumped up with his victory, tossing the pistol down to Ashby, who laid on the floor nursing his eye that had an accidental elbow thrown into it.

Ashby rose, but Phantom felt heavy. The whole no sleep issue was becoming a real problem.

"What the hell was that?" The Commodore spat at him. Phantom reeled, wondering how he was going to spin this. He couldn't tell Ashby the truth, so he'd have to come up with a convincing lie. But damn it, his mind was too slow.

"Do not lie to me, James." There was a growl in Ashby's voice.

Phantom breathed out slowly. "The bloody bird was a message from Indigo."

Damn it.

Ashby's attention snapped as he stood up straight. "Indigo the witch?" Ashby's nose turned up in disgust. It was no secret how witches were viewed by the rich and noble houses of Samsara. It was only a matter of time before the Navy would become witch hunters. The Minister hadn't taken that step yet since the witches often proved themselves useful.

"Yes, I used her help to get into Lord Desmond's estate. Now she's calling in her favor." He wanted to lie, but he was too damn tired. How much would it hurt if the Commodore knew, anyway?

"I'm coming with you."

That much, Sam echoed his own thoughts with a note of amusement.

"What?"

"If you made a deal with a witch, I need to know precisely what that entails." Ashby crept closer to him, a purple bruise forming around his eye.

"Have you ever made a deal with a witch before, Commodore?"

"Of course not," he said so fast and so forcefully, it nearly sounded like a sneeze.

"Then you should know once she has called in her favor. I will have to do as she says. Otherwise, she will curse me."

Ashby blinked and slightly smiled, like that wasn't such a bad idea.

"Don't get any ideas. If you come with me, she'll know you were involved, and she will curse you right along with me."

His smirk fell. "I hate witches."

"Yes, that's the right attitude to have going into a witch's home." Ashby's face turned into a scowl at the mere thought of being in a witch's house.

"Oh no, put the glare and the scowl away. I'm in no mood to be smote down just because I'm walking in with your prejudice ass. You and your two hundred and fifty pounds of pure muscle come in bloody peace. Do you understand that?"

"Fine," he said in a way that didn't give Phantom confidence.

"Good," he forced himself to say. "Now, I'm going to get a nap before we go." He couldn't possibly face Indigo on such little sleep.

"No, we leave now."

"But—"

"What happens if we are late? You already shot her pet."

He has a point, Kayden remarked.

Probably should have left the bird alone, Sam added.

"You're carrying me back, Commodore."

CHAPTER 20
INDIGO'S CIRCLE

The fog had descended to low town by the time they made it to the building with Hect's symbol. Dark clouds filled the sky, a foreboding of rain to come. It would be a wet trek back to the Fortress.

Phantom sighed.

"I don't like it here," Ashby spit out, scowling at every sign and smoke trail, promising readings, spells, and other telltale witch symbolism.

"Remember what I said?" He turned his glare to Phantom. "If your face continues like this, I will leave you out here, in the middle of witch district, in the rain." The Commodore's face refused to change as the rain fell and ran down his face. "I hear they perform rituals on the streets during the rain. All sorts of debauchery and dark art—"

"Fine," Ashby interrupted. There was no such ritual but leaving the Commodore in the street of witch district was a recipe for disaster, especially since he refused to relax his face. He looked like the entire place stunk, which it didn't. The sheer amount of incense used there made sure of that.

Phantom had to stifle a laugh as the Commodore took a labored breath to settle himself. Once he looked only mildly bothered, Phantom decided it was good enough and led the way into the building.

He turned to the left through a curtain of beads to find Indigo. She was dressed in a pale purple gauzy tunic with necklaces, rings, and bracelets. She didn't look behind her to acknowledge who had entered.

"You cannot just call me like a dog."

"Apparently, I can." The woman didn't turn as she began mixing ingredients on the table. Jasmine floated about the room from her incense bowl. The smell reminding him of Rose, but he refused to let it quell his anger.

"You killed my crow," she hissed.

He hoped she felt the sting of loss with the creature. "You should have known better than to send one of your beasties after me." He turned to walk out. This woman clearly had no interest in giving him her attention, even if she called him.

As he attempted to make a step toward the exit, his feet refused to move, planted to the floor like his body was anchored to the floor. He looked up at Ashby, who noted the position he was in, and smiled. The bastard was smiling.

Well, he supposed it was better than the scowl, even at his own expense. Still, he glared at his old friend.

"You still have a debt to pay, Maahes." Phantom's blood boiled in his veins, making him feel hot all over until it felt like burning. It had nothing to do with his monster. That bastard was suspiciously quiet, especially since he'd come in handy right about now. "Don't bother reaching for those stronger than you beneath your skin. You cannot reach them in my presence."

Phantom turned back to her, even if she didn't extend the same courtesy. The burning dissolved the moment he did.

"What do you want?" He bit out, tired of being toyed with.

A dark chuckle escaped her as she finally turned around, but her smile faltered as she caught sight of what he brought to her doorstep. A fire entered her eyes, and the burning returned to his veins, but he welcomed the pain. He had caught her off guard with the Commodore's presence. The thought made him entirely smug.

Phantom glanced back at Ashby, whose scowl had returned, but he wasn't so inclined to scold the man for it. Indigo was getting on his nerves. The least she deserved was a repulsed scowl from the naval Commodore.

"Sacrifices imply that you will lose something, Maahes. Ridding yourself of the Commodore will benefit you more than me." Indigo said plainly, her nose turning up at Ashby as if he carried a foul scent. Remarkably similar to Ashby's expression.

He straightened. "I came here of my own accord, witch. He did not bring me here as a sacrifice."

"He would lead you to believe that now, wouldn't he?" The Commodore huffed at the idea of being fooled so easily, but Phantom had to admit to himself that it wasn't a bad idea.

Ashby took a step forward, pointing a finger at Indigo, who only raised a brow at his bravery. "You better watch your mouth, witch," he spat out the word like poison in his mouth. "One day, when the Minister orders it, I will be at your doorstep to drag you to the pyre myself."

She sighed, as if disappointed by his choice of threat. "Such a pity you must wait for your master to decree your attack. I answer to no one. I could kill you now." He grunted with effort as some invisible force threw him to his knees. His scowl melted to one of pure unadulterated loathing as he struggled to gain control of himself. His arms stayed still by his sides, but he groaned as he tried to force movement into them. Phantom's knees gave out too as he fell to the ground alongside his old friend.

Phantom looked down and chastised himself for being

stupid enough to step into a witch's circle. Below them was a circle drawn in chalk with symbols lining the border. Anyone who stepped into a witch's circle would be under the control of the witch who drew it. Until Indigo was done with them, they would be stuck there. A misjudgment on his part caused by sleep deprivation.

She slowly walked to them, standing before Ashby with her eyes piercing through him. As she lifted her hand, he tried to flinch away, but magic stopped his movement, keeping his head right where it was.

Her fingers trailed over his skin, curling over his cheekbones and grazing along his jawline. "Sweet Macha," she swore. "You are pretty, aren't you?"

An—honest to Nemain—growl escaped Ashby's throat. One that she didn't bother to stop, even though she could have.

"Tell me, Commodore, do you serve the Minister because you want his approval? The glory? The power? Or do you want to protect the people of Samsara?" He only glared at her, clearly uninterested in answering her question. "While you are in the circle, you cannot lie to me, so do not bother. And until you answer, I will not release you."

Phantom watched as the Commodore fought against the binding magic of the witch's circle. The circle urged him to answer because it was her will. His eyes widened, and he groaned at the pain no doubt lancing through his veins, compelling him to speak. Indigo did all of that whilst never lifting a finger.

"I have no interest in glory," he finally spit out, followed by heaving breaths as the circle relieved him of the pain. "My duty is to the people, not the Minister."

The magic released. Phantom felt his weight grow significantly lighter so he could stand again. The Commodore followed not long after that. His breathing labored as his body adjusted to the release of pressure. They shared a long look before turning to the witch.

"What do you want, Indigo?"

She clasped her hands before her in a sign of peace. Witches couldn't access their magic when their hands were together like in that position, so it was a show of respect.

Her gaze was heavy when it turned to the Commodore once more. "We want the same thing, Sebastian of House Ashby."

He scoffed at the idea of them having something in common. "You're telling me you want to protect Samsara?"

"Is that so hard to believe? Did you even consider the people of low town when you said your duty is to Samsara? Or is your loyalty only good for the wealthy citizens?" Her gaze penetrated as if she knew the answer already.

"No, I meant what I said. My duty is to protect Samsara, no matter its inhabitants."

"Except the witches you would see burn?" The words burned themselves, leaving the air feeling heavy and full of smoke. The Commodore snapped his mouth shut on whatever he thought to say. "It's no matter. I would say the same of the officers of the Minister's Navy."

He narrowed his eyes.

Indigo leaned against the table she had been working on. It was filled with a collection of glasses with glowing liquids, jars of spices, pebbles, and bones, along with a pile of silks. She lifted the stick of incense she burned, running a trail of smoke into the air.

"You wish to know what I want?"

"Not particularly, but I haven't the choice as of late," Phantom grumbled, but Indigo only flashed him an amused smile.

"I wish to free the witch's sons," she whispered, as if it were a prayer.

A gong went off in Phantom's head as everything fell into place. Of course, this involved the witch's boys.

"The witch sons? Do you know how dangerous that is?" The Commodore spoke of things he knew nothing of, but Phantom was sure he couldn't avoid the truth. "Do you know where they are?"

"No, someone took them from Kheli, but I don't know where they are being hidden. I only know that they are in the same place as your scaly friend."

Phantom perked up. "You know where Serena is?" The bond itched at him to find her. The bonds dragons made with their masters were akin to familial. He couldn't stop feeling like the beastie's mother if he tried.

"She's on the island, Maahes. When I scry the bones for the location of the sons, I get the sense of icy fire. As if I was burning and freezing all at once." Her eyes locked on Phantom as his blood turned to cold in his veins.

"What does that mean?"

"What do you know of dragons, Commodore?" Her nose turned up at the use of his title.

He caught the look, narrowing his eyes. "Not much."

"Dragons are creatures created by Davina herself and infused with the magic of fate. They can sense when destiny pulls strongly at someone, which is why the last surviving one has imprinted on our dear Captain."

Ashby's brows scrunched together.

"But Serena is no ordinary dragon. She is a white dragon. They are legendarily known for their blue flames, which burn both hot and cold and can create sapphire glass." Indigo waved her hand, the fire pit igniting into towering flames. "When I call on Macha to show me where the sons are, all she shows me is this."

In the flames, an image danced. Serena roared and screeched from inside a metal cage. She was kept in the dark, far from the light of the moons. The image made the beast below his skin itch to break through the barriers Indigo kept on it.

"Wherever the sons are, so is Serena. Your task, Maahes, is to find them and set them free."

"You want me to change them back to human?" Phantom blurted before he could stop himself, but he couldn't believe she'd ask that of him.

"Human?" Ashby noted. "Are they not human?"

"No," Indigo sighed. She likely wanted to keep that detail from the Commodore. The image on the fire changed, like turning one's head in the same room as Serena. On the wall beside her were cages stacked upon one another. Some were in barred cages, like the one Serena inhabited, and some were tanks filled with seawater. In those cages was a variety of animals: monkeys, parrots, snakes, octopi, and crustaceans. But Phantom knew exactly what they really were. A fire burned in his core at the sight of them in cages. It was the last place they belonged.

"How did someone find them?"

"I don't know, but you need to find out and destroy their methods, whatever means necessary. They cannot be disturbed again."

"Wait," Ashby interrupted. "Do you mean to tell me those creatures in cages are children?" Phantom took note that Ashby did not say "witch son". He saw them as innocent, no matter their blood or potential.

"The danger for a witch son is too great on Samsara, as I'm sure you know well, Commodore."

He swallowed at her tone. Before the War even started, the young boys of witches were hunted and killed. Their potential for wickedness was highly feared. So, witches turned their sons into creatures and sent them to Kheli to keep them, and the world around them, safer. Phantom helped ferry them on occasion.

"We do what we must to protect our children. Would you not do the same?"

It was shame dragging Ashby's features down.

Indigo finally turned to Phantom again. "Free them and let them live as creatures that never have to fear the Minister and his officers. Then, your debt is paid."

CHAPTER 21

UNEXPECTED LIAISONS

The sun finally set as they reached the Fortress, but Phantom could only tell by the townspeople, sitting down to eat dinner, or closing their shops. Clouds had officially covered everything that was once the sky as rain beat down in droves, flowing down the streets.

Phantom and Ashby arrived completely soaked and dripping all over the fancy carpeting. They were promptly cursed by a Quarencian maid who had recently cleaned it. The moment brought Phantom back to when they were James and Bash, showing up all muddied to the orphanage and being cursed by Mama Owen, words they would have been punished for using. She had an uncanny ability to know when one of her orphans swore. James had once lost toy privileges for a week straight.

But the maid in charge of Fortress cleanliness had a vocabulary to make Mama Owen blush.

Ashby had to console the woman to calm her down, but Phantom was not needed for that task, slipping away to his less than cozy preassigned room.

Upon reaching his room, he promptly fell onto the bed,

barely shedding his coat and shirt before he did. But on the bed next to him, he noticed a paper waiting for him.

It was folded twice to hide the contents within but written on the outside was a note.

In replacement.
Your Songbird

Phantom smiled at how she embraced the nickname. He knew it was also a way to hide her identity from nosy eyes, but that didn't stop the flush of warmth that swept over him.

Opening the paper, he lost his breath entirely. It was a sketch of him, decked in all his pirate glory, with Serena perched gleefully on his shoulders. He was looking out over the ocean, but there was no smile on his face. A rare moment and she had captured it.

A breath left him as he stared at the beauty of the artwork and the craftsmanship of the design. She had put her soul into the piece, and he could feel her there. It wasn't intrusive like her paintings, but rather a feeling of closeness, like she infused it with her essence.

He marveled at the drawing, but the long day drug at him, calling him to sleep. He set it down on the table beside him before letting his body fall onto the bed.

He was asleep in seconds.

Something was wrong, you could tell in the way the trees moved here, like they were leaning in to get a better look, to listen in. But it was only him, traveling the vastness of Southern Eveleigh. The jungles grew thicker and the animals wilder in this section of the world. A colorful bird with a large beak cawed at him from a branch up ahead.

He followed the woman's trail for weeks. He knew the lost queen would not be traveling to Kalon alone for no reason at all, especially since the world was no longer safe. Necromites flooded these lands and were out for blood. One bite meant death to one's soul even if the body continued to terrorize others.

Lost in thought, he almost missed a shift in the foliage before him. It could have been any assortment of creature. Thunder tigers inhabited this land, and they tore people to shreds, no matter how tough.

Sam raised his spear, aiming it at the bush with a firm hand. He'd slay the beast before it could sink its claws in.

Before he could get close enough, a figure emerged, small and lithe, in the shape of an adolescent boy. He was covered in green and brown paste that made him blend in perfectly with the leaves and trees. Would he not have moved, Sam would have walked right past him.

The boy blinked at him with the signature grey eyes of the Kalonites, but they weren't wide or scared. They were more curious, tilting his head at the newcomer.

It occurred to Sam that these savages might not know Brettanian, and he'd have a hell of a time trying to communicate.

"Hello," Sam said, crouching to seem less intimidating. He knew he was a beast of a man, tall, broad, and strong. It was rare to meet anyone who wouldn't cower in his presence. "Where did you come from?"

Finding Kalon was not a simple task. To the rest of the world, they were so remote, they were as good as myth. They kept their location secret; so wandering would prove fruitless.

The boy, who was likely close to eight, stared blankly at him.

"What's your name then?"

More blank stares accompanied the boy's stoicism. He wondered why the boy even came out of his hiding spot.

"Right, well, I'm going to keep going."

Sam turned to walk due South, crunching leaves and brush

beneath his leather boots. He was going to need to shed layers soon. He was still dressed for the North and the air was growing warmer, more humid.

He pulled off his shirt, stuffing it into the pack he had with him. As he stepped to continue his walk, he felt the prickling sensation of being watched. One look back revealed the boy from earlier, his stare still blank, but his eyes trained on Sam like a target.

"Can I help you?"

Sam was no good with children. Not even when he was a child. He wasn't raised to play in mud and make friends. He was raised for killing and that was what he knew. More than anything, he was raised to find the queen he'd been tracking. He was raised to kill her.

Sam tipped his head back as he lifted a canteen of water to his lips, letting the mild water trickle down his throat and chest while he stared at the boy who had no answers for him.

With no response, he thought the boy would lose interest, eventually. He walked for another twenty minutes before turning again to see the boy still watching him from two paces behind.

Sam stared at him, then moved a hand to gesture him away. "Shoo."

The boy only stood there, staring. Sam breathed out but continued. What else could he do?

Eventually the boy became braver, inching closer to walk beside Sam. At one point, he accepted he had a new traveling companion. He offered the child water from his canteen, which the boy took with eager hands, inspecting the contraption before imitating Sam by sloshing most of it down his painted chest. The paste smudged and ran down in muddy tracks, revealing warm Kalonite skin.

He laughed at the boy, even if he wasted the last of his water. He'd have to find fresh water soon, but with the Kalonite boy following him, he had hoped the boy would lead him to civilization.

Soon the boy picked at things strapped to Sam's person. He didn't blink at showing the boy all the weapons attached to him. His eyes *glittered at the different shaped knives, swords, and the spear. He even had a few darts tucked away in his belt as a last resort.*

He pulled out a dagger worth more than his life, with a clear blue blade. "Now this," Sam started, talking even if he knew the boy didn't understand. "This is the most important thing I have on me. Do you know what this is?" He didn't expect the boy to answer like he didn't for the last fifty questions Sam posed to him. "This is sapphire glass, as rare as the dragons who made it, but it can kill anything."

The boy blinked up at him, listening intently even if he didn't understand. Although Sam suspected he knew what every word meant.

A whistle snapped Sam's attention, but it made the boy run.

A man twisted away from the tree he hid behind. The boy ran right up to him, embracing him as the man lifted him up. Clearly, he was a parental figure to the boy. He had brown and gold hair that was warmed by the sun and a kind smile, but when his gaze shifted from the boy to Sam, the warmth left him.

He was likely in his late twenties, like Sam himself and clearly a Kalonite with his blue-grey eyes and warm skin.

"Who are you?" He asked in clear Brettanian, only slightly altered by an accent.

"Samuel Rourke. I'm from Margari in the North. I'm seeking Kalon." He had to speak the words loudly since the man was still a distance away. "You may call me Sam. I come in peace."

A grim smile flashed on the man's face. "We shall see, Samuel Rourke." He set the boy down before he drew closer. "My name is Mave Ramirez. Come with me."

Phantom woke with a jolt, the room eerily dark from the night and rain still battering against his window. He rubbed at his eyes, banishing the dream he had. It was a reoccurring one. When he first had it, he ran to Ramirez, demanding answers of why he saw the younger version of him in his dreams.

That was when Ramirez had confirmed that the dream was in fact a memory from a past life and he had known Phantom in both lifetimes. Most days it was a hard concept to get around, but when he saw what talking about his son in those dreams was doing to the old man, he stopped bringing it up.

The boy did not survive the Necromite War.

A pang of sadness resounded in Phantom. Ramirez didn't deserve to lose a child. It was likely why he took in Tick years later. The two had many similarities.

It took a moment of collecting himself before he realized he was not alone.

In the bed beside him, a songbird was fast asleep. She wore the cloak and hood he found her in the other day with black close-fitting garments underneath. There was hardly any light from the moons thanks to the cover of the clouds, so he lit the candle on the table next to him to get a better view.

She was absolutely ethereal. Her soft skin was flawless on her relaxed face, her blonde locks falling delicately around her shoulders. With the soft, warm glow of the candle, he could see her black clothing had fallen low around her chest. Something that her cloak would easily cover if she were standing but lying in bed was an entirely different story.

He was tempted to trace his finger along the gauzy fabric but resisted. Just because she was in his bed did not mean she wanted him to touch her. Although, with any other woman, he would have considered the opposite true, but this was Rose Davenport. He needed a star chart to figure her out.

Phantom knew well enough by now that her presence meant nothing when it came to choosing him. Something he was becoming more and more desperate for.

As he thought about that, he remembered the promise he had made to her. The hostage he had caught stalking her was meant to be her investigation. But he had killed himself before she could get to him. Phantom would have to answer for that. It made him dread seeing her beautiful golden eyes.

But as he stared at her face, he knew he'd do anything to make it up to her.

He leaned in, trailing a single finger along her jawline and up her cheekbone, then moving a stray lock of hair from her forehead. She looked so peaceful as she slept. He experienced it before, but he found it was no less captivating than the first time.

She stirred, stretching and waking slowly. Then those golden eyes opened, and he wondered why he dreaded them so much.

"Hello love," he purred, his voice came out rougher with sleep still dragging at his edges.

Her eyes casually swept over him. A small smile graced her face until it faltered, and her eyes widened. Something was wrong. She looked around at the bed she was in, along with her attire, and her eyebrows rose.

"What am I doing here, James?"

Did she have no recollection of coming to his room? He certainly didn't do anything. He'd remember kidnapping her — again.

"You'll have to tell me."

Propping herself up on her elbows, noting the room's darkness, she glanced at her unusually exposed sternum; relief briefly lit her face when she noticed her locket resting there and hurriedly wrapped the cloak around herself, eager to keep some modesty.

Her look of confusion melted into one of annoyance. "Not again," she groaned, falling back onto the bed. She had an awfully calm reaction to waking up in a strange bed.

"If I didn't know any better, I'd say you were used to waking up where you are not supposed to be. Which has me equally curious, jealous, and concerned." He leaned on his side, propping his head up on one hand.

She blinked at him. "I sometimes blackout and don't know how I got there when I wake up."

He smiled. He knew exactly why. After all, he'd experienced it himself.

"Well, that is quite a mess, love. But why my bed?" He lowered his voice, willing it to rumble a bit. "Is it because there is some deep part of you that longs to be close to me?" He wore a smug grin as she glared at him.

"I didn't choose to come to you."

He leaned in, trapping her beneath him with his weight. She sucked in a breath, but he knew she could escape him if she wanted to. There were several knives on her person. The fact that she didn't even try to push him off, or stab him, was enough to tell him she didn't dislike it.

"Do you not want to be here, songbird? Forced to endure my presence?"

Her breathing grew heavy as her eyes traveled his face. "Not at all," she breathed. "As I said, I didn't choose to come here."

"Ah, but you haven't chosen to leave either."

"I," she started, her words breathy. "You think I'm crazy."

"Quite the contrary. I think you are perfectly sane. Who forced you to be here, love? It wasn't me. It wasn't you. I can't imagine the Commodore or Minister prefer you in my bed, so what am I missing?"

She breathed out slowly but didn't open her mouth.

Touch her gently. At the base of her neck, Sam whispered as if she could hear him.

He let his hand wander, finding a small opening in her cloak. He trailed his hand along the bone at her collar, dipping near the middle. Her breath hitched and her shoulders relaxed, allowing the small touch.

A long sigh escaped her as she melted into the bed, relaxing under him.

Phantom didn't allow his hand to move any lower down. As tempted as he was to explore every inch of her body, there was a different effect taking place that he was more interested in. Like the way her breathing lengthened and her eyelids fluttered.

Her eyes drifted closed, as if savoring the calming touch of his hand on her collarbone. He caressed her neck, and she breathed like she had been drowning and he provided her with air.

He hated to break the moment, but he needed her to remember.

With immense effort, he leaned in until his breath drifted over the shell of her ear. "Was it Isabeya who knew to bring you to me?"

Her eyes snapped open, her body returning to its tense state. A pang of guilt washed over him for disturbing her all too brief peace. He'd give it to her again soon, but he had to know.

She rose, pushing him off and climbing out of his bed. Now, he was really regretting it, but there wouldn't have been a reaction if she didn't know.

Rose ran her fingers through her hair, letting her hood fall behind her. She paced, seeming to debate something. It was clear he knew, so what was the point of keeping it secret?

"How?" Her voice was soft, but her eyes were wide.

He rose from the bed to stand before her. He could feel it, the energy coursing through them both, connecting them to each other beyond lifetimes. His hand reached for hers, lifting it to his chest where it had been the night her nightmare came for her. The skin of his chest felt the softness of her hand more keenly than he thought possible. His chest was bare before her, and her eyes drank in the sight.

"Why does the feel of my beating heart scare away the terrors of your nightmares?"

She let her hand drift down his chest, skimming over his stomach and abs. The feel of her skin sent a shiver tumbling through his body so vividly it made him groan.

A smile tipped her mouth, showing him exactly how much she liked that sound.

"Rose, love, if you do not stop, I'll have you pinned beneath me for the rest of the night." Her eyes glittered from his promise, and he nearly fulfilled it. Phantom leaned into her until they were only a breath's width apart.

You need to tell her about Jimmy, Sam reminded.

Phantom winced at the dread that crashed into him, ruining the delicious tension between them. He internally cursed Sam for the reminder when he finally had her to himself.

Her brows drew together, concern making her shift on her feet. "What's wrong?"

His eyes softened when he looked at her, "I owe you an apology."

Concern dissolved into a playful grin. "You owe me several."

He let the mischief in her eyes lift his spirits. "Let's start with one for now." He reached for her hand, and she followed him to sit on the bed. "That man who was following you, he'd dead. I meant to keep him alive, but he chose to take his own life over capture." He swallowed, afraid she would storm out of his room, though he wasn't sure if that would have been through the door or the window. "I should have been more careful, for this, I apologize." He placed his other hand over their joined ones, hoping he wasn't squeezing her delicate skin too roughly.

He waited for her to pull away, to not believe that the man actually took his own life. As a pirate, he was used to lying accusations. Not that he blamed them, he usually was, but not to her.

"Where's the body?" She blurted so fast he had to blink to register her question.

"Love?"

"Did you bury him?" She squeezed his hand back, distracting him until he could remember she required an answer.

"He was taken to the Fortress. Ashby said something about checking him over."

"Sebastian was with you?"

He growled at the way she said his first name, like they were close. Like they shared something similar to what he was discovering with her.

She narrowed her eyes, then a small smile tipped her mouth. "Jealous, Captain?"

"Jealous?" He blurted with a chuckle, pulling on her arm to drag her close. "The betrothed to the woman of my dreams? Why ever would I be jealous of that?"

A breathy laugh left her right before her lips met his. It was a sweeter kiss than what they shared before, but he deepened it, molding her body to his, itching to drag her to his lap and explore every sacred inch of her. The mere mention of the Commodore made the urge to claim her more powerful. "I want *you*, James."

He groaned, taking her lips again, firmly and tenderly.

She pulled away too soon. "If Sebastian has the body, we must hurry. Follow me." She tugged at his hand and although all he wanted was to continue a slow and dangerous exploration of her body, he held back. This was important. He could sense that from her. And he'd follow her anywhere.

CHAPTER 22

DEN OF TORMENT

Rose led him to a shadowy alcove of the Fortress. A door was tucked away behind bushes and moss, but even in its hidden state, there were tracks from where the door opened. The moss seemed to grow away from the lock and handle as a result of its frequent use.

With a weary glance back, Phantom witnessed the very moment she trusted him. A breath of air left him as her voice rang out and her eyes glowed. No words, just a few notes, and the door unlocked before them.

Phantom's eyes widened, coming to terms with the vastness of her power. She didn't just heal. In fact, it didn't seem there were any limitations to her siren song.

She pulled him through the door as his mind continued to spin. Immediately, stairs appeared before them, and they plunged into the bowels of the Fortress. Stone walls encompassed the stairs, leaving very little room for air. He ducked under an arch before they made it to a stone chamber. Darkness surrounded them, but as he was about to call on his beast for vision, the hiss of a match lit nearby. Rose lit a torch and hung it on the wall of the chamber.

The smell hit him first, rot and metal. Death and blood.

His eyes adjusted to the darkness as he took in the room. Blood was everywhere: the walls, staining the stones, the chairs, and the tables.

A locked cabinet leaned against the far wall, but it was clear what it contained, tools used to extract information.

He squinted at the wall and finally saw the chains lining it. Shackles rested there; four shackles, two for wrists, two for ankles. A heavy breath next to him made him all too aware of Rose's increasing heart rate.

Rose's face flushed, her eyes widening. She was on the verge of panic.

"I—" she started. "I've never been down here without them."

"Without who?" The realization hit him like a wave, ready to drag him out to sea and steal the air from his lungs. "Rose," he said calmly. "What happens here?"

She shook as she stared at the wall, her hands moving to come around her waist as if she were trying to hold herself together.

Phantom stepped before her, blocking her view of the wall and raising her chin until she locked her gaze with his. "What aren't you telling me?"

She gazed into his eyes, lost there for a moment, until she breathed in sharply, jerking her head away from his grasp.

"We need to be quick," she whispered, ignoring his question.

He cleared his throat but didn't question her further. He would have to ask her later. Staring at those blood-stained walls, he wasn't so sure he wanted to know.

Finally, he noticed the body on the table before them. Jimmy laid there, his face ashen from death. Cuts and bruises that would never heal littered his body and blood stains marred his clothes where he had plunged the dagger.

"Is this him?"

"Yes, that would be Jimmy. Slippery little bastard."

Rose shot him a look that said she didn't take kindly to his disrespect, but that only encouraged him further. The corner of his mouth curled up.

She contained herself, standing to the side of the table.

"What precisely do you plan to do with a dead body, love?"

Her brows pinched together for a moment before determination set her features to stone. "Sometimes, the dead speak more willingly than the living."

He didn't have time to process that before she began humming. Blue light flashing in her eyes, her humming formed into words.

NEMAIN, I CALL TO THEE
GRANT ME ONE MOMENT OF CLARITY
BEFORE THE SOUL RETURNS TO THE SEA

STOP TIME BEFORE IT ERODES
I ASK ONLY FOR A BREATH OF LIFE
THEN TAKE WHAT YOU ARE OWED

The song continued. There wasn't a convergence of voices like before. This time it was only her voice and no Stone present for the ribbons of light to surface from. Instead, the blue light emerged from the table itself, as if answering her call. But instead of ribbons, the light looked like the tentacles of a sea beast. Like the arms tattooed on the flesh of his neck.

They were so lifelike, twisting and turning in a way that was primal. As her voice echoed off the walls of the chamber, those arms encircled Jimmy's body, dragging him upright until he sat up, facing Rose. Those arms squeezed the body and his eyes popped open.

Phantom jerked backward.

Well that's new, Kayden remarked, amber flames flickering behind his eyes.

Jimmy screamed, but one tentacle came up to silence him before he alerted others to their presence. Jimmy's eyes were completely bloodshot, with only a sliver of his dark eyes showing through the blood. His body was still ashen and cut, his wounds not bleeding from the lack of a beating heart.

Jimmy was not alive, but from the rise and fall of his chest and those alert eyes, he wasn't dead either.

"Merciful Davina," Phantom swore under his breath, taking in the undead criminal before him.

Rose finished her song, but the man still sat bound by her ghostly blue glowing tentacles. "We have little time. He'll be fully dead in five minutes."

Phantom's mouth was still gaping. "Love, he's dead."

"Yes, and I reanimated him. Pay attention."

Phantom rubbed his eyes, staring at the strange wrongness of the corpse before him. Even necromites seemed more natural than this creature.

"Jimmy," Rose addressed.

The undead thing growled at her. "That's not my name."

Rose shot Phantom a look as he folded his lips together to keep from laughing. He didn't care at all what this man's real name was.

She carried on, hurried by lack of time. "Tell me why you were following me?"

It growled again, as if whatever human part left of him was gone completely. "He knows what you are."

"Who?" Phantom blurted. "Lockness? He already told us this, love. Put him out of his misery."

A rumbling came from the creature's chest, too faulty and garbled to be a growl. "The Minister thinks Ravana is working for him, but Lockness visits her."

"What are they planning?"

The surrounding air stilled, as dead as the man on the table.

"War. They are creating an army. The officers are only the beginning. Soon the entire island will be nothing but the Minister's mindless slaves." His voice came out as a hiss.

"To fight who? How can they enslave the entire island?" Rose's voice came out panicked.

"Atlas. Brettania. They need land. Samsara won't last much longer. Death is coming."

Phantom's fist balled together. There were too many random pieces of information. Nothing useful enough to fill in the whole picture. "How do they make an army of slaves?"

"Ravana knows the way. She—the grimoire—" Jimmy shook his head, expelling the death that crept up to claim him properly.

Did he say grimoire? Kayden interjected.

As in, the *grimoire?* Sam added.

Phantom's blood went cold.

Rose repeated one line she sang before, causing the tentacles around Jimmy to squeeze tighter, milking the last bit of life within him. He growled at the pain but seemed more alert.

"Witch sons, a white dragon, the pendant of Davina," he mumbled, as if it was a recipe. A witch's ingredient list. "The blood of Nemain."

"What did you mean 'death is coming'?" Rose blurted before the last bit of life left the man.

When eyes redder than brown rose to meet hers, he spoke softly, "Nemain will claim Samsara in her name and damn it to Hell."

With that, his eyes closed, and the tentacles winked out of existence, leaving his body to fall back onto the stone table.

The night ended with Rose growing more jittery by the minute. She kept looking over her shoulder, searching for monsters unseen. He reached for her hand, squeezing it to quell the nightmares haunting her. Her shoulders dropped marginally.

They reached her balcony, sticking to the shadows and dodging officers occasionally.

"Rose, can you tell me one thing," he pleaded, taking her attention. "The Commodore, does he have anything to do with what happens in those chambers?"

Hope was a tricky thing to have. Phantom tried to not grasp it too tightly while Ashby worked for the Minister, but still he couldn't help but want his friend back.

There was a hesitation that seemed to come up anytime he asked her a question. He wondered if she had ever willingly trusted anyone before.

"No, he's never there, and my father doesn't seem keen to give him access." Phantom wondered about it the entire walk back. Whatever happened in there was vile, he could sense it in the atmosphere of the place and how tense Rose grew there. It must have been something truly terrible for it to affect her so.

It made him want to tear the Fortress apart until someone admitted to their crimes against his songbird then separate their spine from their body.

But dread crept in on him. On his list of suspects, the Commodore was near the top. He couldn't imagine Ashby not knowing of such acts that took place in those wretched chambers. But the idea of torturing and killing him—

It left Phantom with a pit at the bottom of his stomach, making him feel ill.

Even when he remembered the blood Ashby spilled on Bashtir and that it belonged to Robin. Phantom wasn't convinced the Commodore would go through with it. That if the threat needed to be carried out, Ashby wouldn't take the boy's life. But if he did not, another officer would have.

But if there was a chance Ashby hurt Rose, Phantom would no longer question him and carry out his threats.

"He's talked about smuggling me off the island."

"What?" A ring of hope came through his voice faster than he could stop it.

"But I don't think it's for my sake," Rose whispered almost too quietly for him to hear.

"Why else would he try to help you escape?" Rose blinked, clearly having more to say, but stopped for some goddess-forsaken reason. "Rose, please," he begged, putting both hands on her head. "I need to know what happens in those damned chambers. I need to know what's holding you here."

A tear escaped her eye, but her resolve strengthened by the set of her jaw; content to keep her secrets.

"I saw your power tonight. You have the power to end all of this yourself, don't you? You just need the right songs, and you could end everything here." Another tear confirmed what she would not say.

"It's not that simple," she breathed.

"What could possibly mean so much to you to sacrifice everything for it?"

She sniffled and he didn't need his beast to witness the fear in her eyes. Something haunted her worse than that chamber.

Phantom shifted, placing his hands on the sides of her neck and leaning his forehead against hers.

"You can trust me. Tell me. What will you lose if you take your freedom?"

She drew back, looking into his eyes, searching them.

"You," she breathed, and it felt like an anchor dropping. "The Minister will kill you if I leave. And if you leave, he'll send his soldiers to Kheli, wipe out the entire island, and hunt down every devil until they're all dead." Her tears streamed down her face. "I—I can't be the reason that you die."

He shook his head, his dark hair sliding over his brow. "Oh,

Rose." That's when he finally felt it. The feeling of belonging to someone. He loved his devils, but he was a means to an end for them. A way for them to live. A freedom they couldn't find elsewhere. Or even a last resort. But no one had ever sacrificed their own future, their own sanity for his sake.

He crashed his lips into hers, the sweetness of her kiss overwhelming him in an instant. With her face cupped in his hands, she reached for him desperately, running her hands up his chest. There was nothing soft about this kiss, but rather it was like breathing for the first time. He scrambled for more and more of her, like he couldn't stop the slow descent into the madness that came with the feel of her.

Phantom swept his tongue in, and she moaned with the new intimacy. He groaned at her eager acceptance of him, her hands finding their way under his shirt to feel his skin beneath.

Before things could get too interesting, a crow squawked, startling her away from him. A look around told them the sun would soon be arriving.

Phantom inspected the crow, glaring at it and it glared back. *Indigo.*

"Bloody Indigo," Phantom cursed under his breath.

Her eyes widened as she took in the lightening sky. Phantom reached for her again, pressing his forehead into hers, letting their passion die out before it cost too much. "We will find a way out of this. Together."

She nodded. "Before I go," she said, clearing her throat. "Don't go to the feast."

"What?" He hadn't even heard of this feast yet, so he didn't think his presence was required.

"It's in a few days. Please, just don't."

She was intent on keeping secrets, but there was no time to get them out of her. He'd have to try again later.

"If you insist, love."

She released a breath, then pulled away from him. He held

onto her hand, unwilling to see her go so soon. She stared back at that hand, sighing with so much resistance, it pained him to see it.

"I'll see you again soon," he promised.

"Yes, you will," she agreed, smiling at him so brightly, every weight on him seemed to evaporate. She climbed up the wall to her balcony and disappeared inside.

CHAPTER 23

BLOODY CROW

Phantom hated mornings and he was seeing too many of them. The silver and lilac sky faded to yellow and blue.

In truth, he was in a foul mood due to Indigo's interruption. Even now her crow cawed at him as it jumped from tree to tree, leading him away from the Fortress. He was inclined to shoot the bird again, but he had no pistol to do so. And he doubted shooting another of her pets would go unpunished.

He growled his displeasure at having to obey another's whims, but the crow had him curious. It did not fly into town as he expected. Instead, it veered towards the Temple where Ravana's loyal acolytes were lined up to begin morning prayers.

Phantom kept to the tree line, calling on his quiet counterpart to help him go undetected. As he thought it, orange like the last rays of a sunset licked at his vision and shadows drew to him. Phantom released a slow breath of relief, Draven didn't always answer his call, content to hide in the recesses of their mind, but when he did, it was like walking in thick darkness.

"Thanks, mate," Phantom whispered since he didn't trust

Draven would hear it if he only thought it. As usual, there was no response.

The crow soared above him, landing on the side of the Temple wall, its talons digging into mortar. It pecked at the brick, willing it to open.

"What did you find?"

Phantom leaned into the wall, placing his hand on the side.

Air. It was flowing out of the wall, warming the outside air. A passage much like the one in Lord Desmond's estate. Of course, there would be a secret entrance.

He gazed down at the bird, the urge to shoot it evaporating. "How do you feel about becoming a devil?"

The bloody thing squawked loudly before releasing its talons and flapping away.

"That's what I thought."

He turned his attention to the wall, pressing in until it budged. The wall opened, sliding in then shifting to the side so he could roll it far enough to slip past.

Darkness enveloped him in the narrow passageway. It was small enough to make Phantom feel trapped, dread pooling in his stomach.

But he leaned on the beast, who perked up at the attention.

Phantom blinked, red swimming in his vision before he opened his eyes, seeing an outline of the walls around him. He didn't need light. He was a creature of darkness, that much was clear even if he couldn't remember his original life.

He followed the passageway for several minutes before hearing a moan. At first Phantom mistook it for a moan of pain, but as the sound continued and lengthened, it was clearly from pleasure.

Following the sound, he found a mesh covering replacing the wall, meant to spy on the inhabitants of the Temple. He peered through the mesh and a sheer curtain to see an extrava-gant bed amid a lavish room. Tapestries, candles, statues, furniture, and everything the materialistic mind could want was scattered about the chamber.

And there, on the bed was an unmistakable sheet of red hair and a very naked body attached to it, which he could — thankfully — see very little of from this angle.

Ravana faced the opposite direction as she rocked back and forth atop a man's body. She cried out in ecstasy as she fiercely rode the man below her.

Phantom's face etched into a grimace, and he snapped his eyes shut, turning away from the image that would surely haunt his nightmares. Wisps of memories from his young years gnawed at him, reminding him how her clammy hands felt upon his skin. How she used her power to get what she wanted from him.

He banished the memories away, wishing he could erase them from his skull.

She cried out again, loudly finding her pleasure. He resisted the urge to cover his ears, but knowing there was a reason the bloody crow brought him here.

When she finally recovered, she climbed off her latest victim, pulling a long satin robe around her naked flesh. It glittered in lilac, a mockery of Macha's moonlight.

"Return to your duties, Commodore."

Phantom attention snapped to the man on the bed. Ashby sat there, his pants loosely hugging his hips and his broad chest bare. He sat at the edge of the bed, his head in his hands. Ashby's fingers dug into his skull, seeming to tear at the strands.

"Commodore?"

Ashby stood sharply, as if his hesitance never happened. He slung his shirt over his head before seizing his longsword which rested against the foot of the bed.

"Yes, my lady."

He stepped out of the chamber as if he couldn't get out fast enough. Phantom stared after his old friend. He was never sure what to believe when it came to Ashby. Was it foolish to hope Bash was in there somewhere? Or was there only the Commodore now?

Does it matter? Kayden barked, clearly unwilling to supply hope.

He's still on the wrong side, Sam calmer tone still held a note of cynicism.

But Phantom couldn't shake the feeling that something was off with Ashby.

"My lady," a meek voice interrupted Phantom's inner conversation. "Lord Lockness is here to see you."

She sat at her vanity, brushing through her hair delicately. "Send him in."

Lockness entered a moment later, his suit immaculate and his hair perfectly combed back, but there was a grimace spoiling his image. "It reeks of sex in here."

Ravana moved from brushing to stringing glittering diamonds to her ears.

"Perhaps you could join us next time."

Lockness paced about the room, looking suspiciously at everything, including the wall Phantom hid inside.

A scoff escaped his mouth. "I wouldn't touch you if you were the last woman alive, Ravana. Keep your pets." He squinted at the curtain shielding the tunnel from view, Phantom held his breath.

"Yet, here you are, in my room."

He rolled his eyes. "Your slaves insisted. Apparently, you didn't wish the morning worshipers to spot us together."

She twisted in her stool, raising a single finger to her lips. "I know you can keep a secret."

Lockness groaned. "What do you want?"

"When will my next shipment arrive?"

"You need *more*?"

She dropped a necklace in her lap, glaring at him. "The last batch you brought me was a bunch of sea creatures and rodents, not the magic blood I needed."

Witch sons. Lockness had them?

He rose his brows, annoyed with her. "Then, perhaps, your enchanted sexton doesn't work."

Her eyes narrowed as she rose from her seat, stalking after him. "It works. Perhaps it is your motivations in question. But you wouldn't betray me. Not unless you *believe* in the Minister's vision?"

His upper lip pealed back. "Never," he growled.

"Then get me the sons or I will find them myself. Then I will owe you nothing and you can plead with the Minister."

His nose turned up, flicking at his displeasure. "I will get them for you, and you *will* honor our agreement."

"I will when you do." He raised his head, looking down on her with something akin to hatred. Phantom felt an odd relief that the lord disliked her so much. "You're dismissed, my lord."

She turned her back on him, leaving him no choice but to leave, his shoulders dropping by a fraction on his way out.

Phantom finally let out the breath he held, unable to hold it in any longer.

Ravana's attention turned to the curtain, narrowing her eyes at him. She couldn't see him. Could she?

"Hello darling," she drawled.

Bloody hell.

He bolted, running down the tunnel as he heard her call for the guards.

The tunnel was too narrow to move quickly, but he was highly motivated to ignore the pain of scrapes and bruises. The beast's vision helped when he walked slowly but it was nearly useless as he ran.

Finally, he reached the entrance, sunlight beaming through the single crack he left open. He pushed the brick aside to skim through, the sun warming the air and grass beyond the Temple.

Of course, the bloody sun would shine right now.

He surged out of the tunnel entrance in time to hear booted footsteps from both directions.

He called Draven to his aid, needing the shadows more than ever.

Nothing.

Bastard.

Phantom never slowed, running quickly into the forest beside the Temple, even if there wasn't much in the way of trees to hide him. It was something. He ducked behind a tree to assess the threat.

Looking back, he watched as Ravana's personal guards swarmed the forest, entering at various points and cutting off his exits. He ran through the list of his assets.

Other than his personal effects, he had his powerful counterparts.

The beast would take out the guards quickly, but killing two dozen men would lead to a witch hunt he couldn't afford. With the beast being suppressed for so long, he'd have little control over it.

Draven's shadows would have been useful for a stealthy escape, but he wasn't responding, content to leave Phantom to Ravana. He growled at his useless past self.

Kayden was fireproof. Immensely helpful now.

I'll remember that when you're facing the flames, Kayden grumbled.

Phantom ignored him, then cursed himself for forgetting what Sam did.

Fighting. I fight and I win.

"Against two dozen guards without killing them?" Phantom whispered at himself, forgetting to mind-speak to his past selves.

Yes, Sam answered. There was no arrogance accompanying the words, only cold truth, as if he hated it. *Let me out and I'll take care of them.*

"Fine. But no killing. The reins are yours."

Phantom felt himself slide away from consciousness, slipping into the recesses of his mind. He thought he heard a shout before it all went dark.

CHAPTER 24

THIRD MISSION

The Commodore rapped on Phantom's door. He groaned, leaning forward in his bed. Memories from the night before came to him, and the period where he blacked out. His mind was completely blank from the moment he gave Sam control.

He didn't even remember getting back to his bed. But the splitting headache was akin to being hungover; along with the blackout, he wondered if that's what happened.

Ashby knocked, "Get your ass out here, James."

Well, he was in a foul mood today.

Phantom leaned down to look at his clothing, still the drab civilian clothing he sported last night, but with rips and tears strung about. He looked like he'd been in a brawl. But somehow, there was no blood.

You said no killing, Sam supplied.

"Suppose I did. I just didn't expect you to take it to heart."

"What?" Ashby called from the door.

"Talking to myself." Phantom squinted at the harsh sunlight. "Come in," he amended.

Ashby barged in, narrowing his eyes at Phantom's poor

state. "Let me guess. You got piss drunk and took a swing at a man twice your size."

Phantom sported an upside down smile. He couldn't argue that's exactly what he looked like.

Ashby looked to the ceiling, seeming to ask for patience from Davina.

"I can explain," Phantom said too quickly, realizing he couldn't. He wasn't even sure which part the Commodore would be most appalled by: a past life taking control of his body, Ravana's ill intentions with children, or Phantom's witness to their intimate relations. He'd strike those images from his head if he could. "No, I can't."

Ashby scoffed. "I don't care. Just put your uniform on, the Minister requires your presence."

Phantom groaned at his luck. The last face he wanted to see was the Minister's. "Of course he does. Shall I bring the salts and soap or do his servants have those ready?"

Ashby crossed his arms. "James, this is important. Testing the Minister right now isn't wise." For a moment, Phantom could see Jon in the way Ashby stood. The sharp pain of home-sickness stung.

He searched Ashby's eyes, watching them soften.

Seeing the concern in Ashby's gaze reminded him of Rose's words. He tried to get her out of the Fortress before. Whatever his reasons may be.

He pulled on the Commodore's bulging arm, dragging him deeper into the room and shutting the door for privacy. A single brow rose on Ashby's face.

"I need to know something," Phantom whispered, only loud enough for Ashby to hear. "Do you intend on getting Rose off the island?"

The Commodore's eyes grew wide for a fraction of a second before he schooled his features into neutrality. He stilled for a moment, assessing his old friend.

"Yes, I do."

Phantom let out a breath, hope building in his chest.

"How long have you been planning this?"

Ashby swallowed, seeming to understand he was scheming with a known pirate in the Minister's own Fortress, yet he didn't try to move away. "A year." Was all he said, not giving Phantom vital information. The Commodore was not a good liar, and Phantom could tell when he withheld information. There was something to the set of his jaw that gave him away.

"You let her stay here all that time?" The rage found him again. The push and pull between happiness and rage dizzying.

The Commodore's eyes narrowed. "What do you mean?"

"Why, exactly, do you want her gone, Commodore?" There was a deathly note to Phantom's voice.

A resignation fell over Ashby's features. "If you don't know, it's best you don't find out."

Before the Commodore could turn his back, Phantom's arm snapped out, halting his old friend. "You don't want to help her. You want to be rid of her?" Memories returned to him, ones that made more sense now. "That's why you boarded my ship with only two men."

"James," Ashby warned, resolve solidifying his features and giving nothing away.

"You weren't going to fight your way to her. You didn't *want* to succeed. It had nothing to do with tricking me about her value."

Ashby's stoney gaze sharpened on Phantom. "Yet you brought her back." He pulled his arm out of Phantom's grip, then took a step into his space. "You want her, James? Take her. Spare us all."

"Spare you? How?"

The Commodore's features hardened again as his mask set firmly into place. He grunted heavily but ignored Phantom's question. "You're required in the throne room now. If we don't make it soon, the Minister will exact punishment. And I cannot stop him if he does."

With the obvious line the Commodore drew, Phantom's heart sank along with his hope. He might not have to kill his old friend, but he wanted to believe Bash was still in there.

Perhaps he was wrong.

Upon entering the throne room with Ashby, Phantom knew something was wrong. Every officer and every servant was absent. He'd never seen the lavish room so empty as they approached the dais which held the throne and a pensive Minister upon it.

He usually had an air of carelessness about him, but today he was nothing but worries. The Minister's face was stricken with dark, sleepless eyes and a concerned frown. Clearly, something had happened.

"I don't much like to admit when you are right, Lieutenant, but I'm afraid you are." Apparently, there would be no small talk.

"And what is it exactly that I am right about?" The Commodore cut him a hard stare, so he added, "Your Grace."

"You'll have to keep your manners more attuned than that if you're going to have any success," the Minister mumbled in a way that said Phantom wasn't supposed to understand him.

"Success? With what?"

The Minister snapped out of staring at the wall to focus in on Phantom with a frown, annoyed with him for not keeping up.

"The feast."

Phantom felt a shudder slide down his back. Rose was very adamant that he avoid the feast. He knew she would not have risked staying to tell him that if it wasn't imperative.

"I have reason to believe Lord Lockness is planning a coup behind my back," the Minister seethed, a fist pounding into the arm of his throne. It was rare to see the Minister so riled. "You." He pointed an accusatory finger in Phantom's direction. "You will come as a courtier to the feast. I know he knows you as Lord Castellanos. Lord Lockness reported his daughter missing shortly after your departure from his estate. With some convincing, he didn't charge Castellanos, letting the infamous pirate Captain take the blame instead."

"Pardon?" Phantom wasn't sure he heard the Minister correctly.

He sighed dramatically. "When his daughter turned up missing, I convinced Lockness that Castellanos was vetted. Of course, reports came back from a barmaid in low town that his daughter had joined a band of pirates, so Lockness released Castellanos of all guilt."

Phantom blinked. He didn't even think the Minister would bother to cover his trail. What had he hoped to gain from the risk of it? Was it only for peace's sake?

"Luckily, you provided enough evidence that all I had to do was turn his head in the right direction." He rolled his eyes as he reached for a pastry on the table beside him, huffing that he had to attend to them himself since he trusted no one else to be in the room. "Your orders, Lieutenant, are to impersonate Lord Castellanos again and gain Lockness's trust. I want to know what he is planning."

Phantom never thought he would end up in the middle of a political battle between a noble crime lord and the Prime Minister he despised.

Phantom let out a hollow chuckle. "Why would I do that?" The Minister's gaze sharpened, cutting through him like glass. "Clean up your own messes, Minister. Surely some unruly noble isn't getting the upper hand on you." Maybe a small part of him wanted to see Lockness take the Minister down. With freedom from the Minister's threats, he could return to his devils and deal with Lockness later.

Ashby's stare burned. "Watch your tongue, pirate, or I will cut it from your mouth." That hope he had for Bash fell further and rotted in his core. Why did he want to believe in his old friend so badly?

"You really have the stomach for it, brother?"

Before Ashby could respond, the Minister cut in, "Aside from the obvious leverage I have over you, Lieutenant, if you'll be of no use to me, I can just tell Lockness who you really are." The breath stopped in Phantom's lungs. "He'd do much worse than kill you. He'll use you to draw his daughter back to him and kill her for the disgrace she is."

He didn't dare call the Minister out. He wasn't bluffing. Phantom could see it in the desperation clinging to the man. Something happened to truly rattle the Minister and Phantom's execution might be the thing he needs to distract Lockness long enough for the Minister to trample his coup.

Either way, the Minister wins.

It was how he played all his games, by cheating and taking all the cards. Phantom wondered about what Jimmy said, Ravana was a traitor. He'd wager that wasn't the information that rattled the Minister. Phantom would keep it to himself, though. He wasn't sure how it would help him yet, and he refused to supply the Minister with anything he didn't have to.

Rose's warning filtered back to him. There was something about the feast that he didn't understand yet, but he had no choice. Along with countless other reasons, Black's life would be forfeit if he refused.

"Fine, what must I do?"

There was no way to describe the Minister's smile other than cruel.

CHAPTER 25

POOR MANNERS

The phrase "no choice" was becoming more of a regular occurrence in Phantom's life.

There's always a choice. Sam's soothing big brother voice was less than appreciated today.

He paced along the edge of the cliffs near the sea, looking over the setting sun and wishing for the thousandth time that he could find a way to escape the island without hurting the Khelitians with Serena *and* Rose.

The orange sky in the west held no answers for him.

"Being handed over to Lockness to draw Black out is hardly a choice," Phantom said aloud, the air around him having more space than his own head.

Are you certain that's what he wants from you?

"What else could he want?" Phantom bent to pick up a rock, tossing it off the cliff to watch it splash twenty feet below.

Sam's answering silence said enough. There were many things Lockness could want from Phantom, vengeance at the top of that list, but knowing he was working with Ravana, the list grew impossibly longer.

Although, he doubted the Minister knew of their secret

meetings. There were too many enemies surrounding him, not enough answers.

His feet wandered the Fortress grounds as he thought to himself, occasionally Sam or Kayden would answer his thoughts. They took up too much space, he often couldn't tell the difference, their colors blending in his mind. But he supposed it made sense, they were all one once.

A sense of warmth interrupted his thoughts. Glancing around, he took note of a familiar balcony. It was Rose's chambers. He smiled to himself, of course he would end up here.

A few flickering candles dancing in the growing darkness of night.

Perhaps the songbird had some insight.

Yes, that's the reason you're going to climb that balcony. Sam's playful tone only made Phantom grin.

"Among other reasons."

For a human, the balcony was too high to jump to. But for the beast?

Phantom leaned into his beast, and the creature stretched like a cat awakening from a long nap, red misting at the edges of his vision.

He jumped, catching his hands on the pillars of the balcony then hoisting himself upwards until he could roll his back over the railing. His boots came down softly on the smooth stone floor. Phantom had been a thief long enough that light footed landings were habitual.

Warm humid air drifted into the balcony opening, lightly tossing the tulle curtains hanging there. Her room had everything he expected a Minister's daughter would have, a large bed, vanity, and other assorted furniture. All designed by the best money could buy.

He stalked further in when he didn't spy his songbird, but there were too many lit candles for her to be absent.

Upon reaching the middle of the room, he heard water

sloshing. Turning the corner, he confirmed his suspicion to see a bathroom with a large tub in the middle.

And there she was. His songbird with her hair tied up to avoid the water and steam rising around her naked flesh. Some decent part of him thought to look away, but that voice was so very small compared to the scoundrel who couldn't take his eyes off her.

But the lighting was dim, so he couldn't get a good look, especially with her back to him. He squinted at the skin of her shoulders, noticing something different about the texture. He'd seen some of her flesh before. It was always so flawless and pure.

His focus was so drawn to her shoulders that he didn't realize she was humming. His attention turned to the song, but it ended abruptly.

Phantom took a few steps into the bathroom to stare at her shoulders, but they were perfect again, no textures, just clean, flawless skin.

"Spying on a lady is hardly proper behavior."

"I've never been one for proper manners."

Phantom smirked, turning about the room until he could face her. Goddess divine, she was perfect.

The water she sat in was cloudy but did little to hide her curves below. Even if it did, the sight above the water was enough to excite him. Not only was her neck and shoulders on full display, but her décolletage and the swells of her breasts were exposed. At his attention, her nipples hardened, skimming the surface of the water.

He wanted nothing more than to jump into the water and taste every inch of her flesh.

"Yes, I can see that."

His attention returned to her face where a slight smile licked at the corner of her mouth. He leaned forward until his hands gripped the edge of the tub where her feet were submerged.

"There are other improper things I could do." He let his eyes drift again, aware that she watched him take her in. She moved, spilling water and drifting towards him until she was only inches from his clenched hands holding the metal tub like a lifeline. "So many things."

She stared at his mouth, and he nearly took it as an invitation.

The thought of those *many things* had another question popping into his head.

"Are you a virgin?"

She baulked, staring at him with her mouth open. "Continuing the inappropriate behavior, I see." He leaned down, hoping she would close the distance between them. But he kept silent, waiting on bated breath for her answer.

"No."

"No?"

"I'm not a virgin, James."

Jealousy burned in his throat unbidden. He had no reason to feel jealous when his history was hardly pure. Still— "Who do I have to kill?"

She let out a shocked laugh. "I shan't be telling you. For their sakes more than yours."

A thought had him burning hotter. "Is the Commodore one of them?"

Her eyebrows lifted. "And if he was?"

"I'd hate to have to kill him."

"Wha—" Her mouth dropped open. "I will not apologize for my intimacies in the past. And for your information, Sebastian and I hold no passion for one another. So no, he is not one of them."

His shoulders sagged in relief. Not that he planned to carry out his threats, but because he spent too much time feeling jealousy towards Ashby. He didn't need another reason.

"Them?"

Her eyes turned incredulous, finally closing her mouth. Her voice turned deep, dangerous. "You can hardly protest. I've already heard glowing accounts from some of the maids in this Fortress. You're quite popular." Red flushed her skin. In her state of undress, he watched it spread across her chest and up her neck.

He grinned widely, sitting on the floor beside the tub and letting one hand drift to the water. One finger skimmed the surface dangerously close to where Rose's heavy breaths bobbed her breasts in and out of the water. The sight sent blood rushing to this cock, straining against his trousers.

"Jealous, love?"

"I'm only saying we're even. You have a past and so do I. It shouldn't matter in the case of what we are to each other." She was rambling, her nerves getting the best of her.

He let his hand drift closer to her tempting flesh. "And what are we to each other?"

Her eyes tracked his hand as it glided towards her, but when he stopped just short of touching her, she let out a breath. "Friends," she whispered, as if the word pained her.

One eyebrow rose on his forehead. "Do friends do this?" His hand brushed against her peaked nipple that skimmed the water's surface. She sucked in a breath but made no move to stop him.

She didn't respond to his question, but he didn't expect her to.

"What about this?"

He moved his finger along the skin of her breast, caressing the submerged underside until he gently cupped it. Before he got nearly enough of her, she drifted away, retreating to the far side of the tub. He understood. It was too soon.

Yet she made no move to conceal herself from his hungry gaze.

"Who are you, James? To me?"

"A friend, apparently." But the word held no merit, that much was clear.

Her eyes dipped in agitation that was absolutely adorable, but she was still so gloriously naked that it made it hard for him to think.

"I think you know. Or you would not have asked."

"You know about Isabeya," she blurted, some of the lust abating. "What else do you know?"

He stared at her a moment, this time taking in her hopeful features. For the first time in his life, he was afraid he would say something wrong. If she didn't know enough, would he scare her away? What were the maids he'd taken before saying about him? What were her voices saying about him?

This needed to be addressed before they could give into lust. She needed to know she wasn't some conquest he'd set out to achieve. She was so much more than that.

His words would not be enough.

Phantom reached for the robe hanging nearby, a soft white fabric, and held it open for her. "Let me show you."

A curious look crossed her face, her mouth parted, and her eyes widened.

"You won't look, will you, Captain?"

The things that title did to him, especially when she spoke it.

"That would be the proper thing to do."

Her features twisted into annoyance, but before he was about to concede, she hummed. A wind swept through the room, candlelight flickering out until they were left in darkness, too far from the window for moonlight.

"That's cheating," he complained as he heard a splash and the telltale drip of water.

The robe was tugged out of his hand in the next second. "We'll talk about cheating when you tell me how you got in here."

"Well played, love."

He could have used to beast to see in the dark, but she didn't know of that ability, and he doubted she would appreciate it. She hummed in the darkness, and he was tempted to call on his beast to see what she was up to.

Another hum and the candles flickered with flame once more. But instead of the soft robe she stole from him, she wore the black tight-fitting outfit she had on before. The gauzy black fabric was so fitted he could see every curve.

Nemain spare him.

She smiled like she knew. She tossed a cloak over her head and shoulders as he inspected her.

"How did you dress so quickly?"

She only held a finger to those perfect lips to signal his silence.

He let the question go, more important things on his mind, like those perfect lips. Holding out a hand for her, she placed her hand in his before leading him to the door.

CHAPTER 26
CAVE OF STARS

The Fortress was quiet tonight, letting them slip by unnoticed through the service exit.

Phantom led her by the hand. He couldn't stop thinking about how soft her fingers were against his dirty, callused ones. Part of him wanted to let go for how unworthy he was to hold her delicate hand. The dirt caked under his fingernails enough to tell him how far beneath her he really was.

The other part, the one that won out, admired the beauty of their clasped hands. The contrast of dirty to clean, of hard to soft and all the other ways they seemed to complete each other.

Phantom thought about the feast and how she had warned him away from it, yet he couldn't avoid it. He wanted to ask her why it was so important that he didn't attend, but when opened his mouth to ask, her eyes drifted upwards, to the heavens and the stars.

A memory of the sketch she had left him flashed across his mind.

"Tell me why you paint," he prompted. He knew her, but was more than eager to fill in the pieces he didn't yet know.

Her smile faded at the mention of painting, pain distorting her features. She swallowed. "Painting is not what it used to be for me. Now it means image and control."

"What did it used to mean?"

A smile lifted her face again, her eyes drifting back to the stars, and she looked so goddess-damned beautiful. It was blinding. "Once, it meant expression and creativity. It was a way to capture the things I found beautiful in the world. To show people what they were to me in terms words couldn't express. A way to channel what I am feeling into the world." Her eyes became starry, lifted by the notion of something that once held so much passion for her.

"Those stars, I would have painted them among a sky of violet along the horizon of deep blue ocean."

He thought perhaps he should look at the stars she was admiring. Understand what held her attention away from him, but he couldn't bring himself to. There was a small smile tipping her mouth and a glow spreading over her skin. A wonder so beautiful, it put the stars to shame.

He only wished he didn't feel jealous of the glittery bastards.

"Thank you for the drawing," he breathed. It drew her attention to him, along with a faint blush. "Though I do wonder, of all the ways you could have captured me, you chose that moment. Why?"

She started and stopped a couple times. "You looked sad."

His brows drew together.

"I know you have your crew, but you looked so lonely." Her gaze pierced straight through him. He had never felt more vulnerable, like his heart was on display. "I felt like it was the first time I was seeing you. The real you."

"Aye," he said before he thought to stop himself, but the word didn't feel like enough.

Finally, he noticed they had stopped walking. Gently he

pulled on her hand, leading her to the cliff side on the northern-most part of the island.

They started climbing down the jagged rocks when Rose spoke again, "What drives your passion?"

He pondered her for a moment, wondering if she would understand. But if he had any chance of someone understanding him, it would be her. She had proved that. He dragged her body to his until their faces were only inches apart, then pointed westward.

"You see that, the brightest star in the heavens?" He waited for her head to turn in the right direction. "That is the star of Nemain. Legend has it, the star sits above the gates of Hell. I intend to find out." The star was surrounded by the two other stars Ramirez had pointed out to him, that grew closer together.

Rose's gaze turned back to him, a hint of concern etching her features. "The legend also says the gates are guarded."

With her so close, it was easy to wrap an arm around her waist, pulling her flush to him and whispering in her ear. "Not just guarded. There is all manner of traps, terrain never encountered, challenges never defeated, and places never before seen." Her eyes turned to him again, stars reflecting in her irises. "How exciting."

A smile etched her lips, intrigue brightening her eyes.

"Come with me."

Her smile faded, and Phantom's heart sank.

"I can't. James, I can't leave."

He put his knuckle under her chin and returned her gaze to his. "Whatever is holding you here, when you're ready to tell me, just know I will be here to set you free." She blinked, but said nothing else, so he continued, reluctant to release her from his hold, but he reaffirmed his grip on her hand.

Minutes ticked by as they descended to where waves lapped at the shore. The tide was low so they could reach their destination. During high tide or a storm, the cave would flood with no access.

But they were there just in time.

"Close your eyes."

"What?"

"Trust me, love."

She hesitantly handed over control and he led her down the shore to a cave etched into the cliff side wall.

"Can I open my eyes now?"

"Not yet," he whispered, leading her to the perfect spot. Then he adjusted where he stood, taking her waist in his hands again and hugging her back into his chest. His arms locked around her, and she let out a small laugh at how he nuzzled into her neck.

"Open your eyes, Rose."

He felt the breath of air leave her body as she stared down into the hollow of the cave. Inside were a thousand glowing teal crystals, covering the walls and the ceiling of the cave. Water sat in a shallow pool at the bottom, still due to its separation from the sea, reflecting the crystals

"It's wonderful. How? This has been down here the whole time?"

He chuckled at her breathy response, feeling her muscles relax in his arms. "It is normally part of the sea, but on rare occasions, when the tide has lowered enough near a crimson moon, we can see the treasures truly hidden inside the island."

"What is this place?" Gooseflesh peppered her arms, a shudder traveling through her body.

"You feel it, don't you? The power of this place?" He felt it the moment he discovered it as a child. There was a thumping heartbeat radiating from the cave, as if the island's heart itself beat inside. "You feel your breath getting heavier?" He closed in near her neck, placing a soft kiss there at the base of her neck where it met the slope of her shoulder. She had no objections this time. "You feel the drop in your stomach like you're falling?"

He often wondered what it would be like to experience pleasure in this place. With ecstasy running rapt through the cave and the threat of interruption from the sea, he lusted over the experience. But with Rose Davenport in his arms, he couldn't help but think it would be the single most revolutionary experience he would ever have.

But not yet. Not until she was ready.

With immense effort, he stepped away from the warm cocoon of her body, instantly feeling colder. She let out a breath of air as if she could feel his absence as keenly as he felt hers. He reached for her hand, kissing her knuckles while drowning in the pools of her eyes which glittered reflections of the crystal cave around them.

"Let me show you what this cave truly is." She followed as if in a trance. Eventually, her eyes broke from his to take in the beauty of each step. A few paces into the cave and the ceiling expanded and widened. Stalactites and stalagmites decorated every corner. Slowly, the colors faded. Teal turned to deep navy blue to purple, as bright as the sunsets during a Macha full moon.

Rose's lips parted in the pure awestruck wonder.

Finally, he rounded to a chamber of the cave where the ceiling opened with the night clearly visible. It was far off, but when a moon drifted over the cave it created a brilliant display.

On the walls of the moon chamber, the crystals took on a multitude of colors, forming to show two lovers locked in an embrace and surrounded by stars. Several depictions of the same two lovers were shown throughout the chamber, except at the furthest wall.

Rose dropped Phantom's hand to inspect the centerpiece image, as if it was drawing her closer.

The image was of a woman sitting cross-legged with her

eyes closed, as if meditating. Seven of the largest crystals in the cave were arranged vertically over the woman's body, starting between her legs and ending at the apex of her head.

The bottom crystal was as red as Nemain's moon. The second was orange, then yellow, green, blue, violet, and finally purple. He couldn't help staring at the blue crystal located in the woman's throat, reminding him of the way Rose's eyes glowed that very shade. He cursed himself for not seeing it sooner.

"I've seen this before," she breathed, drawing closer to the crystals with a hand raised to touch them. "But only in my dreams." Before she could set her delicate fingers on the cold crystal, she looked back at the man who had brought her here. "How is that possible?"

He reached for her, lifting a hand to her cheek, and drifted his thumb over her soft skin. "Because they are not dreams, Rose." He reached for her hand and lifted it with his own. "They are memories." Both of their hands landed on the green crystal, the one pulsating like a heartbeat. The magic of it shot into him, pushing open the channels buried deep within his memories.

Samuel Rourke had one arm leaned against a wooden post, looking over the sea. He never really had the chance to look at it, but he couldn't now either. His mind was too full of everything he had seen. Kalon was more beautiful than he ever could have imagined, but he wasn't supposed to find things beautiful. He was a killer through and through, trained for assassination and battle, not building houses and staring at waves.

He wasn't supposed to be feeling. He hadn't for the first thirty years of his life. Why now? Why her? He couldn't get this woman out of his head.

From the moment he met Isabeya, she was like a fire, burning so brightly she was blinding, but he couldn't look away. He'd gladly burn in her flames if it meant she paid him any attention at all. He'd take her passion in any form he could get.

He was accustomed to her ire and anger by now but glimpsing what that passion could be was possibly the most heartbreaking thing he had ever witnessed. If she ever found out what he was truly doing there, she'd kill him. And that was if he was lucky. He'd still take death at her hand over being discarded by her, having to live his life knowing he was nothing to her.

The waves crashed harder, and rain started pouring in droves. The house he was in was nothing more than a few wooden posts and fabric scraps draping over the wood. He'd have a lot of damage to mend once the storm passed, if he stayed.

Part of him wanted to leave, tell them *he couldn't find her and let her live her life without ever knowing what she meant to him. It would be the coward's way out, but maybe he was a coward for Isabeya.*

Who was he kidding? He was burning already. Burning for her.

He sensed her before he saw her. The overwhelming presence of her hit him like a blow to the chest, making him breathless.

Turning, he saw her standing, soaking wet from the downpour of tropical rain and surrounded by an angry sheet of fabric flapping in the wind. She looked like a goddess-damned ghost coming to haunt him, her signature dark hair pulled back to a tail and her fighting leathers clinging to every inch of her. In her firm grip was her curved sword, dripping from a recent battle. She was covered in black blood from the necromites she must have killed to get to him. If he didn't know her, he'd say she was a harbinger of death or a bad omen coming to his doorstep. He still wasn't sure he was wrong.

"What do you want?" He couldn't help but to keep up their usual banter. Even if all he wanted to do was claim her for himself. There was some deep part of him that understood. Once he had her, everything would change. Perhaps that would put her in danger, and he wasn't willing to risk that, no matter how capable she was.

"You got what you wanted. I'll leave and you can have every-thing you want here." Sam crossed his arms, towering over her from ten feet away. She was so short for how lethal she was. She didn't move, didn't respond at all. He nodded to the sword in her hand as lightning struck above their heads, a thunder tiger roaring with the storm. *"Finish me off yourself if you'd like."* He opened his arms. He was done fighting her. *"I won't stop you."*

Isabeya breathed heavily, her dark eyes shadowed with the haunted things she had done and seen. He knew her darkest parts because they were his. Even when he had convinced himself he wanted nothing to do with her, the darkness in him recognized the darkness in her.

A loud clang echoed through the air as her sword hit hard stone, mixing with the roars of the thunder tigers nearby. But that ferocity, that fire in her eyes did not abate. Perhaps this was personal enough to her. She wanted to end him with her bare hands.

His heart threatened to beat right out of his chest as she inched closer.

"Kneel," she bit out.

A true execution then. So be it.

He let his knees hit hard stone as he dropped, pain raking up his body, but it was nothing compared to the rage inside of him. He wanted to tell her that none of it was truly him. That he had been falling in love with her all this time and it took meeting her to discover who he truly was.

"I'll find you in the next life, mi reina.*"* His nickname for her never felt more appropriate with his knees on the ground before her. A peasant in the presence of a queen.

She lunged, her hands wrapping around his head as her lips collided with his. It felt like salvation. Like the heavenly fire she was made of, like the air he had been needing for decades, like the water he had thirsted for. That fire crashed into him and burned him from the inside out, but it no longer hurt. Isabeya's fire turned molten as it mixed with his soul.

He reached for her, needing her closer. His large hands wrapped around her tiny waist, pulling her against him with a growl so low, he knew she could feel it rattle her body. She moaned into his mouth in response; the sound of his complete and utter undoing.

He fell back, dragging her with him until she was firmly seated in his lap. He explored her mouth, thrusting his tongue in and claiming her in any way she would allow. Isabeya bit down on his lip hard enough for him to taste blood.

No legion of Hell would ever tempt him away from the queen in his arms.

Phantom was thrust back to the present, his breath still heavy from the taste of Isabeya on his tongue. Rose gazed at him with labored breath, and he knew she was feeling the same effects.

"Do you understand now?" His voice came out much rougher.

She nodded. "I am Isabeya. I'm—" she blinked as the realization took her over. A deeper, truer understanding taking over. "And you're — Samuel?"

Sam snapped to the forefront of his mind, spilling green over his vision and taking over their body. "Missed me, *mi reina*?" Phantom shook his head, expelling Sam to the back of his mind again. He needed this moment with Rose.

"What do you remember?"

She blinked back a flash of green so quickly he almost missed it, banishing her own counterpart. "I remember," she started, looking down at her hands and the colors of the stones next to her. "Davina blessed us with eternal life through reincarnation, so we could never join the dead."

"Cursed actually."

Her light brows drew together, disappointment flashing across her features. He stopped it by taking her face into his hands, cradling her chin.

"I have to lose you just as many times as I find you." He could see it all in her eyes, every death and rebirth playing out. It was a cruel fate to anyone. Not to mention the beast that laid dormant in his chest. "Rose, we are not cursed. I am. Fate follows me, and She has not been kind. You are unfortunate enough to be tied to me." Confusion flashed across her face as she studied him.

He took a steadying breath. "There is a monster inside me that craves bloodshed. One that could have only been born in the depths of Hell. It's why—"

"That's why you worship Nemain. You think you belong to her." She wasn't asking, she didn't need to. Her hands came up his chest until they rested on his neck. "You're not a monster, James."

A hollow laugh left him. "I wouldn't be so sure."

"You're not." Her face was all hard lines, reaffirming him with her faith.

"You don't know what I've done," he whispered because he hoped she would never find out. Even if he had his reasons, he wasn't proud of the man who had unleashed the beast upon his enemies.

"It doesn't matter." Her hand pressed harder into his chest, grounding him to her. "You're here with me now and I'm not letting you go."

His thumb brushed over her cheek. She was so beautiful, so precious.

Warmth overwhelmed him, and he understood what his first mate had with his wife.

"*My tresora*," Phantom whispered, and she smiled in response.

He pulled her to him, crashing his lips against hers and giving into her thrall. She tensed and relaxed against him at once, sinking into the kiss and giving into him completely. She opened her mouth, inviting him to deepen the kiss. He did so without a moment's hesitation, his arms traveling around her waist to her back and pressing her into him. She sighed, melting in his arms.

Rose's hands skimmed along his chest, then around his shoulders until she dug her nails into his hair, lightly pulling. The feel of her hands and the taste of her lips was explosive; like the magic circulating the chamber, his heart thrumming in his chest like a wild animal.

He pushed at her until her back hit the cold stone and the churning, glittering crystals surrounded her. With one hand on the stone behind her and the other gripping her waist tightly to him, he broke the kiss to explore her neck. She moaned deeply as his lips hit that sensitive spot above her collarbone. He felt like an animal himself, her scent and moans driving him feral. The sweet smokiness of her overwhelmed him, a growl escaping him.

She sighed at the pleasure it gave her. He pressed into her, his knee firmly between her thighs. His hard length pressed into her stomach, but he knew he should pull away. The moment he claimed her as he wanted to, he wouldn't be able to leave her back in that Fortress. He'd steal her away again, and she wasn't ready for that.

Still, he couldn't pull away. The intoxication of her kiss, the sounds she made in response to him, the magic of the cave seeming to push them to consummate their bond. It was all too much and not enough.

Phantom's hands drifted back to her waist, slipping under her shirt so he could feel more of her. His thumb grazed over a line of raised skin, and he froze.

Pulling his head back, he stared at her as she realized exactly what his hands had found under her shirt. There was a fear in her eyes that made him even more angry.

She tried to pull her shirt down to cover up the scars, but it was too late. He felt at least one and with her reaction; he wagered she had several more where that came from.

"Rose," he pleaded, his voice coming out almost threateningly. "Let me see."

Her eyes snagged on his, and she seemed to decide. He wouldn't push any further than that, but he had to know how many scars he needed to pay back.

Reluctantly, she pulled up her shirt, only stopping before her breasts and exposing every inch of her stomach to him. The monster slammed into his head so quickly that everything turned red at the sight of so many scars. He'd have an easier time counting the stars in the heavens than counting the marks made on her.

A deep vibrato took over his voice. "Who did this to you?"

There were scars layering over other scars in patterns that showed someone's relentless attention to detail in carving up her skin.

A small sob escaped her, which calmed the beast enough for him to see straight. She was crying, ashamed of letting him see her scars.

"No, no, no, no, no," he said so quickly the words ran together as he refocused her attention on him with both hands on her face. She blinked away tears he promptly wiped away. "You are beautiful, Rose. There is not a single inch of you I don't hunger for. These scars," he said, releasing a hand to drift over the scars of her stomach. The feel of them making it even more real. "They make you more beautiful because you survived all of this, and you are still kind. You are still strong. They did not break your spirit and they never will. I'm sorry you endured it and I promise I will make whoever did this pay so severely that even Nemain will reject their soul. But don't for one second think that I want you any less."

She collapsed in his arms, tears streaming down her cheeks as she accepted his words. He was honored that she found solace in his arms, but the thought that there was someone out there who touched her so cruelly made him shake with wrath.

"Rose," he whispered as her sobs slowed. "Give me a name."

She sucked back a breath. "Ravana."

His anger rose up like a tangible entity, yellow fire licking at the edges of his vision and mixing with the red he was used to. The beast rose at every threat, but Kayden—

Kayden's anger was reserved for the vilest of creatures.

Phantom burned from inside, the potency of rage reaching a level he didn't know was possible.

"Wait on the shore for me," he ordered Rose, but it wasn't his voice, it was Kayden's graveled tone.

CHAPTER 27

LAY DOWN YOUR ARMS

The heavens opened and rain poured down Phantom's hot skin. He refused to be shoved inside his own body, he wanted Ravana's blood on his hands. He wanted to hear her pleas and begging. Kayden and the beast fueled him, urging him into action.

Never had his counterparts teamed up with him like this, but the yellow burning and red licking at the edges of his vision was proof enough. But it was the rage in his stomach, boiling to the point of pain that brought everything into focus.

Ravana was a monster vile enough to belong in the depths of Hell.

If she used the grimoire, her soul belonged to Nemain already. He need only to kill her, and her true torment would begin. But not before he got his fill of it first.

Lightening flashed overhead as he made it to the top of the cliff, rain washing over his body already soaking his hair and clothing. It was fitting he chose to wear all black tonight. It embodied the harbinger of death he'd become.

Phantom heard her heavy breaths before she climbed up behind him.

"I told you to wait for me," he growled, not completely in control of his speech.

She sucked in air greedily, her blonde locks plastered to her face. "I can't let you do this."

He squinted through the rain as she staggered to his side. "You can't what? Let me destroy the monster who has been tormenting you? Who has had a hand in all our nightmares?"

She took a step back, the air abruptly stopping in her lungs. "Wh— what do you mean *our*?"

He reached for her, pulling at her waist and pressing her against himself. "She took my innocence, Rose. Just as she took away your control, with lies and power given to her by the Minister."

The burning in his own stomach eased marginally as he watched her eyes glow, not blue as he was used to seeing, but red as deep as the blood moon and yellow as bright as fire.

A sadistic smile etched his face, watching the rage burn her too.

"She touched you," she bit out, her hand shaking as she gripped the collar of his coat.

"She did much worse than that. If you come with me, you can punish her for what she did to me then I'll cut her to ribbons for what she did to you." He didn't recognize the voice vibrating in his throat, but he didn't care. Ravana had to be punished, then sent to Nemain.

The flames in her eyes flared for a moment as she considered taking him up on his offer. Then she shook her head and the flames abated.

"No."

"No?"

"You can't kill her. I've tried, there's some sort of spell protecting her."

"We haven't tried together," he growled, liking the sound of it too much. He wanted to do this with her. The idea that she could stand beside him as an equal as they eradicated their enemies was a thought all too appealing.

She pushed away from him. "Even if we succeed, Khelitian lives would be forfeit."

"Not if we get there first."

Her fists balled, shaking beside her. "It's too risky."

Why would she ever try to stop him? If anyone deserved his wrath, it was Ravana. His rage returned tenfold; some of it, frustration at the songbird for trying to stand in his way. She occupied the space before him, right in the direction of the Temple.

"Out of my way, Rose," he warned. He didn't want to hurt her, but Kayden and the beast were too close to the surface, and he didn't trust them not to.

"No, I can't let you do this and get yourself killed." He scoffed at her little faith. Ravana was no match for him. "You aren't thinking clearly. Once you kill Ravana, how will you get to Kheli and fend off an entire army by yourself? You don't know where your devils are, you don't have a ship. I want to kill her same as you, but we need to be smart about this."

It might already be too late, Sam reminded.

He'd read that grimoire cover to cover; he knew exactly what Ravana was capable of and what she must have been seeking next. It was the one thing that could save one's soul from the price of using the grimoire.

We must get to her first, Kayden barked, taking the body's reins and steering them onward.

Rose took another couple steps back, keeping distance between them. "I don't want to do this, James. Don't make me." She reached into her cloak pulling out the Stone. It glowed faintly silver, but mostly lilac as Macha's moon grew to its fullest.

He ignored her threats. He'd walk right past her, straight to the Temple and the priestess waiting inside. She wouldn't dare stop him.

As he thought it, he heard humming.

His eyes snapped to her just as vines grew out from the ground to wrap around his legs. They tightened, holding him in place.

He tugged at them, but they were stronger than they looked.

"These won't hold me for long," he promised. With enough force, he'd tear straight past the rope vines.

"They aren't meant to," she responded, a glint of darkness shadowing her eyes.

GIVE ME STRENGTH

He tugged at the vines around his ankles, but more came around his wrists, tightening with every second.

GIVE ME LENGTH

Rose's eyes glowed blue as the Sumerian Sea in summer, an aura of blue mist surrounding her. She was damn magnificent.

OH CREATURE OF THE SEA

Lightning flashed behind her, highlighting her silhouette. She was so beautiful, he ached to touch her. A need purer than the anger that rose up in his body. But the vines began to lose strength, bending to his movements. He laughed through her song, the sound hollow.

LEND ME POWER

"Love, you've made me ravenous. You best find another way to keep me back."

FOR THE HOUR

"Because the moment I'm free of these, I'm going to claim every inch of you, slowly, intimately, until you're begging me to stop. Then I shall unleash myself on your enemies."

FOR YOU, GODDESS THREE

Her song stopped, the unmistakable haze of lust clouding her eyes.

He broke free, slicing his arms through the vines and lunging for her. With one hand on her throat, the other on her back, he swept her legs out from under her, landing in the mud. The Stone knocked from her hand, landing just out of her reach.

Phantom leaned down, his breath coasting over her lips. "I told you to keep me back, little songbird."

But her eyes weren't full of fear, nor lust. Rather, a smirk tipped her lips.

"I am."

Before he understood her meaning, a large arm wrapped around his waist pulling him off her. It jerked him until his back smashed against stone and mud, rain pelting his face. He groaned, lifting his head up to see an arm, but not a human one, pinning him to the ground.

It was a blue glowing tentacle the size of a tree trunk, the illusion as solid as a true kraken arm. He squirmed below it, rearing his back to slip past it, but more smaller tentacles sprouted from the ground around him. One seized his wrist like a manacle before slamming it to the ground. Next was his ankles, then his other wrist, until he was spread out in the mud.

Rose's eyes glowed brilliantly as she stalked toward him, her cloak was gone, the tight fitting, wet clothing leaving nothing to the imagination as it clung to her legs. Her nipples peaked from beneath the fabric, begging for his touch. It was quite possibly the sexiest thing he had ever seen. His body responded to hers as she lowered herself to sit on his lap. He noticed too late the blade as it pressed against his throat.

His blade.

His smile returned as rage simmered away, replaced with something equally as burning.

"You are glorious."

A smile tipped her lips as she stared down at him. He was completely at her mercy.

"You will take Ravana's life, but not today. We will take her on together when we are ready."

"I'm beginning to believe there isn't anything you can't do."

Logic finally broke through his rage haze as a realization came to him. The sight of those scars flashing across his memory. If Rose couldn't handle Ravana on her own, could he?

She pressed the knife into this skin. "Is this a fancy of yours, love?"

"I need your word, James. You won't go after her until *I* say so."

He nodded. "Aye, you have my word."

She leaned back, sheathing his knife back to her thigh, but all he could focus on was her delicious hips straddling him. The tentacle arms still had him pinned, otherwise his hands would be all over her body.

"Rose darling," he purred.

Her attention lifted to him.

"Unless you plan to use these extra arms, would you banish them? I'd like to make good on my other threats."

Desire glazed over her eyes, but it was still pouring down rain. Not ideal for their first.

She stood, backing up a couple steps, before the tentacles winked out, releasing him. But this time he caught it, the wince, the way her shoulders slumped.

"Love?"

Those heavy breaths returned. She was breathing too deeply.

He lunged, catching her just in time for her to fall into his arms.

"Rose?" He eased her to the ground, putting a hand to her wet face. But there was no response.

"Rose!"

CHAPTER 28
ONLY A FEAST

The sun set low in a mosaic of purples and yellows on what promised to be a lovely night. Phantom entered from high town with the rest of the nobles invited to the feast. Apparently, there hadn't been a feast in a long time, and they buzzed with the opportunity to see inside the Fortress. The Minister's lavish lifestyle enchanted many of them.

Phantom had brought Rose back to her chambers, laying her in her bed before slipping back into the night. She had used too much power fighting him off. He was ashamed he forced her to such action that would harm her.

Even thinking about Ravana now had his blood boiling with red and yellow tinting his vision.

He hadn't seen Rose the day after, when he planned to hunt her down to ask about the feast. Though, he couldn't avoid it, he wanted to understand the cost. He had planned to ask her after their visit to the cave, but he lost the opportunity.

He spent the next day walking by her chambers and searching the Fortress grounds, but never finding her.

Phantom introduced himself as Lord Castellanos repeatedly, surprised to find that no one had met the elusive meat trader who lived on the South side of the island.

The Minister ensured that Castellanos' hermit ways had continued once Phantom had abandoned the role. He wondered what he held over the lord's head for such a feat.

Phantom wore a ridiculous blue tailcoat and a silver silk scarf. His undershirt was filled with ruffles and lace that peeked through his other layers. The scarf, of course, was to cover his tattoo. With his hair styled back and his beard shaved, he truly felt like a nobleman. Dread pooled in his stomach. Or maybe that was the fact that he knew going to this feast was a bad idea, yet he had no way out of it.

He'd meant to ask Rose why he should avoid it, but his time with her had been cut short.

The Commodore insisted on teaching him what he should know to pull off a convincing noble. He only paid attention to half of it, distracted by his songbird's absence in the Fortress.

Besides, he'd fooled Lockness once before without help. He also had to avoid the gaze of Lord Desmond, who had seen him as an officer.

But Ashby's attention prevented him from warning Black and Clare if they were still at the inn. The chances were unlikely, and he wasn't sure how the warning would help, anyway. If Black knew it, they'd be there to save Phantom and they would both pay dearly for it.

A couple of servants entered with him instead. They had only just been assigned to him, so their names were already forgotten. One was an older, meek man with glasses who seemed more inclined to spend his time in libraries than trivial feasts. He named the man Alejandro.

The other was a younger woman with a permanently scrunched nose, as if she smelled something bad. He'd call her Sonia.

The ballroom was magnificent. Fabrics draped the edges of

the room in reds, blacks, and golds, with tapestries depicting roses and other beautiful plant life. It all reflected Quenceria, the mother country for most of Samsara, even if the Minister himself had no ancestry there. The Minister had been sent to the island before the War, as an occupation from Brettania. But with Brettania cut off from them and Quenceria long gone, it was best to celebrate the culture most of the people knew.

Candles littered the ballroom in droves, making sure every square inch of the glittering ballroom was lit, from the magnificent chandelier to the table centerpieces. Phantom's brow raised. The amount of wealth in the room really shouldn't be possible, and the ogling stares of the nobles confirmed it.

They were rich, yet they stared.

He'd seen some of their houses. It was old money and family heirlooms that made their homes lavish. All this however, was new money, so where was he getting it from?

Phantom took in the people arriving. Lord Desmond was in attendance, and he didn't want to risk recognition. Lockness needed to have no reason to doubt Phantom's validity.

Black's life depended on it.

Then he spotted Rose, and air rushed out of his mouth. Relief washed over him at seeing her unharmed.

She was in a shimmering lilac gown with her air delicately curled and hanging around her face. The dress was perfect for dancing, flaring out at her hips in layers of lace and fabric.

She spun in circles with Ashby and a well of jealousy rolled up inside him. He knew the Commodore's interests didn't lie with her, neither did hers with him. But the mere fact that they were comfortable dancing with one another and that he wasn't the one with his arms currently wrapped around her waist sent a trembling growl through his chest.

"Alejandro, hold my table," Phantom ordered. He could get used to people waiting on him. The devils didn't exactly cater to his needs. He could imagine Jon sending him a choice finger if he dared to try it.

The old man blinked before realizing who Phantom was speaking to. He went to the table marked for Lord Castellanos and stood there. It surprised Phantom that he didn't object to the name. Did anyone bother to learn his name? Guilt washed over him as he realized he was guilty of the same. Maybe he'd learn the man's real name just because no one else did.

The woman he felt significantly less guilty over.

"Sonia, have a bourbon ready at my table." She glared at him, clearly knowing he was talking to her.

"Will that be all?" She seethed through her teeth. Apparently, she had pulled the short end of the stick with this assignment.

Phantom only nodded, his attention going back to the glittering lilac floating across the dance floor. He straightened his back and swept a hand along his styled hair. It was odd, feeling it cling to his head rather that shift and roll about. All he wanted to know was what Rose would think of the new style.

The song ended and Ashby led her off the floor, both clapping at the band. He offered her a glass of water, which she took, smiling gently.

His face was a mask of duty as he spotted Phantom closing in on them, then his eyes narrowed, knowing his old friend too well.

"Commodore," Phantom started, manipulating his voice higher and airier than normal to reflect on how a nobleman would talk. Still, Rose recognized it, turning her panicked eyes to him and nearly spitting her drink on him. "I don't believe you have introduced me to the lady."

The Commodore grunted almost imperceptibly, but Phantom saw the irritation in his eyes. "I have not. This is Lady Davenport, daughter to the Minister himself and *my* fiancé."

The way he said it would have felt like a possessive warning to anyone else, but Phantom knew Ashby.

Phantom raised his brows in mock surprise, but Ashby turned to Rose. "Miss Davenport, this is Lord Castellanos. He trades in the meat markets."

Rose shook her head slightly, as if dispelling her shock. Then he recognized the ire in her eyes. "Lord Castellanos," she nearly gritted out. "I did not know you were coming."

He wanted to explain, but he wouldn't get a chance to, not yet. He took her hand instead, placing a kiss to her knuckles.

"It's a pleasure, love." He let his eyes capture hers in the romantic lighting of the candles. Her chest fell as he watched her melt before him. Maybe there was something about him being cleaned up, the shaven face, the clothes that were making her turn to putty before him. Whatever it was, he hoped he could explore it the next time they were alone.

Her other hand clutched the locket at her chest as if leaning on it for strength. When his eyes found hers again, they were glassy. Something was wrong. So completely wrong.

The music started up again as another dance began. "May I?"

She dipped her head in agreement. The Commodore seemed ready to combust as Phantom stole Rose away to the dance floor. But Ashby's eyes locked on something near the entrance. Lockness had arrived, but his task could wait a moment.

After all, cornering him upon arrival would be suspicious. There were better ways to approach the crime lord.

Once Phantom dragged Rose to the dance floor, he placed one hand on her waist, the other held her hand, but instead of holding it out like the other men did with their partners, he kept their hands close. The position was more intimate.

The two of them fell into the dance like they were made to move together.

"I didn't know you could dance, my lord." Some of the ire had disappeared from her tone, making her sound annoyed.

He looked down at her, taking in the glow of her, the feel of her skin, her waist. "I think you'll find I hold a great deal of surprises."

Her brows rose. "Is that so?"

He leaned in, whispering in her ear. "Surprises like how I intend to worship you like a man seeking penance." She sucked in a sharp breath, nearly faltering in her steps, but he kept them steady. "Or how you will sing for me, gracing me with that beautiful voice as I bring you to the brink of pleasure."

"James." The name came out in a soft whisper, more breath than voice. He felt hot all over. Or perhaps that was her radiating heat. He could feel it, her warmth seeping into him, making him want more of it. More of her.

She broke the spell, looking up at him. "You can't be here."

He chuckled at the breathiness that was still in her voice. "And why is that, love? What is so terrible about my being here?"

She swallowed, the final bit of heat drifting away. The music ended and he reluctantly let her go, knowing that if he lingered too long, he'd draw unwanted attention.

Rose leaned forward anyway, her eyes serious. "You need to leave. I can't stop it."

"Can't stop what?" The panic was back in her eyes and dread returned to his stomach. "Rose, what's going to happen?"

"I see you have met," the Minister's gritted voice came from Phantom's side, breaking their moment and stopping their conversation.

"Ah, yes, she is a beautiful dancer."

"Well, I dare say my daughter has little interest in butcher houses." A small chuckle escaped the Minister before he turned to Rose. "Rose, come with me."

She nodded, heading after him without looking back at

Phantom. Her words rang in his ears. He knew he should leave, but he couldn't. Not with what was at stake.

The cutting glare the Minister sent his way was enough to remind him of that very fact. His eyes darted across the room and Phantom followed the gaze, landing on Lockness. The order was clear enough. He was out of time and had to follow through.

He nodded, dipping his head politely to each of them. "Minister. Miss Davenport." She granted him one last glance, and the sadness in her eyes couldn't be mistaken. He didn't know what this night would mean to her, but he hoped he could still avoid it.

The Minister's punishing grip on her arm was enough to pull her away. A growl rumbled in his throat at the sight.

Phantom took a breath to dispel his monster, then straightened his posture and walked, but he didn't walk to Lockness. No, the man had spotted him. With everything that had transpired between them, he knew the Lord would be curious enough to approach him.

So, Phantom went to his table for that drink.

Sonia stood there with his drink in her hand and her face impossibly more displeased. Clearly, she wasn't a fan of the way he had danced with Rose, but it wasn't up to Sonia. He took the drink and sipped at the liquid gold. It was an expensive bourbon. Not the same as Desmond's, but similar. He missed rum and Goddess spirits. As cheap as those came, they were strong. He could use a good, strong drink for the night.

The sun hadn't even fully set yet; the sky cast in yellow and lilac, but it already felt like an endless night.

"Lord Ferdinand Castellanos," Lockness stated as if he was witnessing a wonder. "You've finally ventured from your abode."

Phantom turned to see Lockness arrive before him in as much lavish glory as he himself adorned. Instead of a drink, he had a cigar in hand, adding to the smoke in the room. The smell reminded him of Ramirez, and homesickness set in.

"Lord Lockness," Phantom addressed as casually as he could, reminding himself he had to charm the lord. "Forgive me for not responding to you all this time."

"No, no," he started, but he seemed irritated. There weren't many who rejected attention from Lockness. "I understand. Your interest was purely a business venture. So, when my legacy was no longer on the table, I expected your absence."

Phantom raised his brows. "Did you? Well, I must admit it tempted me, but when your daughter disappeared, I did not want to be involved. I thought it," he searched for the right word, "inappropriate."

Lockness hummed. "And that little display on the dance floor with the Minister's daughter was what? Respectful?"

Phantom didn't contain his smirk. He wanted the entire room to see them and know she was his. A foolish hope now, but he could be patient. He leaned into the Lockness, showing his desire for discretion.

Lockness willingly lent his ear.

"You called me a businessman, my lord. What kind of businessman would I be if I did not seek the best Samsara has to offer?"

Lockness lifted his head away, searching his eyes. "You plan to steal the Commodore's position as heir?" He said softly enough for only Phantom to hear.

"Can you blame me?" Phantom narrowed his eyes at the man, setting his trap. "If you had a chance to take this entire island, would you not do it?"

A small smile tugged at Lockness's mouth. "Rather ambitious of you."

Phantom sucked in a breath. "I have a dream, my lord, which involves a better Samsara, one that will finally prosper after the fall of mankind."

Lockness stared at him for a moment. "How long are you in town?" He raised his cigar to take another puff.

"I have no plans to return home yet." He let his eyes wonder to where Rose sat next to the Minister. "As you can see, I have much work to do here."

Lockness nodded. "Come to my estate tomorrow. We can talk business, Castellanos. Trust me when I say you'll want to hear what I have to offer."

Phantom realized what an opportunity this was, not for the Minister, but for him to find Serena. From Indigo's vision, he knew Serena was with the witch sons, and that Lockness was charged with their capture.

He'd be a fool to let that leverage go even if he was unwilling to supply Ravana with what she wanted. Seeing Lockness's estate could give him some clue as to the beastie's whereabouts.

Phantom nodded his acceptance.

Satisfied, Lockness left, returning to his table of equally pretentious nobles. Although they were more like flies, clinging to him. They only hoped to gain scraps of his favor. But Phantom knew it was better to capture the attention of a man like Lockness by making him work for it. Lockness will think his eyes are on the Minister, making his diversion a perfect setup.

CHAPTER 29

WHERE THERE IS SMOKE

The party continued, and Rose disappeared.

Phantom was torn between trying to find her and leaving. Clearly, something was going to happen that he wouldn't like, but he was worried that very thing would hurt her as well.

Sonia was more than helpful at supplying drinks, his mind growing fuzzier, which was Nemain blessed since he ended up at Lockness's table. All his noble followers buzzing like gnats with their provincial conversations. Many tried to speak to Phantom about the meat trade, wanting to extend the trade partnerships they had with Castellanos. Apparently, the Lord was known for his strict dealings. He never allowed one more than another, a situation that kept many of the nobles on even ground. It was a smart way to run a business, but it left the nobles eager to earn favor.

Little did they know it would mean nothing to build that relationship with a pirate Captain.

"Have you heard the legend of a jinn hidden somewhere on the island?" William had two too many brandies to be considered of sound mind, but his chosen topics grew more interesting with each drink, so Phantom wasn't inclined to stop him.

Phantom leaned back in his chair, combing a casual hand through his hair. "I'm afraid I haven't heard of someone mention a jinn since I was a child. By all accounts, they are not among Davina's creation."

The man's eyes lit up, his grey whiskers tipping up with his smile. "That's just it, Ferdinand."

Another man groaned beside him, significantly younger. Phantom believed they were father and son from the familial way they spoke to one other, given their ages. "I beg you, do not get him started."

"I will not bore you with my Draiocht theologies. Half this island thinks I'm insane, anyway." His clothes were as fine as anyone else's, but Phantom enjoyed the way he brightened upon speaking of things the other noble gnats considered crazy.

"I don't know, my lord. It is always the crazy ones who see the truth before anyone else does." Gaining the trust of the nobleman might be of some use, and from the way his smile widened into a grin, he hit his mark.

"Davina, spare me."

"Well, the how is not important. A jinn is simply a powerful being, the ultimate power aside from the Goddesses themselves. Granting wishes is the least they can do, but if you befriend one, they will do anything for you."

Phantom blinked at the notion. He'd been told they were creatures that rose from the earth to grant wishes to those true of heart. At least that was the children's version of the story. But a jinn that walked the land of their own free will would be a force to be reckoned with.

"I believe the Minister has one."

Now, that was where the man lost him. Phantom burst out laughing before he could stop himself. If the Minister had a jinn, much would change. Firstly, he wouldn't need a pirate to gain the trust of a troublesome crime lord.

The man frowned at being mocked.

"I'm sorry, you give the Minister too much credit."

"Look," he snapped too forcefully. It drew Phantom's attention. "Look around you." Phantom took in the glittering tapestries, the impressive marble arches, the painted ceiling, things he didn't bother taking in the first time. It was wealth beyond the means of anyone on the island. "Those arches resemble the ones in Magari, and those tapestries are from thirteenth century Favilla, and—and those drapes are from the traveling markets of Carmen."

"What is your meaning?" Yes, the Minister had some impressive trade routes set up to achieve the level of finery in this room alone.

"The Minister doesn't have the means for any of it. Most of these countries are dead. Atlas won't trade with an island that has nothing to offer. Not to mention, marble and many other materials needed for these don't exist here, or the people with the trade skills for it." The man began breathing more heavily. "None of this should exist, so why does it?"

Just as the pieces were tying in, something wet sloshed against his back, followed by the unmistakable sound of glass shattering. But it wasn't the spill or the glass that surprised him. No, it was the voice and the scent of cigar smoke.

"Oh, clumsy me. I'll pick that up straight away."

Phantom's head snapped behind him faster than he intended. Sure enough, there stood his fellow devil, dressed as a servant. Ramirez blended in with a meek voice and a pair of spectacles dark enough to hide his Kalonite eyes.

A towel came upon Phantom's back as Ramirez made a show of cleaning up the lord he offended. Phantom schooled his features into that of distaste rather than surprise.

"Disgraceful. The Minister must see to the insolence of his servants."

"I'm terribly sorry, my lord." Phantom felt the moment a note slipped into his pocket. Ramirez wasn't the best pick-pocket, but he was learning.

Phantom straightened his lapels but winked at the old man when he knew no one could see.

A too subtle smirk tipped the corner of Ramirez's mouth before he relaxed his face, disappearing into the fray of servants.

"Do you know what they say about Kalonites, good sir?"

"Father, he doesn't want any more of your prattling."

Phantom itched to read the note Ramirez risked his life to deliver. He nodded at the men respectfully. "If you'll excuse me, gentlemen."

But the man seemed to not hear, even as Phantom walked away. "They say Kalonite blood is Macha-blesse—" The combined effort of Phantom's disinterest and party goers drowned out the man's latest theory. He could admit the lord was on to something with the finery inside the Fortress being impossible, but Phantom doubted it had anything to do with a jinn.

He found a shadowed corner of the ballroom to inspect the note in his pocket and Earhart's bold script.

I hear there is a festival in low town tonight.

Curious, is it not?

Phantom smiled to himself. His devils were in low town. To anyone who didn't know, this was an innocent enough note, but Phantom knew it meant he'd see his devils tonight. Maybe he could speak to Ramirez and Earhart about all he'd discovered.

The Davina pendant—

Candle lights dimmed all around the ballroom, the room growing darker as the music took on an eerie melody. There was a resonance to the music that resembled Carmen, with deep drums and tambourines. The Carmen troops would circle the world before the War, trading and entertaining, but they were often discredited due to their sensual entertainment.

Sure enough, dancers appeared on the floor. Even in the dim lighting, Phantom could recognize some women who waited on the Minister. Orphans. Same as him but trained for a different purpose.

They wore costumes like Carmenian entertainers, glittering with fabrics adorned in jewels. The bottoms flowed with thin gossamer fabric that was slit in several places to allow their legs a wide range of motion. Their bellies were on full display and their chests barely covered. It was an odd sight to see and wildly inappropriate for an official event.

Rose's warning prickled in the back of his mind. This was it. This is what she warned him about. It had to be, but he had yet to figure out how these women were a threat to him.

They began to dance; sensually, with their hips moving primarily and the rest of their bodies following suit.

Phantom looked at the other men for a clue as to what was happening.

William's hand came down on his back. "Relax, boy. The Minister puts on this show every feast he calls for the nobles. It's the reason many of the men even come."

Phantom brow shot up. There were many wives who came along with their husbands, scowls on their faces. He couldn't imagine this was good for anyone.

William downed the rest of his brandy, and Phantom winced at the casual waste of expensive booze. "During the song, the women will choose five lucky men to come to the dance floor. All you must do is sit there and enjoy them."

William's son gagged beside him. "Father, please."

The old man chuckled. "Dear boy, an old man like me has no business around these girls. This entertainment is for you and for Ferdinand here." At the incredulous looks Williams got, he laughed again. "Loosen up, boys. You are both young and unattached, enjoy it."

A quick glance around had Phantom's hackles rising. Lockness had mysteriously disappeared, along with the Minister and the Commodore.

Phantom stood, taking that as his cue to leave. He had no interest in enjoying the attentions of girls who likely didn't choose this position. Not to mention, the only attentions he sought involved a certain songbird.

As if his thoughts summoned her, the music changed, and she entered, standing out as the centerpiece of the whole chorus. While other women's costumes were colorful, she stood out in stark white with glistening silver gemstones. But it wasn't her outfit that caught his attention. It was her belly, with flawless skin on display.

He blinked, reevaluating her. But when he gazed at her skin again, it was still flawless. Did he dream up that entire night with her? Did they not kiss in the glittering cave? Did he not feel the scars on her with his own hands?

She danced like the others in the room, and he lost his ability to think. Her lips weren't smiling like the others in the room. She looked like this was a death march, not a dance.

He wanted to snatch her away, understand what was happening and why she looked so scared.

He stared at her for so long; he didn't notice when a hand wrapped around his forearm and pulled at him. Glancing down, his gaze caught the eyes of a familiar red head. It was the woman from the bar. The one who tried to get him to dance with her. Her big green eyes looked up at him and he finally noted the emerald Carmenian costume she wore. She was a dancer for the Minister and yet he saw her at the bar.

Alarm bells rang in his head.

"Come, my lord," she whispered, "I know just the girl to pair you with."

He wanted to pull away. Something was very wrong.

But her head tossed to the dance floor, pointing out Rose, who circled her hips with expert skill. The woman pulled him towards Rose, and he couldn't fight the draw. If it wasn't him, some other man was going to be pulled in front of her. His neck prickled at the thought.

He let her pull him to the dance floor but pulled back right before they reached the edge. With a fierce grip, he snatched her back and whispered into her ear. "If I find out you have done anything to endanger Rose, I will gut you myself and spread your entrails out before the Minister, so he knows the cost of spying on me."

Her eyes met his, and they didn't look even marginally scared. Even a smile spread across her lips. "Don't make promises you can't keep, Captain."

He tipped his head up, but she dragged him to the middle of the floor. Phantom glared at the woman, so she knew her days were numbered, but it held no weight. Once he sat in the center most chair, she trotted away.

Around him, four noblemen were placed in similar chairs, all facing the same direction.

There wasn't a correlation between the men that he could tell. Some were old, some were young, but all were noble guests. There were some who looked eager to take part, others who seemed like they were being forced to endure the "entertainment".

Another shiver traveled along his spine, but it dissipated the moment a pair of golden eyes locked with his. He thought she was scared before. Now she looked utterly terrified. He itched to fight whatever caused that hopeless look in her eyes, but the only thing that seemed to cause it was him.

That couldn't be right. Had he imagined her attraction to him this whole time? He must have imagined the scars as well, because her skin was perfectly clear and untouched.

Perhaps she's the spy, Kayden supplied.

Phantom shook his head, dispelling that thought.

Part of him appreciated the costume she was in, but he couldn't escape the feeling of wrongness souring the moment. His hands gripped the arms of the chair. Phantom wouldn't dare make the fear in her eyes worse, but this entire show was designed to tempt him. The curve of her waist to the flare of her hips had his mouth salivating. He tried to expel the thoughts, but he knew she could see the hunger rising in his gaze. It was too long. It was taking too long and every inch of him begged to claim her body. He wanted her more viscerally than he ever wanted anything.

Still, the fear in her eyes refused to fade, and he noticed how she had stopped dancing, as if rejecting her participation. He furrowed his brow, wondering if she was about to stop whatever was about to happen.

Another dancer grabbed her wrist, whispering into her ear. He didn't recognize the woman, but whatever she said was enough to steel Rose's features. All the fear vacated her body, replaced by a cool detachment.

The other woman left as Rose's eyes locked onto Phantom's like a target. The music changed once more and Rose's eyes changed with it, her hips moving to the rhythm. Her eyes glowed a brilliant cerulean blue, but she was not singing. Instead of ribbons of light or kraken tentacles, a blue dust lifted off her jolting hips. It swirled in the air, lifting like smoke and traveling about the room. It landed on a man next to Phantom and he breathed in the blue smoke, his eyes changing to the same color as Rose's. But the rest of him went blank as if he were no longer present in his own body.

Fear and betrayal pierced his heart as he refocused on the songbird coming steadily towards him. Would she do that to him? Turn him into a mindless servant like that man in the mess hall.

He saw the blow land, and she saw the betrayal in his eyes, a tear streaming down her cheek, but she did not stop. It was too late. The smoke was all around him. Eventually, he'd have to take a breath.

Phantom opened his lungs, and the blue smoke came rushing in, eager to make him bend to the Minister's will. No more fight. No more chances left. He felt the smoke wash over him, forcing him to submit, to abandon himself to the trenches of his own mind. Blue traveled across his vision. He knew his eyes looked like hers when Rose let out a nearly imperceptible sob at the sight.

But another part of him answered.

The beast rushed up to meet the intrusive blue smoke, extinguishing its hold and burning away any submission, any will beyond his own. The monster rushed so quickly and forcefully that it eviscerated the blue in his vision, replacing it with red so vibrant the room appeared to be bathed in blood. A growl deepened his voice, making Rose flinch.

She looked down at him, within arm's reach, witnessing the beast come forward. She stepped away, a fresh fear entering her eyes.

Flames of yellow flickered at the edges of his mind.

Yes, let her be afraid of us. She betrayed us.

The growl came back, and she jerked away, seeing violence in his eyes. Phantom fought the rage. She wouldn't have done this to him. She could have last night when she had him pinned to the ground, at her mercy.

The only reason she did so now had to do with the Minister.

But one voice bellowed above the chaos in his head, reaching to take the reins.

She just tried to take everything *from us.*

Yellow swarmed his vision like all consuming fire.

CHAPTER 30

THERE IS FIRE

Rose ran before the dance finished, but her part was over. The four men around him were only defanged necromites, ready and willing to follow orders.

A glance around the room told Phantom that it affected every man there, but not as deeply. The other men went about their conversations, laughing like nothing had changed, but the blue glistening in their eyes told another story. Could no one else see the blue? Maybe that was the monster protecting him, because the wives looked bored or angry, but no blue tinted their eyes. Yet, they didn't notice the change in their husbands.

He didn't have time to ponder what it meant. He needed answers from the songbird.

And teach her what it means to betray us.

"No," Phantom bellowed as he slipped out into the empty hallway. His new expensive shoes clicked against the marble floor. He shed them, cantering down the hall in the direction she went. He scented burning flowers and followed it.

He abandoned his scarf, his tattoo on full display, but no one was in the halls to witness it. There were entirely too many layers covering his body and he needed them off. He left a trail of clothes behind until only his billowing white undershirt and dark trousers were left. He undid the top couple buttons so the fabric wouldn't suffocate him so much.

Marching through the Fortress halls, he sniffed out the songbird as her scent drew closer. She was close, so he stopped and turned, barreling through a door and entering a tearoom where Rose sat alone, sobbing into her hands.

Her head shot up as she stared at Phantom, half undressed and fuming. Kayden's rage too tangible to ignore. His eyes blazed crimson and amber like he was drowning in blood and fire.

"What? How—" she tripped over her words.

"Confused?"

Her mouth opened and closed as if she wanted to say more but couldn't unscramble her thoughts.

"Confused why I'm not a mindless solider? Why your spell didn't work on us?" Kayden's voice came through with his, mixing them together until he wasn't sure where one began and the other ended.

"It really didn't work?"

He growled, low and deep in his throat. The anger that he felt was too strong, too raw. He sprung on her, pushing her back until her back collided with the wall.

"Do I look tamed to you?"

More tears flowed, but he finally could see what they were. Relief.

She smiled faintly as her hands came up his chest and landed on the sides of his head. "You're okay. You're still you?"

Something inside him softened at the raw emotion in her eyes. "Yes, love. All five of me."

The words broke her as a sob tore from her throat and her knees gave out. He caught her before she fell to the floor, cradling her to his chest. Her salty tears fell to the skin under his open shirt and her sobs broke his heart.

Damn it.

It was difficult to stay mad at her.

She tried to take our free will, Kayden whispered.

After a few moments, she righted herself, sniffing and standing up straight. He couldn't help but wipe her tears away. He couldn't bear to see them anymore.

He leaned into her a little deeper, with his hands on either side of her head. His monster was too close, too ready for blood. He could smell and hear every beating inch of her. He could smell that unmistakable smoky sweetness that he wanted nothing more than to drown in. Was it fear that got her heart racing? Or something else?

The beast seemed to understand it too, and he realized there was another scent on her that made his beast crave something else. It aroused her. Very much so. The knowledge had his heart beating faster.

You would have been the Minister's mindless slave and it would have been because of her. Kayden demanded action from him.

He growled deep in his throat, expelling the rising desire, or at least abating it, until he had his answers.

"What. Happened?" He bit out the words.

Her mouth opened and closed, not wanting to tell him, but ultimately sighed as she gave in to him.

"He forced me to do it. When I refused, he threatened your life." He ground his teeth. The Minister would kill him eventually, anyway. It was the only happy ending for the Minister, becoming the hero and slaying the pirate who tormented the people, but Phantom intended on retaining his mind when he faced the gallows. "But that didn't work."

His eyes drilled into hers, demanding her truth. "I know your life means more to the Minister right now than my obedience. But when I called his bluff—" Another sob caught in her throat. "They took Lara. She's my only friend and she'll die because of me. With both of you gone, I didn't—I couldn't—"

He heard the pain in her voice and remembered the scars that were supposed to be all over her body. The ones suspiciously absent tonight.

"Rose," he said, deathly calm. "Did they do something to you?" With one silver lined look from her, he knew they used more than threats to get her to cooperate.

A fresh wave of tears flowed down her cheeks, and he knew it was bad. With his beast senses so close, he should smell the metallic scent of blood on her. His eyes drilled into hers, a fear more powerful than his anger taking over.

With great effort, she let out a series of hums, but no words accompanying them. Then her skin faded from flawless and glistening to marred and mutilated.

Right in the middle of her chest was a new one. It trailed from the apex of her collarbone all the way down to her naval. It was jagged and highly raised, as if the nightmare that inflicted it was trying to kill her slowly. He blinked as if he could deny its existence. That wasn't a wound that people came back from.

Before his fury hit him completely, his fist went directly through the wall next to her face. Bits of brick and mortar covered his hand, then crumbled to the wall beside them. Rose didn't even flinch.

His beast was close, ready to tear from his skin, too close to stop it. Not with the sight of how close he came to losing her, and he didn't even know it.

If they had killed her—

His fangs sprouted from his mouth, ready to tear flesh open and seek vengeance for the songbird himself. He might have let it happen if she had not been in the way. Although, he was becoming less sure that he had any choice in the matter.

A growl, deep and primal, erupted from his throat. "Run. If you don't, I'll kill you."

She stared at him, not an ounce of fear in that beautiful

face. Her lips parted as she watched him struggle to keep the beast back.

He felt a hand on his chest, and he flinched away, snarling with the movement, but the hand paid no mind. It caressed his chest until two hands circled around his neck, flesh flush to his skin. He opened his eyes to see her only a breath away from him, staring at him like he was a miracle, not a goddess-cursed monster.

Rose's thumb drifted across his cheek where hair normally dusted his jawline with heavy stubble. But with the bloody disguise, it was smooth, freshly shaven.

A small, amused smile tipped her full lips. One he couldn't stop staring at. "I think I prefer the beard."

A flicker of amusement traveled through him, making the beast easier to restrain. It eased enough to let his own smile grow. "I'll be sure to grow it out."

Something just as strong, but infinitely sweeter, filled him and he became aware of every inch of her pressed against him. He wanted to feel her skin on his lips, imagining his hands on her bare hips, digging his fingers in hard enough to see her flesh bend with him. He wondered what her moans would sound like, what her desire would taste like.

As if she could see everything that flashed across his mind, she let out a heavy sigh that was so bloody close to a moan.

His eyes caught on that long, jagged scar again, and he wondered how she was so incredibly brave. If she had agreed to what they asked at any point, they would have stopped the torture, but she held out to the absolute limit of her body. All so she wouldn't have to enslave his mind.

Before he realized what he was doing, he moved a hand to feel that scar. The proof someone endured agonizing pain for his sake.

When his fingertips grazed the raised scar at the base of her throat, she sucked in a breath that drove him bloody insane.

"How did you heal so quickly?" If it had been his wound, Smith would have stitched him up and he'd be confined to his bed for days, at least. She was walking around, *dancing* without hinderance.

"I sang," she said breathlessly.

His brow furrowed as his hand came to rest on her collarbone and his thumb felt the very real raised skin of her scar. "But when you sang to Angelica, she was mortally wounded, and you healed her without a trace of a scar."

His thumb moved lower, and her eyes drifted shut, soaking in the intimate touch.

"I didn't finish the song. Ravana will only do it again if she doesn't see the scars on my body." He froze, beating back the rising beast again. His lack of movement gave her the breath to speak. "They're supposed to be reminders of my failures; I fail every time I try to fight back. I fail when the pain overcomes me. I'm not strong enough to resist her."

"And yet, you still fight." He studied the scars, not just the new horrific one, but the layers of scars on her stomach. He didn't see someone who was weak. Her eyes opened, but her breathing came in heavy sweeps. "Rose, you are the strongest person I know."

She sucked in air, a sob wrenching from her throat. They stayed there for a moment, but he'd stare at her for eternity if he could.

Until she broke the silence. "Kiss me."

Her body moved, bending to his hand, begging it to continue its descent.

A small chuckle left his throat, but it sounded more like a growl. "If I kiss you now, love, I'll scarcely be able to stop. Can't you see how you've completely bewitched me?"

Her eyes grew heavy but intense. She had no intention of stopping him.

"That's precisely the point, Captain."

He let a smirk tip his lips as he obliged to her demands, continuing the descent of his hand. "I knew I'd get you to beg for me one day."

His hand shifted until it was trailing right between the swells of her breasts. Even with the presence of that reddened scar, her skin was soft. Her heartbeat raced in her chest, matching the rhythm of his own. His thumb crept inside her barely existent top to graze the underside of her breast and she moaned.

It was his complete and utter undoing.

His other hand retracted from the wall to catch her head as he crashed into her. Phantom didn't understand how it could be possible for her to taste even sweeter than she did before, but she never failed to surprise him. Her mouth opened, inviting him. His tongue swept in the same moment his hand closed around her breast. Her breath hitched, and it resonated with him, charging him on.

He devoured her mouth, and she met him with just as much intensity, her leg coming up around him to draw him closer and her desire permeated the air like his very own aphrodisiac. He wanted to reach for that leg, feel her thighs and hips for himself, but he also couldn't bring himself to remove the hand at her head or her chest.

His desire pressed against her and with her leg around him, he felt her heat against him.

"James," she breathed like a prayer when he broke their kiss to trail more along her neck.

Finally, he moved his hand to her leg, feeling the thickness of her thigh, ready to rip the fabric directly off her skin. His other hand remained on her head as he nipped and kissed at the delicious skin of her neck. It reminded him of honey, the richness of her skin, and he wanted to find out how much of her tasted that way.

Phantom fell to his knees before her and her arms came

around his head, clutching him closer and tugging on the strands there. She was completely and blessedly ruining his perfectly styled hair.

He kissed her chest, keeping one hand glued to her thigh, which clung to his waist, the other reaching to free her perfect breasts from their sparkly white cage.

He paused, staring up at her like he was praying to a Goddess. Worship was exactly what he was planning to do with her. Exactly as he promised.

"You want this?" He had to be sure. He'd get one delectable taste of her, and he'd be addicted for the rest of his life, but if she didn't want it, it meant nothing. But by her heavy breaths, and the whimper complaining that he stopped, he knew what the answer would be.

He still needed to hear it.

"I want this, James. I want you."

With a growl and little strength from his monster, he ripped the fabric from her chest, baring her before him. She moaned at the bite of pain from the release of fabric, then nearly screamed when his lips closed around the sensitive peak of her breast.

"Uh, Captain?" Hyne's cursed voice came from the door.

Phantom growled deeply; he was almost certain it scared the devil back to whatever drain he crawled out of. Rose snapped to cover herself, but Phantom rose to block her from view. Then, with his gaze locked on her panicked eyes, he released the rest of the buttons of his shirt. He chuckled at the switch in her eyes as they looked at the devil behind him, then at his newly exposed chest.

"Wait for me in the hall, devil." The door closed to signal Hyne's obedience.

"Don't fret, love." He shed the shirt and raised it to her. "This is for you, since I destroyed yours. Though I could hardly call that a shirt." She snatched the shirt and clutched it to her chest, but before she could put it on, he leaned in. "This isn't nearly over."

The panic finally drained from her eyes enough to return his smoke. "Promises, promises, Captain." The sultry edge of her voice made his skin crawl with anticipation. Hyne had better be prepared for an early grave.

He backed away from her, even if the effort was nothing short of painful. "Call it a promise. Call it a vow. But I will draw every drop of pleasure from your body, and then some." He smirked as she sucked in a breath, reveling in the sight before he went through the door. He shut it to give her privacy, immediately dropping his smirk as he faced his devil.

Hyne wore a servant uniform like Ramirez had, a simple white and black pairing that was entirely too clean for the devil that didn't even deign to wash his face. But it was the sly smile on his lips that had Phantom's frustration paramount.

"If you say a bloody word—"

Hyne raised his hands. "Don't worry, Cap. Trust me, I wouldn't have interrupted you if it wasn't important."

"Then get on with it."

Instead of cowering at Phantom's rough tone, he chuckled at the bubbling irritation, knowing why he was drawing it from his Captain.

"You got Ramirez's note?"

"Aye."

"Well, there's something else. A woman approached Clare and begged her to find," he tossed his head to the door, "you know who. Apparently, there is a sick child."

As if he summoned the songbird, she emerged from the sitting room with his shirt on. An intense wave of masculine pride overcame him at the sight of her in his shirt. Even if he didn't own the shirt, or steal it, it was on *his* skin and now it wrapped around *her* body.

"Sick child? Where?" Her eyes locked on Hyne.

"The Wet Cat. The woman said you could help, and that there wasn't much time."

Rose raised her brows, then snapped to Phantom. "I need the Stone. It's in my rooms."

"Then we'd better hurry. I doubt you want anyone catching us in our current state."

"Where are your rooms?" Hyne blurted.

"Up the stairs, a few doors down." Rose pointed to the staircase that was in their view.

He smiled devilishly. "No worries, miss. I'll cause a distraction, and no one will be looking for you."

Phantom's lip curled, his frustration ebbing a bit with the new urgency. He grabbed her hand, and they ran for the stairs.

CHAPTER 31

CAPTIVE KNOWLEDGE

Rose changed quickly into her black clothes and cloak. Phantom did the same in his own chamber, opting to meet back at her room. He chose black for the sake of discretion. With Rose dressed in black as well, they looked like harbingers of death roaming the halls of the Fortress.

Or a pair of assassins.

Phantom liked the sound of that even if he much preferred the idea of both of their bodies without clothing present.

But that would have to wait. There wasn't much that could keep Phantom from making good on his promise immediately, but a child's life was one of them. Amongst another urgent issue.

Leaning against the wall outside her room, he waited for her. She exited without even noticing him, and he swore he'd have to teach her perception skills.

"Where do you think you're going?" She froze completely, then turned to face him. A ghost of a smile touched her lips.

"I was going to find you." She took the few steps back to him and he had to restrain himself from reaching out to her. Time and urgency kept his arms crossed.

He inspected her clothing, his eyes roaming over her waist, cinched in the tight clothing under her cloak, the flare of her hips that he didn't get nearly enough of earlier, and the small curve of her breasts which had him eager to pick up where they left off.

Finally, he noticed her devouring him with just as much hunger, sending delicious heat warming his body and coloring her cheeks.

His voice took on a deep vibrato. "Love, if you keep looking at me like that, I will forget every urgency keeping me from you."

She sucked in a breath, then shook her head to dispel the lust encircling them. "How are we getting out? The halls downstairs are crawling with guests and servants."

He tossed his head back to her room. "If I'm not mistaken, there's a particular balcony I remember you traipsing down frequently."

Her brows rose. "You think you can get down?"

He chuckled. "Of course I can."

***

"Bloody hell, how do you climb this, woman?"

She snickered as he glared at the smooth stones that made up the side of the Fortress, as if they were especially designed to prevent climbing.

"Do you sing to the stones in offering for a better foothold?" He was about to laugh at the ridiculous nature of his inquiry when he turned to face the songbird and her expression didn't protest. "You do?"

"Something like that." She climbed off the ledge of the balcony with a soft hum on her lips. Her foot reached the stone and somehow caught on an invisible ledge he couldn't see.

His mouth dropped open and she let out a breathy laugh at his expense. "Afraid of heights, Captain?"

He tilted his head in her direction. "Why don't you fly down then?"

Her smile faltered. "I don't know the right song."

"I shall need the details of exactly how that voice of yours works." He paused, remembering back to the ballroom where she hadn't been singing when his beast blocked her influence. "Or hips, it seems."

"And paintings," she blurted, her eyes widening as she realized what she gave away.

His brows knocked together as he recalled the paintings in the halls of the Fortress. The ones that weren't there when he lived in the Fortress before. His beast had a similar reaction to those images as it did to her dancing.

"Rose," he whispered dangerously. "How long has the Minister been trying to get ahold of my mind?"

Still dangling on the wall, she stared back at him with glistening eyes. "Since the moment you arrived." Instead of holding his eyes, she continued her descent down the wall, humming as she went to create new invisible footholds. Footholds that weren't there when he reached his foot out for one.

With a gruff groan, he returned to the balcony to look over the edge. Fine, she was using her goddess-given power, so would he.

He called on the beast, which was all too eager to answer his call. It had been waiting for action, even if bloodshed wasn't on the menu tonight. Although, the Minister was becoming dangerously close to the main course.

Red tipped the edges of his vision as he took a running start, using one hand on the railing to jump over the edge of the balcony. He bent his knees to absorb the shock.

Rose cried out as his boots hit the rocks below. The monster lent him enough durability and strength to land without more than a jolting wave through his legs.

Phantom glanced back at Rose and flashed a smile as fangs sprouted from his gums. "You're not the only one with secrets, love."

She made it down to the rocks with a crunch and gaped at him. "I would have helped you get down."

"Not my style." He enjoyed feeling the wind in his hair, the weightlessness in his limbs, and the thrill in his blood. Most would call him fool hearted to be addicted to the rush of energy, but he called it living.

"Oh no. You much prefer falling off things like cliff sides and women's balconies." Irritation rattled her tone, but there was an undercurrent of amusement.

"You like that I'm unpredictable. It keeps the thrill in your veins."

He gave her credit for trying to keep her face stony, but with a smirk from Phantom, it melted away, replaced by a bright smile.

Goddess that smile.

He pulled her to him, wrapping her in as much of him as he could, his lips crashing into hers. She leaned into the kiss, begging for him to deepen it. He obliged eagerly. It was so bloody intoxicating; he kept forgetting their urgency.

Phantom broke the kiss too soon and caught sight of her breathless wonder.

"We need to get going."

"Aye."

But he hadn't let her go yet.

I believe you were in a rush, Sam reminded.

He released her with a barely contained growl. She smiled at his show of restraint, pleased with herself for making it so hard on him. She turned towards the main road where she could find her way to low town.

But he cleared his throat. "This way, love."

"Low town is this way."

"But that infernal den of death and torture," he pointed in the opposite direction, "is that way."

"Why would we want to go there?"

"I presume Lara is there, waiting to be used as a tool against you."

Rose's eyes widen. Phantom had no intention of the Minister having anything to hold against Rose. He could hardly do anything about himself, but her friend, he could help.

"But where would she go? They'll find her and take her back. Not to mention, punish her for escaping."

He reached for her hand and laid it upon his chest, her eyes narrowing to where their skin was flush.

"Trust me." Her eyes blinked up to his, filled with equal parts despair and hope. "Lara will come aboard Nemain's Revenge. From there, it will be her decision where she goes next."

Silver lined her eyes and told of someone who didn't know how to ask for help. He'd make it his life's mission to be the person she counted on. She flung her arms around his neck, the force of her embrace powerful enough to knock him back a step, but he closed his arms around her.

"Thank you," she whispered.

With another tight squeeze, he released her. "We haven't the time to waste, love. We have too much to take care of in one night."

<hr>

They got in the same way as last time, with a soft hum from Rose and an immense amount of self-control. The beast could scent the blood from the accosted room before they ever managed their way in. It was much stronger this time and Phantom didn't want to understand why.

A twinge of guilt struck him in the back of his mind, and he wondered if it was wise bringing Rose back to her place of torture so soon after what had happened to her. Even if she didn't feel the physical pain of it anymore.

He kept his eyes off the walls as Rose pulled him through the room that reeked of blood and death. They reached the opposing door and Rose hummed again. She would have been a fantastic thief with that ability; not even hindered enough to pick the lock. He envied her talents.

Reaching the hall outside the torture room relieved him of the pungent smell, though it had a way of lingering.

"This way."

A few steps later, the hall turned into a cavernous expanse. Phantom had to keep his mouth shut. He expected prison cells and there were barred cells, but they contained endless bookshelves. He couldn't count the books present, but the rows took the shape of circles that tunneled down into the ground. The darkness that enveloped the bottom let him know there wasn't a way to know how far.

It was a prison *and* a library.

"My father considers this knowledge too powerful for Samsarans to possess. He has me sing the song of blocked perception to all the officers allowed in here. To them, all they see is prison bars." She stopped herself for a moment. "But he never has me sing to the prisoners."

The Minister had no intention of letting any prisoner survive a visit. Including Lara.

He squeezed her hand. "We'll get her out."

She responded with a quick breath to seal off her emotions, just for a moment, so she could accomplish what she came to do. He hated watching the habit take place. He hated that his songbird knew how to make herself numb, but he knew she needed to focus, he'd beat her walls down again later.

They crept along the walls of the prison library, and he couldn't help but think Ramirez would kill to get a glimpse of these books. He'd get his devil the chance. Besides whatever knowledge those dusty tomes possessed; they were dangerous enough to scare the Minister.

Why doesn't he burn them? Kayden was all logic and ambition. *It's what I would do with dangerous things.* The statement curdled Phantom's stomach. Kayden wasn't known for his kindness when he lived.

"She's going to be in the dark levels. That's where he sends people he hopes will go mad." She said it too casually, and he knew why she shut herself down. It was a horrific thought for anyone, but to someone who didn't have a sense of hearing, it was hell. He kept finding reasons to end the Minister's regretful existence.

Rose hummed softly, a different tune than before, with a few words littering the song. It didn't take him long to realize it was a tracking song, a way for Rose to pinpoint which cell her friend was in. Again, another useful trait. Compared to the missions he had performed before, doing a mission with Rose felt like cheating.

She stopped before a cell that reeked of old dried blood, enough to raise Phantom's beast to the surface, like a shark to a wounded animal. It purred as it woke under his skin, mixing with the sharp hum of Rose's unlocking song, her eyes glowing brightly in the dark.

It was no wonder Lara screamed.

"Hush, it's okay." Rose said, but immediately cursed at herself, but Lara quieted anyway. Perhaps from knowing screaming wouldn't save her. "I'm an idiot. She can't hear or see us, besides the eyes. Which, yours are glowing right now."

He balked, his beast rolling in — laughter? It could laugh?

"It's not so easy, love. And yours are glowing as well." As he said it, they faded until all he could see of her was a red lined silhouette, courtesy of the beast. He walked a step toward her, running into something that clattered on the stone floor.

"Mine look like the sky. Yours look like the death moon," she retorted. But the conversation was hysterical enough to expel the beast, anyway. Especially since he enjoyed the idea of her eyes glowing like the sky, vast and beautiful.

He jumped when she gasped, eager to draw her away.

"No, it's okay. It's Lara." A moment passed in the dark before he heard her again. "She's trembling. She's so cold. We need to get her out of here."

"Hey! Who's there?"

Bloody hell.

An officer's steps were distant but growing louder. It would be difficult to communicate with Rose in the dark when they had to be quiet, but he reached out a hand and found her elbow. She didn't flinch. A second later, her hand clasped in his and he could lead them out.

Rose probably knew a song for seeing in the dark, especially with the Stone growing heavy in her pocket, but last time she used it, she passed out. They couldn't afford that happening in a library prison cell.

He squeezed her hand, briefly bringing it to his lips for a kiss, hoping to make her smile.

"I know someone is down there. Show yourself." The guard was closer, but his voice was shaky. The depths scared him. Phantom heard metal unsheathing and knew it would be a fight to get out. He didn't want either woman in danger when blades clashed.

He pulled Rose forward until his breath brushed the shell of her ear. "Keep her back. I'll take care of this."

Her hand snapped to his coat, holding him hostage. "No," she breathed. "I have a better way."

Before he could object, Lara's freezing hand ended up on his arm, where she clutched him like he was her only lifeline.

"Rose, wait," Phantom pleaded.

Her singing filled the prison, echoing off the walls and casting an eerie effect.

> ARE YOU NOT WEARY, TRAVELLER?
> DO YOUR EYES NOT BEG FOR REST?
> DIP YOUR TOES IN A BATH OF LAVENDER
> LAY YOUR HEAD DOWN
> FOR YOU ARE DAVINA BLESSED

The song continued its eerie chant, reverberating off the rounded walls of the unending tunnel. The edges of Phantom's mind grew weary as the song enveloped him like a warm blanket, demanding him to sleep. But before Phantom could even flutter his eyes, the beast roared beneath his skin and the spell broke.

The next second, a body hit the floor. Phantom braced for Lara to fall in his arms next, but it never came. He tugged on Lara's arm until her feet moved.

Rose came into view as they peeled away from the thick darkness.

"Rose darling, it is a wonder to hear your song and not be pulled under by its power, but would you mind explaining why this one did not fall prey to it?"

Her silence was enough to worry him. There was too much left unsaid between them and not nearly enough time to explain it all. Not to mention, a moment alone with her would result differently than a conversation.

"Lara can't hear me. For the song to work, her ears must also work." A note of sadness lowered Rose's tone. They walked upwards, towards brighter light.

"What aren't you telling me, love?"

An audible sigh left her. "She could hear once. My father took that from her so I couldn't use her against him."

A pit of dread entered his gut.

The moment they could see each other, Lara's arms flew around Rose's neck and clung there like she might die if she ever let go. But the moment Rose's arms came around her friend, Lara squeaked.

Rose gently coaxed her friend off her, using her hands franticly.

Are you hurt?

Lara breathed heavily, but responded with her hands, albeit slower. *Some officers get eccentric with their roles as prison guards.*

Rose's gaze found his over her shoulder and understanding filled him. Her song didn't work on Lara because she couldn't hear it. That included the healing benefits. It was another means of control the Minister had over Rose. He could hurt Lara and Rose couldn't do anything about it.

Phantom nodded, confirming her silent question. Smith could help her.

Rose took a steading breath, then returned her attention to Lara. *We're going to get you far away from here.*

Lara's eyes lit with as much panic as hope as they found Phantom. She inspected the plain clothes he wore and remembered that there were red eyes in the cell with her, too.

Who is he?

She had turned back to her friend, but Phantom lightly touched Lara's arm to get her attention again before Rose could answer.

My name is Phantom, Captain of the Eleven Devils and Nemain's Revenge.

At that alone, her eyes turned wild, clearly trying to decide if she fell into the hands of an even more terrifying villain. She did, but luckily for her he was here to be her savior.

You're welcome aboard my ship where you may stay aboard or, find a life elsewhere. Either way, my men will secure safety for you.

She stared at Phantom with her mouth parted, deciding if he was truly offering her freedom. Lara turned to her lady. *What about you?*

This was a question he wanted to know the answer to more than anything else in his life. It was all that mattered in that moment.

A soft smile graced the songbird's lips. *I will join you as soon as I can.* Although her hands moved in response to Lara's question, her eyes traveled to Phantom's, knowing the answer mattered to him too.

A glance at Lara revealed a smug grin and a soft giggle. Her dark lashes fluttered at her friend, who blushed profusely.

Phantom shot a wink to Lara before baring down on Rose, crashing his lips to hers and drawing her up by her waist. Whatever embarrassment she felt at choosing a lover would be absolutely crushed by the time he was through with her.

He didn't linger nearly long enough, though. There was still a little girl in need of their help.

Lara's playful dark eyes glittered in response to Rose's smile when Phantom pulled away. But there wasn't any more time to lose, so he grasped her hand, and she took Lara's. They crept through the prison library as a chain.

The stench of death and dust left behind.

CHAPTER 32

OUR CHILDREN

Phantom wondered how many people he could save before Nemain deserted him. He could hardly call himself a disciple of death with all the preventative measures he went through to preserve life.

They made their way to the inn to rendezvous with the devils. Lara had fussed about her dirty, ripped dress, but Rose had to explain their haste and that too much was at risk to retrieve a new one. If anything, she'd fit in better in low town with a dirty dress than a clean one. Though the blood stains might attract attention.

Phantom had offered her a coat to shield from the cold and cover the blood that had seeped through her dress. She needed Smith.

Lara nodded her appreciation with a sad smile.

It was a busy night at the inn, the festivities only beginning even if the night was no longer young. Banners spread across the main hall with drinks being poured by the dozens.

The moment he arrived, a short burly man crashed into him, but it only took Phantom a half second to recognize the musky olive oil scent his first mate carried.

"Earhart, you finally made it." He embraced his old friend, patting him firmly on the back.

Earhart pulled back to punch his Captain in the shoulder, in an amiable nature, of course. "This is what happens when I leave you alone for one day?"

Phantom lifted his brow. He wasn't entirely wrong, but Earhart's presence would not have made a difference on Bashtir.

Still, he humored his first mate. "You know you can't leave me unsupervised, mate."

With a nod and a grunt, Earhart's eyes shifted to the women who stood behind Phantom. Rose had lifted her hood over her head, hiding her face from the masses.

Phantom shifted the attention to the trembling woman at her side. "This is Lara. She'll be joining us." Earhart nodded, understanding the discretion required for a refugee.

"Come along Lara."

Phantom held up a hand to his first mate. "She won't be able to hear you, mate." Turning to Lara, he let his hands talk for him, but of course, he spoke out loud as well for Earhart's understanding. "This is my first mate. He will take you to the ship and get you settled."

Her brown eyes turned panicked as her hands moved franticly. *I'm not leaving without Rose.* She made her finger curve to represent "r" then drifted it under her nose as if signifying the pleasant smell. Phantom attempted to contain his smile as Lara used the sign for a rose rather than spelling her name out.

The hand signal suited her. Something sweet smelling, beautiful, but covered in thorns.

As if on command, Rose's smokey sweetness hit him and he wanted to draw her away from everyone else so he could bask in the scent.

Rose moved to face her friend, reading Lara's hands to know why she resisted.

I have things to take care of here. But I will see you again.

With a tap on Lara's shoulder, Phantom received her attention again. He signed and spoke. "I assure you; I will protect her with my life. And I will bring her to you as soon as possible."

Lara nodded curtly before accepting Earhart's outstretched hand.

"She can have my quarters," Phantom breathed, wanting to be sure Rose's reason for staying was properly taken care of. "At least until we find a more permanent solution."

As they walked away, Clare took notice of the recent addition. She rounded the bar counter and stood before Lara, her signature red barmaid's dress swaying with her steps. The woman was a few inches shorter than Clare, but there was a sense of awe as they locked eyes. As if a sense of belonging was finally falling into place.

Clare put her hands on either side of Lara's head, then her eyes found Phantom. "This one is mine, Captain."

With a grin Phantom nodded, "I was hoping you would say that."

He put a hand to the small of Rose's back to guide her towards the rooms, giving one last command to his first mate. "We'll be up in the rooms. Absolute discretion is required."

"Aye, Captain. You need not explain your nocturnal activities to me." Although there was jest in his tone, his eyes were serious. He could kiss the man for how well he made a cover story for his Captain.

Rose stepped up, ready to explain that was not the intention, with a rosy, pink blush flushing up her neck, but he clasped her hand with a squeeze before she could.

Rose fought against his pull, eager to correct Earhart as her mouth opened, but Phantom swept her up in her arms. She squealed, but he whispered into her ear. "Play along, love."

Eyes were on them as Phantom gave them a show, careful to keep Rose's hood up and identity sealed. "Do not disturb us, mate." Sending a wink Earhart's way, Phantom sauntered away.

Earhart gave a false laugh and an even falser salute as Phantom inched to the door at the side of the inn that lead to the rooms.

Once the door swung closed, Rose's stare was on him. He could feel it like a bonfire at his side, heat licking up the side of his face. He dropped her on her feet before she could protest.

"You really followed me here that night?"

They passed rooms as he recalled strangers' conversations. "Aye, though I might add, I did not know it was you until I was already in pursuit. I simply saw a cloaked figure shift through shadows, then come in here. You looked like you wanted so badly to go unnoticed that I got curious about what you were hiding."

She huffed out a sigh. "I don't suppose you have any tips for blending in."

He let a smile drift his lips upward as his eyes fell on her. "You weren't meant to blend in, love. Give them a reason to notice you other than your secret. It's the same with picking pockets." He drew on a black velvet pouch containing the Stone he snatched off her at the Fortress and her eyes narrowed into slits. "A dose of misdirection and a soft touch." The object dangled from his grasp by its ties. He winked, but instead of balking like he expected, her eyes grew darker, heating the glistening gold into molten.

She leaned into him with a single damned hand to his chest while her other drifted behind him and tapped on the wood of a door. The one she had entered before, but the knocks came out in code.

One. Three. Two.

But that damned hand kept gliding across his chest, finding the opening of his shirt and sliding in to contact his skin. Delicious heat drifted over his body as her scent overwhelmed him.

When she finished her knocking rhythm, her lips parted as those mesmerizing eyes flicked down to his mouth, then back up to his eyes.

Bloody hell.

He was instantly hard and beginning to forget what he was doing there. She had that effect, to make him forget everything, as if his entire world began and ended with her.

His hand came up to rest at her neck, ready to pull her lips to his if she didn't break this bloody tension, but her arm was stiff at his chest, as if holding him back and keeping him waiting.

You invented that, you imbecile. Kayden's voice barely registered in his head.

Footsteps cracked against floorboards, and he vaguely remembered that they were standing there for a reason.

She stepped away as soon as the doorknob rattled, and a low growl escaped him. Then her other hand lifted, revealing a black velvet pouch hanging from her fingers. His mouth parted. He hadn't even felt her other hand on him. Not that he would have even questioned it with the mesmerizing look she held against him.

"Perhaps keep a better eye on your treasure, Captain." An amused smile graced her tempting mouth at her victory.

A smirk teased his lips. "Oh, I intend to."

The door opened, revealing the woman from before who let out a relieved breath. "You came," she breathed.

"Sorry it took me so long, I had to be sure I wouldn't be followed."

The woman glanced down the hall, spotting Phantom standing at the wall next to the door.

"It's alright. He's with me," Rose amended before the woman could shoo him away.

"Then come in, quickly," she whisper-shouted, pulling Rose in. Phantom followed closely behind. Once they were in, the woman checked each direction of the hallway before closing the door. "Those officers have been relentless lately. I've had to hide her twice since you were here last."

She turned to Phantom with a raised finger. "If I find out you're a spy of some sort, or mean harm to my lady or the child, I will inform Mrs. Owen."

How did she know Mama Owen or to threaten him with her?

"Don't look surprised, boy. I could recognize one of her lot, anywhere. And by the pirates occupying the dining hall below, I would assume you're her little phantom?"

Rose's eyebrows flicked upwards. He hadn't told her, or anyone, where he got the nickname from, for good reason. Childhood names weren't known to strike fear into an enemy.

Phantom nodded, an amused smile curving his lips.

"Aye, ma'am." A bit of his pirate and the gentleman Mama Owen raised coming out as one and clashing with just two words.

"Good," she breathed out. "You may call me Mrs. Brock." The woman turned her attention to Rose, but Phantom felt two feet tall after Mrs. Brock threatened to tell his orphanage mother, of all things. It made him feel worse that it worked. He didn't want Mama Owen putting her life at risk by coming after him.

"I don't think she has much time left. Do you have what you need to help her?"

Rose nodded, not taking her eyes off Phantom. When he winked, she broke her stare to turn into the bedroom.

The room reeked of death. Nemain was nearby, monitoring the child with labored breaths on the small bed. The red welts had returned with a vengeance, as if the disease was getting retribution from being temporarily cured.

Although death clung to the child, there was a reluctant energy to it. Something Phantom had never sensed before.

Nemain did not want to claim this life. She was ready to give the child eternal rest, but waiting, lingering in case her fate changed.

Rose rounded the bed, placing a hand on the girl's forehead, fear splitting across her face. Mrs. Brock followed inside to stand at the footboard while Phantom remained at the threshold. He'd do his best to stay out of the way, knowing the only thing he could offer the child was protection if officers beat down the door while Rose worked.

She pulled the Stone from its pouch, this time, her eyes lit blue instantly, her magic melding with the Stone. He could feel it, the relation the Stone had to her touch, as if it were part of her. He furrowed his brow, perplexed why he didn't feel it before.

A series of hums came from her throat as she found the right pitch.

SLEEP THE NIGHT IN PEACE, OH CHILD OF GRACE
LET ALL THAT AILS YOU RELEASE, IN THE MOTHER'S
EMBRACE
ALL THE PAIN WILL CEASE, WITHOUT A TRACE
UNTIL DAVINA CALLS YOU HOME

The girl's welts and boils disappeared before his eyes. He'd seen what Rose's magic could do with the aid of the Stone when Angelica lay dying. But that was a stab wound, this was surreal, watching the infection slip back into her skin like it never happened.

While Rose sang, he took note that she didn't look as overpowered by the Stone, but many voices still sang with her, as if lending her their power. He kept a watchful eye on her in case she passed out after using the Stone. Inching closer to her side, he'd gladly care for her if she needed to recover.

Rose was so focused on the song and the girl, she didn't

notice, but Phantom couldn't stop staring. It was a wonder to see the girl's skin return to a rich brown, to see the blue ribbons of light circle around Rose's arms and the girl, but that wasn't what he stared at.

He watched his songbird sing the healing song with all the air in her lungs, those glowing blue irises calling to him. Like a siren's call.

It was only then he noticed the blue ribbons circling around him, swirling around his arms, sliding along his chest and neck as if it were her own hands. A smirk rose on his lips as he remembered those ribbons of light doing the same when she had the nightmare in his cabin. Only now, they seemed bolder, more persistent.

A small laugh escaped him, enough to draw Rose's hazy gaze. Those blue irises glowed brighter than the sky, snagging on his form and the light that wrapped itself around him, trying to possess him. A pink flush crawled up her neck.

Before he could tease her about it, Mrs. Brock cleared her throat, making it clear she saw and understood what was happening. Rose broke her stare and finished her song, the ribbons winking out of existence.

Rose placed the Stone on the bed before her eyes fluttered closed and her body slumped. Phantom caught her before she fell to the floor.

"I've got you, little songbird." She stirred for a moment, attempting to hold on to consciousness before slipping into darkness. He enveloped her in his arms, kissing the top of her head as the little girl stirred.

"Oh, Mira, I'm here *mija*." Mrs. Brock rushed to the opposite side where she had a meal laid out with water for the child. Mira's eyes opened slowly, blinking rapidly and taking in the world around her as if she had never seen it before. He supposed if she was near death, she likely hadn't opened her eyes in some time.

Her eyes were the deepest brown, like melted chocolate as they widened, looking upon Phantom with a sleeping songbird in his arms. The girl scrambled back against the headboard.

Phantom extended his hand in what he hoped was a reassuring gesture. The girl was likely taught to fear men, considering any of them could be an officer ready to turn her in.

"Easy girl. I'm not here to hurt you."

Mrs Brock's tone was abrupt. "There is a room she stays in to recover down the hall. I will check on you, pirate."

The little girl's eyes widened at the mention of a pirate, but more intrigued than fearful.

Phantom hoisted Rose into his arms, catching Mrs. Brock's glare.

"I assure you, Mrs. Brock, my intentions are entirely honorable." Whether it be the fact that he was a pirate or the grin he shot the woman, he couldn't tell, but something made her eyes narrow.

"Like I am to believe you. Not in my rooms, Captain. I can assure you of that."

He let a breathy chuckle leave his lungs at the stout woman's sternness. He imagined this was what it would have been like to meet Rose's mother. The woman was a version of her mother, like Ramirez was a version of his father, even if he never met the man himself.

With what he hoped would appear as a respectable nod, he left the room so Mira could recover and deal with Mrs. Brock's fussing in peace.

A few booted steps across creaky floorboards and Phantom used his back to push open a door he assumed was correct. Sure enough, there was a bed and a glass of water ready for Rose's recovery.

He frowned at the small bed on its creaky frame. It would not be enough to hold both their weight. It was a shame, since all he wanted to do was hold her.

He laid her across the small mattress with her head on the near flat pillow. But it would have to do. A chair sat beside the bed, likely for Mrs. Brock to treat a patient in need. He pulled the old wooden chair up as close to the bed as he could. Gently, he brushed a lock of hair from her face.

Macha's moon was full, which caused the celebration in low town. It shined brighter than Davina's silver moon, bathing the room in lilac moonlight. It seemed the clouds hanging over the endlessly rainy island took a break in honor of their Goddess. The festivities outside radiated through the room, filling it with sweet notes of a mandolin and the heavy beating of drums. The streets would be full of dancers, swaying with the music and stumbling with the rum in their veins.

Phantom had no doubt Clare kept the good people there well stocked with booze for the occasion.

His devils loved to celebrate the Macha holidays, mostly because the people of Kheli did so religiously. Although dancing naked around a bonfire appealed to his wild nature, there was something magical about being in low town Samsara during a lilac full moon.

As he stared at the songbird, he wondered what their future looked like. Love had never been something he considered as a pirate or an officer. Women were beautiful. Men were dashing. But none truly spoke to his soul. Of course, he knew that one day his destined love would appear and ruin his life as she had in each of his past lives, whether he chose to be with her or not.

She will be the end of you. Don't think your presence will cause her anything but strife and death, Kayden warned. He scarcely spoke of his time alive and what truly happened between him and his version of Rose.

Scarlett. A woman of pain and fire.

Phantom only felt pity for that version of himself, no matter how much Kayden screamed at him to run from her. It was clear he made the wrong choice in his own life. A mistake Phantom was unwilling to repeat.

Rose stirred, her eyes blinking rapidly.

It snapped him out of his thoughts, leaning him forward until his elbows rested on the bed next to her. It was like her very presence was water and he was a man dying of thirst.

She groaned, closing her eyes and tipping her head back, a hand landing on her forehead. "*Mierda*, this blasted headache."

His smirk came quick and fierce. "Did I just hear you swear, love?" He lifted the water glass next to them, handing it to her.

She released a huff, accepting the glass and sipping its contents. "Of course you did. If you could feel this, you would understand."

He winced, knowing what a magically induced headache felt like, very similar to how a hangover felt. A night of too much drinking and a full experience with his monster held very similar morning reactions.

"I can't say I don't know what it feels like."

Her eyes snapped to his, narrowing suspiciously.

He tipped his head at her, black hair falling to his forehead and partially in his eyes. "We have much to discuss. First, tell me what helps with these headaches of yours." He gently took the empty glass from her hand and set it on the nightstand. She could reach it easily enough, but he wanted to do it for her. The urge to provide for her every need was instinctual.

"Food," she blurted. He raised a single eyebrow. Not what he was expecting. "My magic and my body get energy from the same places, water, sleep, food. Fuel my body and my magic will grow as well." The inn below would be serving all kinds of delicacies tonight. They'd have to venture into the festivities. "The Stone isn't truly a power source as much as a knowledge source. It provides me with the correct song to use, but the magic is still mine. The Stone requires some of my energy reserves in exchange for the knowledge."

"The Stone steals power from you? What if it takes too much?"

She swallowed. "That night in Kheli was a bit too much for me."

He blanched as he remembered what little she ate or the fact that she trekked across the island and back the same night.

"You were running low on energy."

She nodded.

"Why didn't you eat the food I provided for you?"

Her brows knocked together. "I didn't trust you."

Another memory surfaced of her eating the fish Wilson made the next morning with Ramirez.

"Then Ramirez brought you food."

Rose nodded, confirming how much that one meal did for her.

Of course, Ramirez would know what she needed. He remembered her past life as vividly as he remembered his younger days. After all, Ramirez didn't have to rely on the memories of a past life.

He rose from his seat with one hand out. "Can you walk?"

She nodded again before taking his hand and rising from the bed.

"We're going to get you as much food as you can handle."

Her mouth twisted into a smile. "That would be quite a feat, Captain. I can eat a lot."

He smiled at her brazen attitude towards food. He shouldn't have been surprised. She got those gloriously thick hips from somewhere. His eyes drifted to the very part of her he was thinking about, but when his eyes returned to hers, one of her eyebrows shot up. It was so bloody adorable.

He kissed her knuckles before pulling her out of the room and down the hall where Mrs. Brock was still fussing over the little girl.

"Goodnight, Mrs. Brock. Mira," he acknowledged before

pulling Rose to the door. Just as he did, a whistle belted from the window.

Two quick spurts and a long one.

It was a signal from Hyne. Officers would be on them in minutes. Rose read the panic in Phantom's eyes a moment before he whispered to the women. "Can you go out the window? Officers are coming."

Mrs. Brock's eyes widened before she snatched Mira out of her bed. She picked up a small pack at the window before climbing through the seal. "I'm prepared for anything, Captain."

He nodded to her before she refocused on Rose. "Take care, dear." Then the woman's eyes were on Phantom. "Visit your mother," she added harshly before descending into the lilac darkness with Mira clutching onto her.

Without another thought, Phantom traveled to the main entrance with Rose's hand still clasped in his own. He resisted the urge to glance at her before opening the door and checking the hallway.

The hall was quiet, not a soul in sight. Which was more unnerving than the officers being at the door. Tapping into his monster's hearing, footsteps pounded against the stairs. There wasn't enough time to climb out the window too. They might have led the officers directly to their target. But they couldn't casually walk by the officers either, not with such recognizable faces.

An idea crossed his mind.

He pulled her into the hall in the opposite direction of the stairs. There was no exit this way, but there were other rooms. Rose opened her mouth to protest, but he held a finger to his lips to silence her. There was only one way this would work. He pulled her cloak hood over her head to hide her face.

Just as the officers rounded the hallway, Phantom pushed her against the wall, their lips colliding. How did it feel better every time he kissed her? Like drowning and breathing air for the first time. They had so much unfinished business. He didn't want to push her too far, but the taste of her and the passion she was giving back made that thought melt away.

One officer whistled. "Get a room, lovebirds."

Phantom ignored them, but he felt Rose stir as if the embarrassment was enough to drag her away from him. He couldn't have that, not with the officer's eyes on them. He reached a hand to her face, with the other arm on the wood of the wall behind her, right next to her head. It focused her enough that she melted into him once again. It reminded him of only hours ago when they were in a similar position, and he was about to bring down the surrounding walls.

Was that only hours ago?

He needed her skin on his. He needed to drown in the taste of her. He needed everything.

Here was not the place and now was not the time.

The officers stepped into the room. No knock, no warning. They knew exactly where to go, meaning someone had betrayed Mrs. Brock. He was thankful, Hyne warned them first, but they wouldn't take long to realize they entered an empty room.

With painful reluctance, he pulled away from Rose, his breath heavy. But he couldn't pull away completely, both his arms now on the wall, on either side of her head. Her pupils dilated; the gold reduced to a thin strip. Her breath was ladened, raising her chest up and down, drawing his attention to the swells of her breasts.

She needs to eat, you idiot. He felt Sam's voice in his head as powerful as if it were his own thought.

The urge to take care of her finally overpowered the need to claim her, but he couldn't keep putting their passion on hold.

He leaned in until his breath coasted against her neck. "Next time I kiss you, Rose." He felt her shiver at the sound of her name on his lips. "I won't be stopping. No matter how inconvenient the location."

He pulled away to find her eyes glistening. "Promises, promises, Captain."

Phantom growled at her sultry tone. He nearly pulled her into a room without regard for who could be in there, but he picked up on footsteps coming back to the door.

Time had run out.

He took her hand again and pulled her down the hall before the officers could see, leading her down the stairs and into the bustling dining hall where they could disappear into the crowd.

CHAPTER 33

A DEVIL FOR YOUR TIME

T he inn bustled and boomed with dancers, drinkers, and general merriment. A drinking game had started with the bard in the corner of the dining hall.

"Ho, hey!" the drinkers shouted before taking a swig of their respective steins.

Phantom pulled Rose along the crowd, dipping them behind the counter before the officers could emerge from the inn doors. They glanced around franticly, clearly trying to track down their target, or the passionate couple in the hall that disappeared.

One officer, a burly fellow with a frigid gaze, narrowed his eyes over the crowd, then his arm clamped down on the nearest shoulder, which belonged to Phantom's powder monkey. But Robin had gotten himself out of stickier situations.

"Oh, hello, officers. Come by for a drink, eh?"

The officer grunted, his whiskers tilting with his upturned nose. "Don't play with me, boy. Did you see anyone come through these doors?"

Robin made a show of thinking, putting his free hand to his chin and scratching. "Aye, I believe I did. There was this skinny, scarecrow looking fellow and his companion, a meaty chap with a mustache larger than his brain." Robin shot them his finest grin.

The officer's eyes narrowed into slits as his fist dug into Robin's shirt. "What did you just say to me?"

"Hey, you look just like him. Say, are you two related?"

Phantom would have worried for his monkey had the devils not been surrounding them.

The officer fisted Robin's shirt, lifting him clean off the floor. "Maybe we'll see if the Minister can get you to talk, boy."

Robin snickered, his freckles dancing on his face. "I'd take that back before—"

"Hands off the boy."

"Before that."

The officer slowly turned to come face to chest with a grim *cerbalus*, also known as Jon. The skinnier officer behind him turned sheet white while looking upon Jon with his enormous arms crossed, staring down at them. Jon truly must have giant's blood.

Slowly, the officer set Robin back on his feet, but his mind was slower to catch up. "What will you do about it, Draiocht scum?"

It might have been the first time Phantom saw a cruel grin paint the brute's face. He made a show of cracking each knuckle individually, then his neck as Robin drifted to his side. The mustache officer still stared down the giant, but his skinner companion tugged on his sleeve.

"Markus, come on, it's not worth it."

"Yes, Markus, run to mama," Jon rumbled.

Markus pulled his sleeve away, taking a stand before Jon. The idiot didn't even pull his sword, cocky enough to believe his fists would be enough. "I can handle this trash."

"You really can't," Robin teased, mimicking Jon's signature stance by crossing his arms.

Markus didn't wait any longer, smashing his fist square into the middle of Jon's hard chest. Jon didn't even flinch. "Was that supposed to hurt?"

Finally, fear caught up to Markus, staining his cheeks and widening his eyes, but it was too late. Jon's fist collided with his face, sending him flying into the far wall. The man fought to stand before his eyes closed and his body slumped. The crowd erupted, cheering for Jon. No one in this area held respect for the Minister's Navy, so it was no surprise when they threw food at the officers.

The skinner companion didn't even check if his mate was alive before running out the door. Truly, was there no camaraderie in the officer ranks?

Phantom snickered before looking back at Rose. She wasn't laughing. In fact, her eyes were drooping as if she would pass out at any moment. She needed food.

"Come on. Let's get you something to eat." He hoisted her up and helped her into a nearby chair. She panted, as if breathing was becoming more and more of an effort. A familiar white head of hair took the chair next to her. "Ramirez, watch over her while I get her something to eat. Keep her awake, preferably."

Ramirez's eyes turned playful. "I don't know how anyone could sleep in this ruckus." He looked at Rose. "Good to see you again, my dear."

She beamed at him, and they continued to talk as Phantom went to acquire food. He found the kitchens and Wilson at the helm, barking orders at the regular kitchen staff.

"Stir faster and knead harder. It is dough or dog food? Keep your eyes on the fire. Does that look golden to you?"

They obeyed his commands like their lives depended on it. Phantom put a hand to his mouth, covering the laugh that tumbled out, but Wilson heard, regarding his Captain.

The man's hair had grown an inch since the last time they

met. Had it really been that long? He bowed his head slightly, a sign of respect he witnessed many of the villagers Wilson had governed over show. But the gesture was from a life he no longer had. Phantom regretted it the moment he saw Wilson's eyes fill with shame.

"I need something sweet, Wilson."

One of Wilson's thin brows shot up. "You don't like sweet, Captain."

"Aye, but Rose does. Or maybe she does. I'm going on an educated guess." By educated guess, he meant Sam screamed it at him. He supposed Isabeya enjoyed sweet treats often, so it wasn't out of the question Rose would too.

Wilson nodded sharply before pulling out a dish with a swirled round pastry covered in some type of icing.

Perfect.

When he returned to the table, a smile was present on her face, taking in the richness of Ramirez's company. Phantom knew it well, how he could make something ordinary, extraordinary.

"You see, this festival isn't just about celebrating the Goddess of Life, it's about rejoicing in the presence of one another. To realize how lucky we are to have survived when so many did not. It's about knowing that Macha chose us to continue life. She decided our souls weren't only worth saving but were good enough to raise the children who would create the coming future."

"Spoken like a true Kalonite," Phantom mused, teasing, but enjoying the old man's ramblings, nonetheless. Rose's golden gaze snapped to his, drifting with the scent of flowers in her wake. When those eyes latched onto the sweet treat in Phantom's grasp, they glittered. Sam was right. Phantom's songbird has a sweet tooth.

"Is it wrong for an old man to speak of what he knows?"

Phantom took a seat next to Rose, depositing the sweet roll before her. "So long as he isn't speaking crazy."

He shook his head. "I thought I taught you long ago, boy. Sometimes crazy is the word people use when they don't understand the truth. Besides, I have it on a very reliable source." Phantom let his eyes roll back as Ramirez turned his gaze on Rose, who was already on her third mouthful of sweet bread. "I used to know Macha myself."

"What?" she asked around a very full mouth.

"Indeed, she ruled over the Kalonites as their queen for a time." A sadness swept over the man at the memory. Maybe it was his lost son, or the paradise he used to call home, where the thunder tigers roamed.

Rose swallowed her bite. "What happened?"

"Same as everywhere else. The necromites came, and they destroyed."

Rose blinked for a moment. Phantom knew the look. The words brought a memory that had her wincing.

Ramirez caught it too, leaning in. "Yes, yes, you were there. You remember?"

Rose blinked rapidly, then her eyes shifted, flashing green before returning to their golden splendor. But something was different. Her eyes were narrower, looking at the room with suspicion, her chin raised higher, as if accustomed to looking down on people.

Her eyes settled on Ramirez, then softened. "Mave?"

A smile split Ramirez's face so widely, it must have hurt. "Hello, my dear. It's been an awfully long time. It's truly wonderful to see you again."

She jumped out of her seat and flung her arms around the old man.

He laughed joyfully, but she pulled away. "You've grown old."

A sad smile replaced his gleeful grin. "It's what happens when you take the long road."

It took a moment for Phantom to realize it was no longer Rose controlling her body, but another in him knew exactly who had taken over.

Samuel Rourke surfaced in a breath and a flash of green. "*Reina?*"

Her eyes snapped to his, the entire world standing still. She was here, looking at him now. There were so many things he needed to say. So much time he needed to make up for, but the golden irises looking at him now reminded him this was no longer their time.

It was in the past, and they couldn't rob Phantom and Rose of their turn.

Before he could fully succumb to that decision, her eyes blinked, opening again to a flash of blue. She sagged, falling to her seat, the transition of power too much for her weakened state.

He stared down at Phantom's songbird, missing Isabeya like missing part of his soul. She stared at him curiously, but he needed to give control back, let Phantom take care of her.

"Eat, *mi reina.*"

Then his vision turned blue, just in time for Phantom to resurface.

Phantom swayed, taking the back of his chair in hand to steady himself.

"I do believe we lost you for a moment, boy." Ramirez's hand was out, ready to catch Phantom if he fell. He wouldn't— maybe he would. It felt odd being replaced, then restored back into one's body. Like holding your breath underwater.

"Indeed, you did." He centered himself on the seat again, before catching Rose studying him. "Eat, love, you need to get your strength back."

She peeled off more of the sweet bread to nibble at, but even with the few bites she had taken so far, she was appearing brighter, more present. As if the food only needed a moment to fuel her energy reserves.

"How does your magic work?"

His brows knocked together at her question. "Pardon?"

"To refill your power. I saw your eyes flash when you jumped off my balcony, and when you changed just now." It made him uneasy. How little she knew of the monster, of what he was truly capable of. It had been present. She'd witnessed some of it, but not to the point of understanding the danger she had been in.

He cleared his throat, leaning back in his chair and putting a hand to his mouth. He knew how his power replenished, knew it well. It was another reason he believed he was a servant of Nemain.

"Blood."

Her eyes snapped to his, taking in the truth there.

"Not consuming it like the creatures of Hell but spilling it. Every death I take powers the magic in my veins. But I need only one death to fuel myself for months."

Rose seemed unaffected by the idea of him killing, and he wondered if she had sent souls to Nemain herself. She took another bite, that sweet sauce dribbling on her chin, making him want to lick it off her before she wiped it away.

"Yet you tried to spare the trespassers on Kheli. Why?"

He leaned in, whispering, "I do not kill just for the thrill, nor will I sacrifice lives for power."

A smile split her lips. "Captain, careful. Some might think you are not as ruthless as the stories say."

"Oh, I am. But only to those who deserve it. The innocent have no place perishing by my hand." He drew a stein to his lips, letting the ale wash into him. Goddess, he missed rum. That's when he caught it, her face falling, haunted even. But it was gone so fast, Phantom wondered if he imagined it.

"What if your magic runs low?" She whispered.

He smiled sadly. "I wish it would. Sadly, fate finds me before that's ever a concern." Pressing his lips together, he lowered his stein. "My usual concern is limiting myself. Too much and—"

"And what?" She whispered, keeping her voice low in the crowded room.

Ramirez watched them with calm fascination. He would not interfere, but his company held Phantom accountable all the same.

Phantom glimpsed into those eyes again, so enraptured by him. Could she truly accept him as he was?

"Too much, and the power controls *me*."

A mix of sympathy and confusion wrinkled her face. Perhaps she never had to experience too much power since her body made use of the energy one way or another.

"How does it control you?"

He cleared his throat, taking her free hand in his. "It singles out one emotion in my head, channeling that and that alone, until I can see nothing else. Or a past life persona takes over, which is just as likely to be devastating."

Earhart leaned into Phantom's ear. "Our little officer friend is waking up."

Right. There was still work to be done. There was always work to be done.

He leaned into Rose a moment, his body urging to at least kiss her, but he would keep his promise and now was not the time. "Eat your fill, love. Wilson is in the kitchen, should you need more."

Her hand reached out to his before he could pull away. "Where are you going?"

He smirked at being the one she didn't want to leave. Phantom knew it wasn't because she felt unsafe, not with the devils mingling around her, but that she simply wanted him next to her.

"I need to handle the vermin. Don't worry, I'll be back soon." His gaze flashed to Ramirez. "Watch over her and make sure she eats."

Macha smiled on Samsara. No rain came down upon tonight's festival goers. Instead, the streets roared with a unique sound. The sound of unbridled joy and songs, reflecting the blissful evening. Couples took to dancing in circles to the cheery beat.

Phantom and Earhart deposited the half-conscious man in the mud and stone beside the inn. A great splash surrounding him. He blinked up at the devils, taking in where he was.

"Ah, awake I see," Phantom taunted. "Well, I don't suppose you know where a fat officer with a giant mustache could have gone?" The man didn't answer, clearly sensing he was in trouble. "I aim to kill him."

The man snapped up, not as groggy as he first made it seem, jerking to take off down the alley. But Earhart cocked his pistol, pointing it at Markus's head before he made it two steps.

Phantom let out an exaggerated sigh. "I suppose you'll have to do." He leaned on the monster's strength to push him to the wall, his head cracking against the wet stones. Phantom had a knife to the man's throat before he could utter a word. "I'll make it simple for you. Answer my questions and I won't slit open your throat. Deal?"

He spat at Phantom. "I don't answer questions from filthy pirates."

"Do they not teach you manners at the Fortress anymore?" The man grunted as Phantom wiped the officer's spittle off his face with his sleeve.

Markus steeled his features.

"Tell me, who do you work for? Lockness or the Minister?"

Markus laughed, his throat bobbing, nearly hitting the knife in Phantom's hand, as if he didn't care for his life. "You think you have it all figured out, don't you?"

"Enlighten me," Phantom demanded while pressing the knife into the man's neck, drawing a bead of blood.

Fear tipped the edges of the man's eyes. Every man had his breaking point. Phantom just expected Markus's to come much later with his endless bravado. But he supposed the cocky ones broke the fastest.

"They're working together, with the Priestess."

The world bottomed out, like seeing a bear standing on its legs, to find it much larger than expected. He shared a glance with Earhart.

"What?" It was Earhart's voice that spoke the question. Phantom suspected it, but the two were still at odds with each other. Enough to send Phantom to Lockness as a spy.

"How could that arrangement work? I doubt the two came to one another." Phantom couldn't understand how two men who wanted to rule the island, who craved power, would ever agree to an alliance.

"They didn't. The Priestess is playing them both."

Phantom arched a brow, gazing at Markus. "The Priestess? To what end?"

"She has Pike's grimoire. It promises men power, but to her—"

Phantom knew its promises well. He'd searched those pages, the magic of every paper calling to him like a siren song. It promised much to whoever beheld it. To Phantom, it promised endless life, freedom, and victory over his enemies. What more could a pirate want? Though in those days, he was not yet a pirate.

But what could a book promise a priestess of the moon Goddesses?

"Immortality," Phantom whispered before he realized he said it aloud. It made sense. Ravana was no fool, nor was she ignorant of her crimes. Once one used the grimoire, they were required to pay its price. Eternal punishment. Damnation. Immortality was the grimoire's one loophole.

Rage ripped through his core fast enough for the beast to come shooting up, a graveled growl erupting in his throat. "No," he snarled. Phantom hardly noticed he had dropped the knife to wrap his hand around Markus's throat.

Awe replaced the fear in Markus's eyes, his scent clearing of its tanginess for a fraction of a second.

"It's true." His muddy brown eyes collided took in Phantom's reddening ones. The beast coming on too strong to contain. "You're the Lion in all the legends."

Phantom's elongating nails tipped into the man's neck, beads of blood dripping down his skin. The scent of fear and urine mixing with the man's stale breath. Phantom pulled his victim forward until his mouth was close to Markus's ear.

"Ah, you recognize me. Then know your death will be far from quick. Even Davina will not recognize you when I'm through with you."

Before he could make good on his promise, Markus laughed deeply, as if he couldn't contain himself. Phantom knew there were men who laughed as a sign of stress or fear, the body unable to handle the trauma. But this was nothing like that. Those men laughed like drunkards, unable to understand what was so funny. Markus laughed like he had revealed his hand in Kazeboon and came up victorious.

"I am but a vessel, Captain. Thank you so much for admitting who you really are. The Priestess will be by to collect the Lion's blood."

Phantom slammed him into the wall, his nails digging deeper. "Well, you won't be around to tell her, will you?" He wasn't sure what all of it meant, but if there was one person to keep secrets from, it was Ravana.

Markus smiled, blood coating his teeth. Phantom blinked.

He didn't even hit the man. He shouldn't have been bleeding from his mouth.

"She already knows."

The tangy scent of fear evaporated from the man's scent, as if his fear was never there.

"But thank you, James, you've been most cooperative." It was not Markus speaking, but Ravana through him. As if it was her throat he held. He squeezed fatally at the thought of her, but Markus smiled wider.

The sight turned Phantom's monster ravenous, red swarming his vision. He wanted Markus bleeding on the muddy ground, yanking Ravana's soul from him and forcing her to Nemain's carriage himself. Whatever Ravana wanted with him, it had to do with that damned grimoire and the promises it made her. Promises that cost more than they gave. A cost he'd have to pay, or his devils, the island, Rose—

Crimson soaked his vision.

"Captain," Earhart's voice of reason came through his haze of red. "Stop, we could still get information out of him."

"No," Phantom growled low, the monster barely poking its head out. "Ravana is using his body. His survival only serves as a spy for her."

Markus laughed again, but it was light, like a woman's. His mouth coated in even more blood. His body was already dead, poisoned by whatever magic Ravana forced into him. Even witches possessed nothing this strong.

No, this kill was his.

He snapped the man's neck with one hand, breaking off the abhorrent laughter with a sickening crack, leaving Phantom and his first mate in silence as the body fell into a puddle of mud.

CHAPTER 34
SIREN'S HEART

Phantom cleaned off Markus's blood before venturing back into the inn. Earhart, always prepared for every-thing, had a wet cloth and bucket for him to do so. Perhaps his first mate was too used to cleaning blood.

The well of his magic was getting too full. He'd worked hard to contain the beast and to only use morsels of its magic to not draw attention, but without an outlet, he feared it becoming too powerful. He had planned to let Earhart finish Markus off, but when Ravana's laugh came from the very throat Phantom held, that kill was his.

Phantom fought back the beast, its rising resistance only feeding into his many worries. One thing was for certain, he'd have to hand over the reins to the beast fully in a controlled environment. Lest it happen when and where it would do the most damage, leaving Phantom powerless to stop it.

Then there was the matter of Ravana. A matter he had to think about and couldn't all at once.

"Captain." Earhart's brow creased in concern.

"I'm fine," he growled out, sharper than intended.

"No, you're not." Earhart stepped front of him with a handout, as if he could stop his Captain from walking out into the street. Phantom released an impatient sigh. He needed to be doing something, anything, that would stop Ravana. He couldn't tell if it was Nemain urging him to stop the Priestess from cheating death, or his own instincts, knowing nothing good would come of it. "You are far from fine. Jon told me of what happened."

A flash of red came across his vision, not the beast, but the memory of it ready to tear through his own friends. Jon suffocating beneath his palm, the fear coating Black's scent, the failure in Wilson's eyes.

"What would you have me do?" Phantom rose his brows, knowing full well how bloody fucked he was. "Have me leave and doom the entire island? Even if we found somewhere they could live, are we to abandon this island to tyranny?" Perhaps Rose's words were getting to him. "I can't even tell which officers are from Kheli because they've been enchanted to forget everything but obedience."

Aren't you a pirate? Some get left behind, Kayden whispered to him.

"How is that possible? The witches don't have magic of that magnitude."

He knew. He had understood for a long time but didn't want to admit it. The signs were staring him in the face. All the officers had to listen to her sing during the weekly mass. The paintings in the halls, paintings he knew she made after finding her in the sunroom. Then her dancing, the blue dust like smoke coming off her, infecting people like a toxic cloud.

He'd still be furious with her for attempting to take his freedom had he not seen the relief on her face when he hadn't succumbed to her. Although in other ways, he already had.

"Rose," Earhart breathed. He owed the woman much, considering his wife was still alive due to the songbird. But he had seen it, witnessed Rose's power when she healed Angelica.

Phantom should have known then, that was only the tip of her power, a well much deeper beneath the surface.

Phantom nodded.

"Who is she?"

Phantom didn't have to answer. Just like Ramirez and Jon, he knew this could happen. That one day the woman of Phantom's past lives would arrive.

"I didn't realize she was this powerful."

"Nor did I."

Earhart's head bowed. "Why is she helping the Minister?"

Flashes of those scars came across his mind. The price Rose paid for defiance. "She doesn't have a choice, mate. She never has."

"And now?"

"I will do whatever I can to ensure she comes out of this with her freedom. Whether she chooses to save this world or burn it, I will be there, fighting at her side."

Earhart soaked in the seriousness of Phantom's gaze, searching for jest or hidden meaning before his eyes widened. He understood what it meant, what the cost could be.

Then the first mate's eyebrows scrunched, a line forming in the middle.

"Did he say, 'Pike's grimoire'? As in *the* most fearsome pirate Captain to ever sail the seas? The book crafted by demons to entrap greedy souls with the one loophole of immortality that could give the owner limitless power?"

Phantom glared and Earhart raised in hands in surrender. "Other than you, of course."

One eyebrow shot up on Phantom's face, choosing to ignore his first mate's placation.

"Aye, and now Ravana has it."

The festivities grew louder as lilac moonlight spilled into the street. Macha's moon would expand in size during Her fullness, as if peeking in on the world below, drinking in the sight of Her people in merriment.

The street outside the inn was filled with colors, not just in tribute to the lilac of Macha, but to the many colors of life. Yellow, blue, orange, green, red, and many others filled the space and cobblestones in banners, flags, and fabrics, while music filled it with echoes of tambourines, flutes, and other homemade instruments.

The bard had made it outside, but Phantom couldn't hear him over the abundance of voices singing along with him.

People clapped towards the sides of the street, drinking and shouting, while a collection of dancers swerved in and out of each other towards the middle. And right in the center was Rose, swinging with Ramirez, who was light on his feet for one so old.

Someone had given her a dress to blend in with the locals, a white gauzy material that was layered with an assortment of colors reminding Phantom of the fish off the Khelitian shores. But nothing could ever compare to the beauty that was her smile. She beamed so brightly it hurt.

Every eye was drawn to her, centering her in the celebrations, as if they knew she was more than merely human.

Not that he was human either, but while he carried demonic energy like it was a coat of arms, she radiated Goddess energy like it seeped out of her pores. One only had to be near to soak up the rays coming off her.

Phantom let his back hit the wall, watching his songbird enjoy herself. He wouldn't dare disturb her, not with her smiling so brightly. Although all he wanted was for her to look at him like that, for now, he'd take that smile existing at all.

Earhart leaned against the wall on one side of him, Black on the other. Black was back to normal, coal smudged over his face, his hair tucked far enough under his hat to forget he had any.

Another look to the dance floor, Phantom spotted a head of ebony hair sporting her signature red dress. Clare's form bounced up and down with the beat of the song. She was louder than most the others, her voice a force to be contended with all its own. Her dress was low enough that her breasts bounced with her.

Not that he was looking, but he knew someone else was. Black's gaze locked onto the dark beauty.

"Go dance with her," Phantom whispered to his swordsman. Black didn't like the attention of dancing, preferring to exist in the background, but Clare was born to be front and center. If he wanted to keep up, he'd have to let the moonlight shine on his skin occasionally.

A nervous laughter left him. "I don't think so, Captain. She's far better off without me."

This wasn't about a dance.

He tracked Black's gaze back to the barmaid, only to find her hand outstretched, beckoning Black to her, a glimmer of promise in her eyes. It was a dare, clear as day. Clare wanted Black out of the shadows, facing his fears, unafraid of the eyes around him.

A smug smile plastered on Phantom's face. "She doesn't seem to think so, mate."

Black was too stunned to decide, but Phantom could see the temptation on his mate's face. Jon drifted to Black's other side, witnessing the interaction, Phantom nodded to Jon once, and the brute understood.

They each put a hand to Black's shoulders, but before he could shake them off, they pushed him out to the middle of the street, straight into Clare's arms. The moment her hand grasped his, he was under her spell, falling into step beside her.

Phantom laughed deeply along with Jon and his first mate.

He let his eyes drift to Rose again, and she looked even more brilliant than she did a moment ago, as if she was the sun that shouldn't exist at night.

"Is it her?" Jon said only loud enough for Phantom and Earhart to hear.

Earhart answered for his Captain. "Sure is, mate. Captain has found his one true love. You owe me fifty crowns." His brow dipped to the brute who chuffed at the idea of losing a bet.

"Bloody hell, you two wagered on this?"

"The whole crew bet on it, Captain." Phantom couldn't contain his laugh at his first mate's smug grin. Of course, Earhart would bet on the side of love. He was a true romantic at heart, no matter how much blood he spilled.

Phantom's gaze traveled to the brute, a frown present there, but it was something more than losing his coin. Jon's gaze snagged on Rose. Phantom never asked if there was someone in his past. Maybe seeing his friends happy was bringing up painful memories.

Phantom followed the man's gaze to the songbird and stargazer she danced with. A pit formed deep in his gut. Maybe it was Kayden's warnings, or even Sam's. One thing was certain: their story never ended well. Although he didn't know the details of each ending; he knew his past lives were full of heartache, anger, and death.

Ramirez's half smile reminded him of that. The old stargazer witnessed how Sam's story had ended. He could feel the devastation and failure coming from his heart in shades of green, not a feeling he had earned in this life. It was almost cruel to have Ramirez around all the time, but he needed the reminder all the same.

"I should let her go," Phantom breathed, his heart heavy as he thought of parting ways with the songbird.

Earhart's gaze snapped to his. "What kind of urchin shit is that?"

He let out a heavy breath. "Mate, we're cursed to be together, not destined. We're not soulmates, no matter how much I feel it. Soulmates don't get ripped apart the way we do. She'll be taken from me, one way or another. If I have any say over it, then I can make sure she is happy and safe."

His first mate put a hand on Phantom's shoulder, pulling him in until they locked eyes. "You think she's going to be happy in a life without you?"

Phantom tipped his head back to the songbird in question. "Look at her, Joseph." Earhart blinked at the intimacy of his first name, knowing the pains it took for Phantom to say it. He looked at Rose, dancing and singing, not only in Ramirez's arms, but the merry men and women of low town Samsara. Her smile was wider than he had ever seen it. "She's happy right now. She doesn't need me to feel that."

Earhart pulled on Phantom's shirt. "No, no, she's happy *because* of you. You don't think I saw the shadows in her eyes when she was on the ship? She looks like an entirely different person now. You did that."

"Even if you're right, I could be the death of her. I will not allow that."

Earhart's eyes narrowed. "Fuck Davina. Since when did the Captain of Nemain's Revenge start believing in destiny?"

"He's got a point," Jon piped in.

Phantom knew his reputation for hanging fate and the rules She made. It didn't mean he could escape it.

"Listen to me," Earhart demanded. "That girl is the only one for you. You know that. If you let her go, you'll spend the rest of your life wishing you hadn't." Phantom frowned at his friend. "Start acting like the pirate you are and steal yourself a siren's heart."

Phantom tipped a smile, amused at his mate's word choice. Before Phantom could register what had happened, Earhart nodded to Jon who prompted shoved him into the fold of bodies. Before Phantom could step away, Ramirez pushed Rose the rest of the way until a golden gaze locked with his and her soft hands were on his.

Saw that coming, Sam remarked, but Phantom ignored his inner voices.

The smile he thought was the most brilliant thing he had ever seen transformed into the very sun before him, melting every wall and boundary around his heart. They were useless anyway. He was too selfish to let her go. So long as that was what she wanted, he'd be right beside her.

She pulled him into the fray, his body knowing the movements well, but his mind was far behind. It took a few steps into the boisterous dance before he found his footing and his mind could wrap around the idea of dancing with her.

He had danced with her earlier that night, but it was nothing like this. Then, they were both wearing a disguise. Now, she was more real than he had ever seen her.

The beat increased, and he snagged her hand to keep up, floating through the arms of other dancers. The beat of the drums and the clapping bled through Phantom, pumping his heart rate faster. Black and Clare danced beside them, Black looking more than a little uncomfortable and Clare laughing at his expense.

They danced and weaved through the streets of low town. Many knew Phantom's face easily there. They saw and loved him, even if high town sought his hanging. Low town would never tell of the phantom who saved them.

But now, they smiled at him, dancing with a girl they did not recognize, a girl who shined brighter than the Goddess moons. Her hair was sunlight incarnate. Golden cores of the stars were her eyes. He couldn't stop staring at the girl Davina meant for him. Even if it was a curse, curses could break, and he was strong enough to mete out every threat to her.

Music lulled his senses, tempting him to forget everything

outside the songbird in his arms, pulling him with the music and looking up at him as if he was the world.

He almost let it, especially when the music slowed, centering him to her. He remembered what it was to kiss her only moments ago. Was it so recently? Why did it feel like it had been centuries since their lips met? He wanted to be lost in her, to feel her against him and show everyone exactly what she was to him.

Phantom stared at her lips, then back to her eyes and caught them trailing his face the same way. He'd never heard a siren's call so strong. Temptation urged him to pull her into his arms, throw her over his shoulder, and demand a room in the inn.

Before he thought to do so, his hand caressed her neck, his thumb brushing across her bottom lip, then along her cheek. Her skin was so incredibly soft, so at odds with his callused hand. She was not some delicate flower, wilting at the slightest inconvenience. She was a force as strong as the winds and tides, the very things that directed his life.

He leaned down and time slowed with them, begging him to close the distance as her lips parted and her eyes gently closed.

"Clear out."

Phantom's eyes snapped up, even as Rose waited for him. Officers plowed through the crowd at the end of the street. They were tall lads, looking over the vast crowd for their targets.

Phantom let his hand drop, curling around her hand instead.

"We are looking for the Minister's daughter. Have you seen her?"

He leaned in, his breath trailing across her neck before reaching her ear. "Run."

Her eyes snapped open in time for Phantom to wink at her,

then pulled her hand. She joined his urgency with her own, running with him even as the dancing around them continued. As if the people understood their need to blend in, the music picked up, signaling the most chaotic dance they would know.

The clapping grew tenfold, more dancers piling onto the street. He'd give it to the people of low town. They knew how to hide someone from the officers. Then he realized they knew exactly who she was. That's why they all turned a blind eye when the officers asked questions. They knew her, and they loved her.

After all, she healed and cared for their children.

Phantom pulled her into an alcove, watching the officers from a safe distance, Rose leaning into him to see too.

His devils had poured into the street, dancing or singing. Hyne looked to be in a drunken stupor, but by the control he had, Phantom knew better. He ran straight into an officer, stumbling back into the man and knocking him to the ground, laughing hysterically.

"Off me, low town scum," the officer retched, tossing Hyne to the ground as a stumbling Tick pulled his weapon, looking confident, yet unsteady. That too, an obvious act. "A Kalonite? I should have you detained." To his credit, Tick didn't look the least bit affected. He lifted his chin and wobbled his sword at the man. Too distracted, the officer ended up in the sword fight with two drunken fools.

Further down the street, Clare wiped down an officer's uniform, cooing some fake apology as she "accidentally" spilled more wine on his jacket.

"Oh dear, I'll clean this for you straight away."

"Unhand me, woman!"

She pulled at his jacket just for it to tear under their combined efforts.

Rose giggled like a schoolgirl beside him as his own laughter tumbled from him.

One more officer raced through the crowd like a shark parting a school of fish. But in the middle of the street stood a giant, his arms crossed before him, feet apart. An unstoppable force. Jon.

The officer huffed. "You think you can stop me?"

Earhart came from behind Jon, completely hidden by the mountain of a man. "I'd like to see you try to move him."

Jon didn't have to lift a finger. The moment the officer took a step, Robin slid by so low, the man didn't notice until his legs were knocked out from beneath him. The moment he was down, Earhart removed the officer's sword and the crowd descended on him.

"More a'comin'!" Someone shouted from the opposite end of the street as five officers swung into the crowd.

A whistle came from the first direction. "Here too!" Another group came from that direction as well, the Commodore leading the way.

"Bloody hell," Phantom bit out, gripping Rose's hand as she sucked in a breath. The Minister clearly knew they were both missing. Phantom bit his tongue. There was no way out they wouldn't be caught on the street, especially since he turned them into a dead end.

Rose pulled at his hand before his mind could find another way out. She pulled him to a ladder beside the building, very similar to the one he climbed with the Commodore. It was old, rusted metal, but functional enough to use. She didn't look back to ask his opinion on the decision. It was clearly the only way out.

She gripped the bars, hauling herself upwards. Too tempted to stop himself, he put a hand on her ass to "help". She glared back at him to show him how much she appreciated his assistance. He let out a low chuckle before releasing her.

He climbed after her, keeping the ladder as silent as possible. They made it to the top with hardly a sound, looking over the edge and down on the street. Officers had seized the bard and many of the dancers as Ashby addressed the crowd.

"Anyone who gives up the Minister's daughter, and the pirate known as Captain Phantom, will be rewarded greatly."

Silence answered his old friend.

"Don't believe me? The Minister is willing to offer a position in his household in exchange for any information." To Samsarans, that was offering the best wealth they could acquire. Everyone knew that those who lived inside the Fortress were the richest on the island aside from Lockness's men and working for Lockness was only meant for the vilest of creatures.

Yet still, silence answered, not a soul willing to lift their voices. Phantom did not know the people cared about him. He avoided pillaging from low town, knowing they were suffering the same as Kheli, but he had no idea he earned such loyalties.

"No one?" Ashby prompted. "Fine, but know, I don't want to do this." He pulled one man from an officer's grasp, a head of brown hair, enormous arms, and a short frame coming into view. Earhart.

"No," Phantom whispered. It was a surreal anger, seeing Ashby hold Earhart with a knife to his throat. Once, they were friends, before Phantom's decisions tore them apart.

"Come out, James," Ashby shouted loud enough for the entire street to hear, though it was eerily quiet. "You know I don't want to do this."

Earhart didn't say a word, but anger flushed his neck and cheeks red. Ashby would throw his life away for what? Duty?

There was so much life left for Earhart. Angelica. Anna. Maria. His girls needed him more than anything. Phantom would not be the reason his first mate didn't make it home.

He looked over to Rose, resignation settling in his heart, and she saw it, shaking her head against it as he rose, ready to give himself over for his mate.

He didn't get the chance. Earhart threw his boot hard

against the Commodore's foot, his head slamming back into Ashby's nose.

Chaos ensued, every devil reacting to their first mate's lead, the rest of the crowd responding in kind. Banners and instruments flew, knocking into officers. Bottles of beer and rum crashed against the officers along with the walls and the ground.

A woman older than time jumped on a short officer's back, yelling like she had conquered the world. Hyne laughed, punching the man in the gut before he could throw the frail woman off. As the officer fell to the ground, Hyne offered the woman his hand like she was a queen dismounting her steed.

A group of dancers picked up where the bard had left off, whistling and clapping to make up for losing the music. They twirled and jumped around officers, pushing them back and forth in a circle like a game, until they drew their blades. But the dancers had silk ribbons from their performances earlier that evening. Ribbons of lilac, green, yellow, and orange tied around the officer's eyes, disorienting them enough for others to relieve them of their swords.

Clare had resorted to punching the nearest officer, breaking his nose, then she screamed in his face before Black knocked him out with a glass bottle.

The street was an absolute mess of chaos. Phantom grinned at the sight of it, Rose gaping beside him.

He tried to spot who had a hold of the Commodore, but Ashby had disappeared. A jolt of trepidation sung through his veins. A glance over the side of the roof confirmed his fear. Ashby was untouched, standing at the end of the ladder, knowing very well which way Phantom would have gone.

Their eyes met, and his breath caught in his throat. He thought he saw his old friend in those eyes once again before they narrowed. "Got you." He took to the ladder, climbing two at a time.

Phantom turned to Rose, grasping her hand again. "Run."

Her gaze widened a moment before Phantom pulled her across the roof. "Where do we run to?"

Sure enough, the roof ended, and the next building was a couple of stories taller. They could hardly get a running start with the slanted roofs, but heights were Phantom's specialty.

He snagged the clothing line that connected the buildings, pulling Rose by the waist into his body. "Hold on, love." Her eyes widened with panic, taking in exactly what he was about to do, but they were out of options and time. The Commodore had made it to the rooftop, barreling towards them. He looked back at her. "Don't let go."

A smile tipped her lips. "Never."

"James, don't!" Ashby bellowed.

She closed her eyes tightly before he jumped off the roof, leaning on the monster's strength to keep himself and Rose on the rope. It loosened, letting them fall freely before going taut and swinging them towards the tall building. He pulled his feet up so his boots hit the glass of the window, breaking it in an instant before they flew through it. They separated, rolling on the rugged floor of an inn room.

Phantom let out a hollow laugh. Rose glared at him with heavy breaths before she laughed, too.

Phantom hurried back to the window, looking up to find the Commodore standing at the edge of the roof, snarling like a caged bull. He watched the decision take root in his old friend's mind.

"Don't try it, brother."

Rose rushed to the window, witnessing Ashby crouch for a jump, his hand around another clothing line.

"He won't make it."

"No, he won't."

The position of Ashby's line was all wrong. Still, Ashby jumped from the rooftop, determination setting his features to stone. The wind whipped at the stray hairs around his face as he fell and swung. But the Commodore was too heavy.

The rope strained, then snapped.

Quicker than should be possible, Phantom's hand snapped out, closing around Ashby's wrist before he could fall too far. The Commodore slammed into the brick with a smack and a groan.

Phantom grunted with the Commodore's weight, using his other hand to keep his hold. He's couldn't lean on the monster too much. The beast was too powerful right now.

The Commodore's eyes snagged on Phantom's, a moment passing between them as Ashby's eyes softened. The surprise was evident. Ashby didn't think he would save him. Phantom was surprised himself, but he pulled on the Commodore's arm, hoisting him to the window.

Rose was right there, lending a hand and strength to their aid. She continued to surprise him with her strength until he heard her soft hums and knew where she was getting it from.

Ashby used his feet to help climb up the bricks until he fell through the window, and all three of them fell back on the ground, panting wildly.

"You saved me," Ashby whispered, almost to himself.

"Don't count on it happening again, brother."

Ashby leaned up on his arms. "But it will. If there was ever a time to let me die. That would have been it, yet you risked yourself. You risked *her* for me." His eyes trained on Rose, who only watched and waited. "Why?"

Phantom let out a heavy breath, knowing the real answer. "Because I still believe in *you*, Bash. You're in there, somewhere."

The Commodore blinked once. Twice.

Then he stood, Phantom standing with him, blocking Rose with his body, prepared to take her hand and run. He might not have let his old friend die, but he was still the enemy.

Ashby leaned in, facing his cheek to Phantom. "Punch me."

"What?"

"Punch me in the face and make it bruise."

Phantom let his fist fly, landing hard against Ashby's cheekbone and making him step backwards. His hand throbbed from the impact.

Ashby shook his head, expelling the pain. "Is that all you got, Hawk—"

Phantom's fist found the other cheek, throwing Ashby to his knees.

He spit blood from a busted lip. "Now, run. I won't be able to hold them off long. Consider my debt paid."

Phantom leaned down, patting Ashby's large back. "Thank you, brother."

It was Bash who nodded.

CHAPTER 35
CALLS YOU HOME

The sun rolled over the horizon, mixing lilac moonlight with newborn sunlight as Phantom and Rose weaved through the streets of low town. The streets were crawling with officers, some with egos and demeanors the size of Jon, some with blank stares who traveled the street unfeelingly. He wasn't sure which would be worse to run into.

"Where do we go?" Rose whispered as she pressed against him in the smallest alcove he could find. Her warmth raked over him, comforting him.

"Well, we can't very well turn back up at the Fortress. It's clear that your siren call didn't work on me." Her eyes gazed at him. "Well, at least not in the way they expected." An amused smirk tipped her lips, making him think of that bloody promise he made.

He wasn't sure which, but one voice in his head snickered.

"I imagine that was the Minister's last attempt to control me. He'll try to kill me the next time."

"Let's sail away, get your ship and leave this place behind."

A breathy laugh left him. He'd wanted to hear those very words from her, and now he was the one tied to the island.

"Can't, love. I made a deal with a witch. Until I fulfill my end, I can't leave the island. That, and the Minister won't wait for long to deploy a ship to Kheli. If I can find out what he and Lockness are planning, perhaps I can stop it." Not to mention a beastie to find.

Earhart had informed him of Clare's plan to evacuate the island, but he never got the details of how successful they were of that. The alleyways of low town were no such place to discuss delicate secrets. Phantom would have to stall the Minister somehow, without getting killed.

"But you can."

"What?"

"Leave with Earhart, the devils will take care of you until I can get to you." He'd pray to any Goddess who'd listen that she'd accept his offer, but he knew it was a long shot. From what he'd seen, she was possibly the most powerful creature in the world, let alone the island. She was also stubborn.

She lifted her head defiantly. "Absolutely not."

He took a steadying breath, placing his hand in hers and squeezing. "Rose, I couldn't bare it if something happened to you. I wouldn't survive it. More than that, I would become the very monster my reputation claims I am. Consider that, if you stay, I won't be able to protect you as well as my devils can on my ship."

"I can protect myself."

A sad smile curled his lips. "I know you can, but your power makes you a target. More power means more enemies."

She squeezed his hand harder. "I am not leaving you. You stay. I stay."

He nodded, lifting their joined hands to kiss her knuckles. If he couldn't kiss her, he'd have to settle for this. "I don't deserve you."

Rose smiled sweetly. "Then live long enough deserve me."

Of course, she wouldn't deny it. She rather give him a reason to keep fighting. His reason.

"I intent to. I'll fight to deserve you everyday you let me."

Since he couldn't kiss her, not yet, he glanced back out of the alcove, looking for a clear opening. He could feel her trepidation buzzing beside him.

"That's it? You aren't going to make me go with them?"

"You always have a choice. I will do everything in my power to ensure we succeed, and we make it out of this alive."

"Then what do we do?"

He glanced around. "I can't explain here."

"Where then?"

He closed his eyes, taking a steadying breath. It was the one thing he never wanted to resort to, but he knew it was the one place he could go.

"It's about time I visited home."

During the walk there, rain poured with the early morning mist. Phantom had snatched a couple cloaks from a nearby vender. Rose was less uncomfortable with the constant drip of rain on her face than he expected. In fact, she smiled with the feel.

She assured him the Stone was still safely tucked away in her dress. The Priestess must have discovered the false one they planted by now. It would be yet another reason to track them down, though he knew the officers had no lack of motivation.

Water pelted them from above, an inconvenience and blessed cover. The officers would have a more difficult time tracking them down in Samsara's rainy conditions. Phantom held Rose's hand the entire night. It felt right, always having contact with her skin, even if he couldn't hold her in his arms. Not yet, but he needed it as soon as possible.

The orphanage was more run down than he remembered it. Shingles falling from the rooftop making the fresh rain run in sporadic ways along the top. There were leaks, no doubt. Usually, during the rainy mornings, the orphanage would bustle with restless children who itched to play outside but were denied due to the tearing heavens.

But the orphanage looked more like a ghost from his past now. It was quiet and dark, only a few candles lit on the bottom level. The level where Mama Owen would spend most of her time. She always expected guests, so she had to be close to the door.

Phantom let out a heavy breath and Rose's arm wrapped around his in a comforting gesture. He wasn't used to it, someone using physical touch for comfort. He resisted the urge to flinch, her warmth steading his nerves.

When he took too long, Rose raised a fist to the door. He promptly stopped her.

"I'm afraid that will do no good." Phantom lifted a hand to pull the string next to the door, tugging on it for a few minutes. Bash had installed it all those years ago. Several multicolored small flags were attached to the strings. They littered about the ceiling of the bottom floor. It was a signal to Mama Owen that someone was at the door.

It must have been terribly hard to always think about who was at the door without being able to hear them.

Soon footsteps groaned against the wooden planks of the floor before the door opened, the old hinges complaining.

There she was, the woman he considered his mother, her big brown eyes staring up at him. He expected a disappointed frown, or a tongue lashing. Instead, a smile spread across her lips.

"Aye, *mijo*, you're here." Her voice came out a bit jumbled, a side effect of not being able to hear herself combined with learning Brettanian and Quencerian. Sometimes, he swore he only understood her because he was raised to.

"I need your help." He signed the words along with saying them. Sometimes Mama Owen needed to read lips along with hands.

Her eyes went to the blonde beauty, who leaned in enough to meet Mama Owen's eyes. Rose lifted her hands to sign too. "Please, *señora*."

Mama snapped out of her shock before pulling them inside. "Come in." She signed as well, too, knowing that sometimes her spoken words didn't come out correctly. "What are you doing here, *fantasma*? There are officers crawling everywhere." She blew on the nearby candles, extinguishing all but one and setting that one on a table for them to sit. They both understood the silent command and took their seats as she shuffled about the room, closing curtains and blinds.

Phantom took in the run-down orphanage he once considered his home. It was as if the walls were crumbling around them, water stained the ceiling, paper peeling off the corners. But the biggest difference was the silence.

He waited until her eyes were on him. "Where are all the children, Mama?"

Her eyes fell flat, haunted, but her hand moved. *The Minister has decreed all orphans be sent to the bloody Fortress.* This time she did not speak the words as if that would make them more real. *Without the children, the Minister has ceased my payments.*

Anger curdled in Phantom's gut. Mama Owen was a good woman who dedicated her life to ensure all the orphan children from the War had a family.

"Even the young ones?" Phantom's signing was sharp. The Minister wasn't supposed to take anyone younger than thirteen.

Solemnly, she nodded. *The Minister believes raising the children in the Fortress will create more loyal soldiers.* Phantom's heart ached. He shouldn't have been exposed to half the things he was at such a young age. He couldn't imagine what they would do to five-year-olds.

Mama Owen's voice returned. "I know who you are, child." Her eyes fixed on Rose, who fidgeted in her seat. "I know those officers are looking for both of you." There was a judgement in her eyes, and he knew. He was the reason her orphans were taken from her. He was the infamous rebel who stole a ship and slaughtered the crew. It was his disobedience that caused drastic measures, assuming it was the kindness of the woman before him who shaped him in such a way.

"I'm sorry. I did not mean to take this away from you." He hung his head, unable to look her in the eyes. In those three years, he never thought about what his actions would do to her. Maybe he did, and that's why he never visited, but seeing her now and the way she was living because of his decisions was nothing short of devastating.

"No, *mijo*."

His eyes shot up to hers. She scanned the room, ensuring no one else was there before sitting across from him. Her hands clasped in his. She gave up signing so she could keep contact with his hands, but if anyone could understand her, it was him.

"You started something here." Her eyes were wider than ever, even beneath her full dark lashes. "The people are restless. They want to be free of the Minister. The measures he has taken in response to you have opened their eyes to how little freedom they have. We needed you to show us what we were missing. We've been told the world out there is too dangerous for us, that this island is the only mercy we could hope for."

He remembered people telling him that when he was a child. That he should accept the island as a sanctuary and that there was nothing but death beyond it. What liars they turned out to be.

She shook his hands. "You started it, *fantasma,* do not apologize. Soon enough, the people will fight back, and they will follow you."

Finally, it made sense why all those people protected him when the officers came. It was what he represented to them. The very thing he promised every person crewing *Nemain's Revenge.*

Freedom.

He didn't realize he promised it to the entire island. Or at least, low town. The people of high town still hated him as far as he knew.

He stood, signing as clearly as he could manage. "I don't want them to follow me." He already felt weighed down by the burden of the devils. Every time their lives or freedom were in jeopardy, he felt it. Adding another thousand souls to his roster?

Absolutely not.

"I can barely help my crew. What makes you think I can take on low town?"

She shook her head. "It's too late, *mijo.* You may not accept them as your people, but they are yours nonetheless." He breathed in the words, eager to deny them, but could he? Mama's eyes turned to Rose. "If you're here, running from your father, same as the rest of us, then I know it's time." She looked between Mama's lips and her hands as if one would deny the other. Rose didn't sign up for a war, either. They both wanted to run away. "You've left him vulnerable, child."

For a moment, Phantom thought she meant the Minister, that not having the songbird to control his soldiers made him vulnerable. With all the scheming he did with Lockness and the Priestess, he wasn't sure that was true anymore.

But Mama's head turned to Phantom, and he knew she meant him.

"No," Rose breathed, forgetting to sign with the realization that she could lose him before they ever began. A fear he had never seen before flashed in her eyes and he thought he spied red in them for a second. "No." She repeated, shaking her head this time.

Phantom reached out to her. She leaned away from his touch. "I'm right here." He pulled her into him, embracing her as she came to terms with the danger they found themselves in. "I'm a survivor, love. I won't leave you." As he said the words, he knew he couldn't promise it and not because of the danger he exposed her to, but because of the curse on their lives. He may not know truly what it meant, but their past lives had failed at a happy ending repeatedly.

He took a breath of her smokey sweetness before pulling away and pressing his head to hers. "We will make it out of this. You hear me?"

She nodded as a single tear fell down her cheek. He wiped it away before turning back to Mama. She examined Rose, indecision clear in her taut features.

"I will provide you with a room, *mijo*. But there is one thing you need to take care of first."

Curiously, he stared at her as she lifted from her seat, taking the candle with her in an iron holder. They followed down the hallway to another candlelit room toward the back of the house. She opened the door and there was an officer sitting at the desk.

Commodore Sebastian Ashby sat with closed fists on the wooden desk before a candle, the gloom of the closed curtains making even daylight hard to reach. The Commodore's body raked with tension, but he did not move.

Every fiber in Phantom's body told him to run, to take Rose's hand and run as far as they could.

"Hear him out, *mijo*. He came alone, knowing you would come."

"It's a trap," Phantom said breathlessly, forgetting to sign, but she knew what he would say.

"It is no trap. He would not disrespect me in such a way."

Phantom's eyes locked onto Mama Owen's. "He would if he had to."

"Listen, *mijo*. It may save your life," she pleaded, her big brown eyes enough to melt him. She was so much smaller than he remembered. She swatted his shoulder like she used to do when he was an unruly child. "Perhaps you give him back his life, too."

His brows crashed down. His life? She pushed him inside before he could object, but she stopped Rose. "You can wait, child." Judgement laced her tone. It seemed Rose failed Mama's tests. Though, he knew, no woman would ever pass.

"No," Ashby snapped. He cleared his throat, having difficulty saying the words. "I need her."

Phantom growled low in his throat in warning to the Commodore. Rose was spoken for. He didn't care about formalities. The Minister doesn't decide engagements, and he had plenty of reason to believe who Rose would choose.

"*Mijo*," Mama warned. "You play nice in my house, remember?"

Phantom didn't take his eyes off the Commodore as Rose came up beside him.

Ashby's eyes softened as they traveled to their adopted mother. "May we have the room, Mama?" He signed as he spoke.

She nodded before closing the door.

It reminded him of so many times before when she'd lock them in a room together until they worked out their problems. Though their petty arguments were nothing compared to their issues as adults.

Phantom itched with the feeling that something was wrong. Ashby couldn't possibly be playing nice. Not now. Not after everything, even if he let them go once for saving his life. Even now, he stood with his fists balled at his sides, riddled with tension that made Phantom jumpy. He stood in front of Rose, scanning the room.

"Such a good little knight, handing us over to the Minister without even thinking of what that would do to Mama. Is everything truly lost between us?"

Ashby sucked in a heavy, albeit shaky, breath. "Please, James, I don't know how much longer I can hold it off."

Phantom narrowed his eyes, searching for the trick. "Hold what off?"

He didn't answer, instead his eyes shifted to Rose. She retrieved the Stone from her bust, hesitant to remove it.

Ashby's eyes widened, realizing what she had. He took a step back, backing himself into the desk he had sat at, nearly tipping over the candle there.

"I don't know if this will work," she breathed. "I don't know if I can undo it. I've never tried."

"Try," he bit out, pleading in his eyes, even as his hands gripped the desk edge like it was a lifeline. Her eyes softened. "I can't stay like this, Rose. I'd rather die."

"What? What's going on?" Phantom wanted to shake the answers out of his old friend, but it was his songbird who spoke.

"Sebastian has been under my enchantment for some time. I don't erase his will completely, so he must get regular doses to prevent—" She paused, the words getting caught in her throat. "To prevent disobedience." Shame, it was unadulterated shame lacing her eyes. How did he not see it before?

"When you rebelled, killing the crew, and liberating the Kalonites, it started. Other naval officers rebelled, burning their uniforms and taking up arms against the Minister." He choked on his own words, like his body rejected them, denying that he was telling the truth, forcing him to stop. "Then one by one, they were subdued, taken into the Minister's underground prisons, but when they came out, they were no longer rebellious."

"He brought them to me."

Phantom snapped his eyes to hers, realizing how heavy those souls weighed on her. Those beautiful eyes lined with silver. "I—" a sob tore through her throat. "I don't know if I can change it. I don't know if I can give it back."

"Try," Ashby pleaded again.

"I could make it worse."

"Do you know how it feels to hold something in your hand that you know is delicate? Your instinct is to protect it, at all costs, but your body disobeys you and destroys it instead, and there is *nothing* you can do to stop it." His hands reddened from gripping the table. "Right now, my body wants to take you both out and deliver you to the Minister. The only reason I can hold off is because I haven't had a session with you in quite some time. But I am *losing*." The desk moaned under the amount of pressure he applied. "Rose, free me before I do something else I'll regret."

Without another tear, she reached into the pouch, and her hand collided with the Stone. But something was different. The Stone reacted immediately, bursting from her in ribbons of blue light. Her knees hit the floor as she struggled to contain it. She was too tired. It was too much.

"Rose," Phantom yelled, landing at her side to keep her upright.

"*We're fine*," she said with many voices.

He put his head to the side of hers. "Please, don't use too much." He couldn't imagine what taking too much would look like. Would she shrink before him as if she starved to death? Would he be able to stop it?

Her glowing blue eyes landed on him. "*We will not*." Then those eyes, both Rose and not, focused on Ashby. Fear filled his eyes, watching her use the Stone.

Instead of dwelling on it, he shut his eyes tight as she stood up again, her voice coming out smooth and confident.

DAVINA, I CALL TO THEE
CHANGE THE FATE I MADE
SET THE CAPTIVE FREE
LET THE CHAINS FADE

Ashby grunted as ribbons swirled around his body, pulling him from the desk. He nearly ripped into the wood to hold on, but he stood no chance against the solid light. Some of the light strayed, wrapping around Phantom's chest like a purring cat soaking in his scent. This time she did not notice, did not blush.

She's too far gone, Sam remarked, concern lacing his voice.

Ashby shook, his body rebelling against the reversal. The hold of the magic, not wanting to detach from him. He heaved, falling to the ground on all fours. His fists squeezed until his knuckles turned white, his breath rapid and choppy. Phantom could tell the man wanted to scream, but he held it in, unwilling to give away their location to any passing officers.

Maybe Bash really was in there, screaming to get out.

Ribbons of solid light retracted, floating back into Rose like the tide returning to the sea. They both fell to the ground, Rose into Phantom's arms. She'd be out for a while. Ashby fell like a sack of potatoes, hard and loud, but his breath still heaved.

Phantom checked his songbird's pulse, finding it alive and steady. She needed rest and a meal when she woke up. He lifted her up, taking her to the nearby bed. It was a small bed meant for a child, but she would fit. He just couldn't fit on it with her. He moved a stray piece of hair from her face, letting his knuckle trail over her cheek.

"You love her, don't you?" Ashby sat up, leaning against the wall with one hand on his propped-up knee, but his breathing was labored.

"Don't you?" He was engaged to her, spending years with her before Phantom had ever met her, even if they both lived in the Fortress. She was locked away from the world until the moment the Minister had need of her. He bristled at the idea of a father using his daughter in such a way. Taking away her choice and forcing her to take everyone else's.

That was his fault too.

Ashby let out a hollow laugh. "No, brother, she's all yours. Not that I wouldn't have wanted her had things been different. But I had to watch as they drew her blood until she would sing, locking down my free will." So much about that statement made him want to rage, tear the head off the Minister's shoulders, but another word caught his attention before he could dwell on that fantasy long.

"Brother?" The word was painful and, for once, filled with hope. He didn't realize how much he had missed his old friend. There was a connection he had with Bash that he never earned with his devils. Maybe because his friendship with the devils was conditional. He promised them all freedom and adventure.

When they were James and Bash, he could promise no such thing. Bash could only have been there for him.

Ashby let out a heavy sigh, his breath finally steady. "I won't lie. I hated you for leaving me on that island, for not trusting me enough to believe that I would have gone with you."

It was worse than a physical blow. Phantom hadn't even considered that Ashby would have come, that he had it in him to become a pirate. He would have been his first mate instead of Earhart. A small chuckle left his throat at the image of Ashby in full pirate garb.

"Do you not believe me?"

"Forgive me, brother, but years of death threats and running don't just go away. What makes you think I can trust your word?" Goddess, he wanted to. He felt more and more like he needed his old friend back.

"Lockness is the one who retrieved the Kalonites you restored to Kalon. They weren't even free for a week."

It was likely where those Brettanian soldiers got ahold of so many, but he wasn't about to bring up that vital information. There were still Kalonites on Kheli.

"Let me guess, you helped?"

"No," Ashby snapped, his eyes drilling into Phantom's, the delicate light of the candle softening his face. "I've been getting them out." Phantom's eyes narrowed, still reluctant to trust him. "Lord Casimir, the man you spoke to at the ball last night." Phantom's mind went to the old Reverian man who spoke of a jinn, he glanced at Rose, perhaps the man wasn't so delusional. Was that conversation truly only last night? "He deals in marine goods and owns most of the ships at port. He's also a good man and smuggles all the Kalonites I can find. Although I've only been able to find the men."

Phantom bit his tongue. He knew precisely where the women and children were, and he hoped they were still safe. Though he trusted Earhart and Ramirez to be sure of that.

"Where does he take them?"

Ashby's shoulders rose and fell. "I don't let him tell me. If the Minister were to ask, I wouldn't be able to lie." He let out a relieved breath. "Until now."

"It worked?"

A smile broke Ashby's face, but all Phantom could see was Bash. "It did. For years, I felt this grip on my mind, my heart wanting me to follow a different path, confusing me. Many times, I didn't know if a decision was truly mine or not. But now it's gone. I don't feel so heavy."

"What does that mean for you?"

A haunted shadow fell over Ashby's face. "I can't leave yet. Between the Kalonites and the witch sons, someone needs to stay and fight for them." Phantom nodded, knowing he had that very task to complete as well, and finding an unruly beastie. "Take her very far away from here." Ashby's eyes landed on Rose. "I can't make a difference if she gets in my head again."

The warning regarding Ravana from Jimmy came into his mind. "I'm afraid she's the least of your problems, brother."

Ashby's eyes locked onto his. "What?"

"Lockness. The Minister. Ravana. They are all working together, and I don't think Rose is their only weapon."

Ashby glowered. "Ravana?" He sucked in a sharp breath and Phantom instantly regretted bringing it up. "Ravana," he growled.

"What did she do?"

"She's been taking me to her bed ever since the Minister got control of my mind," Ashby bit out. Phantom shook his head, the memory of seeing them together assaulting him.

"Did you want to be there?"

Ashby struggled with his answer, his head hanging low, the word getting caught in his throat. "No."

Phantom put a hand to his face, horror and guilt washing over him. He should have trusted his friend. If he had known what would have happened, he would have hog-tied the giant man and kept him in the brig if he had to. Instead, he'd been suffering, trapped in his own body, used, while Phantom traveled the seas.

"I'm sorry."

Ashby's eyes snapped to his and Phantom saw the very moment he stopped being "the Commodore" or "Ashby", but he wasn't Bash anymore either. No, that boy died a long time ago. Part of him sticking around until James had abandoned him. The boys they once were, died that day.

He was Sebastian now. The man who stayed on Samsara smuggling Kalonites out, fighting at every turn against the injustice thrust upon him and his comrades. He truly was the hero of the story, the knight in shining armor who came to destroy the villain.

Phantom had seen Rose as the damsel of that narrative. The girl the hero gets at the end of the story. Even growing up, when

Mama Owen told them tales of heroes, he'd always known it was Bash's place and his was the monster. He'd come to terms with that, being the villain.

But Rose was no damsel. In this story, she became the monster, the same as him. His gaze drifted from his old friend to the exhausted songbird.

"I'm sorry I left you on that island and everything that happened to you because I did."

Sebastian groaned as he rose. He took a few steps forward, but Phantom no longer felt the need to be cautious around him. His hand fell on Phantom's shoulder, looking into his eyes, but he didn't have to say it. A squeeze was all the acknowledgement he needed.

As they stood there, something deep inside them snapped back into place. Something that meant far beyond fate, a bond that survived the trenches.

They collided, embracing harshly.

"Glad to have you back, brother," Sebastian whispered.

A pained laugh escaped him. "You too."

They parted with heavy glances. There was still too much ahead of them.

Sebastian's gaze fell to the songbird that made all this possible. If she had not entered his life, would he have known how bad things were in Samsara?

"Now what?"

"I still have a dragon to find. Not to mention the witch sons." As he thought on the memories of Sebastian with Ravana, he also recalled the treasonous conversation between the Priestess and Lockness. "Although, I have an idea of where to start. Is Lockness still expecting me?"

Sebastian's mouth tipped into an all too familiar crooked smile. "I think I can help with that."

CHAPTER 36

LOCKNESS'S GALLERY OF CURIOSITIES

The plan was simple. At least it should have been.

Sebastian had to return to the Fortress, pretending he was still under the influence of Rose's enchantment. Phantom released all the information necessary before he left, particularly about his conversation with a very dead Jimmy and Ravana's growing strength. And the addition of Lockness's hand in supplying witch sons for whatever vile reason Ravana had need of them.

But at his next available moment, he came back to Mama Owen's house to deposit the attire Phantom needed to take on Lord Castellanos's appearance. He didn't have as many tools to do so as he wished, missing the pomade for his hair and one layering vest, but he thought he could pull off a convincing disguise.

Rose had yet to awaken. He slept on the floor beside her, unwilling to leave her side, until night descended on Samsara and Lockness would expect him.

He had leaned over her sleeping form, taking her in one last time. Not that this mission was certain death, but the odds were stacked against him. It was becoming less likely that he'd ever get off this damned island. Even if he snuck away with her and could endure a witch's curse. Could he truly leave Samsara to be enslaved by the Minister and all his partners? Not to mention the witch's boys and Serena. And the reason he was there in the first place, Kheli.

Was there somewhere they could go that the Minister wouldn't find them?

Go to Kalon, Sam chimed.

"Kalon's infested with the dead, mate," Phantom said out loud, not meaning to have a conversation with himself. Or a past life. Semantics.

You'll find that means very little when you're ferrying the chosen people of Macha.

"What?" Phantom said out loud again, thankful Rose slept soundly, so as not to witness him going insane. "What does that mean?"

Silence consumed his head. Not even his other voices chiming in their opinions as if they blocked him out.

"Bloody hell, this is when you choose to be silent? You could be useful voices in my head. I am about to head into danger. Information would be most helpful."

You're not ready. It was the softer voice who spoke, the one incased in orange and shadow. Draven.

"*Los conjones!*" *Bullshit.* Phantom spit out, cursing himself for being too loud as Rose stirred below him. A brief whimper before she drifted to sleep again.

He breathed out a sigh. There was no point in arguing with his voices. They wouldn't show him their memories before they wanted to.

Phantom stared down at Rose again, the smooth skin of her face reminding him of how the Minister wanted her appearance to remain flawless even if her body housed a series of deep scars.

Rage crept up on him again, suffocating in its swift arrival. Amber yellow and crimson like blood fogged his sight.

He was too full, not letting off enough magic lately, but the only way was to let the beast free, something that couldn't happen, not for a while yet. Perhaps after his visit with Lockness, he should tie himself to a cliff side and have Earhart untie him in the morning. The thought made his skin crawl.

Hopefully, he didn't have to kill anyone tonight. His power threshold wouldn't be able to handle it.

He let out a breath before leaning down to kiss Rose's brow, hoping she could feel it.

With one last look, he closed the door to the room and descended into the main living room.

"Oh, *mi fantasma,* you look so handsome," Mama cooed over the red brown suit, complete with coattails, a white scarf, and a black cane. He dressed the way any rich nobleman would have.

She fussed over his clothing, straightening his lapels and dusting off his coat. At one time, he would have brushed her off, but he couldn't find the strength to. She was such a strong woman, loving and fussing over him, even when he caused her current discomfort.

He breathed out, knowing this mission could take his life. His hands moved without speaking, it was always more personal that way, meant only for his mother. The only woman he ever considered his mother. He put a finger to his chest, then both fists across his chest, then pointed at her. Smiling in response, she put an endearing hand to his newly shaved cheek.

"I love you, too, *mijo.*"

Phantom leaned in to kiss her forehead. He wanted to say he was sorry again. Not for what he had done, but for what he was about to do, reentering her life out of nowhere just to disappear again.

Instead, he signed and said, "Make sure she has a meal when she wakes up."

Mama Owen nodded firmly, as if cooking was her life's mission.

Then he slipped out of the door and into the darkness.

That was approximately an hour ago, in which Phantom had dodged officers and weaved through the streets of high town to make it to Lockness's estate. It was even more lavish than Phantom remembered, but that was perhaps due to the "gathering" Lockness spoke of. Noblemen from around Samsara gawked at Lockness's wealth. Although it was a sight to see, the lights, the colors, the newly fashioned tapestries, it was all background noise.

Phantom moved into the foyer of the mansion, littered with white stones and well-dressed guests, many of which he saw at the feast only the night before. Truly, the noblemen would hold a party every night if they could. Lockness's staff easily recognized him, offering him his first drink of the night. The liquid bubbled in its thin glass, so at odds with what Phantom was used to drinking. He preferred a stein of rum over the sickly-sweet libations high town was accustomed to.

But he was no fool. Leaning on his beast, he sniffed the liquid in the glass. His beast could sense even the subtlest of poisons. He once tested it with Ramirez.

He breathed in, his vision flashing red for the briefest of moments before fading away. Not a hint of poison.

"I do hope you're not assessing my choice in refreshment, Castellanos." Lockness's rumbled voice came from Phantom's side, surprising him.

He tipped a friendly smile. "On the contrary, I am admiring your choice of stimulate. Isn't this a Reverian blend? I thought the island ran out years ago." His beast senses picked up on much, including the hint of lemon laced into the wine, a Reverian trait, to be sure.

Lockness lifted his own glass, his demeanor bored, but his eyes filled with mischief. "You'd be surprised what you can accomplish with a bit of extra coin and resources. A fact I would think you knew well."

"Quite." Phantom cleared his throat before taking a drink of his glass, suppressing a wince at the overly sweet taste.

Lockness's unnerving gaze watched him swallow.

"Is it to your liking?"

Phantom flashed him a winning smile. "More than expected, my lord."

More terrible than expected, you mean, Sam teased. He believed there were entirely too many opinions in his mind.

Lockness nodded abruptly, exhaling. He dressed to perfection, not a thread out of place on his completely white suit. If one did not know better, they would say the War never happened.

But of course, it made sense. Lockness controlled the slave trade after Phantom failed to extinguish it. He should have known taking away the Minister's means would only lead to another taking advantage of the situation. The only advantage being that the Minister didn't have full control of the island because of it.

Phantom examined the house and the guests gathered further into the mansion. The man who rambled about the jinn, his son, and Lord Desmond all stood conversing with similar drinks in their hands. Avoiding Lord Desmond in this smaller setting would prove difficult.

"Come with me," Lockness ordered rather than asked Phantom, but he was eager to get out of the small space with Desmond. If the lord recognized him, even if it was as an officer, it could be catastrophic for his disguise.

A servant opened a door for him. He eyed the servant, olive skin and grey eyes, a Kalonite. So open in his estate like a slap to the Minister's face. All Phantom saw was a man stripped of his freedom. It burned something deep inside him, waking the beast. Too early. It was too bloody early in the night to worry about his monster.

Lockness eyed him as he surveyed the room. It was a public room with other parties circling and admiring the various paintings on the walls. Some were of landscapes Phantom had never seen before, rolling hills, lush jungles, and vast deserts. Most of them were priceless pieces, painted before the War destroyed their inspiration. It was like navigating a graveyard, knowing that the places depicted no longer existed.

Some were more familiar than others according to the minds residing within Phantom. A flaming church steeple sparked the interest of one voice in his head.

Everything changed that day, Kayden whispered.

"Ah, that is one of my favorites," Lockness said, swirling the wine in his glass.

Phantom lifted a brow. "I thought you a devout Davinian man, my lord. What interest does the burning of a church hold over you?"

Lockness let out a bitter laugh. "It wasn't the burning itself, but what it represented. It started as a rebellion amongst the people in Reverie all those years ago. Even if it was in a different country, the entire world learned the lesson. Military and religion should never mix."

Phantom let his curiosity show. Although the two weren't mutually exclusive on Samsara, he couldn't say they completely parted ways. "Is that so? I didn't realize your tastes landed in the realm of separatism?"

"Oh, they don't. I believe every type of man has something to teach and something to learn." He puffed up his chest as if the very idea made him the wisest man on the island. "But there is something devastating about a man with the conviction of a priest, the skills of a warrior, and the duties of an officer."

"For a notorious slave trader, you aren't unwise. What

would a man with your ideals be doing in the slave trade? Running it, no less."

"You'll find my methods unnerving." Lockness cleared his throat. "But you should understand, there is nothing I do without reason. We live in a broken world that requires broken methods."

Phantom let his brow drop and his chin raise.

"I don't think I know what you mean."

"My reputation is not lost on me, Castellanos." His head tipped toward the Kalonite at the door, taking coats and providing drinks. "I need you to understand. They are not slaves, they are refugees, rescued from the creatures Nemain cursed upon the land."

Phantom remembered what Sebastian had told him. Lord Casimir was Lockness's rival, even if he didn't know it, undermining the slave trader by freeing slaves. Yet, he stood in Lockness's house.

"Why are you telling me this?"

Lockness breathed out steadily, as if gathering patience to speak to a child. "You still want my succession? Then pay attention," Lockness snapped. "I need to know you agree with me on this. Everyone has failed with their closed minds. Yes, what I do is terrible, but if I did not do it, everyone would die."

"That's a lot of weight for one man." Phantom attempted to make the conversation more lighthearted, the attention of Lockness's passion drawing eyes to them.

Lockness obliged him, lowering his voice. "A leader's burden. I think you know it well." He seemed to suddenly lose interest, turning to a smaller room to the left. He beckoned Phantom to follow him, an action he had no choice between, so he walked, even as the unnerving words settled over him.

Lockness strolled into the small room, nodding as Phantom followed. The door clicked behind him. A jolt of trepidation sinking into his gut. This was very wrong. He regretted his decision to take a cane rather than his cutlass, not that he would have successfully smuggled a weapon past the gates.

The room was still part of the gallery, in addition to paintings, there were also artifacts on pedestals. It was like Desmond's collection, but older and more diverse, as if Lockness cared more about the history of the item than the value of it.

"What do you make of these?"

Blinking out of his reverie, he turned to Lockness, who held up rusty metal manacles. He had them displayed on a pedestal like artwork yet held them like they were a household tool.

Phantom pursed his lips, staring at the strange markings etched into the side of the manacles. He let a glint of mischief enter his eyes. "I worry more about what you make of them, my lord. I'm afraid I don't partake."

A grumble of disappointment slumped Lockness' shoulders. He pointed to a particular symbol that Phantom recognized at last, making the blood chill in his veins. It was the one rune Kazeboon didn't have.

An angled square with its two lower edges trailing down further.

It was his symbol, flashes of his original life coming to the surface, but only ever that bloody symbol. He hadn't seen it outside his own head before. Even in Draiocht, it was erased, as if Maahes never existed. They had torn his symbol down since, according to the legend, he betrayed Ran.

"These manacles once captured the great Maahes from Draiocht culture, as the legend says." Lockness said casually, as if he spoke of the weather. Phantom schooled his features so he wouldn't look so damn unnerved, but alarm bells blasted in his head. He had to find a way out, the mission turning dangerous too soon. But with the glint of suspicion in the lord's eyes, he feared it was too late.

Phantom inspected the manacles closely, his heart rate

thundering in his chest. "They don't look like they can hold a god." Although Phantom knew his original self was no god, the legend was still fashioned around the idea.

Lockness sighed. "I'm afraid they can't." He set the manacles back down on the pedestal, rust falling from the aging metal. Lockness truly must have obtained them recently to not have them cleaned yet.

Phantom lifted his brow in interest, then let out a breathy laugh. "And how would you know of such a thing?"

"There is a crack just here." He pointed to a portion of the manacles where a crack sliced the metal, ripping it apart enough to be ill effective. "For a device created to contain a trickster god, you would think one would make it of better materials."

Phantom frowned and nodded. "One would hope."

"Indeed," Lockness whispered, eyeing Phantom suspiciously. His instincts flared, yet none of his personas had anything to say on the matter.

"You see, the power of the containment spell still exists within the manacles, so in theory, if one could extract the Goddess magic within the metal, then all one must do is adhere it to Maahes. Ravana said it was a simple spell, so I do hope it worked."

A delay fractured Phantom's mind. The truth revealed so subtly; he didn't feel the panic until it settled. He stepped back from the lord, glancing at the wineglass in his hand before dropping it to the floor. Glass shattered as the gravity of reality took hold.

Lockness' eyes darkened, watching Phantom with morbid fascination. He inspected himself, still standing, not coughing, no ill feelings at all.

"What did you do to me?"

But as Lockness smiled at his victory, Phantom noticed what was wrong. The voices were gone. All traces of his past lives — vanished. Not even the monster growled beneath his skin.

It was only Phantom present. For once in his entire bloody life, he was alone.

Laughter poured from him, bitter and unfeeling. "Is this what it feels like?"

Lockness narrowed his eyes. "What?"

"To be human?"

A beat of silence passed as they faced one another.

"It's nice to meet the legend himself. Maahes, although you go by Captain Phantom, don't you?"

Phantom's laughter finally ceased. Without his beast to tear through the mansion, he was well and truly trapped.

"How long have you known?"

"Lord Castellanos? Brave enough to show up at my door? I knew the moment you stepped onto my property."

Phantom blinked, his mind too empty of those voices, too occupied by silence to truly understand what was happening.

"I'd always been curious, Captain. What is it that makes you a god? You seem like nothing more than a man to me. Perhaps you are now. So, what does that make me?"

The door crashed open before Phantom fully registered it, too shocked to reply to the lord. Two guards came up either side of him and he swallowed. Ravana's personal guard.

Finally, he understood the question. "I'm no god." The shock wore off, and a threat hung in his eyes even if his words didn't portray it. He was much worse than a god and Lockness would find out, one way or another.

Manacles locked around his wrists as they forced his hands behind his back. The guards were anything but gentle and he normally had a quip in these situations, but he couldn't find one. His mind numb from the shock, recalling all outcomes and trying to tally how many people would pay for his mistake.

"Not anymore, you aren't."

The guards pulled at him, dragging him through the mansion, the guests staring at the spectacle.

At the last moment, he watched Lord Desmond inspect him. Phantom smirked at the man, his eyes widening in recognition, stumbling back a step.

"Think twice, my lord, before you let a devil into your home."

Desmond's mouth dropped, followed by anger reddening his cheeks. Phantom only caught a glimpse of the room before they pulled him to the gate, but he heard the uproar his exit cost.

CHAPTER 37
WHEN THE VOICES STOP

The smell invaded his senses first; the rank of old sea water and dead fish unsettling his stomach.

To his surprise, they didn't knock him out, preferring to put a bag over his head as they dragged him to whatever pit of hell they were going to throw him in. But they would soon be surprised. Hell was where he belonged. He didn't answer to Hell; it answered to him. Phantom didn't know it because of some memory, it was a fact pumping through his blood. He felt it with every fiber of his being, somehow stronger now that his counterparts were silenced.

They'd annoyed him with their prattling, but Phantom found he missed them. He'd never truly been alone with his thoughts before. It left little to be desired.

Before they pulled the old potato sack from his head, he heard a distressed trilling.

Serena.

The bag lifted and only a fraction of light found him, letting him examine the dark room. It was made entirely of stone, making him believe they were in some underground cavern. Water dripped down the walls making the air damp and musty.

Rows of storage boxes lined along the wall, like a wine cellar, but Phantom squinted his eyes, trying to inspect them further.

Those boxes didn't hold dried food or wine. The boxes were in many shapes and sizes, some only had bars. Some were glass-lined cages for marine creatures. Rows and rows filled the wall of small cages, and every single one housed an animal of some kind. Birds, rats, fish, octopus, crabs, snakes — Phantom paused as one creature trapped his gaze.

Monkeys.

He shut his eyes. It's not him. It's not him. He didn't need to add yet another to his list of failures.

Another trill from a familiar beastie had him snapping his eyes open.

Serena was chained to the wall on the opposite side of the cages, screeching out to Phantom to save her. If his freedom wasn't just as unattainable, he would have.

The dragon's purplish blood seeped from the chains around her neck, her blue shimmering scales nowhere in sight. It turned his blood icy. What had they done to her?

"Serena," he called her name, hoping it would help soothe her in such a state, but his voice only spurred her on. She pulled at her chains, digging them into her white scales, still too distressed for the blue to come forth.

"Well, well." The sound of deep, cruel laughter echoed across the stones, and he knew too well who it was. He hated that voice more than any other sound in the world. It grated against his mind, reminding Phantom of a time when he trusted her.

"I did not expect the beast to have taken to you so keenly, James." Ravana appeared, drifting into his vision draped in sheer fabric the color of blood. She was here for violence than, nothing less.

"It's Captain Phantom to you."

She ignored him, floating past him to Serena, who roared

and screeched at her advance. What happened to Serena when Ravana came for her? Anger bubbled inside him at the thought of that, but no colors clouded his vision. The only useful parts of himself within those colors. He had never felt more helpless than with their silence.

"Come now," she tsked, her dark eyes glancing over her shoulder at him, promising pain. "We know each other better than that, Captain." She used his title as mockery, but not in the same way Rose had when she was aboard *Nemain's Revenge*. There was a suggestion underlying every syllable, as if his title were little more than a child's claim to power. She spoke his title like she owned it; him included. It made his skin itch with the need to end her miserable existence. He didn't even want the pleasure of her screams or torment anymore.

He wanted her dead. Immediately.

"Careful *love*, I can't quite tell if you want to kill me or fuck me," she said sweetly, turning back to the growling beast before her. "I can assure you, the former will never happen."

Phantom's own growl rumbled in his throat. "I'd rather gouge my own eyes out then to ever touch you."

Her eyes found his as she released a blade from the fold of her robe. "That can be arranged." Her lips drew into a hard line as if his rejection stung. "Once upon a time, you weren't so repulsed by my touch." She turned to him, reaching out to graze her finger along the skin of his neck. His jaw tensed. His entire body tensed, especially when his mind flashed with images of what she once did to him.

When he was twelve—

He would have preferred her blade to his flesh.

He spat on her, his saliva landing on her cheek, and she flinched at the contact. "Anyone," he growled out, "but you." He wasn't about to tell the Priestess his interest had become entirely singular. She likely knew far too much already.

She wiped away the wetness on her neck with a swipe of

her sleeve, but kept her eyes narrowed on him. "You should not curse my kindness."

"*Kindness*," Phantom hissed at her. It seemed Ravana had tired of the conversation since she turned back to the snarling beastie.

"I always knew there was something special about you, James. I could feel the Goddess magic running through your veins. When you rebelled, I was sure of it." She held the blade to her hand, cutting it open as a stream of blood coated her hand. "But Maahes?" She laughed, drifting to a pedestal in the room's corner. A book laid upon it. One he recognized with absolute clarity.

Captain Pike's grimoire.

He once had the pleasure of destroying the old pirate and his wretched crew. They were now at the bottom of the sea with *Macha's Demise*. The cursed book had ended up in the hands of the Minister, no doubt supplying Ravana's access to it.

Ravana opened the book, letting her blood drip across the pages, the sacrifice required for information. "Do you know what you're capable of? What you were created to do?"

She said the word *created* like he was only a tool, fated for a purpose than living. He'd suspected it was true, though. Lineage had been suspiciously absent from each of his lives.

"I imagine it has something to do with the Goddess of Death." His tone turned light, attempting to regain some of the control.

"Oh yes. Nemain put quite a bit of magic in you. Luckily, that makes your blood very potent." She picked the book up, the monstrosity taking up so much space in her small arms, but she took a breath before reading loudly. "*Immunitatem*. This ritual is difficult to replicate considering you need the blood of an immortal, but when siphoned in the light of Davina's pendant, it can grant immunity from all ailments, including manipulations of the mind."

Her eyes brightened with excitement as they shifted to something behind him. Footsteps came to the side of him as Lockness stepped into view, having changed from his brilliant lord attire to something much more subtle.

His mouth twisted, showing his displeasure. "Remember why you're here, Ravana. You have a job to do." A threat laced under his words.

The thought made Phantom's blood chill. Clearly, he was part of whatever they wanted. Immunity? Were they searching for a way to block themselves from Rose? There had to be more they wanted. The cages before him told him as much. Those poor creatures were there for a reason. So was Serena.

Ravana's jaw tensed, her only sign of discomfort before reaching for a nearby wine glass and handing it to Lockness.

"The honors, my lord."

It was enough of a command for Lockness to bristle. Phantom was at least grateful to see the lord weary of her rather than bending to her whims. He wondered if Lockness knew about Ravana's plan to become an immortal.

But even as he thought it, he wondered if that were true. Lockness had stalled, knowing who Phantom was and tried to explain himself. Maybe they didn't understand each other, but every fiber of his being told him Lockness's motivations weren't as selfish as they appeared.

Lockness leaned down to Phantom, slicing into a vein on his arm, blood flowing freely. Phantom bit his lip, refusing to groan from the pain, but he used Lockness's proximity to whisper into his ear.

"Don't trust her," he said as loud as he dared.

Lockness didn't look at him as he filled the wine glass with Phantom's blood. "What makes you think I trust her?"

Had he misjudged the situation? He didn't dare turn to see if Ravana suspected them, looking to the glass that Lockness held. It was about a quarter full as he passed it to Ravana, then knelt back down to wrap up his wound as the Priestess turned to a table to work, her back to them.

After stopping Phantom from bleeding out in that cave, Lockness took on a more irritated tone. "How long is this going to take?"

"Patience, my lord." Her dark eyes flashed to his, and he grimaced at her attention.

She poured the blood down a tube into several vials, setting some aside. She held up the necklace he had stolen from Lord Desmond. The half-light of the silver moon shined from the pendant. His blood shimmered with flakes of precious metal, glimmering through the thick red substance. It swirled in the vial, mesmerizing Phantom.

"It's ready." She raised the glass, then brought it to Lockness, who promptly turned up his nose.

"I'm not just going to drink something you've enchanted without seeing it work first," he growled out.

An exasperated look drifted across her features. "Fine." Her head nodded to a guard at the entrance of the cave. No light protruded from the entrance, so he assumed it went further into the building rather than outside.

They waited a moment before the guard came back with a man struggling in his arms. It was an officer, his hands tied back, and his mouth gagged as the guard pushed him to his knees beside Phantom.

Familiar honey eyes and freckles looked at him with a hint of hopelessness.

No no no.

He just got his old friend back and now Sebastian was about to face it all again. But he held his chin high, defiance proudly on display. Perhaps the first time he'd truly seen his friend proud to be breaking the rules.

"Sebastian, my dear," Ravana cooed, putting her hand on his chin to make him look at her. "It's a shame we have to do this to you." Phantom's anger burned so hot in his core that he thought he felt the beast flicker for a moment before it died away, snuffed out by the spell in his system.

She carefully untied his gag. "If this works, no one will alter your mind again." She let her fingers linger on his cheek, grazing his strong jaw. "Do you think you'd come to my bed without such persuasions?"

He stared at her, his eyes narrowing. "I'd rather die," he spat out.

She snapped up straight, as if the words physically hurt, but her cool mask of detachment never once faltered. "No matter. I'll find another once you've found an early grave."

A snarl left the man, but all Phantom could focus on was the actual possibility that he would lose his oldest friend again.

Ravana turned her back on them before wrapping her hand around the vial, her long nails clicking against it. A gruff guard pulled Sebastian's head back while another pulled his jaw open, readying him for the liquid.

Phantom attempted to crawl to his friend, but Lockness's hand clamped around his arm and pulled him in. "Let it happen. If it works, he'll be immune to what is coming."

A growl rumbled in Phantom's throat. "And if it doesn't."

"He's due to die, anyway. Same as you."

Phantom struggled against his hold, cursing for the thousandth time his human strength. "Awfully comforting."

But it was too late, anyway. The enchanted blood poured down Sebastian's throat, and he had no means to stop it. His friend gurgled with the unwanted liquid as it slid down his throat. Once Ravana pulled back and before he could spit it in her face, the guard to his side slammed his jaw shut, then covered his nose and mouth, forcing Sebastian to swallow.

Sebastian coughed, confirming that the potion was gone, the magic working its way into him. He breathed heavily as the guards released him to his knees.

Ravana crouched before him, hands on either side of his face. "Why do you make me do such things? All you have to do is obey."

Sebastian spit on her face, Phantom's blood splattered across her flawless features. She flinched at the impact.

"Fuck. You."

Phantom suppressed a smile, proud of his friend for using foul language, but the urge left him as he saw the murderous gaze in Ravana's eyes. This was the woman who occupied Phantom's nightmares, forced herself upon Sebastian, and butchered Rose like she was a pig for slaughter.

There wasn't a single person he would hate more in all his lives than that woman.

She didn't bother to wipe her face as she grabbed Sebastian's lower face, digging her nails in and drawing blood. "Already did, my sweet. Don't tell me you didn't enjoy it."

Only hatred burned in his eyes.

She tossed him away like discarded food before stepping around him, her guards and Lockness following.

"We'll be back to test if it worked once it settles in your system. Do refrain from killing him in the meantime, James."

Before exiting, two of her guards came for them, dragging them away from the cave.

CHAPTER 38
MAN OR MONSTER

P hantom and Sebastian were dragged into a dungeon. The walls were still misshapen, like the cavern, but this time chains lined the wall behind a fence of metal bars.

A muffled cry drew Phantom's attention further down the line.

There, with streaming tears down her face, her wrists manacled to the wet cave wall, and a gag firmly locking down her siren song, was Rose Davenport.

"No," Phantom whispered, pulling on the arms of the guard holding him back. But his beast was too far away, only a rumble in the back of his mind. "Let her go," he growled, "Or I swear to Nemain, I will feed you your own entrails."

A soft chuckle echoed from across the dungeon, drawing shivers down his spine.

"And how will you do that, *demonio*?" Felix's stare was icy, unfeeling, yet filled with cruel amusement. His hands were busy sharpening the shining metal of a new blade. "I hear your tricks are concealed."

Phantom was distantly aware of Sebastian being chained to the wall, but his focus trained on the threat before him.

Felix was playing the game wrong if he thought he was the monster. Phantom let a cruel smile tilt his lips. "And you think what? I'm weak enough to torment now?"

Felix sent a curt nod to the guard holding Phantom. The guard released him, still manacled, but no longer held back. Instead of responding to Phantom's taunts, Felix continued sharpening his dagger.

"I also hear I have you to thank for getting the Commodore out of the way." He laughed hollowly, holding nothing but cruel satisfaction. "Ravana took one look at his face and knew he no longer was under *her* spell. Turns out he's a horrid Kazeboon player." Amusement wrinkled the corners of his eyes in an empty smile. "It would have been nasty business to handle myself. Now, the job is mine."

Phantom shrugged. "You can always count on a pirate for your dirty work." The two guards fixed their positions behind Phantom, blocking him from the exit. Not that he was going anywhere with Rose and Sebastian chained to the wall.

"I can, can I?" Felix inched towards him, doubt etching his words. "Rose here," Felix said, tossing a look back at the distressed songbird. "She seems to think you're a hero."

A fist flew into Phantom's stomach, pain exploding in his abdomen, causing his head to hang between his suspended shoulders. Rose's muffled cry and Sebastian's objections filled the cave. Felix's hand dove into Phantom's hair, digging into his scalp and pulling his face up.

"We both know that's not true. You're no one's hero." Felix sent a knee into Phantom's face. Sharp pain pulsed across his nose as blood streamed down to his mouth.

Phantom spit blood across the stone floor. "You'd throw fists at a restrained man? What a fine Commodore you'll make."

Felix's fist found his gut again, punishing Phantom for his tongue. The flicker of his beast grew stronger, growling in the distance.

"It's only fitting, Hawkins, considering you've had an unfair advantage our whole lives. I'm only returning the favor." Instead of throwing his fists again, Felix straightened himself. "But that's not the point. The point is, I think it's time for the people who are willing to sacrifice *everything* for you, to find out what you really are."

A low growl escaped him.

"There it is. Keep that up. You have a show to put on." Felix leaned to one guard, handing him the blade he had been sharping. "You know what to do."

The next second, hands seized his arms, hauling him into the barred caged where Rose and Sebastian were. Rose's eyes widened, looking over at him as if she were assessing the damage and looking for the right song. But Felix didn't hit harder enough for Phantom to concern himself with injuries.

Sebastian only glared at Felix. There was no love lost between the two. Now, more than ever.

Phantom's heart plummeted as he heard the unmistakable sounds of a cage locking behind them. The two guards strung up his arms right between Sebastian and Rose. If Felix was counting on Phantom's beast, it would not happen. He wouldn't let it. Not this close to them.

"If you think torturing me will get you what you want, you're sorely mistaken."

"Who said anything about torturing you?"

Before Phantom could fully comprehend Felix's meaning, Rose gasped beside him, followed by a fleshy smack and Sebastian's groans.

The guards had split up. One hunched over Sebastian, laying into him with fists. The other held a blade over Rose, right against her cheek as he slowly pressed down.

Red swirled the edges of his vision as he watched a bead of blood drip down her face, her eyes so scared. "Leave her alone or I swear on every Goddess watching that I will tear you apart."

Another groan came from Sebastian. "That goes for you as well."

"Oh, I'm counting on it." Felix grinned from behind the bars. "Go ahead. Rip them apart." It was then he understood. The guards were too far gone to even hear him, only blank stares and empty minds leaving behind the shells of men. "Aren't they magnificent? What Rose does leaves enough free will for survival instincts to kick in. Ravana's power, however, makes them register nothing but orders. They know they'll die in there, yet they still do as I say."

"What's your excuse then? Too cowardly to face me yourself?"

Felix tipped his head, a sneer dragging down his face. "I value my life, *demonio*. Most of the Navy are mindless at this point, but a few of us passed the Minister's tests. Someone must still have a head."

A growl tore from Phantom's throat, too monstrous to be his. "Then it's you I should be threatening." Rose's muffled scream tore through him like the blade was making its way through *his* heart. "Let her go, Felix. Or I'll go to Hell to torment you there, too."

A laugh, that was mostly air, ripped from him. "Right, because you're truly a *demonio*? Morbid imagination."

"Oh, I wouldn't be so sure about that."

One guard threw Sebastian's head into the wall, a sickening crack accompanying it, the sound of his groans the only thing telling Phantom he still lived. But his eyes still went to Rose. The guards had moved onto her neck, satisfied with the deep cut on her cheek. She tried to catch her breath, suppressing her screams when the blade pierced her flesh again. Blood poured down her neck.

Phantom strained against his manacles, the beast roaring

beneath his flesh, ready to emerge. He could easily break the chains, but would he kill them in the process? Normally he could borrow the beast's strength, let the monster rest at the surface of his skin, never fully breaking through.

But his power was too full, leaving the beast hungry for blood. Control was a slippery slope when there was too much unspent power in his veins.

He kept the beast at bay, holding it back. He couldn't risk hurting them.

Rose screamed, and he thought of the curse. This was it. He'd cause her end, just like every other life before this one. He couldn't escape the inevitable fate.

"Tick-tock, *demonio*. I don't think either of them can hold on much longer."

Images rushed to his mind, the lives of Rose's past and how she died in each reincarnation.

Isabeya's blank face as the light left her eyes.

It doesn't have to end this way.

Scarlett's screams as she burned to death on a pyre.

You can stop this.

Lani's hand falling from her round belly.

End the cycle.

Skye's cries as she fell to her death, her wings ripped apart.

I can save her.

Rose's screams broke through, pulling him out of the memories, out of the past.

"We can save her."

We shattered the manacles like they were branches under the weight of a hurricane. One blink and our hand was wrapped around the throat of the guard who dared to touch *her*. We lifted him from his feet before our fangs released to tear out his throat.

Blood and gore spread across the stones of the dungeon.

The faint drip of a silent cave was the only sound accompanying the spraying blood.

We ripped out the other guard's spine like it was only the rope from a sail. His body fell next, leaving the scent of blood and fear mixing in the air like copper and oranges.

"You're next," we growled, staring at the smiling man on the outside of the bars. We crashed against them, but they did not bend. Wrenching on them proved futile.

"Confused? Ravana is full of tricks. More than even you, it would seem."

We roared at him. He should be dead, laying at our feet with the last beat of his heart in the palm of our hand.

"I'll see you soon, *demonio*." Felix walked out of the room but turned at the last moment. "Try not to kill anyone else before Ravana gets back."

Red flooded Phantom's vision as he fought back against the beast. There was no stopping it. There was no stopping him. He could practically feel Sebastian's blood on his hands, dripping down his chin, his body on the floor.

"James." His voice. That was Sebastian's voice, still there. Still alive. "James, stay with me."

There was so much blood, but Rose's stuck out to him. Her blood didn't smell like copper. It smelled like ash.

He opened his eyes not realizing he'd closed them, but it was a mistake. There were too many triggers to set off the beast while trapped in the dungeon. The bodies slowly added to the river of blood across the cave floor mixing with the blood from Rose's face, and the bruises on Sebastian.

Crimson flashed his vision again, the beast needing more action. The carnage sating him for a moment, but those kills only served to fuel his power further.

"What was that?"

A cold laugh left him as he leaned on the bars of their shared cell. "Have you not guessed?"

Sebastian swallowed tightly, the hesitance in his eyes showing that he had guessed enough. "What are you?"

Phantom snapped. "That's a good goddess-damned question, but I'm afraid I have very little information to supply you with."

Rose's tears mixed with the blood on her face. He wanted to rip the gag from her mouth and wipe away the tears, then hold her until everything felt alright. But two things held him back. He was too close to losing control and he would never risk her. The second was the fear in her eyes.

Had he lost everything already?

Sebastian stared at him, waiting for him to continue. At one point, he would have given anything to hide this from his friend, but this was no longer Bash. Sebastian could handle the truth; he could see it now.

"I'm a servant of Nemain."

"I know that."

"Do you?"

Sebastian swallowed, seeming to bite his tongue at Phantom's harsh reply, but his mind was too strained to feel remorse.

"Did you know I was once immortal?" Stillness, Sebastian only offered silence. "Until Davina cursed me to a mortal life. Several, to be exact." A joyless laugh left him. "By my count, I have lived five lives before this one. One of which was not a human existence." Though an argument could be made that he was never human.

"Then what was it?" He breathed out, nearly a whisper.

"A monster, like a lion, but bigger, stronger. It comes out when—" It was a secret he kept for some time. Why the beast really came out. Ramirez was wrong. It wasn't his temper that drew it out.

Relief hit him as Sam's calming voice entered his thoughts. *You know why it comes to you.*

"It comes out when I'm afraid."

Rose's fearful brow softened as she listened, unable to tell him what she truly thought of him now. He took a step towards her. If he could remove her gag, perhaps she could help them escape. But the sight of her blood had the beast clawing its way out. He clung to the cell bars, willing himself to stay away.

Sebastian let out a breathy laugh. "The great Captain Phantom, afraid? Careful, you might ruin your reputation." His eyes grazed over Phantom, landing on eyes that were, no doubt, dilated. "What are you afraid of?"

Phantom let his head drop, a cursed laugh falling from him. Where would he begin? He feared for his crew and the families they sought to protect on Kheli. He feared for Sebastian that the potion would react wrong to his body and if not that, then feared the monster would rip him open just for being in the same room. He feared for Serena, cold and bleeding on the cavern floor. He feared for those boys in cages who would have their lives ripped away if it fit Ravana's whims.

He feared for Rose, that she would die, and he was destined to watch. Again.

That last thought drew a growl from him. He'd see her in the next life, he knew that for certain, no matter what came of their lives now. But they would never be Phantom and Rose again. The notorious pirate and the enchanting siren. He'd never have his devils again, his ship—

He didn't want to die. Not yet. He had so much to live for. More than he ever had before, and that scared him most of all.

"Everything," he breathed out, unable to voice the ramble of things rolling in his head. It was too much.

You can still fight this, Sam urged him. Phantom sagged with relief at hearing the bastard's voice again.

You're not going to die, Kayden said in a rougher tone, less forgiving than Sam.

"What would you bastards know?" Phantom hadn't meant to say it out loud, but a headache was forming, and he no longer cared.

"What?" Sebastian's voice drifted to him in a haze. He ignored him, or maybe he was fading into himself, letting the beast take full control.

No, you don't, Sam hissed. Green flashed across his vision and Phantom was shoved out of his own head, forced down into the depths of his soul. He could still see what was happening, but he no longer had control of his body.

Samuel Rourke grunted, lower and rougher than Phantom would have. Sebastian must have witnessed the changed because he stared, his mouth gaping.

"Hello Sebastian," Sam spoke through Phantom's voice, but it was more graveled, as if he had been screaming.

Finally, coming to terms with what was happening, Sebastian shook out of his stupor. "Who are you?"

Sam reached for Rose, aiming to remove her gag while he was in control. The beast still growled beneath his skin, but Sam suppressed his emotions, as he was trained to.

"My, that's a loaded question. I'm a friend, just not one you've met. But I've known you, watched you with James when you were kids." At the blank look on his face, Sam knew the man needed more than that, but they were out of time.

"Step away from her, or I'll shoot her before she can sing one note."

Sam froze at Felix's unforgiving tone.

The door's hinges creaked as it opened, allowing Ravana and her guards to enter. Clipped footsteps echoed across the cabin as she inspected her prisoners.

"Good, you didn't eat them."

Sebastian's brow slammed down as if he hadn't even considered that was a possibility.

Sam shrugged in response. It was possible. He wouldn't lie to the man, although the beast was a bit more particular about his meals.

Ravana turned to him then and narrowed her eyes. His eyes flashed with green, giving him away.

"And who might you be?"

Sam was hoping for this. To get the chance to be face to face with the bitch.

He willed Phantom's voice lower, almost deathly, as he leaned on the bars of the cell. "Your worst nightmare."

"I highly doubt that." She brushed him off, but he didn't miss the shiver to her skin, the gooseflesh smattering along her arms. It unnerved her. It should. Phantom wasn't the only one with stories to proclaim his ruthlessness.

Only with Sam, they were all true.

"Time to test you," she let out causally before pulling a vial from her robes. It was glittering lilac with white streaking through it like sea foam on waves. She nodded and guards poured into the cell.

He could take them, easily, like he had in the forest by the Temple. But the click of a pistol gave him pause.

Sam turned to see Felix holding the barrel of a gun to Rose's head, her tears and blood still staining her face as she glared up at him.

Sam kept silent while four guards pounced on him. He let them pull his arms back, restraining him. There was nothing he could do at that moment for Sebastian, not if it risked Rose and subsequently, his *reina*.

Sebastian understood his helplessness in the situation as well, letting the guards hold his mouth open and swallowing the lilac substance as it glided down his throat.

Sam held his breath, a tremor coursing through him as Sebastian's eyes went vacant.

"What did you do to him?"

"Oh dear, I was hoping it wouldn't work." A disappointed sigh left the Priestess. "At least we can return to our nocturnal activities again." A giddy laugh left her and sickness filled Sam's gut. That was it, the substance that turned those guards into soulless puppets. The tool that would enslave the entire island.

Sebastian's eyes were vacant, his posture that of a loyal officer. Was there anything left of Phantom's childhood friend? He let the words come out slow and measured. "What. Did. You. Do?"

"Oh, come now, we both know he would have died at your side, James—or whoever you are. I can ensure he will have a long life at my side now."

"As a slave, you mean?"

Her eyes narrowed at him. "Pot. Kettle. Black."

He understood the meaning of the words, but not how she implied them. Neither Sam nor Phantom had enslaved anyone. Phantom *freed* slaves.

"When Nemain takes your soul, I'll be sure She puts you in the deepest circle of Hell." He wasn't sure Nemain would grant his request, but he'd do it personally if he had to.

"Oh sweetness, I have no intention of leaving this world behind."

"How about I put a knife in your chest, and we go from there?"

She laughed at his threat before taking Sebastian's chin in hers. "Now, we mustn't tell the Minister of our failure here today. Understood?"

Sam glanced to Phantom's songbird, seeing her eyes glisten as Felix pressed the barrel of the gun into her temple.

He nodded obediently.

A pit formed in his stomach and Sam could hear Phantom's screams. He felt the pain right along with the pirate.

"Now, onto you." Ravana drifted over to him, glaring into his eyes, not seeing Phantom at all. Instead, she saw a stranger, one she had never sunk her claws into before.

"Think twice, Priestess. I will be less forgiving than my counterpart."

She lifted her chin in defiance. "I care not who's wearing the body. I only care that you get this to work," she bit out. Serena's angry snarl filled the space as she was dragged into the dungeon.

A strange mix of pride and rage overwhelmed Sam. She had grown so much from that little hatchling he found. Once she was small enough to fit in the palm of his hand, now, in length, she was as big as Phantom. And she still had so much growing to do.

He hoped he found her in the next life to see it.

But the blood coating her surrounding chains had him forgetting his pride. That Priestess did this to the young dragon.

"I need her to produce the sapphire flames, but so far, all she's been able to do is bite me." Ravana rubbed her wrist and sure enough, indents from dragon fangs marred her otherwise perfect flesh.

Sam's deep rumble permeated the air. "I cannot teach her what I do not know."

Ravana balked at the laugh, coming to terms with the thought of another being in Phantom's body.

"Perhaps she only needs the proper motivation."

Before he could guess her intention, the guard's hands came around his arms, keeping him in a death grip. Serena bleated and roared, clearly sensing the change in objective.

Ravana grabbed Serena's entire head in her nailed grasp. "I don't know if you can understand me, you little rat, but breath fire or I will make him pay the price." Serena growled, yanking her head from Ravana's grasp before snapping her jaws down on her hand.

Ravana cried out from the shock and pain.

Sam rumbled a laugh at the sight. She deserved that.

"You think this is funny?" she barked, staring up at Sam with a gleam in her eye.

"I think it is tremendously funny. Especially if you think you can torture me. Do your worst." He puffed up his chest, looking down at her, even if she wasn't much shorter. Sam had a way of making everyone else seem smaller than they were. "I'd been trained to endure torture since I was a boy. Better men have tried and failed."

"I'll deal with the little rat later, but for you—" A cruel smile tipped her lips. "I have a better idea. There is a pebble I've been trying to get out of my shoe for some time now. Seeing as you're the only one immune to her, I believe you can help me with my little problem." Ravana's eyes traveled to Rose, whose eyes were hard, another mind taking over the vessel. Sam knew who looked back at him. Only one woman could be surrounded by enemies and glare at *him*.

Isabeya.

His blood went entirely cold. Blue swarmed Sam, tossing him away. Phantom slammed back, his emotions too strong, too relevant to let anyone else have control.

"Ah, I see James is back. Good. For all your disrespect, you could use a lesson."

Phantom growled so deeply it brought his beast to the fore-front, ready to pounce.

"If you touch one hair on her head, I will make you eat your own fingers. One. By. One."

Instead of the fear or even weariness, she laughed, but it was hollow. This wasn't funny to her. She mocked his lack of control.

"I won't be touching her."

No no no no no.

"You will. I don't even have to threaten you." She seized his jaw, dragging his eyes to hers. "I'll just let you out. One more kill should do it. You'll be the nightmare the sailors warn each other about. But it won't be *my* nightmare." He held his breath, denial forcing his thoughts away from the inevitable. "You'll be Rose's nightmare."

CHAPTER 39
RUN

Phantom's fear grew exponentially when they traveled away from the cavern, leaving a broken Commodore lying in the cell alone and without the willpower to move of his own accord. Phantom hadn't even been able to process losing Sebastian. For one glorious moment, he had them both.

Rose Davenport and Sebastian Ashby. The two people he had felt whole with, and in one brief night, he had lost them both.

But he hadn't lost Rose, not yet. That was going to be so much worse, because he would carry out the action himself. There would be no coming back from that.

The man would die with her; only the monster would remain.

Maybe Sebastian would be ordered to finish him off? Wouldn't that be poetic?

Red licked at his vision, reminding him how close he was to breaking, to losing everything.

Ravana's guards dragged him out of the cave and across a field to an outcropping of trees. It was a small pine forest on the edge of Samsara, overlooking the sea from atop a secluded cliff. Just before the tree line was a maze of bushes. The same maze he had followed Rose into.

That first kiss. Now, she would die here amongst her mother's rose bushes and memories of him.

Just as they arrived, Lockness appeared, seizing Rose from a guard.

Anger spiked in Phantom's core. A man who believed he did what was right, sacrificing a woman for his cause.

Rose's hands were bound in ropes, her mouth still gagged as Lockness dragged her by the arm to the entrance of the maze.

Phantom struggled against the guards. He didn't trust leaning into his beast. It was too close and too powerful to control, so human strength would have to do. But there were four guards holding him down and Ravana eyeing him with her hands raised, ready to counter his attacks.

"How does killing Rose help you?" He addressed them both, his enemies lining up to watch his undoing.

Lockness's eyes softened. He didn't want to do this, but something drove him, nonetheless.

"You can blame Sebastian if you wish," Ravana's grating voice made him want to snap her neck. "He failed the test. The immunization potion didn't work. Seeing as I don't want to render my ears useless, this is the best solution for all of Samsara."

Rose's eyes found his, pleading with him.

"As a pirate, I think you can understand our need for freedom," Lockness's emotionless eyes drilled into him, but Phantom could see past the act. He wasn't devoid of guilt like Ravana was. Quite the opposite. It was his compassion leading these decisions. However twisted and broken he was. "If it were my freedom alone, I would not seek these measures, but there are those under my care who are threatened by the Minister's possessive reign." He looked down at her. "I cannot allow that."

Phantom struggled again, grunting as the guards pointed knives to his stomach and throat, halting his movements, a hand shoving into his hair, yanking his head backward.

Lockness's gaze softened, remorse fraying his sharp features. "I'd let her leave with you. You both could find some corner of the world to dwell in, but as she lives, so does her enchantment over me. My goals remain unfinished. My purpose unfulfilled. Her death is my only hope. Even if I am unsure of the result."

"Why not kill her yourself?" Maybe it was a stupid question to ask, but he couldn't get past it. "This seems to me like more work than necessary for the both of you."

"Unfortunately, Captain," Lockness said with deathly calm, pain in his eyes. Yes, he knew how cruel this was. "We cannot." In a flash, Lockness unsheathed a dagger at his hip and plunged it towards Rose.

"No," Phantom screamed, thrashing against the arms holding him in place.

But the dagger stopped as if it had struck a tree right before it could plunge into her chest. She didn't even flinch from the attempt on her life, but Lockness's face reddened with the effort to fight the barrier holding him back.

Ravana leaned into him, whispering like a lover into his ear. "If I could slit her throat, I would have done it every time I carved into her body."

Phantom growled, thrashing against the guards again.

Ravana shushed him. "Calm, James. Save your energy for her."

"If the potion had worked, we would have taken it and this girl," Lockness stared down with pity, "wouldn't have to die."

"We are slaves, Captain. Our chains are simply less visible." Lockness pressed his lips together. "But this could free us. Would you not pay the same price?"

"No," Phantom ground out. Rose's eyes widened at his

confession. Had she really doubted him that much? "Freedom and coin," he started, his eyes deepening, his words only for her, "are nothing compared to you."

Her eyes softened.

"Liar," Lockness snapped.

He was right. Phantom had sacrificed many in the name of freedom. The Naval officers, the Brettanian soldiers, vile pirates, countless Samsarans. The only difference now was that she was *his*. Rose was *his*. Not that she belonged to him, but with him. A kind of belonging he had never felt before.

That curse he was desperate to avoid before now felt like a blessing.

It has never ended well, Sam said hopelessly.

He thought he would at least have a little time before the curse caught up with him.

Ravana swept over to him, leaning in to whisper. "Let me introduce you to my protégé." He was too distracted to notice a woman rounding the guards beside him. Orange hair and so many freckles.

It was the girl who had been following him.

"I call her Minx. She's a crafty little thing." The girl only stood there, a slight smile to her full lips. She couldn't have been more than eighteen. "She told me about a cesspool of an inn she found you crawling around in." Phantom's blood turned ice cold. The devils were there. Had she found them?

Phantom struggled against the guard's grip, trying to face Ravana, but his face was fixed firmly on Minx's face. If he leaned on the beast, he could free himself, but he was too afraid to lose control.

Minx's slight smile widened into a grin.

A growl tore through his throat. Phantom knew what she was doing. One more kill and his power would spill over.

"You're bluffing."

"Am I?" Ravana whispered into his ear, keeping out of his

vision. "Apparently, Captain, you need to keep your secrets closer." The conversation he had with Rose regarding power happened at the inn. Minx must have been there. "She witnessed your heroic and uncharacteristic rescue of our dear Commodore, and his unfortunate mistake of letting you go." Rage burned deep in his stomach, aching for release.

"Really, James. Heroics? You? Please. Your heart is as black as they come. That's why you're going to kill this girl." Minx didn't even blink at the idea of her death. It must have been some trick of Ravana's. "She's the entire reason Rose is here. Minx found her trying to break you out." Red swarmed his vision, increasing his senses until he could pinpoint every heartbeat surrounding him, his own the most frantic. "If it wasn't for my little Minx, Sebastian would still be undercover in the Fortress, and Rose wouldn't have been discovered."

Blood and firelight flooded his vision as his control cracked under pressure.

The small redhead before him didn't tremble at the sight of his changing eyes. She waited for him, greeting her brutal death with open arms.

Ravana's hot breath coasted across the shell of his ear. "Minx is the reason you have to kill the little dove."

A roar barreled from his throat as he lunged at her, the guards releasing him before he could turn his wrath on them. Phantom's hand wrapped around Minx's throat, lifting her from the ground, his fingertips digging into the flesh of her neck.

"You caused all of this?" He demanded of her. He wanted her to beg for her life; give him a reason to let her go. There couldn't be more blood on his hands. His power was already too full, too potent for him to ignore.

One more kill.

"Yes," she choked out. "And I know more." The girl rasped, clearly yearning for death. "I didn't tell her about the other—"

A sickening crunch filled the silence as he snapped her neck. Rose screamed and it only registered now that she had been for a while. Not for the wretched life he had in his hands, but for his own.

Phantom dropped the body in his hands, and it fell to the dirt with a thud.

He felt his power filling, overflowing, and threatening to break the damn on his mind. His control was slipping away.

Ravana had her hands up, a smile splitting her face. Phantom rushed for her but met resistance as he collided with a wall of solid air. Another one of Ravana's tricks.

She moved her hands, pushing her wall of air towards him.

Behind him, Rose stood alone before the maze.

He had minutes, maybe seconds before the beast would be turned loose on her.

"Ravana, please," he groveled, the act of pleading to his worst enemy, the woman he despised with every fiber of his being grating on his soul. "Please don't do this."

She glanced at his eyes, cruelty turning soft.

"There was a time I would have given anything to see you look at me this way, those gorgeous eyes begging for me." He froze for a moment, keeping his eyes on her. If this would save his songbird, he would do whatever Ravana wanted. "Too bad it's all for her."

Ravana pushed again until Phantom was on his knees before Rose. Red. Yellow. Green. Orange. Blue. They all swarmed his vision as if fighting for dominance as the power in his blood demanded action.

He knew he couldn't fight it off, but that didn't mean he wouldn't try. His last breath would not be surrendering to his fate. No, he'd fight until his soul was ripped apart and prayed the next life wouldn't be so cruel.

Phantom's eyes found Rose's, and he promised just that. He promised to find her in that next life and make it better. To not waste time and find a way around this bloody curse. He watched her understand, saw a tear fall down her cheek because she knew. It wasn't just her death today; it would be his as well.

Phantom rooted himself to the ground, digging his hands into the dirt. Anything he could do to hold on.

"Rose," he bit out, his voice rough from the approaching beast. "Run. Don't look back. Don't hesitate. Run."

"No," she retorted, her gag pulled down her face. "No, you can fight this."

"Stubborn woman," Phantom growled out, his rage increased tenfold by the monster. She was so infuriating. Why was he in love with her?

He was in love with her. The realization softened the monster for a fraction of a second. Before the sentiment could solidify, the beast roared to get out again.

The colors assaulted him like a tidal wave, begging for release.

"Fight it!" she screamed at him, witnessing the hope leaving his eyes, knowing what it meant for them. "James, you're stronger than that part of you. Fucking fight it!"

A hollow, choked laugh left him. "Such a filthy mouth, little songbird." The monster clawed at his mind, the pain physically unbearable as if the beast would crawl out of his chest, ripping him open in the process. He doubled over in a pained growl.

"James, please. I love you."

His eyes snapped to hers. The silver and lilac moonlight competing with her golden irises and the tides lining them.

Phantom wanted to say it back, wanted to scream it at her repeatedly until the entire world knew he belonged to her. But Ravana was not so kind.

"You're taking too long. We can't have the Minister finding us out here," Ravana snapped from the safety of her air wall. Every guard aimed a pistol in their direction. Maybe they couldn't kill Rose, but they could shoot her legs, crippling her so she couldn't run.

And running was the only chance she had.

"Rose, go!"

But the shots fired, rushing past him to lick Rose's bare feet. She jumped backwards, avoiding the bite of the metal.

Anger, fear, hatred. All of it bubbled to the surface and slammed into him. He couldn't fight it any longer.

"Rose," he managed as his vision washing with crimson so thick, he could no longer see anything. He wasn't even sure he had control of his voice when he whispered.

"I love you."

CHAPTER 40
KILL HER

The girl in the white chemise had finally run, no doubt seeing his eyes turn the color of fresh blood.

His flesh tore apart to let claws emerge from his hands, growing until they resembled enormous paws, laden with fur. His back hunched over, and he screamed as his spine broke and reshaped, curling and lengthening.

As his body grew, the clothes he wore shred to pieces. Long fur replaced his skin in black tendrils. Blood pumped heavily through his enlarged body, the veins expanding and glowing until they could be seen through his fur.

Longer fur sprouted around his neck and head, marking him as the king of beasts. His maw formed with a pair of saber teeth long enough to slice a man in two.

The beast breathed heavily, feeling the dirt beneath his paws and the breeze ruffling his coat. There were threats everywhere, but he couldn't decipher which was which. He fell into his most basic instinct.

Kill.

Yes, Maahes, kill.

Was that his name? There was no sense of evil or good for

the beast, just fury and blood. He craved destruction like this was his Nemain's given mission.

Perhaps it was. He couldn't remember why.

He roared long and hard, deafening the ears around him.

The patter of a girl's running urged the beast to chase after her, pure instinct driving him. Red washed over everything, the hedges that towered over him, the grass, mud, and rocks covering the ground.

He found a small footprint in the dirt, with a soft curve made from a petite stature. She would be easy prey. He stalked after her with lethal efficiency. He could follow her prints, her scent, or the familiar feel of her presence. Something pulled at the back of his mind, begging him to see clearly.

But this is what he knew. The hunt. The kill.

Another voice reached him, one that was much colder. One that was old.

That's it. Kill her.

The beast recognized the voice. The power all-consuming and too strong to deny. This voice was devoid of fear or compassion, caring nothing for life.

This is your purpose, my sweet. Bring her to me.

He bent to his master, answering the call and drowning out the other voices.

The beast inhaled slowly, catching the smoky sweetness of the girl's scent. She was sprinting, but not nearly fast enough. It wouldn't take the beast long to catch up.

He rounded the corner to see her wild eyes, victory singing in his veins at seeing her panic. Growling, he crouched low.

Before he could pounce, she hummed. A short melody that encouraged the foliage on either side of the opening to grow. They blocked her from view, taking on more thorns in protection of the songbird.

The beast roared as his opening closed. There was no way to reach her, the only path forward now a dead-end.

"Ah ah ah," Ravana rasped like she was in the wind, surrounding them. "No cheating, little dove." As quickly as the new foliage appeared, an opening shifted the hedge to the right, revealing the girl whose chest heaved with fear.

Unhurriedly, he stalked after her and she ran. But she could not keep it up for very long. Songbird hearts were weak. It'll give out, eventually.

No!

The blue voice buried deep in the depth of his mind was emerging, barely holding on to consciousness.

She's stronger than that.

The beast beat back that voice, sending it tumbling back down to the depths again. It would do him no good. The colder voice was his master as it had been in every life. A master that smelled of carrion, the scent surrounding him.

Kill her, pet. Finish this.

He lost sight of her tracks in the grass, but he wasn't worried. Her scent still lingered in the air, jasmine and rose petals urging him on. A fork in the path appeared, and he took the path that smelled most like her, although her scent seemed to be everywhere now. As if it mocked him for not catching her yet.

But that would come soon enough.

Her scent grew closer as the hedges came to a point, another dead-end, shadows filling the space before the beast.

He growled, his tail flicking around the air in agitation.

Screaming echoed in their shared mind, not just the blue one, but the green, the yellow, and the orange, too. A mixture of colors raged behind his eyes. All of them pleading for her, banging against his hold on the body.

But it was too late. The prize was won.

The beast pounced at the shadows, but there, growing from the rose bushes, was jasmine. Potent, sweet jasmine that mixed with the roses surrounding him.

But the girl was nowhere in sight.

Anger flared with a growl as he grew tired of the chase. This needed to end.

A flash of white flew across his red vision.

There you are.

He roared, chasing after her, faster this time. There was no more sense in delaying the inevitable. He was faster than her, so he only needed a second to catch up to her.

But she wasn't the easy prey she appeared to be.

Another sharp hum escaped her, the hedge jutting out to block him. He lunged through the hedge, but it was full of thorns.

Ravana's laughter rumbled through the garden again.

The hedge opened in time to see the girl racing away. He barely saw the tail end of her dress as she rounded the corner.

They repeated the cycle a few more times. Her hums filling the air as she closed off each path one by one to have Ravana reopen the hedge at another location. It became clockwork as the beast grew accustomed to it. The recovery happening faster each time.

He nearly caught her, but a fountain stood in his way.

A memory surfaced, lips collided, words exchanged — the fountain.

Phantom nearly broke through from the powerful memory, clawing his way out, reversing the tides on the monster as if they had switched roles. In a way, they had. But the monster wouldn't give up his prey so easily, not with death's voice bellowing at him.

Kill her. End her and you can return home at last.

He shoved them both away, needing silence as he tracked his prey. They faced each other, the girl standing frozen, her eyes wide and fearful. But she no longer ran, even with his delay in silencing the screams in his head.

"James?" she whispered, a spark of hope filling her,

searching for some sign that he was there. Phantom reacted to his name, screaming her's back from the depths.

A rainbow of colors flashed across her eyes, not landing on a specific one.

The beast tilted his head, clearly intrigued by the trick his pretty prey could do.

She shook her head until the colors cleared. She hummed louder this time, a different tune than he was used to hearing. The hedge beside her opened, revealing a gap in the maze. Beyond it, a small forest at the edge of the island.

He could hear waves lapping against the shore beyond that outcropping of trees. No cliffs were in this area, instead there was a beach. If she got to that shoreline, he could lose her.

She took off running, and the beast jolted, taking chase as she barreled through the new opening, but it shut closed behind her.

The beast roared at the prickling bushes that stood in the way. The foliage reopened in the next breath, the thorny hedges pulling apart and jerking to the sides.

A faded sigh reached his ears. "I shan't waste anymore power. End this." He felt magic evaporate from the air like clearing humidity.

The girl was a blur before him, an apparition of white in the distance, but he would not take long to get to her. There was nowhere for her to go. Nowhere for her to hide.

Just as the beast was prepared to chase after her, Phantom slammed into his consciousness, screaming and echoing within the confines of their mind. The beast bucked, his speed significantly lessened, but that didn't stop him from continuing, moving one paw after the other in pursuit of the girl.

She weaved through the trees, taking every chance to hide, then rush to the next. There was too much chaos in their mind to focus on her. He lost her in the fray.

Growling deeply, he ran to the shore she was headed to.

Phantom tugged on the beast's control, trying to get ahold of him before he caught her, but it was too late.

She had stopped. Just before the beach she stood her ground, waiting for him.

There was a decision in her eyes. Phantom could see it through the haze of red that washed everything. She wasn't stopping because it was a dead end, quite the opposite. She had a chance to get away and chose to remain.

"You think you can hurt me? You. Just. Try."

The beast lunged, paws clawing into the bark beside her head. Phantom felt the beast's urge to shred her skin apart, taking vengeance out on her for everything that had happened on that cursed island.

Her eyes glowed, brighter than he had ever witnessed before.

An arm as solid as steel wrapped around the beast's torso, jerking him back and slamming him to the ground. The beast roared, frantic at the new threat. His giant claws tore into the fleshy light wrapped around him, shredding the slick, rubbery material there.

Eventually, he tore through the arm enough to flip back onto his paws. Until another arm clamped around his back left leg. Then the right, pinning him to the ground.

The sweet sound of a song filled the air.

MY SOUL SHALL TAKE WHAT IT CAN

His front paws were next, forced to claw at the dirt for escape.

I CONTROL THE HUNGER IN THE MAN

The beast used elongated teeth to tear through the rubbery

flesh pinning him down. Salty blood coated his tongue before the taste disappeared.

FREE THE BEAST BY STEALING THE FEAST

Blue light exploded from her chest, dancing away from her in ribbons. They twirled in the air, distracting the beast from his escape as those ribbons shoved into his chest.

The beast whimpered and roared, pain plunging into his chest and lacing his spine. The girl winced at the volume of his roar.

The ribbons caught hold of something within him, pulling at the well of power that made him strong. The beast recognized the threat, straining against rubbery arms to escape. He couldn't lose his power. What could happen then? He'd never been empty enough to know.

The girl sang the line again, deepening her descent into his power. She breathed heavily, until she moaned, taking on his magic like it was pleasure filling her veins.

Phantom broke through the walls the beast had fortified, his magic growing weak enough to let the blue one through.

Pain split his mind, changing the body they shared as blue crashed through his vision like a tidal wave. His spine shifted back into place. Those claws and teeth retreated. Black fur dissolved until only the hair on his head remained.

The beast was still present in Phantom's mind, so he didn't trust the control he had over his body. He looked up through a tuft of unruly hair to see Rose glowing like an angel. She sang beautifully, the words encouraging the ribbons from her chest into his.

He felt the pain of them dissolving his power, but he didn't care. It was working.

The beast reared, pushing to regain control again. He forced Phantom to lunge, slipping out of the too loose tentacle cuffs.

His body slammed over her, his arms bracketing the sides of her head, but not actually touching her.

"No," Phantom ground out, holding enough control that his voice was back.

Hope filled Rose's eyes as she reached for him. The movement made him jolt. That powerful song still linked them together, draining his power into her.

But the beast raged against the intrusion. Phantom slammed his eyes shut, focusing all his energy on controlling the beast. He willed himself to step away from her, but he couldn't. He wasn't sure if that was because of the beast or her song keeping him in place.

Until he realized she wasn't singing anymore.

Her warm hands curled around his neck, skin brushing against his in a way that was torturous. He couldn't let his guard down for a second or it would cost her life. His breathing grew more rapid, his heart more frantic as the beast pounded at his chest, wanting to be released again.

"You can let go. You can't hurt me." Her voice came soft and sympathetic, even if it was her life on the line.

He growled; anger too easy an emotion to latch onto. "Why didn't you bloody swim? You can escape through the water."

Rose ceased breathing. He had figured it out on his own. Her magic wasn't just powerful, it was near limitless. She needed only to memorize the correct songs from the Stone like a witch with a grimoire to accomplish greatness. Seeing her wield that power against him confirmed everything.

He doubted even Rose understood her limits beyond obtaining energy and knowledge. With enough training, she'd be unstoppable.

And he tried to lock her in his quarters.

He laughed grimly for a second before the pull of the beast refocused him.

"Do you know a song that would get you through those waters?"

"Yes," she breathed, pulling herself closer until she was only a breath away from him. Her scent overwhelmed him, the temptation to give into her too much. If he let go, he'd fall into her arms, and everything would be alright.

But that wasn't the case. If he let his control go, the beast would take her away from him, until the next life. Even then, it wouldn't be her. It wouldn't be Rose. She'd be reduced to a voice in someone else's head as he would be, never knowing what became of Samsara. Or Kheli. The devils.

The beast reared at the thought of all he was about to lose. Of what might become of his devils if he left them now. He'd already lost Sebastian. If Ravana did the same to his devils—

Red colored his vision darker, and he knew he was losing control.

Rose watched everything play out on his face, and she sucked in a breath.

"I know you're afraid," she whispered so softly he wasn't sure it was for him at all. "You're afraid you'll lose everyone."

"What do...do you mean...love?" He chocked out, growls interrupting his words as the beast attempted to surface and drown him out again.

Her soft hand landed on his cheek, so close to his mouth the beast could bite a finger off with little effort; yet she stood there, fearless.

"The beast you're holding back. He's your fear. Every time you are afraid, he surfaces to protect you. But he doesn't know the difference between something you fear and something you fear losing. He only knows the object of your fear." She pulled him closer, and he snarled, warning her in the most primal way, but she ignored it.

"James, let your fear go."

"Easier said...than done."

"But it is. The beast is part of you, not some force to be locked up and terrified of. Once you show him you are no longer afraid, he will obey you. You just saw that you have nothing to fear. I can handle you in all your forms. Let your fear go. Trust me."

How in the bloody hell was he supposed to manage that? He'd never been more afraid in his entire life, perhaps several lifetimes.

The beast surged again, and Phantom jolted, trying to keep a handle on the bloody thing.

"You can do this. It's the only way, James. I need you to let go. Please."

Her plea gave him the strength to push the beast back again.

"You have nothing to fear. The beast is you. He's part of you and always will be. Maahes is not your enemy."

The words soothed the beast over as if he were accepting those words for himself. His name. She knew his true name.

Her hands clasped around his neck again, holding him close and filling his senses. He could nearly taste her smokiness on his tongue.

"Phantom, please," she begged. The plea stopped him short. His chosen name was wrong on her lips. He built a reputation on a name that was made of legend. But he wasn't the ruthless pirate to her. She belonged closer to his heart than that.

"I'm not *Phantom* to you," he whispered, more to himself than her.

Then everything fell into place. He'd been battling the beast ever since he learned to fear the world as a boy. All those years ago, when sinister characters thought they could take their anger out on a boy. The beast had come to his aid then and every time since. Because of who he was, his fear looked like anger on the outside, but it was fear, nonetheless.

Red and blue intertwined in his vision like the sea during a

Nemain moon. The pull of the beast was no longer there, even if the beast itself was still present. The colors mixed, but they did not overlap; layers and streams of each color weaving with one another. The same, yet different.

A memory flashed, but it wasn't his own. The memory that surfaced was of Draiocht and an endless sea of sand.

Maahes was surrounded by dunes of sand, not a tree for miles. The sun was high in the sky, beating down on him. The beast ran on all fours, gaining distance in the blink of an eye. He had giant paws, like those of a lion's, but blackened. He ran through the dessert, not in pursuit of anything, but for the joy of it.

The call of a large bird echoed above him. He looked up to the sky, the burning silhouette of a giant bird flew overhead. It was beautiful, with a wingspan as large as two men.

Flames rippled behind the creature, almost as if she was made of them. A phoenix. A bird with golden feathers soaked in flames.

The creature flew through the sky like she owned it while the beast ran after her on the ground, happy to be in her shadow.

The bird called again before diving to the ground before the beast. As she reached the ground, she flipped, landing in a sand dune. The beast ran for her, a subsequent whine coming from him before reaching the dune.

But upon reaching her, he discovered her to be unharmed.

A pleasant, very human laugh resounded from her. A woman with dark brown, curly hair, black eyes, and a deep brown body, rolled from the dune.

"Let's go again!" she shouted at the beast, who lapped the skin of her face the moment he could. His savior. The only good thing to ever cross him. She laughed pleasantly before offering a playful smile. "I won!"

Maahes chuffed, before nuzzling against her neck.

"Oh alright, I'll ride with you this time."

The girl, barely old enough to be a woman and as naked as the day she was born, climbed onto the beast's back before it took off. She laughed again from its back, roaring into the sky.

Phantom's attention returned, golden eyes greeting his. Golden eyes that he wanted to drown in. Hope flooded those eyes as the last wisps of red faded from his vision. The beast's presence was no longer there, but Phantom gained his memories.

He *was* there. It was his past life, joining with his current one.

Memories of sleeping, curled up at the girl's feet surfaced. The beast had been this girl's companion and had loved every moment he had with her.

A breath of relief finally left him as he let himself realize the threat was gone. He didn't have to worry about the beast at all. He could feel his heightened senses, his strength still present without the cost of losing control. The two personas were joined.

He focused inwardly, wondering if his other voices were still there.

Present, Kayden quipped, amber flickering.

Here as well, Sam returned, forest green flashing.

Draven didn't speak, but a shadow of sunset orange drifted over him.

"I'll be needing a moment alone, gentlemen," he whispered to himself and subsequently three others. They retreated into the dark corners of his mind.

Phantom focused on the beautiful, fearless woman before him with so much awe in his heart, he couldn't contain it. She had done this.

"You are the most amazing, stunning creature I have ever encountered," he whispered, leaning in so they were but a breath apart. "You are my life, Rose Davenport. I'm yours until my last breath."

For a half a second, he believed she would reject him. He

wouldn't blame her if she did. All he had done was put her in further danger.

Rose lifted her chin, a challenge gleaming in those golden eyes. "You're mine?"

Everything he was, felt like it was stripped down to this one moment, like the entire world held its breath, waiting for what this would mean. "In this life, and every life after," he vowed.

A small smirk tipped the corner of her mouth. "Then prove it."

CHAPTER 41
SAND & SEA

Phantom reached down, filling his palms with her ass as he lifted her up and slammed her into the tree. Instantly, her legs came around his waist, pulling him as close as she could.

He was completely naked before her. The beast had shredded his clothing, but as she bit her bottom lip, he knew she appreciated the view.

Their lips met in a flurry of heat and passion; the desperation felt all the way to his bones. While he held her legs in place, Rose's hands roamed across his chest, around his neck, digging into his hair. The feeling of her eagerness urging him on.

Her teeth dragged against his bottom lip, drawing a growl from him. Falling into her again, he silently begged she would open for him, and she did, understanding his demand. Phantom's tongue swept in, claiming her mouth. She groaned pleasantly in response, meeting his every move with a passion of her own.

Phantom wondered if she had been waiting for this as long as he had. Was it as inevitable as it felt? Fate drawing them into each other's arms until they were so consumed with passion, the rest of the world fell away.

He didn't care why.

Phantom only knew one thing.

He'd make goddess-damn sure she'd never forget this night, in every single one of her lives. His mouth parted from hers. A small whine of disappointment escaped her, and he chuckled darkly before pressing his lips against her neck and down to her collarbone. She moaned softly.

He whispered against her skin. "Remember what I promised you, love? That I would worship you and I'm feeling particularly devout." He pulled back to watch her eyes, but they were dangerously dark, raking his body up and down.

"I don't see you on your knees."

He growled low, warning her a second before he fell to his knees before her.

Oh, so slowly, he let his hands drift on either side of her bare legs, ascending her body beneath her chemise. The white gauzy fabric was no obstacle, reminding him of that flimsy dress she wore when they first met.

That day she looked at him with fear in her eyes, but not anymore.

He found the heat at the center of her legs and brushed his hand across the fabric there. It was so thin; he could feel the dampness building. She breathed in sharply, but no other sound came out, like she was holding it back.

Every time she sang, the world around her changed. He wondered what would happen if he made her sing. Suddenly, it felt like the only purpose he had. Everything else was put on hold as he drew pleasure from her.

"You'll need to be much louder. The entire island will know exactly who makes the songbird sing."

A smile grew on her face, daring him to try. "We'll see about that, Captain."

He smirked. A challenge he gladly accepted.

In a sharp movement, he ripped her panties apart, the thin fabric landing in pieces on the forest floor. Yet, she didn't seem affected apart from the little bite she made on her bottom lip, silencing her cries.

"You asked for it, little songbird."

He dragged her knee up to his mouth while he pushed the skirt of her dress back to her waist, exposing her. Trailing kisses on the inside of her thigh, he stared at her from his knees, her breath leaving her altogether until a moan slipped out.

He pressed her thigh to his mouth, letting the pressure build as her hands landed in his hair, tugging him closer. A satisfied chuckle left him as he bent to the demands of his woman.

Closing the last bit of distance in a flash, he licked down the center of her and she cried out. He rumbled a laugh at how easily she melted into him. He licked again. His tongue circled around her sensitive bud, and she sank against the tree at the sensation.

He devoured her, licking, sucking, and nipping in every way that made her cries louder and her hands move more desperately in his hair. He lifted that leg onto his shoulder, keeping her open for him, her moans growing louder.

He drew every ounce of pleasure from her, adding his finger to pump inside her while he continued to plunder her most sensitive area with his mouth.

She screamed her release, the sound fading into a moan as her inner walls pulsed and gripped around his finger. He hummed in satisfaction at the feeling of her body's reaction, imaging what that would feel like on another part of him. A part that was begging to be part of the action and a deeper, more primal part of him begged to claim her in the most physical way a man could.

Phantom pulled away to let her catch her breath and gauge her reaction.

Rose stood slumped against the tree, breathing fast, but becoming steadier, with her climax still clouding her. She reached for him, pulling him up. Her hands traveled down his chest, passing down his navel.

"Impatient, are we?" He teased, but that siren quality returned to her eyes, signaling she was far from done with him. Which was a relief, because he was nowhere near through with her. He wasn't sure he ever would be.

"I think we've waited long enough."

"I couldn't agree more."

She reached for the hem of her dress, but he bent to remove it from her body, lifting it over her head.

She was completely bare before him, silver and lilac moonlight mixing to contour her perfect body. Scars cascaded so much of her, but they made her infinitely more beautiful. He couldn't stop staring at how ethereal she looked.

The roundness of her hips curving into her waist. Her breasts were small enough that he consumed them with his hands, but still so bloody perfect. Her hair waved down one of her shoulders like rippling sunlight. And that desire from her eyes, not even marginally sated by one release.

He wanted to devour every inch of her.

Rose's hands grasped his length, and he groaned deeply. She kissed him passionately while running a hand down his length, a new wave of pleasure washing over him.

Phantom chuckled deeply. "No rush, love." He drew away from her enough to place both hands on her face, homing in on the desire there. "I intend to take my time with you. There is not an inch of you I don't want to savor."

He took her mouth again, slowly this time, basking in the feeling of her lips on his. She obliged, taking what he gave as her hand teased the head of his cock pressed between them. The pleasure strong enough to consume him.

He lifted her hand away. "Love, if you continue that, this will be over far too soon."

Mischief glinted her eyes. He moved before she could act on her filthy thoughts.

He removed her from the tree then walked her back until their feet sunk into soft sand and the waves lapped at their ankles. He reached down to lift her up against him and she jumped, wrapping her legs around his torso, but he did not let her body slide home.

Not yet, even as she struggled to do exactly that.

Instead, he teased her, dropping her low enough to slide against that bundle of nerves at the apex of her thighs. A deep resounding moan vibrated in her throat causing a flicker of blue to glow from her eyes.

Phantom lowered her to the sand, letting the water lap at her naked flesh with her head further up the shore. He looked down at her and had to catch his breath again. Blue faded from her eyes, but that made them no less intense.

He seated himself before her entrance, ready to connect them fully. They both understood what this would mean, not because of some fated connection between them, but because he could feel it. In his bones, in his very soul, there was never a woman that would mean more to him.

That also meant he could wait. He placed his head against hers, pained at having to back away. When he did, she whimpered, and it took every ounce of his strength not to return.

He groaned, reminding himself to be smart. "I don't have—"

"I take a tonic for that." Her hands roamed his body like she couldn't stop them. "It stops my Macha cycle."

Phantom let out a groan. "Remind me to thank the witches later for that blessed tonic."

She chuckled sweetly before a flicker of hesitation crinkled her brow. His hand was on her cheek in an instant, his elbow digging into sand as he leaned on it.

"Rose, what's wrong?"

"Did you mean it?"

"Mean what, love?"

He waited eagerly for her response, wondering where he had gone wrong.

"You said you loved me before you turned. Were you only saying that because you thought I would die?" The lace of doubt in her eyes, the vulnerability, it was nearly too much for him.

He caressed her cheek, his thumb brushing over her swollen lips. "I loved you from the moment you placed that old blade against my skin at the Temple. I didn't realize it then, but I knew you. Every moment after proved how much you meant to me." Her breath caught in her chest as she soaked in the intensity of his gaze. "I love you, Rose, deeper than the depths of the ocean and vaster than the skies above them."

Passion drew them to each other again as he pushed in. Her body was ready and waiting for him as he thrust home, filling her completely. She screamed into the night as that blue haze from her nightmares returned. It filled the space around them like a fog, but he didn't dare stop his slow thrusting as her pleas and moans encouraged him, not to mention the waves of building pleasure taking hold of him with each stride.

Phantom felt her clamping down on him, getting tighter and ready to release her into ecstasy again. Normally, he loved to deny pleasure, to build his partner's sensations until the release would be infinitely more intense.

But not tonight.

He'd have that kind of fun with her another time, but tonight, all he wanted to do was ring every ounce of pleasure from her and make her see stars.

Her breathing grew frantic, knowing that was a sign she was close. He reached down between them, letting his hand find the bundle of nerves that he knew would send her over the edge.

But he didn't think it would happen so soon.

He only brushed that sensitive area along with thrusting inside her before she was singing her pleasure, her body pulsating against him, making him want to follow her over that edge. But he resisted, not wanting this to end yet.

The blue haze around them had images he couldn't make out, not with his focus currently on the songbird below him.

He lowered into her as he continued his pursuit towards bliss, kissing her lips, devouring her neck, and nipping at her breasts as her hands explored every inch of skin she could reach.

When he drew back slightly, she pounced, catching his ear with her teeth, sending a shiver down to where he was inside her.

He growled pleasantly, and she shivered at the sound of it.

He nearly remarked on her reaction, but no sooner did her eyes flash blue did her own throat let out a hum. Gaining strength from her song, she flipped them over, landing him on his back in the sand with her seated atop him.

The shock of her sudden strength drew him back.

"Quite the trick, love," he teased, and her smile tipped. There was a switch in her gaze that spoke volumes. She may be the prey, the songbird he would chase, but she could be a predator of her own volition.

"Normally, I don't take to being dominated," he growled, letting her know precisely who she was riding. But the blue hadn't left her eyes as she pushed down on his shoulders with impressive strength, keeping him down. It was incredibly intoxicating. "Then again—"

She smiled brilliantly, but said nothing as she rocked, drawing pleasure from him that urged him closer to bursting.

This. Woman.

He bucked, deepening their connection. Then his hand came around her hips, digging into her flesh and filling his hands. The feel of her body was better than anything he could have imaged. He rocked against her, and she cried out his name, sending it into the fray and drowning out the sound of the crashing waves behind them.

They met with heightened passion. The need of his flesh overwhelming him as his fingers dug in hard and his pace deepened and quickened.

Another one of those delicious cries left her lips, but this time, he didn't stop himself from joining her over the edge. Stars burst across his vision in swarms of blue. He drowned in pleasure from the strongest release he'd ever experienced.

With heavy breaths, they both soaked in the sheer intensity of their climaxes. She lowered herself down, her head landing on his chest, her hair slick with sea water, her body gritty with sand.

The feel of her body was nothing short of heavenly as their breaths synced together with the rhythm of the waves. He stroked up and down her back as she caught her breath.

Placing a finger beneath her chin, he drew her into a kiss that was so much sweeter than what they'd shared before. There was a need to prove that every promise of his body was true.

Phantom would take her anywhere she wanted to go and beg her to let him stay with her.

Her golden gaze met his. "We have to go." She stood, reaching for her chemise.

"If you believe that piece of fabric can contain your sea-soaked glorious body, I think you are mistaken. I suppose it is something, though I do prefer you in this state."

A gleam entered her eyes. "Naked? Shocking."

"Aye, that." He inched towards her, regaining the few feet between them. "And with the glow and grit of a woman who has been thoroughly satisfied."

Her lips tipped. "You haven't even begun to satisfy me, Captain." This time, his title was filled with promise as she lifted the thin fabric over her head.

"Oh, please say that again."

Her hands landed on her hips. "We haven't the time for this. That girl you killed; she knew you were at the inn. She could have told Ravana about the devils."

Phantom's gaze sank. "I killed her before she could."

Rose let out a breath of relief as Phantom realized how foolish it was to trust Minx's word, even her last ones.

"We'd best make sure anyway and get you far away from this island." He also had to figure out how to get Serena out of that cavern. He was confident Ravana needed her enough to keep her alive. But for how long?

Rose nodded, not fighting him on the subject. She examined the uselessness of the thin fabric.

"We must find clothes first."

CHAPTER 42
DRUMBEAT

Phantom and Rose used the cover of the night to sneak around the Fortress. Morning was fast approaching, bathing the island in a deep fog.

Phantom could feel his beast under his skin, but it no longer felt like another part of himself. Those memories of running through the deserts surrounding Draiocht with a wild child turned phoenix were as real to him as his memories of growing up in the slums of Samsara. It was no longer a part of him he had to hold back or coax down. The powers of the beast were present; the smells, the sights, and strength, but none of the overwhelming emotions.

They were one.

There were still three other voices competing underneath his skin, but at least the beast was no longer a problem.

His lack of clothing was inconvenient as they sulked the shadows of the Fortress.

"You wouldn't happen to be able to conjure some clothing for me with your siren song?"

"Unfortunately, I don't know the song for that yet." She blushed as she took in the very little that chemise did for her.

A pair of officers wandered out, laughing over their shared drinks. Not mind bent puppets then. They didn't so much look at Phantom or Rose. Drunk perhaps?

"Well then, this should be fun."

Phantom picked up a fallen branch and knocked one officer over the head with it. His own strength surprising even him as the man hit the ground hard.

The other man's eyes went wide at his fallen comrade, then drew his sword to face the threat. The officer paused, taking in Phantom's state of undress.

Phantom laughed. "Oh I'm sorry, it seems I don't know my own strength."

The officer recovered from his stupor and swiped his sword at Phantom who dodged the blade before it could hit his bare flesh. The man's eyes drifted over Phantom's shoulder, filling with appreciation.

He felt the songbird's presence behind him.

Phantom growled, knocking the man off his feet while he was distracted.

"That's not very honorable of you." He knocked out the man with a kick to the skull, not bothering to be soft.

Rose came running up to him, examining the officers. "What did you do?"

He could hear their heartbeats. "Not to worry, love. They're lucky to be alive with what one has seen."

She glared at him, but he ignored it, examining the clothing the officers wore, hoping the uniforms wouldn't be too small for him. Or too large for her.

***

Rose fixed the collar of her jacket, the clothes too big on her body aside from her behind and hips, which were straining the fabric.

He grinned as he placed the officer's hat on her head, completing her disguise. Not that it helped much. "You're too short for an officer."

He didn't mean it as an insult, but by the twist of her lips, that's how she took it. "And you're too scruffy for one."

Feigning offense, he scratched at his stubble just beginning to sprout. He let the act drop, his eyes lowering instead. "I recall it's a feature you prefer. Though I am curious as to your other preferences regarding my appearance."

She glared at him. "If you keep flirting, we're never making it to the inn."

Tempting as that notion was, he agreed the urgency was too great to ignore. He needed to regroup with his devils and find Serena before the Minister could make good on his threats. Once they were sailing the Sumerian Sea, he'd be sure to give Rose his undivided affections and then some.

Drumbeats stole their gazes towards the entrance to the Fortress. Phantom shot her a quizzical look. It wasn't a good sign.

They snooped around the building, keeping to shadows, but walking more like soldiers now, in case anyone saw them. If passersby didn't look at them too closely, no one would suspect them. Not with the commotion.

A bellowing, self-satisfied voice rose over the chatter; one that he begged Nemain to eradicate from the world.

"My people," the Minister said, standing on a balcony before the masses. Samsarans gathered to hear what the Minister had to say. High town society in their expensive fabrics and umbrellas sneered at the citizens of low town.

Officers littered the crowd in no particular form, some with blank unseeing stares, some with a hunger for blood. Either way, tensions were high, as if the people could sense something wasn't right on their island. Yet none of them looked to the Minister in disgust, nor to the Priestess at his side.

Now that he looked closely at the old man, there was darkness under his eyes and a sweat beating down his face. Whatever the Minister hoped to accomplish wasn't going according to plan. Normally, he would have celebrated the look of failure, but Ravana's smug grin told him it was not so simple.

His eyes narrowed in on her neck. There, the Davina pendant rested on her breast, glowing faintly in the fresh morning light.

"I stand before you all today, with a burdened heart and a saddened soul. My daughter has been murdered."

Gasps littered throughout the crowd.

"Yes, the jewel of my heart, the very centerpiece of my life. My precious daughter has been taken from me this night."

"Oh please," Rose rasped under her breath, quiet enough that it took Phantom's superior hearing to recognize it.

The Minister sniffled, dabbing his eyes with a handkerchief gently, though Phantom doubted any tears fell. It was a poor performance, but the crowd ate it up.

"What happened?"

"Who killed her?"

The shouts rose from the crowd, growing more urgent the longer they remained unanswered.

"It was the pirates who terrorize you." Ravana's infuriating voice broke through the crowd. But the words shook the people, dividing them. The people of high town and the officers screamed louder, but the faces of low town paled.

"Their Captain did it himself, cutting her into unrecognizable pieces," an officer shouted as if he discovered the body himself.

"He laughed as he did it, too," another spoke out, eyes wide like he had been traumatized by the fake murder.

Phantom would have laughed at the obvious manipulation if it wasn't working so well. The crowd stirred, shouts calling for blood, all while the Minister had his face buried in a hand-kerchief.

The Minister pulled up his face, seeming to compose himself long enough to lower his hands, signaling for silence. The crowd bent to his will, eager to hear his words.

"Not to worry, I have captured most of the pirates." Phantom's blood turned to ice in his veins. "Except for the Captain himself. If any of you see him, kill him on sight or take him to me and I will see it done."

"What of the others?" A low town voice bellowed over the crowd and Phantom recognized it as Mrs Brock from the inn.

She was alone in the crowd, her arms crossed before her.

"The devils will be executed once the drums stop. If you hurry, you can make it to the executioner's arena to witness it."

His breath stilled in his lungs. His devils were about to die, and he was stuck in a bloody crowd, the arena on the edge of low town was miles away.

The crowd swelled, heading exactly where he thought they would. The crowd wanted to witness the downfall of the devils. They wanted to see a hanging.

The shouts of the crowd drowned out until all Phantom could hear was the beat of the drums. The sound roaring over him as he dreaded the moment they would stop.

A pull on his sleeve made him look down to see Rose. Her eyes were frantic as she pulled on him, but he couldn't hear what she was saying. He lost them. He lost them all.

"Move your bloody ass," she shouted at him, snapping him out of his despair. He moved, and she ran, dragging him along behind.

She headed straight for the arena, where the devils would hang. His devils.

His family.

The drums grew louder as they ran through the streets of high town, looking for a better route to reach the arena, but every road was packed with frenzied, impatient people. And those bloody drums thrummed in every corner of Samsara, calling to him, reminding him exactly what fate was about to befall everyone he cared about, save the songbird in his grasp.

The crowd surged, thickening like a blockade. He pulled Rose off to the edge near a wall to gain some height over people and scout out a new path.

"Captain," a voice grated against the crowd, hushing chatter and silencing disgruntled citizens.

Lockness.

It was the only man besides the Minister with that kind of sway and power over the people.

"Bloody hell," Phantom swore under his breath, hammering a fist into the wall of the building, causing rubble to tumble down his hand. He forgot his strength was with him now. He no longer had to call on it or cast it away.

He hardly noticed the pain as his gaze landed on Rose.

"Captain Phantom, such a fantastical name for a criminal," Lockness berated, casting his words out into the crowd. He glanced around, knowing Phantom was present, but unsure where. Of course, they knew Phantom would not die in their attempt on Rose's life.

But Rose—

They thought she was dead. Lockness and Ravana had made it clear they did what they believed was necessary, sacrificing Rose to the beast. A plan that nearly succeeded. But if the Minister thought she was dead, they must have too, even if they fed a fabricated story to him.

Her survival wouldn't be taken well.

Phantom examined the officers surrounding Lockness, creating a perimeter, and blocking all the right pathways. But she could get to them if he distracted Lockness.

"Go. Find the Stone and save the devils."

Her eyes narrowed. "What? I'm not leaving you."

"There's no time to argue. Do you know where the Stone is?"

She nodded.

"Good, retrieve it."

Her gaze hardened. "I'm not leaving you."

He placed a hand on her cheek; her round, soft skin beneath his fingertips. "I'll survive," he lied. "I need you to save them if I can't get there in time." Her eyes softened, believing his lie. He took her in. He'd do everything he could to make it back to her, but she needed a distraction. And they were looking for him after all.

"Phantom," Lockness mocked his chosen name.

"Get the Stone. Get them out."

The mission solidified over her face. "I will, and you *will* make it in time."

He grinned. "Always do, love." The words fell flat, but blessedly, she didn't notice.

Before she stepped out, he planted one excruciating kiss to her lips, committing the feel of her to memory. He let his grip on her go and the air turned cold as she stepped away, disappearing into the crowd.

Phantom breathed in once before removing the officer's cap and loosening the scarf at his neck, revealing his trademark tattoo that would be recognized from any corner of Samsara.

The whispers began before he could even make it to Lockness, and the crowd parted.

"Ah, there's the lost sheep." Lockness regarded Phantom, taking in the officer's uniform and his hateful gaze. The man before him attempted to kill his songbird. Even as she survived, he'd rip the man's throat out for it. Phantom's low growl was warning enough to promise that.

Lockness remained unfazed as he nodded for a nearby officer to clap irons over his wrists. They removed his weapons, forgetting to take the knife in his boot. The metal shackles bit at him as the drums increased in volume.

"You hear that, Captain?" The drums continued to beat, a steady unrelenting sound Phantom both despised and prayed would never stop. "That's the sound of your demise. Not to worry, you'll join them. I'll be sure you get a front-row seat to the action."

Phantom narrowed his eyes. It was an act. Something about his words weren't right. From what he understood of the man, Lockness was not needlessly cruel. Everything he did was for a purpose.

He had pondered the lord's words from the gallery. Lockness wanted him to understand, and part of him did. Enough to understand that Lockness thought himself the hero.

This was an act.

For who? The people?

Phantom got his answer as Ravana appeared beside Lockness on a drift of red shadows like airborne rivers of blood. Her pale skin was akin to silver moonlight, her eyes gleaming with lilac light. There was something otherworldly about her, and utterly unnatural.

The crowd gasped at her arrival, almost in unison as they bared witness to the display of Goddess magic that should only be possible by a Goddess. It was blasphemy of the highest order.

Her red dress blended into the surrounding shadows, clearly some of her trickery at play, the Davina pendant glowing brilliantly at her neck.

"My, David, have you caught me a pet?"

Lockness' nose wrinkled at the mention of his first name, clearly not wanting her to call him that. But Phantom's interests landed on the dutiful officer that followed through Ravana's red mist.

Sebastian's eyes were empty and dazed as he followed

loyally. Ravana's sickening gaze drifted over him like the chill of a nearby spirit, lifting the hair from Phantom's back.

She pouted at his appearance. "An officer uniform, truly James? I would have thought you more creative than that."

She drifted closer to Ashby, a hand landing on his shoulder. Most would see his apparent boredom and think him unbothered by her presence, but Phantom noted the way his hands flexed at his side, then curled into fists.

He resisted the smile that played at his lips. His friend was not gone. Not completely.

"I hate to disappoint," Phantom mused, playing along with her game. It was Kazeboon with four players, all lying to produce the effect they wanted.

Ravana turned up her nose in disgust, apparently disliking the evidence of her villainy. At least he would own it, but she always preferred to be seen in a good light.

"You will pay for your crimes," she stated plainly, like it was scheduled.

"You mean your crimes, Priestess. Let's not pretend you did not orchestrate this," Phantom purred, letting her see his fangs. The promise of death.

Silence encompassed the crowd around them. Samsarans surrounded them, listening to their exchange.

She laughed deeply, yet it was hollow. "Who do you expect to believe that, Captain? The Minister? Perhaps the Commodore. Oh." She made a gentle high pitch sound, her grasp on sanity slipping with whatever she had transformed herself into. "Oh, I forgot. He won't be of any use to you, will he?" She jeered, before raising a hand to Sebastian. "Come, pet, I think the Captain has a date with his precious Goddess."

The Commodore obeyed swiftly, marching to her side and withdrawing the sword from his hip. Before he could reach them, Lockness wrapped a firm hand around Ravana's arm, jerking her to him. But his eyes were on the crowd, with good reason. The crowd stirred with murmurs and unease.

Those blasted drums adding to the tension.

"I promised he would see his devils die first," Lockness gritted out. Phantom couldn't tell if the man was trying to buy time or didn't like to be undermined. "I always keep my promises, Priestess." He bit out her title like it was a curse, and Phantom had to agree. Whatever she was now, it was not a priestess.

She glared at him, tearing her arm from his grasp, daring him to challenge her. "Then you shouldn't promise what isn't yours to give, my lord."

He let out a frustrated sigh, but his eyes traveled back to the crowd. Phantom followed his gaze to see a mix of emotions circling the people.

Disbelief.

Fear.

Anger.

Restlessness.

Part of him hoped the people of low town that mixed heavily into the crowd would come to his aid, rise against their captors and take the island back. But they thought he killed Rose, and they loved her more than they admired him. Even if they believed he was innocent of that crime, there were still too many high town nobles and merchants around them. Victims of Captain Phantom and the Eleven Devils.

They'd probably start calling for his head soon enough.

Phantom turned to the crowd, apprehension running through him. But he ignored it. The immediate future was his only concern.

"Don't you see what's happening?" The crowd silenced, looking to Phantom with an array of feelings towards him. "The Minister has a witch that has disgraced every Goddess you pray to. Don't you see? A priestess she is not."

"James," Ravana cooed. "What are you doing?"

Sebastian halted next to her, awaiting orders. She hadn't yet asked for Phantom's head, but she would.

Scanning the crowd, Phantom spotted Lord Desmond flanked by his own personal security, clearly unwilling to brave the mob without them. He locked eyes with the lord, recognition spreading over him, but the next second his eyes were on the necklace encircling Ravana's neck, glowing brighter than the moon itself.

"The Minister has tricked you. He seeks to take away the free will of everyone on this bloody island."

Gasps littered the crowd, along with a few laughs.

"Why would we listen to a pirate?"

Phantom's anger coiled. He had half a mind to let the Minister have them. But a face in the crowd stopped him. Beside Mrs Brock was the little girl he helped save, bundled in scarves to hide her face, but her eyes poked through.

They don't deserve this, James, Sam reminded.

"Where are your sons? The ones you enlisted into the Minister's oh-so-noble Navy? Hm? Have you seen their dead eyes and cold answers? Do they seem like the same sons you sent to the Minister? Have you even questioned what he has done to them?"

Murmuring filled the street. Ravana shifted from foot to foot, clearly uncomfortable, even as the corner of Lockness' mouth tipped up.

"It's true," Lockness bellowed loud enough to be heard over the chatter. The crowd silenced easily, willing to listen to him. Lockness took a few healthy steps from Ravana, who glared at his back like she would stab him. "The Minister seeks to enslave the minds of anyone who would dare defy him."

"David!" Ravana snapped, a ring of desperation in her tone. Things were not going according to her plan.

The crowd continued to grow uneasy. They pushed against the line of officers keeping them at bay.

"Now's the time. Take action for your families. For the island," Phantom shouted over the crowd, watching as several stares pinned to him, believing him.

A silence took over everything for a second, a calm before the storm.

"Kill him," Ravana commanded Sebastian. The Commodore marched after Phantom.

Lockness leapt to protect him — oddly. But he was soon tossed away as Ravana's eyes glowed with brilliant lilac light. Lockness fell on his back without a visible force pushing him down.

"I was going to wait for this, but your presence has become a nuisance." Ravana retrieved a long dagger from her cleavage. Gemstones of all sizes encrusted it, a ceremonial dagger. But she wasn't talking to him, it was Lockness she was after.

He couldn't pay attention to their scuffle as a sword was about to separate his head from his shoulders. He lifted his irons for the sword to catch on the chain. The metal clanged as the cuffs rubbed on his wrists, chaffing and bruising his skin.

"Come now, brother," Phantom mused. "We aren't back to this, are we?" Even as he said it, he knew they would always come back to this.

A feminine grunt returned Phantom's attention to Ravana. Lockness disarmed the Priestess by knocking the bottom of her hand and dislodging the dagger. Lockness reached to retrieve the dagger, but a gust of wind tossed it aside before his fingers could grip the hilt. Ravana's imposing cackle clarified that it was no coincidence.

Phantom backed up a step to wrap the chain of his irons around the tip of Sebastian's sword, and rip the metal from the Commodore's hands, the sword coming loose too easily. If it had been any other officer, he wouldn't have questioned it.

But Sebastian Ashby didn't lose his sword.

Phantom tipped his head at Ashby, who drew the knife tucked away in his boot, the same place Phantom always kept his. His eyes widened for a moment, staring at his old friend, praying for a sign that he was fighting his compulsion.

The crowd surged, growing louder, shouts littering the air along with the steady drums. Officers barely kept them all at bay. Some called for his head, some for Ravana's. If they slipped by the line of officers, chaos would ensue.

Perhaps that's just what we need.

Sebastian lunged for him, missing Phantom's neck, but he barely flinched. A small smile crept up his face, he was beginning to understand. Phantom was chained and weaponless. It would be no feat for the Commodore to unarm him. It should have been easy, which meant Sebastian was only trying to *look* murderous.

This time when he struck, Phantom wrapped his chain around the knife's blade, knowing Sebastian would have avoided such a maneuver the second time if he were truly the enemy. A small chuckle left him as he drew Sebastian close enough to whisper.

"Break the line," he commanded, pulling back to see if he understood the order. Sebastian nodded without breaking his cold and emotionless demeanor, but it was all the confirmation he needed.

They continued to struggle together, making their way to the crowd and the line of officers. Phantom pulled a blade from one officer holding the line. The officer turned back enough to allow the crowd leverage. Phantom and Sebastian jumped out of the way.

The crowd surged like a storm wave into the street, flooding every step with shouts and angry town members. Many reached for Ravana, who shrieked at their approach before disappearing into a cloud of red mist.

Lockness was nowhere to be seen, but he was hardly the problem now.

Drums still beat furiously; unyielding and mercifully still going.

Sebastian pulled Phantom from the street before the mob overtook him completely. Once they hid away in a shadowy alcove, Phantom fell into his brother's embrace.

"I thought I lost you."

Sebastian's arms came around him. "You almost did." But he pulled away just as fast, reaching to unlock the irons and let them fall to the dirt. "You need to go, or your crew will die."

Phantom stared out at the racing mob. "How?"

Sebastian nodded his head to a spot behind Phantom. A ladder like the ones he climbed before rested on the side of the building. It seemed he'd be bypassing the crowd altogether.

"Come with me," Phantom demanded.

But Sebastian was already shaking his head. "I heard why she wanted it to work. If she knows I have my free will, she'll know the immunity potion worked. She and Lockness want to take it and free themselves of Rose's control and subsequently Ravana's mind control potion." Phantom thought back to the men he killed in the cell. They had no will of their own, not even for survival. According to Felix, even Rose's songs weren't that powerful.

"Ravana doesn't trust the Minister not to use her own potion on her, so she needed the immunity before giving it to him."

Phantom's stomach dropped.

"She plans to give her potion to the Minister to dispense. He'd enslave the minds of anyone who defies him, the entire island if he had to, but she'd be immune to it."

That was why Lockness was working with her, to gain immunity.

Until it was off the table.

"So what? You're going to do whatever she says instead?"

The drums beat louder, and Phantom could swear the space between each beat was faster, as if building to a crescendo.

"I have work to carry out here." He pushed his old friend to the ladder and Phantom sheathed the officer's sword and grabbed hold of the ladder without taking his eyes off Sebastian.

"I'll come back for you," Phantom promised, reaching for Sebastian's belt and pulling out the Commodore's pistol. "I shall return this to you, then." He placed the pistol in his own belt before lifting himself up the ladder, climbing as quickly as he could. A glance down confirmed Sebastian had already taken to the mob, returning to Ravana's side like an excellent guard dog.

But Phantom knew better now. He'd do what he had to.

The selfless bastard.

Phantom made it to the roof. Looking out towards the sea, he spotted the arena. It was a stone walled circle right next to the cliff side. Only the barricades protected the arena from the sea, which was raging, a storm on the way. The waves crashed furiously against the cliff outside the arena and battered against the barriers, threatening to breakthrough.

The drums became a heartbeat in Phantom's chest as he shed the officer's coat and took off running, leaping across the close-knit rooftops with ease. With the monster's talents belonging to him now, his steps were faster and stronger.

All the while, he silently prayed.

Hold on, devils. I'm coming for you.

CHAPTER 43
STORMY BLUE

Phantom could hear it now.

OH WHOA THE SUN'S NOW SETTING

His crew was singing the song that damned pirates and sailors sang when the world ended. Now his devils were singing it, not in celebration like they once did, but in somber realization. The notes took on a much deeper tone, giving them a sense of pride as they faced death.

OH WHOA THE END'S NOW COMING

Singing one last song together.

OH WHOA THE SHIP'S NOW SINKING

They knew death well, sailing on Her tides for years.

IN THE STORMY BLUE

Phantom picked up his pace, running along the rooftops with the mob of angry citizens following him on the street below. It would not end today.

He jumped onto the last building in the row before leaping into the street below. The dirt and sand kicked up at his disruption. The clearing before the arena was empty since the mob was still a few blocks behind him. He was close to shore now, only a few hundred feet away from the arena and his singing crew.

He recovered from his jump in time to spot a flurry of blonde hair running for the arena as well.

"Right on time, little songbird."

He crashed into her, taking her by the waist, pulling her back to his chest, and putting a hand to her mouth. She yelped into his hand, struggling against her captor.

"It's alright, love. It's me, you're safe," he whispered into her ear.

She relaxed, and he released her. When she turned to see his somber face, he had a finger pressed against his lips. Normally, he would have smiled at seeing her, but with the sound of his devils giving up hope, he couldn't manage it.

"Did you retrieve it?"

She nodded, tapping on the coat pocket of her stolen uniform. "I had left it with Mama Owen, and I told her to hide."

With the Stone back in her possession, he breathed a bit easier, returning his attention to the arena before them.

Phantom scanned the wall of the arena, knowing the entrances would be filled with officers, and the mob due to descend on them. After examining the wall, he tipped his head to the side. Rose could do it, and with his newfound agility and strength from the monster, it would be easy.

"Hurry, love. We haven't much time."

She understood instantly, grasping onto a stone jutting out and lifting herself up. He followed suit while the song of his crew filled his ears and the drumbeats increased in pace. They were running so dangerously low on time.

It didn't take them long to scale the wall, especially with Rose's humming that produced handholds in the rock when they needed them.

Reaching a window in the wall, they both toppled through as the singing and drums continued.

"What's the plan?"

Phantom looked out the adjacent window to the arena floor below. The arena was a large circle, spanning the length of two ships with rows of pews on the opposite side for the gathered audience to watch. On the side near the sea, a portcullis protected the arena from the raging sea, but would be opened to relieve flooding during low tide.

Phantom's breath caught in his throat as he bared witness to what lay in the center of the arena.

His devils lined up in a row, their necks in nooses attached to the gallows. They were seconds from being hanged. A pyre stood on the opposite side of the arena, Black and Clare tied to it like witches at a trial.

Both had been stripped of their normal clothing, replaced by a thin chemise like what he found Rose in. His stomach hollowed out when he spotted who was in the middle of the hanging line. Robin had to have a stool to reach where the noose hung, his face red and tear streaked.

Phantom couldn't mourn them yet. They weren't dead, and he'd see to it that they lived long and happy lives.

His head was empty as he turned to Rose. He'd yet to come up with a bloody plan. With the song of the damned and the drums beating furiously, he could hardly think. He reached a hand into his hair, pulling at the strands, willing his mind to come up with a solution.

Rose's panicked gaze flushed as she realized they might have climbed up there to watch the devils die.

All he had to his name was a sword he stole off a nameless officer, a pistol, a knife, and Rose.

"Can you stop this?"

Her head shook before the question had fully made it past his lips.

"The drums make it impossible. They must hear me for the song to affect them and it wouldn't discriminate between officer and pirate. Every target has to be within listening distance."

He growled, running his fingers through his hair and cursing the beating of the drums. A multitude of possibilities ran through his head like grains of sand, all ending with the deaths of his crew. Until his eyes caught onto a rope pulled wooden wheel.

That will do, Sam remarked.

Phantom locked eyes with his songbird. "Do exactly as I say."

She nodded.

He scooped up a pile of ropes and laid them in Rose's arms. "Tie these off here." He motioned to the opposite side of the chamber where another set of wheels rested. She went to work as he made his hands busy too, tying another rope around a rock slab in the middle of the chamber and testing his weight against it.

As she worked, he barked orders at her as if she were a devil aboard *Nemain's Revenge* and there was an oncoming storm.

The song grew louder, drums beating faster. His heart pounded rapidly with each note. The bloody thing would beat out of his chest soon.

Phantom jumped to Rose's side, finishing the last change before handing her the line.

"When I say so, pull this with all your strength."

She stood tall. "I will." Her face was so cutely determined and her eyes so wild, that he couldn't help brushing his lips against hers briefly. That was all he could afford before he gripped the rope with one hand and jumped out the window.

He heard Rose gasp the same moment the drums stopped.

Breathe in.

For one painstakingly long second, everything was silent. The song was over, and the drums ceased.

The burly executioner curled his sausage fingers around the lever of the platform, about to take the floor from under the devils. Another officer held a torch over his head, leaning down to light the pyre. It wouldn't take long for the pyre to burn, but it was more time than the men at the gallows had to spare.

Phantom planted his feet on the stone wall inside the arena and with one hand gripping the rope, he aimed Sebastian's pistol at the executioner.

Breathe out.

The shot rang, and the uproarious crowd silenced, looking for the culprit and victim. The executioner took too many seconds to fall from the bullet that went through his eye socket.

And he fell the wrong bloody way.

Phantom jumped from the wall, landing in the arena's sandy floor and blocking out the hopeful faces of his devils as the officer fell onto the lever. He pulled the hidden knife from his boot then shot towards them with inhuman speed. The structure holding them must have been rushed to completion with the amount of ropes holding it together. He threw the knife at the rope steadying the cartoon above their heads.

As the floor fell out beneath them, so did the beam above them.

The gallows collapsed completely. Everything fell to the sand, including the devils. The ropes around their necks didn't draw taught enough to cause damage. But he prayed the creaking wood of the structure wouldn't finish the job.

It crashed spectacularly, a cloud of dust curling around them. But Phantom couldn't stop to examine the damage and who survived. He drew the sword from his hip, turning to the officers barreling towards him. He caught one blade, pushing that officer off before parrying another, using methods Black had taught him.

He needed his best swordsman on the ground, who was currently coughing from the smoke of the pyre with Clare.

He abandoned the officer immediately, jolting towards the pyre and confusing the officers enough that they were slow to follow.

A figure rose from the dust of the hanging structure. Jon's large, shirtless form emerged like a necromite rising from death, but instead of snapping jaws, Jon pulled a sword from the very dead executioner. An officer came to restrain him, but it was too late. He struck the blade in the officer's gut before the man could block.

Phantom made it to the pyre, jumping onto the dais and holding his breath.

Black's eyes were bloodshot from smoke exposure, face pale with all the coughing. Clare seemed to be holding out better, but only out of sheer stubbornness. He didn't waste time on words, cutting the sharp blade against the fraying fibers of the rope holding them to the pyre stake.

Flames licked at Phantom's backside, burning. He gritted his teeth as the rope finally gave, and the three of them jumped from the fire. Slamming into the ground, they landed in the sand with more than a few burns on their skin, but nothing too bad if they got out of the smoke.

Black reached for the barmaid. "Sophia, are you hurt?"

She coughed furiously, only now letting herself breathe. "No, but someone's going to be."

An officer came upon them before Phantom could react.

Metal sang against metal as Black retrieved the sword and crouched before Phantom, stopping the blade inches away from his neck. She screamed a battle cry in the man's face, putting enough force behind the weapon to have the man faltering.

Even in a thin dress, Black was nothing short of ferocious.

Phantom leapt to his feet, taking the only weapon he had left and handing the pistol to Clare. Her dark eyes lit up as her hands wrapped around the base.

"Don't miss."

Those dark eyes thinned, regarding him. "I don't miss, Captain."

He grinned for half a second before turning to the wreckage of the gallows, shots firing behind him where Clare felled officer after officer.

Phantom ran to the rubble, a few more devils popping their heads out of the debris. Wilson pried a plank of wood from the platform, swinging it ungracefully at the officers, knocking them on their asses and yelling like a madman.

Earhart searched through the scraps as Jon and Wilson kept the officers busy. Russet rose from the ground with a bloody gash on his forehead, but nothing serious. Hyne and Tick crawled out together, Hyne pulling Tick up and supporting his weight. Tick was having trouble walking.

A pang of guilt shot through Phantom as he realized his devil was hindered by a leg injury.

They were still missing three men.

Phantom reached them as Earhart pulled Smith up and supported him, his wooden leg missing. The doctor's limp was exaggerated by a gash on his side. He winced, placing a hand on the wound and leaning an arm over Earhart's steady shoulder. The moment he caught his Captain checking him over, he waved him off.

"I'm fine, boy. I would know. Find the others."

He nodded to the doctor before digging through the debris pile to find the rest of his crew. Where was Ramirez? Robin? The old stargazer and the boy too young for the pirate's life.

Blood pounded in his ears; a residual steady beat left over from those bloody drums. Finally, he spotted a hand, wrinkled from age and sun exposure. Pulling final beams away from Ramirez, he noticed his head was bruised and bloody and his eyes were closed, but his chest still rose and fell.

Ramirez coughed, expelling dust from his lungs.

"You gave me a heart attack, old man," Phantom said, relief resounding in his voice. "Can you stand?"

Ramirez nodded. "I reckon I can."

"Robin," Ramirez breathed, realizing who was missing.

He put a hand to the man's forearm, lifting him to his feet. A quick glance told him no one had found Robin yet.

"Robin!" Phantom shouted, hoping the sound would wake the boy and make him struggle against the weight of the boards. Nothing moved.

"Robin!" Phantom shouted again, Ramirez echoing the call. Officers poured into the arena from the direction of the audience. They were out of time and down a devil. A very important devil.

Earhart joined their search for the boy, calling out his name too, tangy fear consuming his scent.

Phantom's hands came away bloody as splinters of wood sunk into his skin, but he hardly cared. Not with Robin under there somewhere.

Finally, he lifted a board that revealed a freckled, ashen face and thin frame. He pulled the boy from the wreckage, but he was unconscious, and Phantom couldn't tell if he was breathing. He had been buried the deepest.

"Kill them all." The order came from the dais of the arena. The Minister stood at the tallest point, commanding his army of mindless officers.

Without a moment's hesitation, they came for Phantom and all his devils.

Jon was there in an instant, scooping up a limp Robin before turning an expectant eye on Phantom.

"Go to the rope," Phantom shouted at his devils. The window he had jumped from was on the opposite side of the audience seating and the Minister's private box. His devils obeyed, running to the rope ahead of the army of officers. Time was not on their side, but Black and Clare downed every officer that got too close. Wilson bludgeoning some with a plank of wood.

The crowd shouted a series of profanities; many aimed at Phantom and his devils, others at the Minister and the officers, as if this was a game to bet on.

They reached the wall and climbed one by one up the rope. The pause they took to get Robin up lost them precious moments.

This was it. The last second Phantom was waiting for.

He put a hand on either side of his mouth, directing his voice to the window above. "Rose! Now!"

He prayed to whichever Goddess would listen that she heard.

Black still fought a few feet ahead of them, slicing across two midsections at once and spilling their entrails as two others came to take their place.

"Black, come on!" Phantom trembled with anticipation.

Then it happened—

Wood creaked and moaned as the portcullis rose, but not as it should have. It was meant to release excess water into the sea during low tide. But it was high tide and there was a storm approaching.

Seawater poured into the arena in a mighty wave, sweeping up all the officers and forcing them aside in its wake. The others moved swiftly, most getting out of the way by jumping into the audience. But those in the middle — he hoped they could swim.

"Black! Run!" This time it was Clare who shouted.

The roaring wave was enough of a distraction for Black to get away. Clare climbed up the rope, Phantom climbing after her. Only Black remained. The water sloshed as Black lunged for the rope, climbing a few feet before Phantom and Clare caught her arms.

The wave crashed against the wall then, flattening Black to the wall as they pulled. Black was completely soaked, pulling deep, strained wheezes from running so fast and suffering from smoke inhalation.

But the devil smiled at the exhilaration.

Phantom didn't share the sentiment, his gaze turning to the boy slumped against the rock slab in the middle of the chamber. Smith stood over him, checking his pulse, a somber look on his face.

"No." Phantom shook his head, as the world tilted. "He can't—"

"He's not gone yet, but he was crushed badly. I fear his spine is broken."

Phantom knew what that meant. They all did. No one could survive if their back was broken, even if they were still alive for the moment. Most sailors would put a man out of his misery if their doctor dared to call such an injury.

It was cruel to keep them alive, suffering until the end came.

Earhart's eyes grew wide. "No, no, he can't be dead. He's meant to outlast us all." Phantom recognized the denial setting in with his first mate, the man already grieving the loss. They all would.

Nemain's Revenge would not be the same without its powder monkey.

It was his fault for choosing that method to free them. If he had only run faster, arrived sooner, shot the officer in the chest rather than the head, maybe he could have prevented the structure from falling on Robin.

A cry of rage came from Jon as his fist collided with the wooden wheel keeping the remnants of the bridge intact. A heavy smash echoed in response to the loss of the mechanism.

A sob wrenched from the barmaid behind him. The only moment he ever witnessed Clare shed a tear. Now they flowed freely as Black comforted her.

Smith then held out the knife to Phantom. "Make it swift, Captain."

It was happening too fast, his mind not catching up to the tragedy. He knew he could lose a devil, but not so soon, not this way, not this one. Robin was altogether too young. He was a witch's son. Powerful blood ran through his veins and a misstep on Phantom's part would kill him? It wasn't right.

Still, it was too late for what ifs. Not as Robin's breath came in labored pants, whimpering even in his sleep, his body too traumatized to wake. It was no use waiting for him to wake for goodbyes, either. If he ever did wake again, he'd be in too much pain to manage it.

A lone tear fell down Phantom's cheek, cutting through the ash and dust. He crouched down to Robin, holding the knife to the soft freckled skin of his neck, but he froze, too cowardly to end it.

Then a delicate feminine hand landed on his.

Rose's eyes glowed a brilliant cerulean blue and a collective gasp went through the chamber. She looked like an angel sent by Davina herself as she took the knife from Phantom's palm and tossed it to the floor.

HEAVEN NEED NO MORE

Words poured from her in a melody so sweet he lost himself in the notes. Nothing existed but Rose's song and the ribbons of light filling the chamber and wrapping around Robin's limp body.

HELL CLOSE YOUR GATE

The song intensified as Rose flinched under the weight of all the magic she carried. It poured into Robin, healing his body. Her gaze was entirely fixed on the powder monkey below her.

HEAL ALL THAT WAS TORN

He had somehow forgotten what she could do, the power she possessed. How had he forgotten that the salvation of his powder monkey was standing in the room with them?

BREAK THE LOOM OF FATE

If she hadn't stopped him—

NEMAIN REST IN BLISS

For one painstaking second, he thought Rose's magic wouldn't be enough. The damage was too extensive, the weight of that thought crushing his soul.

MACHA GIFT YOUR KISS

Robin's pained breaths evened out as Rose's magic repaired his back. The brilliant ribbons of light surrounded his devils and Phantom finally let himself see them.

DAVINA REWRITE THE STARS

His crew gaped at Robin, mesmerized by the ribbons. Hyne reached out to touch a tendril of light, but instead of being solid, his finger drifted straight through it like a beam of moonlight. Rose trusted them enough with her secret to let every devil see what she could do.

BUT LEAVE US WHAT IS OURS

Robin jolted, rising to a sitting position as he coughed, expelling the dust and ash from his lungs.

Rose's song cut off along with the ribbons, her eyes returning to gold as she laid them on Robin to check him over.

Those eyes caught his again, and he felt it. He wasn't simply in love with her. No, love was too easy of a word. She was far more precious.

"*My tresora*," Phantom whispered, but with the silence, every devil heard it, and knew he was staking his claim on her.

Clare broke the silence first, a squeal coming from the barmaid. She jumped at Robin, taking Rose down with them. She laughed, even with tear-stained cheeks, relief falling over the devils like fresh air.

"Captain," Earhart started, recovering first, because they weren't safe yet. "We need to go."

"Aye." Phantom nodded at his first mate. "Can everyone climb?"

Hyne pipped up. "Ah, missy?" He regarded Rose, but held Tick in one arm, holding up the hobbling man. "Can you help him with his leg?"

She smiled softly, nodding. There was a new respect for the songbird amongst his devils. Pride beamed in his chest.

"No time for that," Russet announced, leaning on the outer window, looking to the ground below. "We've got company."

CHAPTER 44
WINGS OF FREEDOM

Phantom leaned out the window to see not only officers, but the crowd following them. The mob had grown unruly, his supporters mixing in with his accusers.

It hadn't been hard to guess where the devils had disappeared to when the sea took control of the arena and now citizens raged at the officers, throwing rotten fruit, shoes, and rocks at the men. The naval forces froze in place, adhering to the commands of their master.

He spotted Sebastian at the helm, his face passive and controlled, but Phantom knew what the Commodore faced for the good of Samsara.

Phantom looked for a way out, glancing further up the wall, but officers pointed pistols at them from the rooftop across from them, others throwing ropes into the chamber. Phantom and his devils were surrounded. The sea still ebbed and flowed at the window behind them from the now flooded arena.

Storm clouds bellowed and cracked above them in a tempest. The clouds broke, a deluge washing over everyone outside. If he didn't know better, he'd say Davina was preparing for war.

He searched for anything. Thought of every outcome, but there was no way out. The only chance they had was to fight their way out and not every devil would make it out alive, not with the entire Navy's mindless soldiers surrounding them.

"Give it up, Hawkins!" The Minister shouted over the roar of the storm and the crowd, the latter quieting enough for Phantom to hear him. "You cannot win."

He knew that. The moment Rose failed to take control of his mind completely, he knew it. It was control or death.

Ravana materialized through the rain beside Sebastian, curling a hand over the Commodore's shoulder and whispering into his ear.

"Surrender, and I'll let the boy live. Fight and all of you will die," the Minister continued.

Phantom swallowed, looking to his devils. Most of them were worse for wear. They had five weapons between them. Tick was limping. Robin was still heavily breathing. Clare and Black were in nothing but thin chemises and coats they had stolen from officers.

His eyes lingered on Robin the longest. If he took the Minister's deal, he could at least save one of them.

Phantom gritted his teeth before examining the raging crowd. They pushed against the officers, ready for a fight. Could he rile them up further in contempt for the Minister and his disimpassioned Navy? Would he only add their deaths to his already burdened heart?

The crowd pushed harder, some raising their weapons. Many were careful not to hurt the officers. They were still citizens of Samsara, many of them facing their family and friends in the fray, even if their minds didn't allow recognition. They were as much a part of its people as the townspeople were. They were fathers, brothers, husbands, and sons. And now the people knew what the Minister had done to them.

A shrieking roar filled the air, followed by a blast of blue fire cutting through the stormy winds in spurts as a dragon flew above the chaos below.

Serena shrieked again and the whole of the crowd stopped to witness the mythical creature before them: a white dragon spitting blue fire like she was goddess-damned meant to.

Phantom laughed, bright and full at the sight of Serena flying and breathing blue flames like a full-grown dragon. She really would be fearsome to behold one day. But by the collective gasps and shouts of the people, she already was.

A flock of parrots and toucans flew in a herd behind her, as if following her as their leader. A shout from the edge of the crowd confirmed his suspicions. Monkeys were pouncing on officers. Those too close to the shore found themselves faced with snapping claws or tentacle arms.

The witch's boys. Serena freed them somehow; not only that, but they were following her into battle. She swooped down, aiming for the Minister's head, a line of fire hurtling through the rain.

Ravana deflected the blow with an air shield of her own, scowling at the dragon like she was only a bothersome bird.

"Show me your true colors, you winged rat," she screamed at Serena, who attempted another blow at the Priestess before flying away to attack from a different angle.

Rose came up beside Phantom, but he tucked her under his arm and dipped her down so no one could see her alive. "They think you're dead. Your best chance is that knowledge remaining with only us until you can get away."

"No," she protested.

"Rose—"

"They're dying," she bit out, tears streaming down her face. Phantom's brows scrunched together. "Look," she pleaded, and he did. The creatures and the crowd attacked the officers with not much in the way of weaponry, but the officers fell due to the sheer numbers they faced. The Minister's confidence faltered as he begged the crowd to stand down.

Finally, he looked closer. The officers. She meant the officers were dying.

He met her gaze to see that they were no longer gold, but blue light overtook her irises. "They didn't choose this. I chose it for them. In my fear and pain, I enslaved their minds."

He could feel her decision rattling through him. "No."

Rose pulled on his arm. "I did this to them. I can't give them back the years I took, but I can make goddess-damn sure they have a future they can choose."

His words to Earhart at the festival came back to him.

I will do whatever I can to ensure she has the choice. Whether she chooses to save this world or burn it, I will be there, fighting at her side.

He let his head fall to her forehead, his eyes falling closed, wishing he could extend this moment for eternity. So she never had to face this.

"I'm coming with you."

"We all are."

Earhart stood with every devil at his back. Some had pried off pieces of wood from the bridge mechanism as weapons. Wilson, of course, claiming the longest one to use as a makeshift staff.

Hyne had made a cast out of scraps of clothing and wood to make it easier for Tick to walk. It wouldn't do much more than keep him upright, but that seemed to be the point.

Even Smith had fashioned himself a makeshift wooden leg from mechanical parts.

Phantom nodded to them.

"It's time then."

Earhart grasped Phantom's forearm, his Captain returning the gesture. "We're with you to the end, Captain."

"May you have smooth waters," Phantom recited their goodbye, as if it might be the last time he ever said it.

"And open seas for all days," the entire crew replied.

Phantom nodded, if the Eleven Devils met their end tonight, there was no better way to go than fighting.

Rose reached for her pocket and drew out the glittering Stone, swirls of lilac and silver pulsing in her hand, reacting to her magic as her eyes glowed brighter.

"Stand back." Her voice filled with many voices as power overtook her.

The wild girl who flew over the sands of Draiocht.

The maiden made of sunlight who loved to tell stories.

The ferocious lady who burned brightly.

The warrior queen who fought for her people.

And the songbird, whose depth of caring and bravery were unmatched.

Phantom saw as each part of him recognized every part of her. Her blue gaze mixed with shades of red, and he knew what she saw. The same thing he did when he conquered his fear and allowed his beast to run wild. Except her beast didn't run—

Rose's smile grew wider, and she took a page out of Phantom's book, letting her weight take her backwards and falling out of the window to the fast-approaching ground below.

He rushed to the window, blood rushing in his veins. But wings spread out from her back, halting her descent. She caught wind, aiming her body towards the sky. She raced by him, climbing into the air at incredible speed.

His gaze shot after her, but there was nothing but rain pelting his face. Then the telltale sound of bodies hitting the floor came from the building beside them. The officers vanished.

Through the mist and rain, he saw her. Rose stood on the rooftop, shadows stretching out behind her, showing off the sheer size of her wingspan.

Brilliant cerulean blue wings folded, then spread out behind her as her eyes glowed the same color. His mouth opened, catching rainwater as he stared at the most beautiful sight he'd ever seen. The crowd finally noted her, halting their attacks to look up at the angel descending upon them.

"Look!"

"Is that another dragon?"

Rose fell again, diving to the ground below, the crowd screaming at her fast approach. In the last second, she swooped, narrowly missing the dispersing citizens.

"Come on devils," Phantom ordered, Russet letting several ropes glide down the side of the wall for them to climb. Phantom, Russet, and Jon being the first three to go, descending the stone structure in under a minute with the help of the rope. The crowd below them parted to allow them access.

The moment Phantom's boots hit the sand; he heard it.

Rose's voice rang among the rain and the wind. He couldn't hear the words, but he could see her hovering a hundred feet above the crowd, Stone in hand, singing to the officers below her.

"Not dead, are you, daughter?" The Minister spat, seemingly unsurprised by her appearance. Had he known all this time what she was capable of? What he was holding her back from becoming by living in fear of her.

Behind the Minister, Ravana still battled with Serena, batting off her blasts of fire.

As Rose sang, blue filled the air with cracks of lightning. She was utterly magnificent, but she couldn't last much longer, not with the Stone draining her. Phantom wondered how much of his power she took. He would give her all he had left, but he had to get closer for that.

"Move," he shouted at the crowd, his voice bellowing louder and deeper than a human's would.

The crowd parted instantly, jumping away from the dirt

before him like it was hallowed ground. He ran through them, yelling at them to move every so often, blue filling the air making it appear like the sea, even with the dark clouds above them.

Rose continued to sing as he approached, halting just under her. He watched the faces of the officers, their eyes turning blue like hers until their stony expressions dropped. One by one, she freed them, releasing them from the enslavement of her magic.

A heartbeat passed as they regained themselves and who they really were.

Disoriented from the weight of their imprisonment lifting off their shoulders, they opened their eyes to the scene before them. Many dropped their weapons instantly, refusing to attack the townspeople now that they could see clearly again.

Rose's wings folded suddenly; no longer holding her up as she lost consciousness and her wings disappeared altogether. She fell, coming closer to the ground as all her energy was spent.

Phantom caught her, cushioning her fall and holding her form to his chest. The devils crowded around them, shielding them from potential attackers.

The officers became more aware, looking to each other, their own hands, their gazes turning to the Minister.

The Minister faltered a step backwards, understanding sweeping over him. He had made every person on that island his enemy and they wanted retribution.

The officers inched closer, a reckoning heavy in their gazes.

"I had to. You think you would have survived without me?"

"Kill him!" An officer shouted.

They jolted, running for him, but no one paid attention to the battle still locked behind him. Ravana got her dagger in the line of fire, the little beastie growing frustrated from missing the slippery woman so many times. She threw the last of her blue flames at Ravana, curling around the blade in her hands, remaking it.

Serena, with nothing left to give, drifted to the sand on heavy wings as Ravana's cruel, bellowing laugh filled the air. She raised the dagger in the air and it glinted blue.

Sapphire glass. The strongest, most powerful substance in the world, made only by white dragons.

"Finally," she growled as the Minister backed into her, but she was ready, pulling his back to her and slashing the blade across his throat. Blood poured over the blue blade, then rushed down his chest as shock erupted in his eyes.

The officers halted, not a soul willing to aid him.

She let the Minister's body fall as lightning cracked overhead, bathing the sky and cracking across the ground before her.

An officer threw a knife at her chest. The knife took root, plunging straight into her heart. She staggered backwards, looking at the protruding steel in her chest, but she cackled louder.

"You think you can kill me?" She violently wrenched the blade from her chest, tossing it to the singed ground around her. The wound didn't bleed, as if she was already dead.

"We'll see if you can survive if your limbs are separated from your body," one officer hissed, his face red. The officers charged, running to the Priestess like she was their last meal, and they were starving men.

She laughed like the entire world was hers before sweeping a hand in the air, red swirling around her and Sebastian. When it dissipated, they were gone.

I'll come back for you.

And he would. But the crowd was too riled, too angry.

They needed to get out.

"Jon," Phantom called, but the brute was already at his side. "It's time to go home."

He grunted in agreement.

Phantom spotted Smith curling Serena into his arms like a nursing babe.

"Come on, devils," Phantom shouted loud enough for all of them to hear. "We've got a tide to catch."

They banded together to form a makeshift shield, with the most injured directly in the center, navigating through the mob. But they paid the pirates no mind, turning their rage towards the Fortress. The air thinned as the rain subsided and the clouds became less dark, letting a sliver of sunshine through.

He nearly let himself enjoy the moment, freedom within his grasp and Rose's deep breaths reminding him she was alright.

The devils chased after him, but as they were about to take the bend to the docks, a familiar voice cut through their victory shouts.

"Uh, Captain?" Black said uneasily. Worry prickled against Phantom's spine. He knew it was too easy. Something was wrong.

Black held a handful of sand, letting the granules fall to the ground again, but Phantom saw it. He knew the signs Nemain sent to warn when death was approaching.

Through the grains of sand, bits of black rot sifted through.

Wilson stepped up to the sand, crouching low and inspecting the particles. The burdened man lifted his eyes to his Captain, then nodded grimly.

CHAPTER 45

ONCE A DEVIL

It took only a handful of minutes to dispatch the officers guarding *Nemain's Revenge*. Since those at the docks weren't present to hear Rose's song, Black was careful to spare the officers clearly still under influence.

Per Captain's orders.

Black's gut clenched at the idea that she had been disposing of officers who had no choice but to attack her. Had she known, she would have taken greater care with them.

Lara crawled out of her hiding spot in the Captain's quarters, Sophia leading her. She mercifully was recovering in the ship when the devils were captured. It seems she understood the need to hide.

Black passed them by, slipping into the main cabin and taking up the one private room there was to collect her thoughts.

They saw her. Every one of the devils saw her without her armor. That's what it was after all: protection. Against them? The disguise had gone on for so long that she wasn't sure if the mask was her or the girl underneath.

She hadn't made the choice before the Minister stole them

away and forced it on her. He had striped her bare before the devils and called her a witch. As humiliating as it was, she thought they were going to die. It was over anyway.

But standing back on *Nemain's Revenge* with the devils creaking the floorboards above her, it mattered again.

Everything changed now.

The door opened behind Black, and she tensed. The footsteps behind her were too soft for a devil. They were closer to the stalking silence of a trained huntress.

"It doesn't have to change," Sophia's voice was so uncharacteristically gentle that it caught Black's breath. She remembered Sophia's eyes when the Minister had his crueler officers strip her.

It was only thing keeping her from falling apart completely.

"Look at me. Just at me." Sophia's voice was so steady, it grounded Black, keeping her attention away from the officers laughing at her, or the devils shouting expletives. She couldn't listen. She couldn't bear to hear what they were saying. It was too much. Instead, Black chose to drown in the dark sea of Sophia's eyes. "That's it, baby. Just look at me. Everything is going to be alright. All you must do is look at me."

Sophia's hand came around Black's waist, pressing herself against her back, snapping her out of the memory. Black turned around to look at the huntress she adored. There was something in her other hand, a pile of clothes.

"I brought two. One is the fearsome man who sails *Nemain's Revenge* as the greatest swordsman on the Sumerian Sea. The other is a blank page to fill in as you see fit." She placed both sets of clothing in Black's hands.

"What if I can't go back to this?" Black held up the coat *he* always wore. She was beginning to hate *him*, the persona she believed she had to take to sail away from her father. She could see now, the bits of her father she put into the disguise.

His anger. His logic.

Kill first, ask questions later.

Now, there was blood on her hands thick enough to make the air harder to breathe around her. How many men would have returned to their families once Rose lifted their spell? Men who met their end at her blade.

"You can," Sophia said with so much confidence, Black had to hold back a bitter scoff. Sophia's warm hand slid against Black's bare cheek. A cheek that felt oddly naked without her kohl shadow. "The choice was not taken from you. Whichever way you choose to walk out of this room today is *precisely* who you are. Just as it will be tomorrow and the day after that."

"You make it sound so easy."

A small smile spread across her face. "I imagine it gets easier each day." She pressed her lips against Black's knuckles before returning to the door she came from, leaving Black with the decision.

CHAPTER 46

ALWAYS A DEVIL

With Phantom's boots firmly planted on the wood of the deck, he took a long breath.

He was finally home, with Rose in his arms, Serena recovered enough to fly up the mast, and the Khelitians safe for the time being.

It was a start at least.

He placed Rose in his chambers, kissing her forehead and leaving her to recover. But he had something else to take care of before the day was out.

They were well out to sea before he gathered the devils before the main cabin entrance. Clare had informed him that Black would be coming out soon and he had debriefed his devils thoroughly. Though he had every confidence in their intentions, their teasing could be ill placed.

She rose from the steps of the main cabin, a sword strapped to her hip as it should be. But the devil who emerged was not the same Black they knew. She was covered in silver and gold adornments, from earrings, to rings, to necklaces. Her black shirt fell loosely around her chest but was cinched at her waist with a belt and tight-fitting black pants. Her leather boots hugged her legs all the way up to her thighs.

Phantom smirked as she had taken a page out of his book. Instead of kohl shading her jawline, it was smudged around her eyes, deepening the darkness of them. With her sharp jawline and angular features, her gender was indeterminate, but entirely *Black*.

Upon spotting every devil staring at her, she froze.

"Alright men, what do we say?" Phantom prompted them.

They spoke in monotone unison. "It doesn't matter what you wear or what you are called, you will always be a devil."

Phantom nodded proudly.

Black jolted, as if preparing to run back to the cabin and never emerge again. Until her eyes landed on Clare draped against the ship's mast, watching with amusement in her eyes.

Black didn't speak for several moments.

"I'm sorry," Robin said, breaking the silence. "Were we not supposed to know that you're a girl?"

Jon smacked the back of his head immediately, drawing laughs from some of the devils and easing the tension.

Black's brows drew together. "You knew? You all knew?"

"Of course, we knew," Wilson spat, his impatience showing.

Hyne spoke before Wilson could continue, "We only thought that is who you wanted to be, miss."

Black's nose crinkled in disgust. "Never call me that again."

Hyne smiled like he just found something to annoy her with, but Phantom interjected before he could.

"What shall we call you then?"

Her eyes finally landed on his. An understanding reaching them, his promise to her all those years ago finally coming to fruition.

"Mate. She. Black. Any of those work just fine."

Phantom let an amused smile lift his face. "Shall I call you, my swordswoman?"

Black smiled, finally releasing the tension in her shoulders. "I'll always be your swordsman, Captain." He reached out a hand that she accepted, bracing forearms. "Now and always."

"Good, because we have work to do."

***

Rose stretched her arms above her head before opening her eyes like a sunbathing cat. It was so adorable, he wanted to curl straight into her arms and never let her go.

Tresora. Treasure.

She blinked rapidly, expelling the sleep still clinging to her, but then a groan left her throat and she rubbed her eyes.

"How long was I asleep?"

He let out a sigh. "Two days, I'm afraid."

Her blinking eyes widened. "Two days? Davina, spare me. What happened?"

A small chuckle left his lips at the small profanity she used. He'd have to make that mouth much filthier if she was going to survive his devils for long.

Breathing in, he sat on the bed next to her. "First," he started, tipping his head to the table next to her, where mutton and potatoes waited, along with fresh water. "Eat. I want to be sure you are strong." She eyed the potatoes, but a resounding grumble told him exactly how she felt towards the meal.

Rose sat up, taking the plate into her lap and shoving meat and potatoes into her mouth. It was better food than they usually managed, the recent supply fill from Samsara keeping their storage filled for now. But Phantom was reluctant to take too much. The people there needed food.

A responsibility he accepted in the last couple days whilst he debated with Jon and Earhart regarding their next steps.

Jon suggested Draiocht. If they set up a trade route, it would keep Samsaran bellies full. Problem was, Samsara had little to trade.

As she shoveled heaping piles into her mouth, she motioned with her opposite hand for him to continue. He nearly forgot she was expecting him to say something.

"Samsara is adjusting. Your father is dead." Her brow furrowed, a mix of emotion towards the news, but he continued. "Lockness and Ravana survived, sadly. Lockness has seized control of the island, but Ravana has more sinister plans, I imagine." He took a breath as the weight of what he was about to say next settled on him. "She ascended as an immortal." A flash of that blade embedded in her heart came to his mind, then the smile on her face as she extracted it. "I don't know if anything can kill her."

"And Sebastian?"

A chill trickled down his spine. "He's undercover, pretending to be under her control."

Her eyes softened, and she dropped her fork, reaching a hand to his arm. She could see it. How could she see him so clearly? "We'll get him back."

Phantom's chest clenched at the idea of leaving Sebastian behind, but he ignored the emotion. The Commodore was the only reason he knew what was taking place in Samsara, sending doves after the ship with news. It drew him back to the island's problems.

"Love, exactly how much did the Minister owe to you?"

Her chewing stopped as her eyes locked with his. She swallowed before answering. "Everything. He had me enchant Lockness's mind to never rise against him, along with other nobles. My paintings alone did the trick without the buyers being any wiser."

It must have been what Lockness had referred to as "freedom" before the maze. Not freedom like the officers needed, but freedom to form a coup. Phantom had a sickening feeling as Rose continued.

"Every tapestry. Every column. Every silk and velvet. Every piece of finery in that Fortress is because of a song. I've been singing for him since I was four."

The air seized in Phantom's throat. Draven's shadows curled around his vision in sunset orange. That counterpart had been more active than usual with the integration of Maahes.

Draven didn't feel like the beast did though. He felt like a weight of crushing rocks trying to smother him.

"You mean to tell me, the Minster provided himself with every luxury, but never provided food for his people?"

"I cannot produce edible food. But I can make the ground better for crops. He forbade me from doing this, saying he would burn the crops and punish me for it."

It made no sense. Why make his people suffer?

"He told me it made the people dependent on the Navy to provide for them."

"Dependent on Kheli, really." Phantom laughed to himself. A conversation at the feast coming to mind.

"What is it?"

"There's a noble who believes a jinn resides in the Fortress. I suppose I understand his theory now."

A smile tilted the corner of her mouth. "I'm afraid I'm not that powerful."

He leaned on the bed spread before her. "I beg to differ. I've seen you do some impressive magic, little songbird."

Rose blushed before returning her eyes to her food.

He kissed her forehead. "Eat up, then get dressed and meet me outside."

A single delicate eyebrow rose as she looked to the clouded window in the room. "But it's dark out."

A grin pulled at his mouth. "That's when we travel best, love." He stood, walking to the door. "Come out and I'll show you." He watched as an alluring smile spread across her lips, marveling at her before drifting through the door of his quarters to the deck beyond.

The deck was a flurry of commotion. Sails filled with promising winds as the rigging moaned and creaked with movement. The sea tossed and turned along the sides of the ship. Phantom breathed in deep, taking in the ocean spray and the smell of saltwater. Even if she was not in the same room, burnt flowers lingered with him.

It smelled like home. He was finally aboard *Nemain's Revenge* with his devils and his songbird.

A weight he couldn't quite let go of crept in on him.

Samsara was marked for death.

He didn't have the heart to tell Rose. She had worked to heal the sick in low town, but they were now doomed by Davina and warned by Nemain. He had thought a lot over the last two days, trying to find a way to save the Samsarans and the Khelitians.

He had a plan. It was stupid, even he knew that, but there was no better option as desperation clawed at him. Every devil had agreed to it, knowing what kind of danger they would face.

Sophia Clare leaned against the railing of the ship, looking out to where the clear night sky met the rolling waves of the ocean, reflecting the twinkling lights and drowning them in stars. She wore her signature red barmaid dress that hung over her shoulders with some embellishments, including a leather vest that cinched her waist in a mock corset. One edge of her skirt was tucked into the leather, creating room for her legs to move. Tall leather boots poked out beneath all the layers. She even managed to get ahold of someone's hat, looking the part of a pirate.

He leaned on the rail next to her.

"Sure you want to join us?"

She didn't turn, only stared at the sea. "The answer will remain the same no matter how many times you ask it."

He hated putting her in danger, especially since his focus would be on Rose, no matter that she was the most powerful one on the ship. But Clare was human.

"Can you blame me for being uncertain?"

Finally, her eyes found his. "If Samsara falls, Kheli won't be far behind. I'm here to ensure you prevent that from happening."

He saluted her mockingly as he flipped his body, leaning his back on the railing instead.

And there, Black stood, watching them with one hand on the pommel of *her* sword. Her hair flowed freely around her face, curling around her nape and neck while a hat, larger than Clare's with a feather decorating it, sat on her head.

"I reckon I have you to thank for this," Phantom whispered low enough only Clare could hear.

"No, you don't. She did it all on her own." Clare spun, landing her back against the railing beside him. A heavy look passed between Black and Clare, full of longing and unsaid words.

"She did it for you," he pointed out.

"No, she didn't." Clare broke the spell they were under before turning, striding away from both him and Black.

A frown pulled at the devil's face right before Phantom mouthed the words. *Good luck.*

Then the sun rose.

Not truly, but with Rose's beaming smile, it felt like the sun with the rays of it warming his blood.

Rose Davenport had emerged from the cabin, dressed head to toe like the pirate she was. Her hair flowed freely down her back in waves along with a white loose shirt and brown trousers. She was covered with leather straps, necklaces, and rings. Some of which he knew she stole from him, but he wasn't complaining.

Her smile captivated him as she approached, hope spilling from her eyes as he held out a hand to her.

She grasped it, squeezing gently. "So? What is it you must show me?"

"Soon, but first—" He jerked on her hand, sending her flying into him before he claimed her lips. Phantom's arm encircled her waist, pulling her closer to him in a tight embrace as he plundered her mouth and she relaxed against him, soaking in his kiss.

"Ahhhhh!" Earhart cheered, drawing out the note in a teasing manner. The rest of the devils joined in, hooting, whistling, and hollering like monkeys.

Rose's mouth tipped in a smile before she broke the kiss with a laugh, red flushing down her cheeks and neck. She was so beautiful. He could have kissed her for the rest of eternity.

Her eyes scanned around her, taking in the smiling devils, then they narrowed on him.

"Where are we going?"

Phantom twisted her in his arms, facing her to the front of the ship towards their destination, but kept his arms locked around her, pulling her back to his chest and leaning his head against hers.

"You see that star? The brightest one in the sky?" His breath coasted over the shell of her ear as he whispered to her.

"The star of Nemain."

Just as Ramirez had predicted, the two stars beside it had joined, rivaling the intensity of Nemain's own star.

"Yes, and do you know where it sits in the sky?"

She sucked in a breath. "Above the gates of Hell. Necropolis."

"That is where we are going."

"But isn't there—"

"According to legend, one must face tests of all kinds to face the Goddess of Death herself." He knew the legends as well as she did. Some said the jungles and waters outside the gates tested one's very soul. To what end? No one knew, but few came back with enough wits to say.

"And you think we can face that?"

"If anyone can, it would be us." She shook her head, but his voice lowered, knowing the stakes and why he made this choice. "Ravana is immortal now, and if there is anyone who could do something about it, it would be Nemain. The Priestess cheated Her out of a prize after all."

"Do you think She will help us?"

"I do," he said, even if a knot in his stomach told him otherwise. What did a Goddess care for a band of pirates and a damned island? But it was Nemain's warning after all, maybe She had a way to reverse the effects.

Rose pulled away from his chest, unease wrinkling her features. His chest felt cold as she drifted to the railing beside Jon. She looked over at the sea and the star they followed. "I'll do what I can to help." She pulled a bundle of black velvet from her coat and handed it to him. "Hold on to this. Even being near it drains me."

He wished he had known that sooner, but he had a feeling he had a lot more to learn.

Phantom nodded, deciding to stow it away in his cabin. He'd keep it far away from her if it helped.

"As you wish, love," he said before striding to his cabin and securing the object in his desk. It would need a better perch, but his desk would do for now.

The ring of a blade being drawn drew Phantom's attention back to the deck. He emerged from his cabin to find the devils all facing one direction, swords drawn, their faces a varying mix of shock and fury. When his gaze caught on the object of their attention, his blood ran cold.

Rose was being held against Jon's chest, one hand over her

mouth to silence her siren song, another holding a blade to her throat.

"Jon," Phantom yelled. "What are you doing?"

Black lunged for him, but Jon pressed the knife deeper into her skin, drawing a trickle of blood. A growl crawled out of his throat, a warning of the power of Maahes.

"Keep back," Jon ground out.

"Do as he says," Phantom commanded, and the devils took a collective step back, but anger still flashed in their gazes.

Phantom turned his gaze back to the brute, a man he trusted time and again.

"Jon."

"No, Maahes, don't speak."

The words died in his throat, seeing a tear drop from Rose's eye as she realized what was happening.

But it was Jon's face that had him stunned. "I am sorry for what I must do."

Phantom flinched as Jon lowered the knife long enough to throw a palm sized bag at the ground before them.

A loud crack ripped across them as smoke filled the air, covering Jon and Rose from sight.

"No," Phantom shouted, jumping into the smoke, not caring what it could do to him. The only thing that matter was her. He searched through the smoke and debris left behind. A small hole was carved from deck and railing as if a shark had taken a massive bite of his ship.

But Jon and Rose were gone.

There wasn't a trace left of them.

Shock froze Phantom as he stared at the space before him.

A devil betrayed him.

A bloody *devil* betrayed him.

He fell to his knees as the rest of the devils ran to help. She was gone. He just got her back, and she was gone.

"Captain, what do we do?" Earhart's face came into view.

Something deep inside Phantom rattled, but it wasn't one of the voices that cluttered his thoughts. No, it was something deeper, something truly — him.

The weight of Samsara and Kheli lifted off his shoulders as his mind singled down to one thing and one thing alone.

"We find her. Whatever it takes."

THE FIRST MATE OF NEMAIN'S REVENGE

A prequel novella
Coming Soon

Acknowledgments

We did it again! I'm so grateful to all the lovely people who made this book into a reality. Unlike my approach to creative writing, I will be keeping this short and sweet.

My God for giving me the creativity and inspiration to write.

My husband to be, Brenton, for supporting me, being my creative sound board, and encouraging me on bad days. You may not think you've done much, but your love and support has made this possible for me.

My wonderful editor, Rachel, you have been multiple editors for me during this process. You've corrected my grammar, my word choice, and my plot holes. More than that, you've helped me believe in my own work and watched me grow as a writer.

My cover artist, Maria Spada, for doing it again and creating a beautiful cover that my readers are already obsessed with.

My sensitivity reader, Sam @boundbymischief on Instagram, for reading my work and letting me know if I represented my characters well.

To my beta readers, Trish D.W., who is an author herself, and Alex Kettell for making my work better. Your feedback truly helped and your positive comments gave me life!

To @azurityart for bringing my characters to life!

To @sovana.art for bringing my scenes to life!

I've ended my last three sentence with "life!"... Rachel, I need you.

Also by McKenzie A Hatton

The Captain of Nemain's Revenge

The Siren of Samsara

The First Mate of Nemain's Revenge - Prequel Novella

Nemain's Revenge Book Three (Coming 2024)

McKenzie A Hatton's ideal night is a glass of wine and a good book. She grew up in the rolling hills of Oregon, spending time with family at the beach, and petting every animal who would let her.

McKenzie is a world traveler with a town in Ireland, Killarney, being her favorite. She is lucky to have the chance to travel and to write, the two things that make up her passions.

For book updates visit her website and sign up for the newsletter.